"HOW LIKE A MONOFORM YOU ARE," LAAS SAID.

Odo did not rise to the taunt. "Why are you acting like this? I'm not your enemy."

"At this moment, I consider the entire Great Link an enemy of the Hundred," Laas vowed. He indicated the dead changeling. "This one adrift, alone for centuries, then found by humanoids, experimented on, and finally killed in a paranoid frenzy. Me—" He pointed a finger at himself. "—living among monoforms for two hundred years, tormented, miserable. The same story for the other two." He motioned to either side of the islet, evidently to include the other two changelings he'd brought with him, though they'd already glided back into the Link. "For what?" Laas concluded, in a way that did not invite an answer, but Odo volunteered one anyway.

"For knowledge," he said flatly, again reiterating the justification he'd been given for the Hundred. But as with Laas, he found that he could no longer countenance that explanation. Right now, he wondered why he had never questioned it.

"How can you say that?" Laas asked sharply.

"I don't know," Odo confessed now to Laas. "It's what I was told. I had no reason to disbelieve it."

"Don't you see," Laas said, "that we have *every* reason to disbelieve it?"

"That may be," Odo allowed, "but *I* never lied to you. You don't have to fight me."

Laas stepped forward. "You've lied to yourself, Odo," he said, "and that means you've lied to me as well." He circled around and headed for the edge of the islet. "And the Founders have lied to us both."

WORLDS OF
STAR TREK
DEEP SPACE NINE®

VOLUME THREE

SATISFACTION IS NOT GUARANTEED

KEITH R.A. DeCANDIDO

OLYMPUS DESCENDING

DAVID R. GEORGE III

Based upon STAR TREK®,
created by Gene Roddenberry,
and STAR TREK: DEEP SPACE NINE,
created by Rick Berman and Michael Piller

POCKET BOOKS
New York London Toronto Sydney Ferenginar The Dominion

An *Original* Publication of POCKET BOOKS

POCKET BOOKS, a division of Simon & Schuster, Inc.
1230 Avenue of the Americas, New York, NY 10020

STAR TREK is a Registered Trademark of
Paramount Pictures.

This book is published by Pocket Books, a division of
Simon & Schuster, Inc., under exclusive license from
Paramount Pictures.

ISBN 13: 978-0-7434-8353-7
ISBN 10:   0-7434-8353-7

First Pocket Books printing February 2005

10   9   8   7   6   5   4   3   2

Planet art by Geoff Mandel
Cover design by John Vairo, Jr.

Manufactured in the United States of America

For information regarding special discounts for bulk purchases,
please contact Simon & Schuster Special Sales at 1-800-456-6798
or business@simonandschuster.com.

FERENGINAR

Satisfaction
Is Not Guaranteed

Keith R.A. DeCandido

ABOUT THE AUTHOR

Keith R.A. DeCandido has been very handsomely paid for his prior forays into the world of *Star Trek* fiction. Those lucrative publications include novels *(Diplomatic Implausibility, Demons of Air and Darkness, The Art of the Impossible,* and *A Time for War, a Time for Peace),* duologies *(The Brave and the Bold* and the first two *I.K.S. Gorkon* books, *A Good Day to Die* and *Honor Bound),* comic books (the four-issue miniseries *Perchance to Dream),* eBooks (the *S.C.E.* novellas *Fatal Error, Cold Fusion, Invincible, Here There Be Monsters, War Stories,* and *Breakdowns),* and short fiction (stories in *What Lay Beyond, Prophecy and Change, No Limits,* and *Tales of the Dominion War).* Forthcoming work includes a third *Gorkon* novel entitled *Enemy Territory;* the stories *"loDnI'pu' vavpu' je"* in *Tales from the Captain's Table* and "Letting Go" in *Distant Shores,* the tenth anniversary *Star Trek: Voyager* anthology; and *Articles of the Federation,* a novel about politics in the United Federation of Planets.

Not content to make a profit solely off *Star Trek,* Keith has also written in the media universes of *Gene Roddenberry's Andromeda, Resident Evil, Farscape, Serenity, Buffy the Vampire Slayer,* Marvel Comics, *Xena,* and more. Upon realizing that he retains more rights to original fiction, he also put out the high fantasy police procedural *Dragon Precinct* in 2004, and edited the acclaimed novelette anthology *Imaginings.*

Keith lives in New York City with his girlfriend, two adorable cats, and way too much stuff, some of which he was unwise enough to pay retail for. You can read his self-serving propaganda at DeCandido.net, or just e-mail him at keith@decandido.net.

*Dedicated with fondness and sorrow
to the memory of Cecily "Moogie" Adams,
taken from us much too young.*

ACKNOWLEDGMENTS

Primary thanks must, as always, go to Editor Supreme Marco Palmieri, who keeps coming up with brilliant ideas, keeps pushing his authors to do more than they think they can accomplish, and keeps insisting on taking no credit for it no matter how often we gush about him. I'm especially grateful to him for letting me run with the idea I came up with way back when I was writing *Demons of Air and Darkness* and flesh it out into the story you're about to read.

Secondary thanks go to my wonderful agent, Lucienne Diver, about whom there aren't enough good words to say.

Tertiary thanks go to the wonderful actors who played some of the characters seen in the following pages: the late Cecily Adams, Hamilton Camp, Jeffrey Combs, Michelle Forbes, Henry Gibson, Galyn Görg, Cirroc Lofton, Andrea Martin, Chase Masterson, Josh Pais, Wallace Shawn, Tiny Ron, Nana Visitor, Lou Wagner, and most of all, the Big Three, the ones who made the Ferengi cool again, Aron Eisenberg, Max Grodénchik, and Armin Shimerman.

Additional thanks to the various reference sources, primary in this case being the invaluable *Legends of the Ferengi* by Ira Steven Behr and *The Ferengi Rules of Acquisition* by Behr & Robert Hewitt Wolfe, as well as some of the usual suspects: *The Star Trek Encyclopedia* and *Star Trek Chronology* by the tireless Mike & Denise Okuda, and the *Star Trek: Deep Space Nine Companion* by Terry J. Erdman & Paula M. Block.

More thanks to all of *DS9*'s fine Ferengi forays over the years, from the first season's "The Nagus" by David Livingston & Ira Steven Behr to the seventh season's "The Dogs of War" by Peter Allan Fields, Ronald D. Moore, & René Echevarria, and all the ones in between. Special mention also must go to the excellent *DS9* novel *The 34th Rule* by Armin Shimerman & David R. George III, with Eric A. Stillwell, the gold-pressed latinum standard for Ferengi-focused fiction, and to the Ferenginar section of Michael Jan Friedman's excellent

New Worlds, New Civilizations, from which I borrowed liberally. Gratitude also to Tracy L. Hemenover.

The usual thanks to the Malibu Gang, the Forebearance, the Geek Patrol, the folks on the various online bulletin boards, and the readers who've sent e-mail over the years—you all keep me going.

Final and most important thanks go to Terri Osborne, whose support has always been of more value than latinum. . . .

HISTORIAN'S NOTE

This story is set in late November, 2376 (Old Calendar), approximately seven weeks after the conclusion of the *Star Trek: Deep Space Nine* novel *Unity*.

Satisfaction is not guaranteed.

—RULE OF ACQUISITION #19

Females and finances don't mix.

— RULE OF ACQUISITION #94

"Dabo!"

Quark looked up at the baritone cry that indicated that someone had just won at Hetik's dabo table. Again.

What was I thinking when I let Treir talk me into hiring him? The honest answer, of course, was that he *wasn't* thinking, at least not with his brain, but rather the appendages on either side of it. It was difficult to be reasonable or to think things through when you were talking with a two-meter-tall Orion woman bred for sex appeal and wearing one of the skimpy outfits that Quark himself insisted his dabo girls wear.

Not to be confused with the sleeveless V-neck tunic and tight shorts that his dabo *boy* was clad in as he handed over a considerable pile of winnings to a Boslic woman. It was, in fact, the third time the woman had won, and if she kept up at this rate, Quark would be bankrupt.

With a brief hand signal to Frool to keep an eye on the bar, Quark navigated among the tables, which were fairly crowded. Three Starfleet ships were in dock at Deep Space 9—one about to head into the wormhole to the Gamma Quadrant, one on its way to deliver supplies to the ongoing Cardassian relief effort, and one simply stopping over for shore leave after a patrol of the sector—so the bar was full to bursting with gray-and-black-uniformed personnel, along with the usual collection of traders, cargo carriers, and travelers of all kinds that paraded through DS9 every day. Plus, of course, the regulars.

If Quark had his way, there'd be fewer Starfleet; they weren't the biggest spenders in the galaxy, and they didn't imbibe nearly enough to suit him. There wasn't a lot he missed about the days when the Cardassians ran the station, but one was that you could always count on members of the Cardassian military to be heavy drinkers.

Still, it was a decent day for business. *So I'm not about to let that Bajoran simian ruin it by giving all my latinum to that Boslic!*

As he drew closer, he noticed that the Boslic woman wasn't looking at the winnings that were piling up next to her arms, which were folded neatly at the edge of the dabo table. She wasn't looking at the other players—a Lurian freighter captain, a human Starfleet officer, and a Tellarite civilian—who *were* looking at her winnings, and rather dolefully at that.

She was looking at Hetik. More to the point, she was *staring* at Hetik.

Quark knew that stare very well. It was one that was all too often etched on his own face whenever Ro Laren was in the room. Or Kira Nerys. Or Natima Lang. Or Treir. Or Ezri Dax. Or pretty much any other beautiful woman.

In a gentle voice that sounded like honey over *hasperat*, Hetik told the Boslic woman to put all her winnings on double down.

Without even hesitating, she did so, barely looking at the latinum strips she moved across the table.

Quark, who knew his dabo table, relaxed and stopped in his tracks.

The human and the Lurian both bet triple under, and the Tellarite, spitting and cursing to a degree that irritated Quark—not so much the cursing as the spitting on the table, which he made a mental note to tell Broik to polish later—put what little money he had remaining on double down as well.

To Quark's lack of surprise, triple under won, and both the Tellarite and the Boslic were cleaned out. The Tellarite immediately got up and stormed out, which suited Quark fine, as he had bought only one drink, finished it hours ago, and refused every offer of a fresh one.

However, the Boslic woman simply stood up, ran a hand over Hetik's cheek, said, "Thank you for a divine evening," and slowly exited, making sure to give Hetik several backward glances as she departed.

Okay, so maybe a dabo boy wasn't such a bad idea.

Quark worked his way back to the bar. On the way, he was intercepted by Treir. The Orion woman towered over him and favored him with a seductive smile. "You didn't trust Hetik, did you?"

"I just wanted to keep an ear on things." Quark spoke defensively, which caused him to wonder why he felt so defensive. "Rule of Acquisition Number One-Ninety: 'Hear all, trust nothing.' "

As they got to the bar, Quark took his place behind it. Treir draped herself over the bar so that she was at eye level with the much shorter Quark, and also gave him a very good look at her very generous cleavage, most of which was visible in her very skimpy outfit. Quark knew she did it on purpose, since she was as aware of the Fifty-Third Rule as he was—"Never trust anybody taller than you"—and also knew the deleterious effect her cleavage had on his higher brain functions.

"You know," she said in her sultriest voice, "you never gave me proper compensation."

"For what?"

"Hiring Hetik. You didn't think hiring a dabo boy would be a good idea, but he's drawn in a huge number of customers. I think I deserve some kind of reward for that."

Two Bajorans departed; Quark grabbed their empty glasses and put them on the shelf to be cleaned. "It's true, he has added bodies to the dabo table."

"And yet, you haven't—"

"—given you compensation? No, I haven't." Quark leaned forward on the bar, his large nose close to Treir's small green one. "You had that idea while in *my* employ to service *my* bar. 'You pay for it, it's your idea'—Rule of Acquisition Number Twenty-Five. Since I paid for it, it's *my* brilliant idea, and I don't owe you anything."

Treir stood up straight and looked down that small nose at Quark. This put her torso at eye level, which didn't bother Quark all that much. Treir had a magnificent torso, and the outfit she wore today left it entirely exposed, from the bottom of her breasts to the middle of her pelvis. She folded her arms over her chest. "You know, Quark, when you sold me on this job, it was as an *improvement* over being a slave."

Quark spread his arms. "Isn't it? You don't have to have sex on demand with whomever your Orion master says you have to. You're free to come and go as you please, and you actually earn a wage. Now, if that state of affairs is no longer to your liking, you can walk out that door and that will be that—aside from the breach-of-employment fine, of course."

Treir smiled sweetly. "Of course." The smile fell. "You do realize that if I leave, the dabo tables will empty out in an instant."

"Nonsense. I'll still have Hetik and M'Pella."

"Oh, don't be so sure of that."

Quark felt a tingle in his lobes. He couldn't help it; he *loved* it when Treir pretended she had some kind of authority over the bar. She didn't, of course, but that didn't even slow her down. And, it was true, she had made several good suggestions for improving business.

She's so invigorating.

Brushing a hand across his lobe, he started to speak, when a customer in a Starfleet uniform called out for two synthales.

As he went over to the replicator, he said, "Anyhow, I can't afford to trust Hetik or you or anyone else. These are dangerous times." To the computer he said, "Two synthales."

Treir scrunched her face up in confusion. "What're you talking about? Profits are up, and have been since Bajor joined the Federation."

He handed the synthales to the officer and his companion, also in uniform. They raised their glasses in salute and drank. Quark turned back to Treir. "No, *revenues* are up. Profits are barely holding steady."

"That doesn't make any sense. You've got people pouring in here, you gave us all a pay cut, and the dabo tables and holosuites are packed."

"Which reminds me, shouldn't you be at your table?"

"I'm on a break."

Quark sighed. Instituting breaks was the biggest mistake he'd ever made.

Treir continued. "Look at those two." She pointed at the officers to whom he'd just given the synthales. "They can get those same two synthales for free in the replimat or in their quarters, but they're willing to come here to pay for it because they like the atmosphere. Let's face it—Quark's is the hot spot of the Bajoran sector, and everyone knows it."

Bowing his head, Quark said, "Thank you for that lovely demonstration of the Thirty-Third Rule, but—"

"I'm not sucking up, Quark. I gave that up when you and Ro took me off Malic's ship. I'm telling the truth."

That brought Quark up short. Telling the truth went counter to every instinct he had. "You see, you've just perfectly demonstrated the source of my problems."

"I don't understand."

"Of course not, you're a female. And—"

Treir pointed at Quark, which was disappointing on two fronts. For one thing, it was a fairly menacing gesture from a two-meter-tall Orion; and it meant she unfolded her arms, thus reducing the drool value of her cleavage. "So help me, Quark, if you quote the Ninety-Fourth Rule at me, I'll rip your ears off."

Quark refused to be intimidated or aroused, though it was a close call. "Well, it's true! Females and finances *don't* mix, no matter what my mother *or* my brother says." He shook his head. *"Yes,* we've got more customers and we've got more revenues. But the only reason we're able to stay in business on this Federation station with their"—he shuddered at the very thought—"moneyless economy is because dear old Grand Nagus Rom decided to make my bar the Ferengi embassy to Bajor."

The sweet smile came back. So did the folded arms, which made up for it. "I know all this, Quark. The bar's Ferengi soil, so you can—"

"Pay taxes."

Treir frowned. "Huh?"

"My brother has continued the 'reforms' that Grand Nagus Zek put forward before he retired." He walked over to the back of the bar and pulled down a bottle of Aldebaran whiskey. "That includes income tax," he said as he poured the green liquid into a glass. "I *didn't* lower your wages. I have to take a certain amount out for taxes, which I didn't have to do before this bar became part of Ferenginar."

Rolling her eyes, Treir said, "So now you have to actually pay taxes to support your government."

Quark rolled his eyes right back. "I *don't* support my government. My government is run by an idiot—I should know, I was *raised* with him. He's driving Ferenginar to ruin, and what's worse is that I have to help *pay* for it!" He took a sip of whiskey, the emerald beverage burning his throat as it went down. "And the only way I'm going to be able to pay for it is for you to stop wasting my money by standing at this bar and distracting me and getting back to your dabo table. Break's over."

She leaned over again. Quark's eyes involuntarily went to the cleavage. Her voice now sounding like a waterfall on Bajor, she said, "What makes you think I haven't been working all this time, Quark?" Ever so gently, she traced a finger along the edge of his right lobe.

Then she sashayed her way back to her dabo table.

Seven men and one woman followed her as if she'd hit them with a tractor beam, and within seconds, all eight were putting money down on the table.

For several minutes, he just stared at her. As good as Hetik had been with that Boslic woman, Treir was several orders of magnitude better with *all* her customers. She was like a Terran chameleon, always changing to suit the needs of whoever she was speaking with. She could be seductress, best friend, confidant, opponent, herald—whatever was necessary to get people to play her game.

Let's face it, Quark, he admitted to himself as he slugged down the rest of his whiskey, *without her, the profits wouldn't be holding steady, they'd be in the waste extractor. Rom managed to save my bar and destroy it at the same time.*

He sighed. The truth was, Rom *did* save the bar. If he hadn't made Quark's into the Ferengi embassy, there would be no Quark's at all. He wasn't some Federation stooge who could somehow survive without profit. *A Ferengi without profit is no Ferengi at all, and I'm nothing if I'm not a Ferengi.*

"What was that, Quark?"

Quark looked up to see Elias Vaughn. He hadn't realized he'd been speaking out loud. *This is what happens when you drink on the job.* "Just quoting the Eighteenth Rule, Commander. What can I get you?"

The old human squinted at the bottle Quark held in his left hand. "What's that you've got there?"

"Aldebaran whiskey." He put the bottle down on the table in front of the commander so he could examine it.

"Don't think I've ever had it."

Before Quark could extol the drink's virtues, he saw a very small Ferengi with very large lobes enter the bar, holding a package under his right arm.

It's about time. He'd been waiting for this for *weeks.*

Without even looking at Vaughn, he said, "Have the bottle on the house, Commander."

It was rare that Vaughn looked surprised, though the expression barely registered with Quark. "That's unusually generous."

Still not looking at Vaughn, busy as he was observing the new arrival's perambulations through the bar to a back table under one of the staircases, Quark said, "It's an unusual day. Excuse me."

Signaling Frool to once again take over the bar, Quark worked his way to that same back table. Before he arrived, he made sure to inhale deeply several times, so he could hold his breath as long as possible.

Gash was the best forger in the Ferengi Alliance, but he had never been well acquainted with the concept of bathing.

Or, Quark noticed as he approached, dressing. The green shirt he wore was out of style ten years before it was first replicated. Not that he could see it all that clearly, since Gash's body odor was making Quark's eyes water. The two Sulamids at the next table over skittered away within thirty seconds of Gash's arrival.

However, Quark could forgive the lost business. If the package—which Gash had placed on the table—was what Quark thought it was, the loss of the drinks tab of two Sulamids was a drop in the proverbial bucket.

"I hope that's what I think it is."

"Well, whatcha think it is, eh, Quark? Heh heh." Gash sniffled, then ran an ugly green sleeve across his bulbous nose. "Course it's whatcha think. Toldja I'd get it, didn't I? When've I ever letcha down, eh? Heh heh."

Quark could, in fact, think of half a dozen times when Gash had let him down, but didn't think it would be politic to bring them up now. Besides, those complaints were always related to timeliness, not quality.

Gash touched one filthy finger to a section of the package he carried. The outer casing folded outward and then contracted under the items inside the package: three pieces of yellow parchment of a type found only in the Grisellan system.

Quark reached for the parchments, but Gash stopped him by slapping his hand away. "Now now, don't be touchin' them with your bare flesh. You know what Grisellan parchment's like now, don'tcha? Turns all crumbly if fleshy oils get in 'em. S'how y'know they're genuine."

"Of course," Quark said. "I was just eager to—"

"Eager t'getcher profit, s'what you are, Quark. You kids today, you don't know nothin' 'bout patience. Rushin' around all over the place, y'don't 'preciate the work it takes."

Smiling, Quark said, "Oh, believe me, I appreciate the work you did forging these provenances. And they'll fool those Yridians bidding for the totem icons?"

Gash snorted, which sent a drip of snot flying toward the table the Sulamids had abandoned. "Oh, they'll fool those Yridians. Heh heh. Fool the Grisellas, too, you betcha."

Leaning over the table, Quark looked at the work Gash had done. The script was in the old Grisellan style, of a type not used in thousands of years. The first letter of each sentence had an extra curl in it, an affectation particular to the Hrabotnik period in Grisellan history. Quark also noticed an odd scratch across the bottom of the parchment. He'd seen reproductions of Grisellan provenances, and none of them had that scratch. *He'd better not have ruined these.* "What's that?"

"Heh heh. Was hopin' you'd notice that. See, them icons you showed me's from the early Hrabotnik period."

Shrugging, Quark said, "So?"

"Durin' the *early* Hrabotnik period—but *only* the early period, not the middle or late, nor never the times before or after—all the icons' provenances had this scratch. Had to do with the monks who were makin' the parchment, y'see. The plants used for those ten years all came from the same grove, an' they had impurities in 'em. If your Yridians know their Hrabotnik-period icons, that scratch'll be the first thing they look for."

Quark found himself reminded not of a Rule of Acquisition but of an old human saying he'd heard Vic Fontaine use: "Sometimes it's worth paying the extra nickel for the good stuff." Gash embodied that saying. He cost considerably more than any other forger Quark knew—and Quark knew all the good ones, as well as several bad ones—but he was worth it. This was precisely the sort of detail that most forgers wouldn't bother with, and it was forgetting that sort of detail that led to far too many forgers getting caught.

Reaching into his vest pocket, Quark pulled out his personal padd. He tapped in the security code—necessary to activate the padd if it lay inactive for more than thirty seconds—which Quark changed every day, and which would work only if typed with Quark's fingers. He had originally put a DNA scanner in, but that proved less useful than he might have hoped, as it meant that Rom, and possibly some other family members, could also get at the padd's contents if they ever learned the code. So he added a fingerprint scanner, which was fairly cheap, and which guaranteed that Rom could never get at his private accounts.

Not that it matters. Before, Rom would never do such a thing, and now Rom's Grand Nagus and can get at my accounts anytime he wants, fingerprints notwithstanding. But it's the principle of the thing.

After entering the code to activate the padd, he then accessed his account. "All right, I'm giving you half the money now."

Gash's beady eyes went wide. "Half?" he cried, spittle flying out of his mouth. "We agreed t'seventy-five percent on delivery, an' twenty-five when you sold th'icons! You double-crossin' me, boy?"

Calmly, Quark called up the contract on his padd, highlighted the terms of payment, and held the display up to Gash's face.

"Oh," Gash said after he squinted at the glowing letters. "Guess I misremembered."

Quark nodded. "Guess you did." He stood up. Breathing through his mouth for so long was going to have him hyperventilating soon, and breathing through one's nose around Gash was tempting fate. "I'll take this."

"All righty, then." One strip jutted out from under the three provenances. Gash touched it, and the packaging sprung out from under the parchments and wrapped itself around them once again.

With a polite nod to Gash, Quark picked up the package and moved toward the bar again. *Now I just have to let the Yridians know that the Grisellan totem icons they've been asking about have arrived. Of course, they arrived three weeks ago, and they're as Grisellan as I am, but the Yridians don't know that, and with these provenances, they'll never guess.* The market value of the three icons was ten times what Quark paid Gash and the person from whom he'd bought the fakes. With two Yridians bidding against each other, whoever walked away with the icons was likely to pay considerably higher than market value.

Within minutes, he'd secured the provenances along with the fake icons in the floor vault, and gone to his comm unit to let the Yridians know that they could come anytime to inspect the merchandise.

Before he could make the call, however, a message came over the comm system. It was addressed to Ambassador Quark at Quark's Bar, Grill, Embassy, Gaming House, and Holosuite Arcade, a wholly owned subsidiary of Quark Enterprises, Inc., in cooperation with the government of the Ferengi Alliance. *Well, nice to see they got the whole title right.*

The message was from a Ferengi named Chek, who requested an immediate return reply. Quark racked his brain—the name was very familiar—and then he placed it. Chek Pharmaceuticals was one of the leading providers of medicinal drugs to the Ferengi Alliance.

What would the chairman of one of the leading pharmaceutical companies want with me? Of course, Quark realized, it could very well have been some diplomatic matter. In general, he liked the title of ambassador, as it gave him a certain clout that the title of "bartender" just didn't convey. It was also the same title that Worf carried, and having equal rank to that prune-juice-swilling oaf gave Quark a perverse satisfaction.

Either way, Quark heard profit in the wind. Putting the Yridians in the back of his mind, he returned the message, which got him a bored-looking functionary at Chek Pharmaceuticals.

"This is Ambassador Quark, returning Chek's call."

"I'm afraid Chek is very busy right now," the functionary droned. *"You will have to try back at another time."*

Normally at this point, Quark would forward a modest bribe to the functionary, but not this time. *Let's take this diplomatic post out for a test ride. Besides,* he *called* me. "If Chek is too busy, then obviously his need to speak to me was of no import. Tell him not to waste the embassy's time again."

That, as expected, got the functionary's attention. *"Wait! Uh, hold on, I think he's coming out of a meeting right now. Please, don't cut the connection!"* The screen then switched to the Chek Pharmaceuticals logo, along with their most recent jingle.

Quickly, Quark said, "Computer, mute!" but it was too late. The jingle was now running through his head. *It'll be hours before I get this blasted tune out of my brain.*

Still, that was a small price to pay for not having a small price to pay. Using his ambassadorship to get out of paying standard bribes was a very nice perk.

Chek himself came on a moment later. A Ferengi of medium-sized lobes, he had wide eyes, a thin nose, and particularly sharp teeth. He spoke for several seconds but no words issued forth from the speaker.

"Computer, sound," Quark said quickly. "I'm sorry, Chek, I'm having some trouble on this end, could you repeat what you said?"

Looking nonplussed for a moment—Quark suspected that the man was not used to being interrupted—Chek then recovered and said, *"I was simply saying, Ambassador Quark, that it is a privilege to speak to you."*

"Not at all. My comm lines are always open."

"That's very good to hear. I understand that the embassy is available for private functions—for a small fee, of course."

Quark smiled. "I wouldn't call the fee all that small."

"I don't doubt it. After all, you offer a unique service: a piece of Ferenginar that isn't actually on Ferenginar. As it happens, that's precisely what I need. I've arranged for a group of ten businessmen to meet one week from tonight, and the embassy is the ideal site."

"The standard price for such a—"

Chek interrupted before Quark could quote a figure that was in fact forty percent over his standard price. *"I will pay you two bricks for the exclusive use of the embassy for all ten of us for the entire evening, including your games and holosuites."*

Quark managed to control his reaction. Two bricks of gold-pressed latinum was a hundred and fifty percent higher than his standard price. "And what do you expect the extra latinum to buy you?"

Giving Quark the most insincere smile he'd seen since the last time he looked in the mirror, Chek said, *"All I ask is that you join us for our meeting."*

Having expected the answer to be something like free use of his dabo girls or unlimited food and drink, Quark was taken aback by the condition that was applied. "Me?"

"Yes, Ambassador. I believe you will have much to contribute to our discussion."

"And that discussion would be what, exactly?"

"Ferenginar. I assume you have a standard contract agreement for such a use of the embassy?"

Quark had to admit, he liked the way Chek made sure to refer to "the embassy," rather than "your bar" in the dismissive and condescending way most people referred to it. Pulling out his padd, he entered the code, then called up the very contract to which Chek was referring. "I'm preparing to send it right now," he said as he filled in Chek's name, the date, and the price. "Food and drink will be extra, you have to provide your own gambling stakes, and certain holosuite programs are off limits unless the user pays an extra fee." Before Chek could object, he said, "Rights issues, you understand."

"I understand when I'm being gouged, Ambassador. Food and drink will be supplied at no extra cost, and all holosuite programs and all holosuites will be available."

"All but one, yes. We have one holosuite that is permanently given over to a particular program. It's an open program, and you're welcome to use it, but it's set to stay on continuously."

"What is it?" Chek asked, sounding curious.

"A human program. I doubt you'd care for it."

Chek's face contracted. *"Humans. Scourge of the galaxy."*

Having adjusted the food-and-drink clause, Quark transmitted the contract.

"Thank you, Ambassador. I'll have my legal people look this over and get back to you within the day."

That surprised Quark. *What self-respecting Ferengi would trust someone* else *to look over a contract? Especially a lawyer.* The lowest profession on Ferenginar that didn't actually involve physical labor was that of lawyer, as lawyers were the worst kind of vermin: earning profit solely through the means of other people. One could argue—indeed, most lawyers *did* argue—that they were no different from investors, but few Ferengi bought so self-serving an argument. That he used such a creature brought Chek down several notches in Quark's estimation.

"I look forward to the signed agreement," Quark said.

"I look forward to signing it. See you in a week, Ambassador."

With that, Chek signed off.

An interesting conversation, Quark thought. Of particular interest was Chek's use of the word "businessmen." No "businesswomen," apparently, despite the new reforms.

It had been a couple of years since Grand Nagus Zek instituted his sweeping reforms, many of them inspired by his relationship with Quark's mother, Ishka. That madwoman had put several insane ideas into Zek's head, including the notion that females should be allowed to wear clothes, do business, talk to people outside their family, travel freely, and commit other obscene acts. Zek had named Rom as his successor in part because he expected Rom to continue those reforms. Now, a year after Rom's appointment, females were all over the Ferengi business world. It was enough to make one's lobes shrivel.

Chek says he and his businessmen want to talk about Ferenginar, and they want me there: the brother of the Grand Nagus. Quark wondered if Chek was familiar with Quark's diatribe after Rom's appointment, declaring his bar the last outpost of *true* Ferengi values.

By making this place an embassy, Rom has made a mockery of those words.

Now, he shoved those thoughts into the back of his head. There'd be time enough to curse his brother for being the biggest idiot in four quadrants later. Right now, he had a couple of Yridians to fleece.

No good deed ever goes unpunished.

—RULE OF ACQUISITION #285

Rom hated meetings.

Put him alone in a room with a computer terminal, a bowl of tube grubs, and a problem to solve, and Rom was in his element. Under those circumstances, he knew he could make anything, build anything, solve anything. He worked better by himself—it was why he was such a good engineer and such a terrible waiter.

Unfortunately, the one thing being Grand Nagus did not afford Rom was solitude. His days were spent meeting with people. His evenings were spent meeting with other people in order to discuss the day's meetings with the first set of people. His nights were spent sleeping off all the meetings. It was an endless cycle.

The only relief was the time he spent with his beloved—and very pregnant—wife, Leeta. Right now, while Rom sat in another meeting, Leeta was being checked up on by Dr. Orpax. The best doctor money could buy, Orpax was the only physician Rom would even consider for Leeta. One of the perks of being Grand Nagus was that he not only got Orpax's services, but was entitled to a fifty-percent discount. Of course, Moogie had had to remind Rom to request that discount, and then she had to remind him again to tell Orpax about the financial ruin that would accompany a denial of his request.

Rom always forgot that part. Being ruthless gave him a headache.

Now he sat in the meeting room in the Tower of Commerce reserved for the Economic Congress of Advisors. The thirteen congressmen sat in chairs, six to a side and one at the foot of the table made of gold that sat in the room's center. The nagus's chair—the only one that actually had proper cushions—was at the head, and it too was made of gold, with jeweled decorations. Small computer terminals sat in front of each chair, and a large viewer—framed in gold—sat on the wall to the nagus's right. On the left was a shelf containing all manner of expensive objects. Also on that shelf was the machine that made a visual record of this and all meetings of the congress, which were closed to the general public when they occurred. However, copies of the visual record were sold afterward for a good price.

Rom stared at the tapestry sewn in latinum that hung on the far wall depicting Grand Nagus Gint, the first nagus, ascending into the arms of the Blessed Exchequer in the Divine Treasury. Rom had heard rumors that Grand Nagus Smeet had sold the tapestry and replaced it with a fake, but he had never believed those rumors. The cost of producing a fake would be almost as much as the sale price of the original. *Still, that may not have stopped Smeet. He wasn't the most financially bright nagus— that's why he was assassinated.*

Rom turned his mind away from thoughts of Smeet. They hit too close to home.

The president of the congress, an eager young Ferengi named Fal, sat to Rom's right and was tapping commands at his terminal. "The next order of business is the resolution to create an investigatory arm of the police force."

Kain, the oldest member of the congress—Rom had heard that he used to babysit Zek—grumbled, and coughed twice, hacking up a considerable amount of phlegm. When he was finished, he carefully wrapped the handkerchief he'd coughed into and put it in a case he removed from his pocket. *He's probably going to try to sell it,* Rom thought. Kain had retired to a moon that he bought a few years ago—ironically, from Rom's own cousin Gaila, who was in desperate need of quick cash at the time—but Zek had lured him out of retirement to join his new congress. According to the records, Zek's lure had been another moon.

His coughing fit over, Kain asked, "Whadda we need *that* for? We've got a police force *and* a military."

"Our police force is a collection of whip-wielding thugs," said Nurt, a wide-eyed, round-stomached male of middle age, who had been one of the major proponents of Zek's reforms over the past few years. "They don't know how to solve crimes, they just know how to take bribes and beat people up."

"Isn't that all a police force is supposed to do?" Kain asked.

Not answering the question, Nurt instead said, "As for the military, their jurisdiction is purely extraplanetary—they don't have the authority to act on Ferenginar itself, and I don't see any good reason why they should be allowed to."

"This is insane," Kain said. "We've got the FCA to regulate financial malfeasance."

Fal said, "The idea isn't to regulate malfeasance, it's to solve actual physical crimes—assaults, murders, that sort of thing."

"Whose lame-brained idea was this, anyhow?" Kain asked.

Fal stared at Rom. Rom stared back, wondering why the young president felt the need to stare at him.

Then he realized he was being prompted. "Oh! Uhh, it was my idea."

"Oh, and an excellent idea it was, Grand Nagus," said Liph, another of the congressmen, and several others followed with similar groveling.

There was a lot about his new job that Rom didn't like, but he really enjoyed the groveling.

Kain, however, was not among those in suck-up mode. He pulled on one of the tufts of hair in his left ear. "It's a stupid idea. What'll it accomplish?"

"Well, uhh, it'll get more people who commit assaults and rapes and murders and robberies off the streets."

Sitting up straighter in his chair, Kain coughed three times, then said, "Since when is thievery a *crime?*"

Nurt shook his head. "We're not speaking of the noble art of theft, Congressman Kain, but rather outright robbery. Why, for the last month, a succession of homes in the city of Kope have been broken into, with valuables being stolen. There's no art to this, no financial acumen being shown, just blundering into profit like some kind of Klingon."

"Worse," Liph said. "Even a Klingon wouldn't violate the sanctity of a home."

"With a proper investigatory agency," Nurt said, "those crimes can be stopped, as well as even more heinous ones."

"Besides," Rom added, "it would provide job opportunities for Ferengi who have intelligence, but, uhh, don't have the lobes for, uh, business." *Like me*, he managed to avoid adding. Not that it was necessary, as everyone in the room filled in the blanks.

Silence fell over the room after that, and then Fal said, "If there is no other discussion, we shall put it to a vote."

Each congressman voted. The tally appeared on the wall viewer: nine in favor, four against.

Fal then took the next step that was a vital part of any vote. "Would those voting against wish to attempt to financially influence the vote with bribes?"

Apparently none of the four—Kain was one them, Rom was sure of that—felt strongly enough about the issue to try to buy the vote. That was, if anything, a stronger mandate than the nine favorable votes.

Then the final step: "Would the Grand Nagus want to use his veto?"

This time, Rom didn't hesitate. "No." It was *his* resolution, after all.

"Very well." Fal cleared the viewer. "Congressman Nurt, as the cosponsor of the bill with the Grand Nagus, you have right of first refusal to supervise the assembling of this new division."

Smiling, Nurt said, "I accept. I already have several recruiting offices bidding for the staffing rights."

Fal nodded. "Moving on to the final bit of business."

Oh no, Rom thought. *I hate this part.* But he had little choice. *If I don't do this, Moogie will kill me.*

"The Grand Nagus," Fal said, "proposes that Congressman Liph be removed from this august body."

Several cries of outrage came from around the table, the loudest from Liph himself.

Speaking over the tumult, Fal said, "Liph has been diverting tax funds earmarked for several of the Grand Nagus's social programs and used them to invest in quadrotriticale futures. As most of you know, the quadrotriticale crop this year was a disaster."

The congressman sitting across from Liph looked across at him and said, "It's not bad enough you stole tax money, but you stole it for a *bad investment?*"

Fal stared at Rom again. This time he added a verbal prompt: "Nagus?"

"Huh?" Rom thought everything was going just fine. They didn't need him.

Then he realized that he really needed to be the one to make this official. "Oh! Uhh, Liph, you are a disgrace to this congress and I, uhh—want you to leave."

"Leave?" Liph laughed. "Leave where, Nagus?"

"The Economic Congress of Advisors. Now—please?" Rom cursed himself—that *please* ruined it. He was almost approaching aggressive until then.

Liph stood up. "I did nothing wrong!"

Rom tried to summon sufficient outrage. "You took food out of the mouths of hungry Ferengi!"

"So? If they're hungry, let them starve, and cut down on the surplus population!"

"Quadrotriticale futures?" That was Kain, having just completed, and bottled, another coughing fit. "Why didn't you just flush the money down the waste extractor? You've got the lobes of a human."

Liph turned angrily on the elderly Ferengi, and Rom wondered if Liph might try to harm him. Worry for the old man's health warred with joy at the increased sales of a congressional visual record that included a literal floor fight.

However, the three congressmen who sat between Liph and Kain also stood up, apparently not taking kindly to Liph's threatening an old man of Kain's vast portfolio.

Fal spoke quickly. "Why, ah, why don't we vote on this?"

Whirling on Fal and Rom both, Liph barked a laugh. "Vote? There is nothing on which to vote! It is obvious that this drooling idiot we call Grand Nagus has turned you all into lobeless *gree* worms!"

Kain pointed at Liph. "You watch it, boy. I was cheating Yridians when your mother was too young to chew food. And I also know better than to steal money from a *government*—especially a *Ferengi* government—and then invest it in a slug-brained scheme like quadrotriticale. Only lobeless *gree* worm in this room is *you.*"

Liph threw up his hands. "Suit yourself, you old imbecile. All of you can rot. I don't want any part of a congress that would censure me for doing business."

With that Liph stormed out. Rom breathed a sigh of relief. He had been worried that it *would* come to a vote and that they'd elect to keep Liph on the congress. *Then Moogie really would kill me.* Ishka was the one who uncovered Liph's scam when she noticed that the money they'd collected for disaster relief hadn't actually made it into the proper account. It didn't take her long to trace the funds back to Liph and then forward to a dreadful investment on Sherman's Planet.

"If that's everything," Nurt said, rising from his chair, "I have a police force to form."

Holding up a hand, Fal said, "I'm afraid it isn't, Congressman. We're not done with the final bit of business."

Nurt frowned. "I don't—"

"We need a new congressman, you—" Kain interrupted himself by hacking up some more phlegm. Rom idly wondered how much he was selling it for. *Given how much of it there is, it's not like it's a collector's item.* Kain then continued: "And I have just the person in mind. He's a fine man, has the lobes for business, and has served as one of the finest liquidators in the FCA. His name is Brunt."

"Brunt!" Rom yelped.

"Yes, Brunt." Kain coughed a few more times. "Now, I know he's been opposed to most of the reforms—he even opposed forming this congress—but I think he's the best man for the job. Trust me, I've been around since before most of your grandparents were buying their first tooth sharpeners, and if there's one thing I've learned—" Kain then went into another coughing fit. After packing away the phlegm, he went on. "Where was I? Oh, right—if there's one thing I've learned, it's that any good change comes when someone who does things the old-fashioned way sticks around to keep you dishonest. Besides, what better way to prove that the new way of doing things is right than by having its biggest opponent on the congress and being voted down every time? It'll do *wonders!*"

Several of the congressmen nodded in agreement. Even Nurt said, "Makes sense, yes."

Rom's mouth dried up. His tongue felt like sandpaper. *Bad enough Kain is nominating Brunt, but everyone's accepting it!*

"I can't think of any good reason not to appoint him." That was Nilva, the chair of Slug-O-Cola.

"I can!" Rom found himself saying.

"Why's that?" Kain asked.

As generally happened when he was put on the spot—and indeed often when he wasn't—Rom's mind went blank. "Uhh—I don't like him very much?"

Nurt chuckled. "He's FCA—you're not *supposed* to like him."

A thought occurred to Rom, and he looked at Nilva. "But—but you were the one who convinced the FCA to deny his petition to be Grand Nagus two years ago!"

"That was two years ago." Nilva shrugged. "Besides, that was for Grand Nagus. This is different. Brunt's got a good set of lobes on him, undersized though they may be, and he knows his greed. He'll be fine. Besides, Kain's right—it's always good to have opposition that you can beat on a regular basis."

Rom's heart sank. With Nilva *and* Kain supporting it, there was no way it wouldn't pass.

"If there's no other discussion?" Fal looked around the table, and nobody spoke up. "Then we shall put it to a vote."

Again, each congressman voted. Rom stared at the viewer in openmouthed agony as the tally came up: eleven in favor, one against. Rom wondered who voted against, then decided it didn't matter all that much.

"Would the congressman voting against wish to attempt to financially influence the vote with bribes?"

Nobody spoke up. Rom was hoping that the nay vote might at least make a token attempt.

"Would the Grand Nagus want to use his veto?"

Suddenly, sunshine came back into Rom's world. *Of course! I can veto it! Yay!* "Yes, absolutely, I want to use my veto right now. I veto Brunt as a congressman!"

Boy, he thought, *that was a close one. Imagine what would happen if Brunt became part of the Economic Congress. We'd be ruined!*

Rom leaned back in his comfortable chair with a smile on his face.

"And now the vote to override," Fal said.

The smile fell. Rom had forgotten about this part. He'd never vetoed anything before, so this hadn't come up. But the congress had the right to vote to overturn the veto. If three-quarters of the congressmen present—which in this case meant nine out of the twelve—voted yes, the veto would be negated.

He could only hope that the power of the nagus's disapproval would be enough to convince at least three of the congressmen to change their votes.

Moments later, the tally showed up on the viewer.

Nine in favor, three against.

"The veto is overruled. Brunt is the new thirteenth member of the Economic Congress of Advisors." Fal cleared the viewer. "That concludes this meeting of the Economic Congress. Visual records will go on sale first thing in the morning. We'll meet again in one week's time."

The various congressmen got up, Kain with some help from the one sitting next to him, and started to leave. Nurt was the first one out the door, apparently eager to begin his work setting the investigatory agency up.

Rom barely noticed.

Brunt is on the congress. This isn't good at all.

It was fully five minutes after the rest of the congress had cleared out of the meeting hall that Rom had the wherewithal to get up from his chair and head back home to tell Moogie.

He took one final glance at the tapestry. Although he saw Gint, he couldn't help but think of Smeet.

*   *   *

"And you just *let* him get elected?"

Ishka couldn't believe what her son was telling her about the latest meeting of the congress. She paced angrily around the nagal residence's sitting room while Rom sat quietly on the *amra*-skin couch that Zek had left behind—it always itched him, he said. Ishka knew it was because Zekkie kept forgetting to apply the *rilaj* lotion she gave him, but it was easier to just leave the couch behind for Rom and Leeta when she and Zekkie went off to Risa.

I should be there now, she thought. Instead of pacing on Ferenginar wearing one of her bulky one-piece patterned outfits, along with the gold-and-ruby neckframe Zekkie had given her hanging from her ears, she should have been lying next to Zekkie on a beach on Risa wearing the latest in fashionable swimwear. *But Rom needed my help, so I came back—and he obviously* still *needs my help.* "I can't believe you let them elect *Brunt,* of all people! He's spent the last five years trying to destroy our entire family—not to mention what he's done to poor Zekkie." Ishka finally stopped pacing and stood over her son. "Why didn't you bribe the congressmen?"

Rom blinked twice. "I, uhh, didn't think of that."

"Unnnh!" Ishka threw up her hands. "Rom, I love you, you know that, but sometimes I think your lobes were stunted at birth."

"I don't think it would've helped, Moogie," Rom said. "Kain and Nilva were the ones supporting it. What could I offer either of them?"

That brought Ishka up short. *"Those* two? I don't believe it. Zek *babysat* for Kain—"

"I thought it was the other way around," Rom muttered.

"—and as for Nilva, he was the one who kept Brunt out of the nagal chair!"

"I mentioned that."

Whirling around, Ishka asked, "What did he say?"

"He said this was different."

Again, Ishka threw up her hands. "Men! How they managed not to drive Fernginar to ruin for the last few millennia I'll *never* know." She sighed. *This day is getting worse and worse.*

She then said words that she knew would upset Rom, but they needed to be said regardless. "We're going to have to tell Krax."

Predictably, Rom winced. "Do we *have* to?"

"He's your first clerk, Rom—and he's got a good set of lobes on him. He *is* Zekkie's son, after all."

Rom then said exactly what Ishka thought he would say. "I know—and I remember what he tried to do to the *last* person Zek named his successor."

Krax had come to Deep Space 9 eight years earlier in the company of his father, Zek. Zekkie had named Quark his successor rather than Krax, and then faked his own death as a test for his son. Krax had failed it—miserably. Rather than try to weasel his way into being the power behind the nagal staff like a good Ferengi, he conscripted Rom to help cause an "accident" that would kill Quark, paving the way for Rom to take over his brother's bar and Krax to be the new nagus. *You'd think a Klingon thought that idiotic scheme up,* Ishka had thought with dismay when she heard about it years later.

As a result, Rom had been rather surprised two months ago when Ishka suggested he take on Krax as his first clerk. Zekkie had been just as surprised when Ishka managed to find Krax, who'd been spending the last few years lying low and staying out of Zek's way.

But Ishka had examined the young male's portfolio, and thought that he had learned his lesson. The two months since Rom (reluctantly) made him first clerk had been productive. The investigatory arm of the police force had been Krax's idea, for one thing, and he had excellent organizational skills. While her son could field-strip a fusion core with his eyes closed, the minutiae of financial paperwork tended to elude him.

Besides which, Ishka needed Krax to eventually take over Ishka's own self-appointed duties. The longer she stayed on Ferenginar, the longer she was away from Zekkie, whom she adored more than anything. Plus, Zekkie wasn't as young as he used to be. Without her around to keep him focused, he tended to wander—both physically and mentally. His servant Maihar'du could handle the former, and luckily the latter wouldn't be much of an issue on Risa—but still, she missed him. On the other hand, she had to make sure that Rom would be able to implement her and Zekkie's reforms, or all the work she'd done for the past few years would be for naught.

Once we get past this nonsense with Brunt, maybe I can finally go back with a clear conscience.

In response to Rom's lament, Ishka said, "That was in the past, Rom. We need to tell Krax."

"Tell me what?"

Ishka turned to see Krax entering the room from the large oaken double doors that led to the sitting room. Ishka hadn't even heard the doors open—but then, she was halfway across the room from them. The sitting room was huge, filled with comfortable seating, opulent statuary, and expensive furnishings. Most of it was too valuable to even touch. The room's size made it easy for people to come in without being heard, a skill the nagal servants in particular had mastered.

"Good news and bad news, Krax," Ishka said. "The investigatory arm of the police force passed with flying colors, and Nurt's going to run it."

Krax smiled and clapped his hands together. "Excellent! And Nurt couldn't be a better choice." He let his arms fall to his side. "What's the bad news?"

"Liph was removed from the congress."

"That's *good* news!" Krax sounded confused.

Ishka couldn't blame him. "I'm not finished. His replacement, by an eleven-to-one vote—and a nine-to-three overturning of Rom's veto—is Brunt."

"Oh. That's not good."

"I know," Rom said. "That's why it's bad news."

"We're going to have to—"

Whatever Krax was going to suggest was cut off by the intercom.

"Grand Nagus, you have a communication from Dr. Orpax."

Rom leapt to his feet—or, rather, he tried to. Never the most graceful individual, he was also sitting on a voluminous *amra*-skin couch that was not conducive to leaping.

Sighing, Ishka helped her son to his feet. Even as she did, he said, "I'll take it in here."

He ambled over to the latinum-framed comm screen and

touched a control. The face of a big-eared Ferengi with very small eyes and a most peculiarly shaped nose appeared. "Yes, Doctor?"

"I'm afraid I have some bad news, Nagus. Your wife, she is not so good. It's the head, you see."

Ishka shivered. She had been afraid of something like this ever since Leeta announced that she was pregnant.

Rom frowned. "What's wrong with Leeta's head?"

"No, no, it is not the mother's head, it is the baby's head. You see, her womb, it is designed for a Bajoran baby. Bajorans have very stunted heads—flat in the back, don't you know."

"So what's the problem?" Rom asked.

"The baby's head, it is too big for the womb. It is turning awkwardly, and occasionally cutting off its own food supply. I am afraid I am going to have to check her into the hospital for the duration of her term."

"How much will that cost?"

Ishka couldn't help but beam with pride at the fact that Rom asked that question first.

"We can discuss remuneration at a later date, Nagus, right now the important thing is your wife."

"Of course, I— Ow!" That last was in reaction to a now-somewhat-less-proud Ishka kicking him. "Oh, uhh, right. You, of course, won't charge the Grand Nagus anything extra for the hospital stay, since the privilege of tending to the birth of the nagus's child should be more than enough repayment. Think of the promotional value."

That's better, Ishka thought.

"You see, Nagus, this is why I wished to discuss this at a later date." Quickly, he added, *"Of course, the honor is more than enough payment, Nagus, and I wouldn't dream of asking otherwise. I will check your wife into the hospital and keep her under close observation. I'll be sure to check in on her twice a day."*

Worried that she would have to kick him again, Ishka was relieved to see that Rom did eventually realize why Orpax was letting that line hang in the air. He touched a few controls on the console under the comm screen, transferring two strips of latinum into Orpax's account.

"Four times a day it is. I will keep you apprised of her health, and you can visit her during regular business hours."

This time Rom didn't hesitate to transfer four strips.

"As I said, you can visit her any time of the day or night. Good day, Nagus."

Orpax's face faded from the viewer. Rom turned to look at Ishka. She could see the agony in his eyes. Ishka wasn't thrilled when she found out that Rom had married some Bajoran sex kitten, and the lack of thrill was only slightly ameliorated when she met Leeta and found her to have more depth than expected. But there was no denying that Rom truly loved her.

"I hope Leeta will be okay," he said. "I didn't realize that the birth was going to be such a problem. Bajoran women have *easy* pregnancies, Leeta said so. I remember when Colonel Kira gave birth to the O'Briens' baby, it was no big deal. I thought it would be the same for us."

Ishka put her hands over Rom's ears and kissed the depression in his forehead. "It'll be okay, Rom—I'm sure your child will be born safe and sound." She turned to Krax. "Speaking of which, how's the raffle going?"

Krax smiled. "We've sold twenty-five thousand chances at one slip per chance. Taking out twenty thousand for the ten-bar prize to whoever comes closest to time, date, and gender, and we're still five thousand slips in the black—with more chances being bought every day." He turned to Rom. "What better omen for your child's birth than to have it be the source of profit for the family?"

Ishka couldn't argue with that. But the worried look on Rom's face nearly broke her heart. *No matter what happens, with Krax, with Brunt, or with the congress, I don't think I can go anywhere until the baby is born.*

Zek lay on the beach, watching the tide crawl up the sand like a profit projection, and sighed with contentment.

Risa's complex weather system screened all harmful solar radiation from those lying on the beach, so Zek was able to enjoy the warmth of the sun without worrying about any deleterious effects. That same weather system kept the temperature warm but not too hot, and provided a slight breeze wafting through the air.

Best of all, there wasn't a trace of humidity. Having lived most of his long life on Ferenginar, he had grown to appreciate dry warmth wherever he could get it.

Decades ago, not long after he first ascended to the nagus-hood, Zek had tried to buy Risa. Unfortunately, the place wasn't for sale, no matter how high Zek upped the offer. He'd tried several times over the intervening years, but he always got the same answer: "Risa's beauty is for all to share."

Zek had the hardest time wrapping his mind around that concept.

He stared out at the beautiful ocean, and leaned over to tell Ishka to look at it.

Ishka wasn't there. *Where'd she go? She was just here— wasn't she?*

"Maihar'du!"

The Hupyrian servant appeared as if from nowhere. Zek had always appreciated, though never understood, how Maihar'du managed to be so quiet and inconspicuous while standing at two and a half meters and weighing more than the average asteroid.

"Where's Ishka?"

Before Maihar'du could reply, Zek suddenly remembered that Ishka had gone back to Ferenginar six months ago.

"Never mind, I know where she is. I want to talk to her right now!"

Nodding in affirmation, Maihar'du helped Zek to his feet. Zek made his way back to the beach house he and Ishka had rented a year ago when they decided to retire here. Zek had tried to buy the place, but the Risan desire not to sell their planet apparently extended to small parts of it. That was a pity, as far as Zek was concerned, as it dashed his alternative plan to use dummy accounts to buy up real estate all over the planet until he slowly but surely owned most of it.

By the time Zek reached the back door of the beach house, Maihar'du had gathered up all of Zek's belongings in his volu-minous arms and caught up to the former Grand Nagus with his greater strides.

Why did Ishka go back to Ferenginar again? Zek racked his brain, but it was so hard to focus. *I need Ishka. Of course, if Ishka were here to help me, I wouldn't need to focus to figure out where she is. No, that's wrong—I know where she is, I just don't know why she's there.*

As he entered the house, he turned to Maihar'du, whose face he could barely see amid the beach chair, drinks container, towels, case of beetle snuff, padds with an assortment of Lissepian erotica loaded onto them, and another padd with his financial portfolio all piled in the Hupyrian's arms. "Why is Ishka on Ferenginar?"

Maihar'du opened his mouth to reply, but then Zek finally recalled it. "Wait! I remember! She wanted to help out that no-good son of mine now that he's Grand Nagus." Zek frowned. "No, that's wrong. It's that no-good son of *hers.*" Then, like a comm signal coming into focus, it all came clear to him. *"Now* I remember! *My* no-good son is helping out *her* no-good son." Proudly, he turned to Maihar'du, who still stood in the doorway, laden with Zek's stuff. "Well, don't just *stand* there! Put a call through to Ferenginar! And make it snappy! Do you want me to send you back where you were—unemployed—on Verdimass?"

Maihar'du wasted no time in moving to the living room, dropping all of Zek's items on the couch—well, most of them on the couch, anyhow—and going to the living-room comm unit to put the call through.

"Damn Hupyrians," Zek muttered. "Can't trust any of 'em. If it wasn't for their beetle snuff, the whole planet would be useless."

Moments later, Maihar'du indicated the companel.

"What're you pointing at that for?" Zek asked in confusion. Shouldn't Maihar'du have been putting away all his stuff? After all, he was done on the beach, and—

Why did I come in here again?

"Zekkie? Is that you?"

"I know that voice!" Zek racked his brain again. Then he recalled: "Ishka! Sweetie-pie, where are you?"

"I'm on the companel, Zekkie. Come over here where I can see you."

"What're you doing on the companel? We're supposed to go to the beach today, remember? The tide'll be coming in, and that means lots and lots of algae. We can make those home-made Slug-O-Colas, just the way you like 'em!"

Zek walked up to the panel and saw Ishka's beautiful face. She was the one who opened his eyes to the neglected half of Ferengi society, and who also kept him alert when the FCA tried to have him deposed. The worst was that one liquidator—what was his name?

"I'm still on Ferenginar, Zekkie. And I'm afraid I've got some bad news."

"Why can't you come back to me here on Risa? It's no fun without you."

Ishka looked so sad, it made Zek's heart flutter. *"I'm really sorry, but Rom needs me now."*

"So do I. Besides, didn't you say my no-good—" Zek hesitated. *Don't undersell him.* "I mean, my incredibly brilliant son was going to help out so you could return?"

"Krax makes a fine first clerk, but things just got a lot more complicated. We had to kick Liph off the congress."

Zek couldn't remember who Liph was. "So?"

"So the congress voted to replace him—with Brunt."

Zek couldn't remember who Brunt was, either. "Well, that's not so bad."

Ishka's mouth fell open. *"Not that bad!? How can you say that?"*

"Well, it's not like they elected that liquidator from the FCA—oh, what's his name, the one who had me deposed two years ago?"

"Zekkie, that was *Brunt."*

"It *was?"* Zek scratched his left lobe. "Well, if you say so, honey-bunch."

"I do. And I don't like it. Brunt's up to something."

"Well, of *course* he's up to something—he's a Ferengi, isn't he?"

"I mean he's up to something that will be bad for Rom."

Zek was confused. "Isn't that Rom's problem?"

"Rom's problems are Ferenginar's problems."

"I don't see why. Isn't your son just some engineer on that

space station where his brother has the bar? Let Brunt go after him if—"

"Zekkie," Ishka said slowly, *"Rom is the new Grand Nagus, remember? You appointed him."*

"I did?" Zek couldn't imagine why he would appoint a Ferengi like Rom to the nagushood. "What did I do that for?"

"To carry out your reforms, Zekkie. You yourself said that the new Ferenginar needs a kinder, gentler Grand Nagus."

"I said that?"

"Yes."

Zek considered it. "Well, it certainly sounds like something I might say. I suppose. Are you sure that was such a good idea?"

Now Ishka sounded as confused as Zek felt. *"Zekkie, we talked about this for months. Don't you remember?"*

In truth, he didn't, but he didn't want Ishka mad at him, so he said, "Of course I do! But even now, the Grand Nagus needs to be ruthless—he needs to make decisions. Rom can't even decide what tooth sharpener to use in the morning. I just— think maybe—well, I mean—" Zek lost his train of thought.

"Zekkie—" Ishka started, but then Zek regained his train.

"We were supposed to retire *together,* sweetie-foot!"

Again the confused look. *"Sweetie-foot?"*

But Zek went on, undeterred, even though he had no idea what recess of his brain that particular endearment came from. "I haven't seen you except on a comm screen in six months! If I wanted to be alone and miserable, I'd have stayed Grand Nagus!"

"I promise, Zekkie, I'll come back to you soon. I just want to make sure that Rom's ready for whatever Brunt has planned." She then broke into a smile. *"Besides, Leeta's pregnancy has almost come to term—I don't want to miss the birth of my second grandchild!"*

Zek found he couldn't argue with that. He remembered the joy he felt when Krax was born—though it was leavened by the complete disappointment the boy had become later on. Still, there was something precious about the purity of a newborn baby who hadn't even acquired a proper portfolio yet. Zek could see why Ishka wanted to be around for the birth.

Then he remembered something. "Isn't Rom's wife Bajoran?"

Ishka nodded.

"Won't the baby look a little strange?"

"We'll find out soon," Ishka said. Zek noticed that she didn't actually answer the question. *"I have to get going, Zekkie—the rates will go up if we're on too much longer."* She stared at him with those beautiful eyes of hers. *"I love you, Zekkie."*

Zek's face broke into a huge smile. "I love you too, sweetie-foot." He decided he liked the endearment. "Talk to you soon!"

"Bye!" Ishka gave him a loving wave, and then her face disappeared, replaced with the logo of the company that provided subspace communication service to and from Risa.

Hm, he thought. *Maybe I can buy them up and use* that *as a way of leveraging myself into a position to buy the planet!*

Pleased with his brilliant revelation, he looked around for Ishka. He never liked to implement a financial plan without her input.

He looked around the room. *Where is she?*

"Maihar'du! Where's Ishka? We were supposed to be going out to the beach today!"

The Hupyrian looked down at the floor and shook his head.

3

*Sometimes the only thing more dangerous than a question
is an answer.*

—RULE OF ACQUISITION #208

Quark had put on his best suit on the day of the meeting. This was, after all, the first big function the bar had as an embassy, and he wanted to make sure that everything turned out right. Besides, Chek had provided a guest list, and some of the most successful Ferengi in the alliance were on it. *Like the Twenty-Second Rule says, a wise man can hear profit in the wind, and the wind is blowing mighty loudly here.*

One thing he noticed was that none of them were in any way involved with politics—nobody affiliated with the Economic Congress of Advisors or with the FCA. These were all private businessmen.

Quark had been right about something else: no females on the list.

On the day of the meeting, he closed the bar early—much to Morn's annoyance; the Lurian complained for the better part of five minutes at a very loud volume when Quark announced the bar's closing, but Quark had long since learned to tune Morn out—but kept the staff on call. For the duration of the meeting, they were to stay in either the back room or their quarters until the meeting was over and Chek and his friends had free rein of the bar, games, and holosuites.

Before leaving, Broik and Frool had set up an entire buffet table full of foods from all over the quadrant, the centerpiece of which was a huge bowl of the finest tube grubs, bred by the Depruu Grub Emporium. Quark had scooped a handful into his mouth before taking his seat at the long table that had been set up for him, Chek, and the nine businessmen Chek had invited along.

"Ferenginar," Chek said, looking at each Ferengi seated at the table in turn, "is in trouble. True, the general economic indicators *seem* to be favorable, and the ship of finance is sailing smoothly—but I fear that that is a temporary state of affairs, and the future will be devastating. Our entire way of life is coming apart at the seams, and once the novelty of these new reforms wears off, we will find ourselves in financial ruin."

Quark found he couldn't argue with anything Chek was saying. He'd argued against Zek's reforms back when they were just Mother's arguments with Father at the dinner table. Even when circumstances forced him to argue in favor of the reforms in order to keep Brunt away from the nagushood—a memory that gave Quark nightmares for more than one reason—Quark had thought the ideas ludicrous.

Chek went on. "We live our lives by the Rules of Acquisition, yet the Ninety-Fourth Rule has apparently been declared in abeyance. Females are roaming the streets, wearing clothes, and earning profit."

Several of the men around the table made noises of disgust and annoyance.

"And where are those profits coming from? Us, that's who. Males who've worked all our lives to gain material wealth. And now these females come out of nowhere and—with the help of a craven government—are giving them windfalls."

At that, Quark had to speak up. " 'Giving'? I can't believe that the Grand Nagus—"

"You yourself, Ambassador, have called the Grand Nagus an idiot."

Laughing, Quark said, "True, but he *is* my younger brother. Is there anyone in this room who hasn't said that about his sibling?"

"Be that as it may," Chek said even as several Ferengi nodded in affirmation of Quark's question, "these are terrible times. My own business has suffered tremendously. Chek Pharmaceuticals' biggest profits have always come from bronchial remedies, salves for runny noses, coughs, and headaches. Now that women are wearing clothes, they're staying warmer and drier and they're not getting sick! Sales of my remedies plummeted this past year. And how am I to recoup it?"

A younger Ferengi named Zoid said, "Surely that isn't our problem, Chek. I made more profits this year than I have in any year since I left home five years ago—am I part of this vast conspiracy to take your wealth from you?"

"That is not what I—"

Zoid kept going. "And why is your great pharmaceutical empire so reliant on this one group of items? Have you focused so much on the Ninety-Fourth Rule that you've forgotten the Ninety-*Fifth?*"

Expand or die, Quark thought instinctively.

"I have forgotten nothing!" Chek slammed a hand on the table.

Another businessman, Vol, spoke up. "Where is Chek supposed to expand to? All the growth industries are run by females. Postwar relief efforts—women's clothing manufacture—ground transportation. All the newest opportunities have been scarfed up by females."

Quark frowned. "How is ground transportation a growth industry?"

"With females able to move about freely outside the home—" Vol started.

"—the need for ground transport increases, of course," Quark said with a nod. He had lived on this station for so long that the realities of planet-based living had moved to the back of his head.

"So what?" Zoid asked. "The Ninth Rule, gentlemen—the opportunity was there, and they had the instincts to point them to it, and they got profit. It's our way."

"Yes," Chek said, again slamming his hand on the table, *"our* way. Not *their* way."

"Are they not Ferengi?"

"They're *females*."

Zoid smiled. "That doesn't answer my question."

Vol added, "And they're being catered to by the Grand Nagus. They get all the choicest government contracts—worse, they're providing good services." Vol's face scrunched up in disgust as he said it. "I had several lucrative contracts in Kope to provide housing. When the latest development was to go up, the nagus gave it to a female-run company—who provided adequate housing. No leaks! No chance of going back to them to fix the flaws and double charge! It's madness!"

Quark shook his head. Short-term, the strategy might have made sense, but providing inferior materials led to quicker replacements and faster profits. That was the most basic commerce that even Ferengi children knew. *This lack of long-term thinking may ruin Ferenginar.*

Chek's words mirrored Quark's thoughts. "We're heading for economic disaster. And it's not just those of us in this room who see it."

"All of us in this room don't entirely see it, either, Chek," Zoid said. "My profits are doing just fine. I've raised my servants' wages, given them more benefits, and you know what? They're more efficient. The quality of the cook's food has improved tremendously, the butler no longer has to be reminded half a dozen times to clean the floors, and my chauffeur actually pilots the aircar cautiously instead of acting like he's at a shuttlepod race."

"He's got a point," another one said. "Productivity in my factory's gone up since I improved working conditions."

"I repeat," Chek said through clenched teeth, "this is *temporary*. Once the dust settles, and these reforms stop being reforms and start being the everday reality of life, the servants will go back to being indolent and the factory workers will go back to being inefficient, only now it will cost more to keep them."

An older Ferengi with wrinkled lobes said in a feeble voice, "You haven't even mentioned the moral crisis."

Quark frowned. "What moral crisis?"

"The institution of marriage is being destroyed before our

very ears," the feeble-voiced old man said. "The Grand Nagus has declared all prenuptial Waivers of Property and Profit null and void. Worse, the females are hiring"—the old man shivered—"*lawyers* to renegotiate their marriage contracts."

"Lawyers?" Quark was revolted at the very notion. "First taxes, now lawyers?"

Chek shook his head. "It's a shame, isn't it? The glory of Ferenginar brought down to this insanity. The Blessed Exchequer is probably laughing at us from the Divine Treasury." Slamming his hand down a third time, he said, "We must end this insanity, now!"

Quark winced. "Would you mind not doing that so much? You'll dent the table."

Bowing his head slightly, Chek also lowered his volume. "My apologies, Ambassador, but my passion on the subject has overwhelmed my better judgment. You see why I felt the need to call this meeting—and why I had to call it here. The Grand Nagus needs to be stopped, and we are the best people to do it. None of us here is connected to the FCA or to the Economic Congress—we have no ties to the nagus, and therefore cannot be influenced by him, or the advisors who whisper heresy in his ears."

"Mother," Quark muttered.

"Yes, as well as the son of Zek."

Quark's head shot up at that. "What, Krax?"

Vol said, "He is now the Grand Nagus's first clerk."

I wonder what that's all about, Quark wondered.

"I also asked you here, Ambassador," Chek said, "because you have spoken out openly against these reforms. Indeed, your speech upon Zek's conferral of power onto your brother has become legendary in certain circles."

Legendary? I like the sound of that. Quark smiled. "Has it now?"

"Yes, it has. And that is why I wanted you here. No one is better suited to speak out against the Grand Nagus and lead our charge against him than you."

The smile fell from Quark's face. "Lead our charge?"

"Don't you wish to stop these foul 'reforms'?" Vol asked.

"It's his *brother,*" Zoid said.

" 'Never allow family to stand in the way of opportunity.' " Vol quoted the Sixth Rule with a sneer.

Quark, however, didn't know what to think. He was no revolutionary, and the last thing he wanted to do was take on the Ferengi government, especially one embodied by his brother and mother. All he wanted to do was make as much money as possible for himself.

Then he thought of another Rule: "Wives serve, brothers inherit." If Rom was brought down, Quark would be the obvious choice to succeed him. Twice, Quark had believed himself to be the next Grand Nagus, only to have it taken from him. *Do I want to try for three?*

He looked at Chek. "How do you plan to bring about this grand revolution?"

"We have ways," Chek said with annoying evasiveness. "In fact, the nagus himself has helped us with that foolish congress of his. . . ."

"Actually, that congress was Zek's insane idea," the old Ferengi said.

Chek made a dismissive gesture. "Either way, we have our methods. Are you with us, Ambassador?"

Quark weighed his desire to return Ferenginar to the values that made it great against his lack of desire to fight his brother—who had, after all, saved his livelihood by making the bar an embassy. All that he weighed against the fact that he hadn't been home in over three years, and would happily allow that figure to quadruple itself a dozen times over.

He made his decision by not making one at all. "Gentlemen, you wish me to buy into your scheme to bring down my brother's government, and all I can do in return is quote Rule of Acquisition Number Two-Eighteen: 'Always know what you're buying.' I only have your word for what's happening on Ferenginar, and," he added with a look at Zoid, "you don't even all agree on that. I prefer to see things for myself. But, since Ferenginar is so distant—"

"Then it's settled," Chek said, once again slamming his hand. As soon as he did so, he at least had the good grace to look apologetic. "Sorry. In any case, you must come to Ferenginar."

"What?" That wasn't what Quark had in mind. "I can't go to Ferenginar."

"Nonsense. Your brother's wife is about to give birth. You must be present for the birth of your nephew."

"Or niece," Zoid said. "I have a girl in the raffle."

"Raffle?" Quark asked, confused.

Vol said, "The Grand Nagus is holding a raffle. The prize is ten bars of gold-pressed latinum to whoever guesses the gender, time, and date of birth."

"Really?" Quark hadn't given Rom enough credit to have come up with that. Quark himself had made quite a bundle on the similar raffle he had run for the birth of the child born to Captains Sisko and Yates. *Must've been Mother's idea.*

"So what do you say?" Chek asked.

Again, Quark put off his decision. "I'll think about it." He pressed a button under the table that would signal Frool, Broik, Treir, M'Pella, and the rest of the staff to come. "In the meantime, gentlemen, please feel free to eat, drink, and be merry, and to avail yourselves of the dom-jot parlor, the dabo tables, or the holosuites."

"Ambassador," Chek said in a low voice, "I need an answer from you."

"You've gotten all the answer you're going to get tonight, Chek." He raised his voice. "Enjoy yourself at Quark's!"

Then he made a beeline for the back room. He had a lot to think about.

Just as he was about to open the door, Frool and Broik walked in. "Quark!" the former said. "You have a message from Ferenginar—it's the Grand Nagus!"

Quark didn't understand how Frool could speak of the nagus with such awe in his voice, seeing as how he actually *knew* Rom, but let it go. Luckily, the two of them were out of earshot of Chek and his cronies. "I'll take it in the back."

It took several seconds of standing in front of the viewer in the back room before he activated the connection. *What am I supposed to say? "Hi Rom, how's it going? Me? Oh, everything's just been peachy since you've been here last. Ezri went back to Trill to watch the entire planet fall apart, somebody wiped out a Bajoran village, and, oh yes, I just got finished having a meeting plotting your downfall. How's by you?"*

Taking a deep breath, he activated the viewer.

"Brother! You have to come home to Ferenginar right away!"

Quark opened his mouth and then closed it again. "What?"

"Leeta's very very sick. You and Nog have to come home!"

"Rom—"

"Don't you want to be here when your niece or nephew is born?"

Deciding not to bother pointing out that he wasn't there when Nog was born, so why should he be there for this one, Quark instead said, "I can't just leave the bar."

"You've left it before."

Before I didn't have Treir and her delusions of grandeur, he thought.

Then he thought about it. *Chek wants me to go to see how things really are. If I do what he wants, I'll be in good with the head of the biggest pharmaceuticals company on Ferenginar. Not to mention the other nine—in essence, I'll be doing them a favor, and it's one I should be able to cash in some time.*

"All right, fine, Rom, I'll—"

"Great!" Rom's unfortunately shaped face broke into a huge smile. *"I'll have Krax send you a transport. It'll be there in two days!"* Rom was then distracted by something to his right. *"What? Oh, uhh, okay. I have to go, Brother. Bye!"*

Rom's face faded.

And that, Quark thought, *was one of our more lucid conversations.*

He reached into his pocket and pulled out his padd to double-check his schedule. Everything for the next two days was still on—including meeting with the Yridians about the totem icons—and everything after that could be postponed.

The only item he regretted having to postpone was dinner with Ro Laren three days hence. *Pity I can't take her with me. It'd be nice to show her the sights on Ferenginar. . . .*

Then Quark got that tingly feeling in his left lobe that he always got when a brilliant idea came to him. *Well, why can't I take her with me?*

Humming the Slug-O-Cola jingle happily to himself, he went back to the front to make sure that Chek and his people were having a good time—and to start formulating his sales pitch to Laren.

"So let me get this straight," Ro said, her hands folded neatly in front of her on what Quark still couldn't help but think of as Odo's desk, even though Ro had been security chief for the better part of a year. He tried to remember how long Odo had been on the job before Quark had stopped thinking of it as Thrax's desk. "You want me to come along as your protection when you go home to Ferenginar?"

"That's right," Quark said, sitting in a guest chair. "It's no different from what you did for me on Malic's ship."

"I wasn't there to protect you, Quark, I was there to try to get information on the Orion Syndicate."

"Which you got, as I recall."

Ro nodded. "Yeah, Starfleet Intelligence has been having a field day with that padd I stole. But I'm still not really seeing the connection between that and this."

"I'm an ambassador now. I'm—oh, what's the human term?—a VIC!"

"That's VIP—which in your case, stands for very important pain in the ass."

"Laren—"

"Quark, look, I've got a lot of work to do. If you want, we can push up our dinner to tomorrow night before you leave, but—"

Realizing that the diplomatic-duty angle wasn't working, Quark went for the security ploy. "I'm afraid for my life, Laren!"

Ro looked at him as if he had grown an additional limb. "What?"

"My idiot brother has hired Krax to be his first clerk."

Nodding, Ro said, "Krax being the former Grand Nagus's son."

Quark blinked. "Uh, right. How'd you know that?"

"I'm in charge of station security, Quark, it's my business to know about potential security risks, and the son of a former head of state whose one and only visit to the station included attempted murder of one of the station's residents is something it's my job to remember."

"Oh." Quark thought a moment, then decided he didn't buy this for a minute. "Who's Retaya?"

Ro frowned. "The name doesn't ring a bell."

"What about Chu'lak?"

"That *does* ring a bell—I think he was a Starfleet officer, went on a killing spree—Andorian, I think."

"Vulcan, actually. How about Fallit Kot?"

"An old business partner of yours who tried to kill you—an instinct I can often get behind. Now, if you're done—"

Breaking into a wide grin, Quark said, "Now I find this *fascinating*. You barely remember a serial murderer who was captured over a year ago. You *don't* remember an assassin who came here to kill Garak over five years ago—yet you remember, with perfect detail, two people who tried to kill *me,* one of them *eight* years ago."

Ro unfolded her hands and put them palms-down on the desk. "Quark, just to warn you, I'm about to hit you really really hard on the nose."

A hand brushing across his lobe, Quark laughed. "I didn't know you were into the rough stuff, Laren."

Now she pointed at him. "Don't get cute with me, Quark, I—" She cut herself off. "Fine, I have checked more thoroughly on people who might hurt you. I worry about you—you're a big security risk with all the enemies you've managed to make over the years."

"Kira's made a lot of enemies, too—I bet you don't have all of them memorized."

Ro smiled. "I don't need to—I trust Captain Kira to be able to handle herself. You, on the other hand, I expect to do a dandy job of hiding under the table."

" 'He who dives under the table today lives to profit tomorrow.' "

"Rule of Acquisition Number Twenty."

"I love a woman who knows the Rules."

Looking up at the ceiling, Ro said, "Spare me the attempt at foreplay, Quark."

Leaning forward in his chair, putting one hand on the table, Quark said, "All right, fine, I'll go straight to the pleading. You just said it yourself—I have enemies. At least one of them is on Ferenginar. In fact, more than one. Someone *else* who came to the station to have me killed is a former liquidator named Brunt, and he's on my brother's Economic Congress of Advisors. For that matter, last I heard, my cousin Gaila went back to Ferenginar, and you've seen firsthand how much *he* hates me."

Folding her arms, Ro stared at a spot on the floor just to Quark's left. Quark sat in silence, removing his hand from the table, and letting her think.

After several seconds, she looked up. "All right. I think I can sell it to Kira this way. Besides," she added with her big smile, "I've always wanted to see Ferenginar."

"Really?" That revelation surprised Quark. "Most non-Ferengi hate the place."

Ro shrugged. "I'd like to make that judgment for myself. Besides, if it's where you came from, it can't be *all* bad."

"Well, I did move away from there as soon as I could," Quark said.

"I assumed you were following the Seventy-Fifth Rule."

Home is where the heart is, but the stars are made of latinum, Quark thought. *I* really *love a woman who knows the Rules.* "To an extent, yes, but—well, never mind, you don't need to know my tiresome family history."

At that, Ro laughed. "Quark, your mother was involved with the Grand Nagus. Most of your family history is public record."

"Don't remind me," Quark said emphatically. "All right, then. I'll be able to show you all the sights—the Tower of Commerce, the Museum of Plundered Art, the Great Marketplace. You'll love it!" He stood up from the chair. "The transport should be here at 1900 to—"

"I know, Quark—that Krax person called ahead to reserve a docking port already."

"Oh." Quark gave her a look. "Is that the real reason why you knew Krax's information off the top of your head?"

"Actually, I remembered who he was when he called—but I did look up his record."

Quark shook his head and moved toward the door. *What a woman.*

"Hey, Quark?"

He stopped and turned around.

"You're not really worried about getting hurt. You just wanted me to come with you, didn't you?"

That caught Quark off-guard. "Well, uh—"

"Why didn't you just ask me? Maybe added an emotional appeal in that sincere voice that you've spent so many years honing to almost-realistic levels in order to convince me that you were serious?"

Quark shook his head. *You'd think I'd have learned not to underestimate her by now.* "I wasn't sure you'd buy it." Then he added with a grin, "And I didn't need it. See, that was Plan C, and you bought Plan B."

Chuckling, Ro said, "Well, it wouldn't have worked anyhow. The only way I *can* go is officially. If I just went with you for fun, I'd have to take leave time."

"So? Doesn't Starfleet lavish you officers with tons of unnecessary vacation time? That's what Nog's using."

"Sort of—you have to accumulate it. Since I've only been back in Starfleet for about three and a half seconds, I haven't really accrued any yet."

Smirking, Quark said, "Well then it's a good thing I gave you a good excuse to sell Kira on."

"I just hope it works."

Quark wasn't worried. Ro had a streak of Ferengi-like ruthlessness in her—besides, she'd earned Kira's trust, which was no easy feat. "You'll pull it off—and if you need help, I have some excellent bribery suggestions."

Ro hit the button that opened the security-office door. "Get out of my sight, Quark."

"Whatever you say."

This time he made it halfway through the threshold before she stopped him again. It didn't surprise him—he'd been on this station for a decade and a half, under the control of the Cardassians, the Bajorans, the Dominion, and the Federation, and the one constant had been that conversations in this office took forever to end. "Oh, Quark?"

"Yes?"

"I was talking with Treir before. She was telling me about your customers last night. Had some interesting things to say about the way the wind is blowing on Ferenginar these days."

Nervously, Quark said, "Really?"

"Yeah. Just thought you'd want to know *why* Plan B worked."

Wiping his suddenly sweaty palms on his jacket, Quark said, "Okay. Thanks."

The first thing Nog did when he came off-shift was go to Captain Kira's office and officially request leave time to go to Ferenginar to be there for the birth of his stepsibling. When Kira expressed surprise that he didn't know the gender of the child, Nog explained the raffle, then tried to sell a chance to the captain, who politely declined. Father had promised to let Nog keep ten percent of any chances he sold, but only if he sold one strip's worth—that was a hundred chances. So far, he'd sold only a dozen, and half of those were to Commander Vaughn.

Once that was taken care of, he went to the bar to double-check with Uncle Quark to make sure all was well. That was when he found out that Lieutenant Ro would be accompanying them.

After that, he made a mad dash to the docking ring to catch a transport to Bajor—he had a dinner date that he had no intention of missing, especially now that he was going to be off-station for an indeterminate period.

Tonight, Nog was finally going to meet Korena, a Bajoran artist who had, to everyone's surprise, caught the heart of one Jake Sisko. Nog had barely had time to register that his best friend even *had* a girlfriend before the announcement came from Bajor that they'd gotten married.

Nog's irritation at Jake's going off and getting married without Nog even having the chance to meet her was ameliorated somewhat by Jake's offer of dinner at Bajor's finest restaurant—Fallert's, in Dahkur Province. Fallert's was located in the midst of a beautiful garden right on the coast. A salty breeze blew in from the ocean as Nog materialized in the transporter station that had beamed him from the spaceport. To his surprise, the station was of Cardassian design, though it had been a Federation transporter that brought him here.

The sun was just starting to set, painting the sky in a variety of colors that nearly stunned Nog into insensibility.

"Nog, your mouth is hanging open."

Forcing his gaze away from the incandescent sky, he turned to look at the source of the voice: Jake Sisko. As appallingly tall as ever, the human had his arm around the shoulder of a Bajoran female of much more reasonable height, though she was still taller than Nog.

Whatever concerns Nog might have had regarding his friend's whirlwind courtship abated at the look on Jake's face. *I haven't seen him glow like that since we got the captain that baseball card.*

"This," Jake continued, "is Rena."

Korena smiled. "It's a pleasure to finally meet you, Nog. Jake's told me all about you."

Nog chuckled. "Well, don't believe a word of it—I'm actually a very nice person."

They all laughed at that. Korena had a musical laugh. *It's like the sound coins make when you drop them into a safe.* He decided not to share that analogy, as non-Ferengi tended not to appreciate its true romanticism.

As the trio approached the front door, Jake said, "I can't wait to try this place."

Again, Korena smiled. "It's wonderful."

Nog was hard pressed to say whose smile was brighter, Korena's or her husband's. *Either way, their two smiles could provide all the light needed to keep the restaurant alight once the sun sets.* Aloud, he asked her, "You've been here before?"

"A few times. I went to school in Dahkur. During the Occupation, this was a Cardassian restaurant. There aren't any roads leading here—the only way to come here was by transporter, and only Cardassians had free access to transporters. Bajorans who didn't work here could only come with the permission of a Cardassian."

Before she could continue, they arrived at the maître d's station. "Reservation for three," Jake said, "in the name of Sisko."

The female behind the station bowed her head. "Of course.

It is our honor to serve the son of the Emissary and his new bride—as well as one of our Starfleet benefactors," she added with a look at Nog. In his rush to get down here, he hadn't had the chance to change out of uniform. "Please, come in."

They were led to a table by the large picture window that looked out over the ocean, providing a spectacular view of the sunset. Three screens rose out of slots in the center of the table and lit up with the day's menu. Touching an entry resulted in a holographic representation of the meal being projected onto the place setting.

Nog, however, paid little attention to that, as he was, again, mesmerized by the sunset. "It's beautiful." At a snicker from Jake, Nog again yanked his gaze away. "Sorry—it's just that I haven't seen that many Bajoran sunsets. On Ferenginar, sunset just means the sky goes from light gray to dark gray, and on the station, there are no sunsets."

"That must've been terrible." Korena sounded sincere and empathetic, which Nog appreciated. "Anyhow, after the withdrawal, one of the Bajoran cooks took over the place. It's become one of the hot spots on the planet. I came here once to paint the sunset for my grandfather."

"Did he like the painting?" Nog asked.

Korena shifted in her seat, and Jake's face fell.

"He died not too long ago," Korena said, then added quickly: "You couldn't have known, Nog, it's okay. He said he always wanted to see the sun set in Dahkur, and he never got to. So I came here, painted it, and put it up in his house. It's still there."

A voice from behind them said, "And one of these days, Rena, I'll convince you to hang that painting here."

Nog turned to see a round, jovial Bajoran male.

Once again, Korena favored them with a bright smile. "Nog, Jake, this is Fallert Kon, the owner. Kon, this is Lieutenant Nog from the space station and my husband—"

"Jake Sisko. It is an honor to have you all in my restaurant. I highly recommend the steamed *asnor* fish. Enjoy your meal."

With that, he walked off.

Nog shook his head. "Fish—when there are probably hundreds of succulent slugs in that garden outside."

Korena looked at Nog. "You're not gonna ask me to chew your food, are you?"

They all laughed once again. "That won't be necessary," Nog said.

"You know, he actually asked a girl to do that on a double date once when we were kids?" Jake said.

That quickly led into a round of reminiscing. After Jake was done embarrassing Nog with the story of the double date, Nog told Korena all about the time Jake suggested they put *frimja* dust in the air vents. Then they both told her about the nascent "Noh-Jay Consortium" that engaged in a few transactions on Bajor.

Pausing only to order, then get appetizers and wine—Korena recommended a particular vintage, which Nog had found to be almost drinkable—they continued to talk of their times together and apart. Korena seemed particularly impressed with the lengths to which the two of them went to acquire a Willie Mays baseball card for Jake's father on the eve of the Dominion War.

Then Jake talked about being part of the resistance movement on the station while the Dominion occupied it, while Nog was serving on the *Defiant*.

"I was scared to death that the Dominion would have him executed," Nog said.

Jake chuckled. "And I was scared to death that he was gonna die in combat without me around to protect him. Let's face it, Nog, I carried you."

In mock outrage, Nog said, "What're you talking about? *I* carried *you*, you stunt-eared hoo-mon."

"Who was the only sane person on the *Valiant*?"

Nog had to grant him that one. The cadets on that ship had become fanatics—worse, they had become *stupid* fanatics—and they had temporarily swept Nog up in their dangerous euphoria.

Korena shook her head as she swallowed the last of her salad. "It's funny—you two really did rub off on each other."

Nog frowned. "What do you mean?"

"Well, Jake's the son of a Starfleet captain, and you're the son of a Ferengi waiter. When the two of you met, which one would you have predicted would wind up in Starfleet and which one would wind up serving on a pirate ship?"

Defensively, Jake said, "The *Even Odds* was *not* a pirate ship."

Leaning toward Korena, Nog said, "Let him have his delusions."

Nodding, Korena said, "Yeah, it's probably safer."

"You two *do* know that I'm sitting right here?" Jake was trying to maintain the defensive tone, but it was swimming upstream against the laugh that Nog could hear building in the human's throat.

"From what you told me about what happened on the *Even Odds*," Nog said, "Uncle Quark would probably say you're a better Ferengi than I am now."

"Well," Korena said, "you did say I didn't have to chew your food."

"Actually, females don't have to do that on Ferenginar anymore."

"I know, I was just teasing you." Before Korena could go on, the main course arrived. Both Jake and Korena had the fish special. Nog, to his surprise, was met with no resistance when he asked about the possibility of sautéed slugs. *It pays to show up with the son of a religious figure,* he thought, wondering if there was some way to make that into a Rule of Acquisition.

The slugs weren't anywhere near as succulent as Nog had been hoping for—they were obviously just taken off the ground, not bred for it at all—but the spicy sautée made up for it. It tasted like a thicker version of the Cajun sauce that he'd gotten from Jake's grandfather on Earth.

After swallowing a few more slugs, Nog spoke in a more serious tone than he'd been using. "Actually, I wanted to talk to you guys about Ferenginar."

Spearing a piece of fish with his fork, Jake asked, "What about it?"

Nog explained about Father's summons. "I was wondering if you wanted to come with me. I've seen your homeworld, when I was at the Academy." He chuckled. "I practically lived in your grandfather's restaurant when I was off-duty. And I was hoping to return the favor."

Jake and Korena exchanged an awkward glance.

As soon as they did so, Nog cursed himself for an idiot for even asking. "Never mind—I shouldn't have asked. You two are newlyweds."

"It's not that we're not flattered," Korena started, "but—"

Nog held up a hand. "No, it's all right. It was selfish of me to ask. I'm sorry."

Jake said, "It's *not* selfish, Nog, I just— We're—"

"You don't have to explain. I shouldn't have said anything. I guess—" He chuckled again. "I just didn't want to be stuck alone in a transport with Uncle Quark and Lieutenant Ro for two days."

At that, Jake frowned. "What's wrong with Ro? I haven't really gotten to know her that well, but she seemed okay to me."

"Nothing's wrong with her—it's the way Uncle Quark acts when she's around."

"How does he act?"

Nog grinned. "The way you do around her."

Korena laughed at that, while Jake looked like he was contemplating throwing his side vegetables at Nog's face. "Hardy har har," Jake said.

"Besides, I haven't been home in a long time." Nog looked up, just realizing how long it had been. "Come to think of it, I haven't been home since before I signed up for Starfleet Academy. I guess I'm a little nervous about it."

"Doesn't your mom still live on Ferenginar?"

Nog nodded as he placed a few slugs in his mouth.

Korena asked, "When was the last time you saw her?"

"When Father and I left Ferenginar. Over fifteen years."

"Are you gonna see her?" Jake asked.

Letting out a long breath, Nog said, "I'm not sure. I don't know what to say to her. Leeta's more my moogie now than my biological mother was. I barely even remember her."

"You should go see her." Korena spoke with finality. "You never know when you'll have your last chance to see family before they're gone."

Jake said nothing, but he didn't have to—Nog could see the words etched on his face. Jake's trip on the *Even Odds* was a direct result of his desperate quest to find his father, motivated in part by his inability to say good-bye to him before the Prophets took him away. It all worked out in the end—Captain Sisko had been returned in time for the birth of Jake's half-sister—but Jake hadn't known that when he bought a shuttle from Uncle Quark and headed for the wormhole.

"I probably will," Nog finally said.

Korena nodded. "Good."

"You know, Nog," Jake said slowly, "if you really *want* us to come—"

Recognizing the typically human gesture, Nog shook his head. "No, it's okay. I'll be all right. Besides, why would you want to leave this sunset behind?"

4

A contract is a contract is a contract—but only between Ferengi.

—RULE OF ACQUISITION #17

Ro Laren hadn't been entirely sure what to expect when she set foot on Ferenginar, but what she got was a soggy, overwhelming, all-encompassing sense of pure humidity. She intellectually knew that humidity couldn't get above one hundred percent, but if it could, Ferenginar would have managed it.

When she, Quark, and Nog boarded the transport that the Grand Nagus sent, they were required to pay an entrance fee of one slip of gold-pressed latinum each. When they arrived on Ferenginar, each of them had to pay a one-slip exit fee.

They disembarked into the Fram Memorial Spaceport; according to Nog, Fram had the spaceport built, and his will stipulated that it remain named after him even after death, regardless of who bought it. The dark blue carpet was plush, and several stands selling a variety of goods lined the walls. Holographic ads for everything from Slug-O-Cola to the latest in outerwear to the finest tooth sharpeners were festooned about the floorspace. A few doors were labeled with a phrase in the Ferengi script that Ro's amateur eye was fairly sure said AUTHORIZED PERSONNEL ONLY.

Walking down the carpeted floor, Ro noticed an odd background noise in the air, a persistent, irregular metallic popping sound that permeated the spaceport. It took Ro a few moments to realize that what she was hearing was the constant rattle of thousands of latinum slips being paid in hundreds of different transactions—most of them occurring by the simple expedient of dropping a slip into a receptacle just like the ones Ro had used on the transport.

Ro asked, "Uh, Quark? What if I didn't have a slip to pay my exit fee with?"

Quark's answer was to point at three Ferengi wearing black leather outfits with white trim, carrying neural whips, and leading a crying Bolian toward one of the doors that was only for authorized use.

"Local law enforcement?" Ro asked.

Nodding, Quark said, "My guess is that Bolian didn't have his exit fee."

"He'll probably have to work the fee off," Nog said. "Actually, the work he'll have to do will be worth a lot more than the one slip he didn't have."

"Do they use those whips?" Ro asked.

"Only if they have to," Quark said. "C'mon, Rom will have sent an aircar."

As soon as they stepped out onto the outer walkway, the humidity—no, the *sogginess*—hit Ro like a phaser blast. A sound like meat sizzling on an open fire assaulted her ears as rain slammed onto a variety of surfaces. The only nearby shelter was a clear enclosure about ten square meters in size, in which stood a few Ferengi and one Vulcan. Quark dropped some slips into a receptacle that hung from one of the enclosure's sides, after which a door opened up.

Once they got into the blessed dryness of the enclosure, Ro's uniform was drenched, her hair was plastered to her head, water dripped off her chin in rivulets, and her entire body felt like it had been dunked in a vat of rainwater. Her *bones* felt wet—and that after less than a minute's exposure. The air-conditioning system in the enclosure was on full blast, evaporating the surface water, and making her shiver. Wiping some wet hair out of her eyes, she understood why most of the life-forms on this world, including the dominant one, had no body hair—that was not an evolutionary path that would be of much use on this soaked planet.

"Why don't you guys have any kind of covering to keep you dry?"

Nog looked confused. He was also in his uniform, but he didn't seem bothered by the fact that he was now soaked to the skin. "What for? It's only *frippering*."

"Only?" Ro wiped the water that was dripping from her eyebrows into her eyes as she asked the question.

Nog nodded. "Oh, yes. You should see it when it's *oolmering*—or worse, *glebbening*."

Ro stared at Nog. "You mean it gets worse?"

"All the time," Quark said. Then he gave her a look of incredulity. "You think *this* is bad rain?"

"Quark," Ro said, "when I was with the Maquis, we had to hide out in the jungles on the southern continent of Volon VI. Half my cell were bitten all over by these bugs that were just *everywhere*. The humidity was abominable. My shirt was so wet you could read through it, and it was *black*. Walking through that jungle was like swimming in brackish, algae-infested waters." She looked at Quark. "Standing out in that *frippering* rain for thirty seconds made me realize just how good I had it on Volon VI."

Before Quark could reply, an aircar pulled up to the enclosure. An opening formed, hitting Ro with another blast of humidity. *I'm going to have pneumonia by the time we get to Rom's place.* The aircar's side door was also open.

The driver said, "I'm here to take Quark, Nog, and their guest to the Grand Nagus."

That earned all three of them looks of surprise from the others in the enclosure—except for the Vulcan, who remained typically impassive.

Ro started to move toward the opening, but Quark stopped her. Reaching into his jacket pocket, he pulled out a slip of latinum, and waved it a few times.

Once the driver saw it, he touched a control, and a canopy arced out from the roof of the aircar and butted up against the enclosure, thus providing shelter for the one meter between the enclosure and the inside of the vehicle.

The three of them quickly moved into the aircar—which

had even more intense air-conditioning than the enclosure—and sat in the aircar's *amra*-skin passenger seats.

Nog was grinning. "Not bad."

Quark dropped the slip he'd promised in exchange for the shelter into a small receptacle on the back of the driver's seat—which, Ro noticed, wasn't *amra*-skin, but plain vinyl.

"We'll be at the nagal residence in twenty minutes," the driver said.

Quark dropped two more slips into the receptacle.

"Make that ten minutes," the driver said without missing a beat.

Shaking her head, Ro said, "Whoever manufactures those latinum receptacles must have made a fortune."

"Fram," Nog said. "The same one who built the spaceport. Those receptacles are the most valuable patent in the entire Ferengi Alliance."

"And he didn't even invent them," Quark said. "Some kid came up with the idea. Fram paid the boy two strips to use the idea, and then made a fortune off it."

Ro regarded Quark with amazement. "What happened to the boy?"

Quark shrugged. "Who cares? He lost."

"The Twenty-Fifth Rule," Nog added.

Leaning back in the chair, Ro said, "I'm starting to understand why you all exploit each other so much—with weather like this all the time, it puts you in an aggressive mood to begin with. For example, I have this tremendous urge to strangle you for talking me into coming along with you."

Staring at her in shock, Quark asked, "You don't like it here?"

"Not so far."

"It'll grow on you, trust me."

"Quark, the only thing growing on me is mold."

Smiling, Quark said, "Food for later, then."

Ro decided not to speak to Quark for the rest of the trip. It cut down on her nausea.

When they arrived at the nagal residence, Ro got out of the aircar—the parking area was sheltered from the rain—and looked up. The mansion looked to be three stories tall. Then, remembering the differences in Ferengi height, she revised that estimate to four or five. The structure was made of solid dura- nium, from the looks of it, gilded with enough gold to keep it glowing—as much as anything could glow in this rain—but not enough to compromise the integrity of the walls. It was a wise precaution for the home of a head of state, and Ro ad- mired the security consideration.

A rounded door parted to reveal a Ferengi of about Quark's age and a middle-aged Ferengi woman. She recognized the former from the signing ceremony on Bajor months ago: Rom. For a Grand Nagus, Rom didn't look the part—he wasn't wearing his robe or carrying the staff with the golden head of Grand Nagus Gint, for one thing.

The middle-aged woman was Quark and Rom's mother, Ishka. She looked more regal than her son, wearing a floral- print skintight outfit that emphasized her shape a little too much, where each flower had a small gem in its center. The gem varied depending on the flower—Ro saw diamonds, ru- bies, Spican flame gems, and *orvats*, at least. She also wore a neckframe—the Ferengi version of earrings—made of latinum and as encrusted with jewels as the outfit.

Naturally, Ro had to duck to enter the place, as it was built for Ferengi. Ro was average height for a Bajoran woman, but the doorway came up only to her neck. She recalled that the last Grand Nagus had a Hupyrian servant. *He must have had to fold himself in half just to get in the front door.*

As soon as they entered, Rom handed each of them a towel and then gave Quark a padd. "Welcome to my home. Please place your imprint on the legal waivers, and deposit your ad- mission fee in the box by the door. Remember—my house is my house."

After thumbing the padd, Quark handed it back. "As are its contents."

Rom then broke into a grin. "Brother, it's so good to see you!" He turned to Nog. "And you too, Nog!" He pulled his son into a warm embrace. Ro heard a squishing sound as the hug squeezed rainwater out of Nog's uniform jacket.

While father and son were reunited, Quark put three slips

into the receptacle. Ro asked, "Do you *really* have to go through all that nonsense every time you go into someone's house?"

Quark gave Ro an arch look. "Do I mock your Bajoran traditions?"

Ro laughed. "Quark, *I* mock Bajoran traditions—so don't think yours are going to get off easy."

Ishka then spoke, looking at Ro. "And who is this?"

"Mother, this is Lieutenant Ro Laren, head of security on Deep Space 9," Quark said formally.

Ro bowed slightly, and put her wrists together in front of her chin and cupped her hands in the traditional Ferengi greeting. "A pleasure to meet you, ma'am."

Returning the gesture, Ishka said, "Likewise, Lieutenant."

"She's serving as my bodyguard," Quark added. "After all, I'm an important diplomat, so Starfleet felt the need to send some protection along."

Ro managed to hold in a bark of laughter, and she noticed that Nog was rolling his eyes.

So was Ishka as she looked at Rom. "I knew giving your brother a title was a mistake. 'Make him an ambassador,' I said, 'and he'll start getting delusions of grandeur.'"

"I wouldn't worry about it, ma'am," Ro said. "Quark *already* had delusions of grandeur."

Quark shot her a look. "Hey!"

Ishka laughed. "Oh, I *like* you." She leaned in close. Ro—who was by far the tallest person in the room—bent over in order to hear her better. Ishka whispered, "A lot more than the last Bajoran that was brought into this house, *believe* me. Why Rom couldn't just find a nice Ferengi female . . ." She stood upright. "But in any case, it's good to see all of you. I just wish the news was better."

"What do you mean?" Nog asked anxiously as they moved into the sitting room. Ro tried not to let her jaw drop at the lavishness—and downright hideousness—of the décor.

"Leeta's gotten worse," Rom said in a tone that Ro could describe only as a frantic monotone. "Dr. Orpax will be calling any minute."

"I'm still not sure you should be using him," Ishka said. "Remember, he *did* misdiagnose Quark."

Ro whirled on Quark. "What?"

Waving dismissively, Quark said, "It was nothing."

"Nothing?" Ishka sounded outraged as she sat down on a particularly comfortable-looking chair. "Quark, he said you had Dorek syndrome!"

"It wasn't a misdiagnosis—exactly." At Ro's questioning glance, Quark said, "Brunt bribed Orpax to tell me I had Dorek as part of a plot to discredit me. He knew I'd try to sell my vacuum-desiccated remains to offset my debt, and he bought the whole lot."

Ro saw where this was going. "When you didn't die, you had to break the contract—that's why the FCA banned you for, what was it, two years?"

"Only one year, actually—just *seemed* like two." He looked at Ishka. "Anyhow, that wasn't Orpax's fault. He's still the most expensive doctor on Ferenginar, and you know that means he's good."

Frowning, Ro said, "I don't see the connection, there."

Every Ferengi in the room stared at her.

Nog quickly said, "She's Bajoran."

Ishka muttered, "We all know how little Bajorans understand Ferengi."

"Moogie!" Rom cried.

"Well, I'm sorry, Rom, but it's true. I know you love Leeta very much, and I'm glad that she makes you so happy, but she doesn't understand commerce at all!"

"What do you expect?" Quark asked. "She's a dabo girl— and not even that good a dabo girl."

Rom redirected his outrage to his brother. "She was a *great* dabo girl!"

Quark grinned. "You haven't seen Treir in action."

Shaking her head, Ishka said, "This is why Ferengi females need to take a more active role in society. Tradition has made us so subservient, so limited, so—so *uninteresting*, that males are turning to other species to find a true life companion."

A beeping interrupted Rom's response. *"Grand Nagus, Dr. Orpax is contacting you."*

"I'll take it in here." Rom got up from his chair and slowly walked over to the gilded piece of abstract art on the wall—which, Ro realized belatedly, was a comm unit.

Rom touched a control, and a big-eared, small-eyed Ferengi with yellow teeth and the oddest nose showed up on the screen.

Before Rom could say anything, the doctor spoke. *"I'm sorry to say, Grand Nagus, that the news, it is not good. Your wife, she is deteriorating—her immune system is weakened because the baby is causing so many physical problems. Unfortunately, the best option to fix the physical problems is surgery, but I cannot perform it in her weakened condition."*

"What *can* you do?" Rom sounded like—*well*, Ro thought, *exactly like someone who fears losing his wife and his child in one shot.*

"For now, we wait and see. If her condition improves, operate we can. I will keep you informed—but I would not allow hope to rise too high, I'm afraid."

"Thank you, Doctor."

"Grand Nagus!"

Ro turned to see that someone else had entered the room. She recognized the pug-nosed Ferengi from the files she'd been re-studying just a couple of days ago: Krax.

Rom didn't even look at Krax, preferring to stare despondently at the floor. He reminded Ro of a child whose pet had just died, and she had to tamp down a sudden urge to give him a hug. "What is it, Krax?"

"The Economic Congress of Advisors has called an emergency session."

Continuing to stare at the floor, Rom said, "I can't. Tell them to postpone until tomorrow. Or maybe the next day."

"This can't wait," Krax said. "That's why it's an *emergency* session. Besides, *Brunt* is the one who called it."

Ishka walked over to Rom and put her arm around his shoulder. "Rom, sweetie—you have to go. If Brunt's up to something, we need to know what it is."

"I guess you're right," Rom said, stretching the "I" out to almost three syllables.

"We'll go with you," Nog said.

"Really?" That seemed to perk Rom up.

Ishka said, "We don't *all* have to go to the Tower of Commerce."

"Yeah," Quark said. "We can just wait here."

"Well, *I'm* going," Nog said, standing up. "He's my father, and I'm going to be there for him."

"You'll just have to sit outside," Ishka said. "All the congress's sessions are closed."

"Closed?" Quark asked. "You don't sell live broadcasts?"

Ishka shook her head. "Visual records starting the day after. The suspense builds anticipation."

Quark nodded. "Makes sense."

Ro stopped herself from saying something snide, and instead turned to Quark. "I'd like to go, too. You *did* promise to show me the Tower of Commerce."

Sighing, Quark said, "I did, didn't I? Fine, we'll make a *trip* of it, then." Quark spoke in his most sarcastic tone, which Ro chose to ignore.

I can't lose Leeta.

That was all Rom thought as he rode the elevator up the Tower of Commerce to the meeting room on the twenty-fifth floor. He barely noticed Quark complaining about the riding fee, saying he wouldn't pay it when it was seven strips five years ago, he certainly wasn't going to pay *ten* strips now. Ro's subsequent assurance that there was no way in hell she was walking up twenty-five flights of stairs barely impinged on Rom's consciousness. Only in the deepest recesses of his brain did he acknowledge the sound of Quark pointing out that Ro's longer legs made her better suited to take the stairs than any of them. And the fact that Nog offered to pay Ro's ten-strip fee, prompting Quark to jump in and pay for both him and her to take the elevator, only registered briefly in Rom's mind.

Mostly, he just thought about Leeta. Thought about how she looked the day Quark hired her to run one of the dabo tables—her big ledger-colored eyes, her lovely *rok*-jewel-colored hair, her pearl-colored smile, and that amazing curvaceous figure that he imagined every night before he went to bed.

Of course, she immediately made a play for Dr. Bashir. Women *always* made a play for Dr. Bashir. When it came out later that the doctor had been genetically enhanced, Rom had been convinced that the first adjustment they made was to give him some kind of pheromone that made women go after him.

But then, after that trip to Risa, they broke up. Leeta was single. For weeks, Rom tried to build up the courage to ask her out on a date, to tell her how he felt, but it wasn't until she was two seconds away from leaving the station with some human or other that he finally was able to tell her he loved her.

They'd been all but inseparable ever since. Even when they were physically apart, as happened more than once during the war, they were always joined at the heart.

And now she's gonna die.

As the elevator finally arrived at the twenty-fifth floor—amid Quark's grumbling that for ten strips, the least they could do is make the thing *faster* than walking would have been—Rom admonished himself. *Don't think like that! I thought Quark was gonna die when he was diagnosed with Dorek. I thought I was gonna die when the Dominion imprisoned me for sabotage. I thought Nog was gonna die a lot of times during the war. Quark lived. I lived. Nog lived. So Leeta will live too!*

As Nog, Ro, and Quark took their seats in the waiting area outside the meeting room, Rom entered, trying to sustain the burst of confidence he'd forced upon himself. *Leeta will be okay.* The words became his mantra. *Leeta will be okay.*

He entered. The rest of the congress was present, and they all rose at his arrival. Rom set his staff of office up against the meeting-room table, took his seat, and pointedly refused to look at the tapestry of Gint.

All the congressmen sat down once Rom was seated, with one exception: Brunt. The wide-mouthed, small-eared former liquidator was holding a padd in his hand and wore the insincere smile that he always employed when he wasn't sneering.

Leeta will be okay. Leeta will be okay.

Fal called the meeting to order. "This session was called by Congressman Brunt." He then nodded to Brunt, who nodded back.

"Thank you all for coming," Brunt said. "Trust me, this will be brief—but painful. You see, in the course of a routine investigation, a rather shocking fact has come to light. You're all aware, of course, that the Grand Nagus's wife is expecting a child. Just two days ago, I purchased a chance in the raffle that the nagus is holding in celebration of the child's birth."

One whole chance, Rom thought bitterly. *How generous.* The other congressmen, who understood the Thirty-Third Rule, all bought at least ten each—even Liph.

"Today, however, I am ashamed to have done so—as you all will be when I reveal what I have learned. An investigator from the new agency that Congressman Nurt has formed came across a fascinating document while investigating a tip from an anonymous informant about a businessman named Dav."

Rom had only been half listening to Brunt's diatribe, but at the mention of Dav, his lobes perked right up.

"As some of you may know," Brunt continued, "Dav has a daughter named Prinadora. For a time, Prinadora was married to the youngest son of Keldar, named *Rom*."

All eyes at the table turned to look at the Grand Nagus.

Brunt went on. "Prinadora and Rom had a standard five-year marriage, during which time she bore him a son named Nog." Brunt said Nog's name as if it were a curse, which didn't surprise Rom. Brunt's disdain for Rom's entire family extended to his Starfleet-officer son. "Rom then signed an extension—an *indefinite* extension!"

This time, the mouths of all the congressmen fell open as they stared at Rom. Rom's own mouth did likewise. *What is he talking about?*

"After five years, Rom and his son left Prinadora, with all his money going to Dav. He went to work for his brother in a bar on a Cardassian space station—but he was *still married*! And the marriage contract did contain the standard monogamy clause!"

The congressmen started to mutter to themselves. Rom didn't pay attention to any of it, choosing instead to stare at the tapestry on the far wall, and feel more like Smeet with every passing moment.

Brunt, naturally, wasn't finished. "I ask you, my fellow

congressmen—is *this* what we want in our Grand Nagus? A man who casts aside a dutiful Ferengi wife who bore him a son in order to cavort with an alien and to pollute the Ferengi bloodlines with halfbreed filth?"

Kain started to talk, coughed twice, then spoke without even bothering to save his phlegm, which right there indicated the depth of his outrage. "You mean to tell me that his marriage to that Bajoran woman is in violation of a contract? A *Ferengi* contract?"

Brunt smiled, and for the first time that Rom could remember, the smile was quite sincere. "Yes, that is what I mean to tell you, Congressman Kain. Our Grand Nagus—has broken a contract!"

5

A deal is a deal—until a better one comes along.

—RULE OF ACQUISITION #16

"What do you mean the marriage is illegitimate?"

Quark had said nothing until they got back to the nagal residence, mostly because he couldn't say anything prior to that. Rom left the meeting holding a padd in one hand and his staff in the other, and was otherwise as silent as the Prime Bank's obelisk.

He finally revealed what was happening when they were all in the living room of the residence.

In response to Quark's rather irritated question, Rom silently handed Quark the padd.

"What's it say, Quark?" Mother asked.

Waving her off, Quark said, "Give me a second." He read the report, which had been filed by someone called Investigator Rwogo. *I didn't even know they had investigators on Ferenginar.* According to the padd, Rwogo didn't work for the FCA. He made a mental note to ask about it later.

"According to this," Quark said, "some investigator was looking through Dav's records."

Nog leaned over to Ro and whispered, "My maternal grandfather."

Ro nodded.

"The investigation included a check on Rom and Prinadora's marriage contract. Turns out the extension wasn't exactly what we all thought it was."

Mother looked at Rom, who was staring straight ahead, unblinking. "Rom, what is he talking about? I thought you signed a five-year extension."

"So did I," Quark said, "and that, when the term expired, Dav would be entitled to all of Rom's assets. That's what Rom told me when he and Nog came to Terok Nor looking for work because he had no money." He held up the padd's display. "But according to this, it was an indefinite extension, and Dav got all of Rom's assets if Rom ever left her. But they're *still* married, and the marriage has a standard monogamy clause."

"Wait a minute," Ro said. "This contract was originally drafted, what, twenty years ago, right?"

"Twenty-five, actually. Why?"

"You mean to tell me that twenty-five years ago, Ferengi marriage contracts had a standard monogamy clause. Why?"

"To preserve family values," Mother said with her usual disdain for proper Ferengi traditions. "Most people didn't care where a Ferengi male went to get his *oo-mox*, but a stable home—and one with as few females actually living in it as possible—was desired, so it's preferred that marriages are one-to-one."

Ro got that look on her face that Bajorans always got whenever the subject of Ferengi societal norms came up. "Gee, how enlightened."

"Tell me about it," Mother said.

"Can we get back to the subject at hand?" Quark then looked over at Nog, who was staring at his father in disbelief. Quark recognized it as the same expression on Quark's own face when Rom revealed that the boy was attending a human school, and again when he announced his intention to apply to Starfleet Academy. *Now you know how we felt, kid.*

"Father, is this true?" Nog asked.

Rom kept staring ahead.

"Don't you remember?" Ro asked Nog.

"I was only seven, and Father never really talked about it."

Ishka also stared at Rom. "I only heard about it, too. Rom, answer your son, *is this true?*"

Rom stood up. He opened his mouth, but then it just hung there.

Quark waited patiently. It often took Rom a few minutes to rev himself up to coherent speech.

Finally, he spoke. "I have to go see Leeta."

With that, he left.

Quark snorted. "What do you think he's gonna tell her?"

"The truth," Nog said defensively.

"Which is what?" Quark asked.

"Rom wouldn't lie to us," Mother said. "He's a good boy."

Nog said, "Grandmother's right. Father would *never* do anything like that. He's not capable of it."

"Isn't he?"

Quark whirled on Ro. "What are you saying?"

"I remember when I was reading the files Odo left behind for his successor. One of the things he said about Rom was that he'd made a mistake about him. I remembered that, because it was one of only about three mistakes that Odo actually admitted to in the entire time he was assigned to the station. His exact words were that he underestimated Rom." She looked at everyone in the room, ending with Quark. "I'm willing to bet each and every one of you in this room has, at some point or other, underestimated him, too."

"*I* haven't," Quark said indignantly. "If anything, I've *over*-estimated him. He's an idiot, always has been."

"He's *not* an idiot," Nog said. "You always put him down, but the truth is, Uncle, your bar would have fallen apart if it wasn't for my father!"

"Oh yeah? Well, if—"

"That's enough!" Mother cried. "Both of you stop it! This whole thing is ridiculous. Aren't we all forgetting something?"

"What?" Quark asked.

"*Brunt* is the one who raised this accusation."

Quark blinked once, then again, then said two words he rarely ever had cause to say in his life: "Mother's right. Brunt's been out to get us for years. The evidence has gotta be fake."

"So where do we stand?" Mother asked.

"In trouble," said a voice from the doorway.

Quark turned to see Krax standing there. *Great, just what we need, Zek Junior here to get in the way.*

Krax held up a data chip. "This is the visual record for the session. I was able to obtain an advance copy for a fee."

Mother stood up. "Well, don't just stand there, play it!"

"I've already watched the important part," Krax said. "The congress is going to review the evidence between now and the next official session. At that point, they're going to vote on whether or not to oust Rom as Grand Nagus."

"We can't let that happen," Mother said with her usual inability to grasp the obvious.

"Why can't we?" Quark said. "Seriously, what would be so wrong about Rom not being Grand Nagus?"

"Rom is a *fine* Grand Nagus, Quark. Just because *you* want to cling to the outmoded ways, doesn't mean—"

Quark stood up and went face-to-face with his mother. He hesitated for a second—the last time they got into a heated argument, she had a major cardiac infarction—but this needed to be said. "They're not 'outmoded,' Mother, they're the way Ferengi society has *flourished*!" Before Mother could counterargue, Quark waved her off. "But leave that aside for a minute, Mother—forget which one of us is right and which one of us is wrong, because you'll never see reason that I'm the one who's right."

Mother grimaced. "Quark—"

Holding up his hands, Quark said, "The point is this, Mother—why are you here?"

That caught her off-guard. "What are you talking about, Quark?"

Nog spoke up. "She's here to help Father, obviously."

"And why is that?" Quark asked Nog. "Shouldn't she be on Risa in happy retirement with Zek?"

He turned back to Mother, and as soon as he saw the look on her face, Quark knew he was right. "It's true, isn't it? You came back because *Rom couldn't handle it*. He needed your help, just like Zek did. At least with Zek, you had an excuse—he was getting old, he needed someone to make him focus. But with Rom, you're fighting his very nature. Rom isn't a great leader, Mother—he's an *engineer*. He sits in small, cramped rooms with computers and solves problems other people give him."

"That's not what an engineer is," Nog said. "An engineer is someone who fixes things that are broken. He makes things better. Some of the finest leaders I've known have been engineers—like Chief O'Brien."

"Nog is right," Mother said. "Rom is just the person to fix what's broken on Ferenginar."

"Ferenginar isn't broken!" Quark cried. *Why can't anyone in this room understand that? Why can't they see what I—and Chek and the rest of his people—see?* "And you all should know Rule of Acquisition Number Two-Eighty: 'If it ain't broke, don't fix it'!"

In that tone she always took when she refused to admit that Quark was right, Mother asked, "So what's your solution, Quark? Put Brunt in the nagus's chair? Because that's what's going to happen. And you *know* it!"

That brought Quark up short. Rom might have been a terrible choice for Grand Nagus—but Brunt was several orders of magnitude worse. He let personal issues get in the way of business, and had no conception of leading by example, as a nagus had to. Twice, Brunt had tried to grab the nagal staff, and both times Quark had been instrumental in stopping him.

It looks like the third time really is the charm.

"You're right," he muttered, pained at having to give his mother credit for being correct twice in one lifetime. "We have to stop him."

From the couch, Ro said, "That may be harder than you think."

Quark looked over to see that Ro was fiddling with Rom's padd. "What do you mean?"

"Well, I've only done a preliminary check, but if this thing is fake, it's a very very good one. I think everyone in this room knows how hard it is to forge a Ferengi contract, and none of the indicators are here."

"Keep checking," Mother said. "We *have* to prove it's a fake."

Ro stood up. "We may not be able to." Before Mother could object, Ro said, "But we may not have to, either."

Nog said, "The lieutenant is right. There's more than one way to prove a crime. One is physical evidence—another is a confession."

Ro smiled. "Starfleet security training at its finest."

"I took Professor Pembleton's course on—"

Quark rolled his eyes. "Can we save the mutual admiration society for another time, please?"

"Sorry." Nog put his hands together. "We need to investigate. I'll go see Prinadora."

Mother shot Nog a look. "Are you sure that's a good idea, Nog?"

"She's my mother—it's my first time back home in years. What could be more natural than wanting to visit with my mother?"

"You'd better be discreet," Ro said. "If Krax got his hands on this, so did other people. Besides, I doubt Brunt's gonna keep it a secret. This will be all over the planet by dinnertime. You going to visit your mother right after your father is revealed to be cheating her won't help Rom any."

Nog nodded. "Good point. I'll be careful not to be seen."

"How you gonna pull that off?" Quark asked.

Grinning, Nog said, "Starfleet security training at its finest. Don't worry about it."

Quark watched Nog depart the living room. Mother went over to the replicator to get herself a snail juice. Ro just looked at him, but Quark didn't return the look right away. He was thinking about his brother, and what his brother had been to him for all these years.

Nog was right—the bar would've fallen to pieces without him.

Finally, he looked up at Ro's gorgeous face. She looked concerned more than anything. He had to admit, she was taking Ferenginar better than he'd expected. Non-Ferengi usually spent days complaining about the rain, but once she got her initial shock out of her system, she hadn't said a word about it. And now that the family—indeed, the entire Ferengi Alliance—was facing a crisis, she was right in there helping out.

Putting a hand on her arm, Quark said, "Listen, Laren—you've got to get to work on that contract. Use all those skills Starfleet taught you, and all those Maquis tricks you picked up—that contract's a fake, and we have to prove it."

"Quark—" Ro hesitated. She let out a long breath. "What if it isn't a fake? What if Brunt's telling the truth?"

Snorting, Quark said, "Brunt wouldn't know the truth if it bit him on his left lobe. Besides, it has to be a fake. Rom wouldn't *do* that."

"I know you love your brother, Quark, but he still hasn't denied—"

"I don't just love him, Laren, I *know* him. I grew up with him, and we spent a long time together on the station, and I can tell you this: Rom isn't capable of what Brunt's accusing him of, and you know why? It would mean hurting someone."

"I don't follow."

Quark took a breath. "The one thing Rom won't do is gratuitously hurt someone. The one thing Rom *can't* do is gratuitously hurt someone he loves, and I can tell you this: He loved Prinadora then as much as he loves Leeta now. Why do you think Rom's so bad at business? Why do you think he's floundering so much as Grand Nagus that Mother had to come back to help him out? He's a *nice guy*. There's a saying I came across a couple of years ago when we were getting ready to play some human game that Captain Sisko liked: 'Nice guys finish last.' It should be added to the Rules of Acquisition. Until Zek made him nagus, Rom *always* finished last because he can't help being a nice guy. It's why he made my bar the embassy, it's why he stayed behind on the station when the Dominion took it over when he should've gone to safety on Bajor, it's why he let Nog go to the human school and attend Starfleet Academy."

He walked over to the replicator. All this speechifying was making him thirsty. "Slug-O-Cola," he said after placing three slips in the slot. The green beverage materialized with a hum. Quark undid the top, looked under the cap to see if he'd won a prize—he didn't, of course, he never did—and took a sip of the refreshingly slimy soft drink.

Then he fixed Ro with a serious look. "If Prinadora was still

Rom's legal spouse when he became Grand Nagus, she would be entitled to all the benefits of being the nagus's wife, and there is no way Rom would deny her that. So I want you to take that contract and put it to every test you know how to put it to, and then I want you to make up a few tests, but you're going to exonerate my brother."

Ro chuckled. "Is that an order, Mr. Ambassador?"

Quark shrugged. "You're my bodyguard—you're supposed to do what I tell you."

"You just keep thinking that."

"Quark?"

He turned to look at his mother, who was now staring at him with wide eyes, her head bowed, and her voice quiet. It was the most properly female she'd been in his presence since she gave back her illegally obtained profits to Brunt five years earlier.

"Yes, Mother?"

"That was the sweetest thing I've ever heard you say about Rom." Then she broke into that know-it-all smile that drove Quark insane. "You know, Quark, I may not like you all that much—but times like this remind me why I love you."

She pressed her nose to his, and despite himself, he returned the gesture.

"Now let's go and save Rom," she said, putting her arm around him.

Bindu was whistling the Slug-O-Cola jingle as he paid the fee to use the aircar shelter. It was another beautiful day on Ferenginar, with the rain *vinkling* down on the city, causing beautiful rivulets in the walkways that flowed in lovely patterns.

It was a good day to be a Ferengi worker.

This day had been like any other. He had woken up, had his usual arachnids for breakfast, watched the morning newsfeed from Ferengi Commercial News, then headed off to the aircar stop.

As usual, Joq was there. They always took the same aircar to work, since they both had offices in the Zalp Building, just down the street from the Tower of Commerce.

Joq was a bit shorter than Bindu, though Bindu mostly attributed that to the fact that he was always stooped over, where Bindu had excellent posture.

"See FCN this morning?" Joq asked.

Bindu sighed. Joq *always* asked that, and his answer was always the same: "Of course. I watch FCN every morning, you know that."

"So you heard about the Grand Nagus."

"I saw what FCN reported about the Grand Nagus, but I don't believe it for a minute. I mean, really, you can't trust everything you see on FCN."

Joq snorted. "FCN reported that Zek was retiring, and predicted that Rom would be made Grand Nagus."

"They also proclaimed that the Dominion was weeks away from victory over the Federation after the attack on Earth, which was several months before the Dominion *lost* the war. They declared Eelwasser the new winner in the cola wars, and that Slug-O-Cola would be out of business within a year."

Grudgingly, Joq said, "All right, I admit they were off there, but—"

Bindu smiled. "And then, of course, they reported that ridiculous story about how the Grand Nagus's paramour was rescued from the Dominion by a team of Ferengi commandoes on some abandoned Cardassian station. I mean really, Joq, you didn't believe *that* nonsense, did you?"

"And what if they're right about the nagus, eh?" Joq asked, pointing a finger at Bindu. "He broke a *contract*. And a contract is a contract—"

"—is a contract, yes I *know* the Rules, Joq."

"Ha!" Joq kept pointing, his finger now digging into Bindu's jacket, which was simply ruining its lines. "You wouldn't know the Rules of Acquisition if they sharpened your teeth for you! I'm telling you, this is just the latest in a series. Do you know the market is down a hundred points? Well? *Did* you?"

Sighing, Bindu said, "I *told* you I watched FCN this morning, didn't I?"

"And stocks are dropping all over the Alliance. It's a good thing I sold my shares in Slug-O-Cola last week, or I'd be destitute by now!"

"My stocks dropped too," Bindu said patiently, "but not catastrophically."

"And you aren't worried?"

Bindu shook his head. "Every time the Grand Nagus sneezes, the market goes down a few points and stocks drop. It'll pass."

"A hundred points is not 'a few'! The last time the market crashed that badly—"

"—was when Zek was sick for a day. It was an unnecessary panic, as Zek proved the next day." The aircar arrived. Bindu pulled his two-strip fare out of his pocket. "Honestly, Joq, you have no sense of history."

"*I* don't have a sense of history?" Joq cried as he pulled out his own two strips and got onto the aircar.

As usual, there weren't any seats. There never were this close to the capital city.

Joq continued his harangue once they'd settled into the aircar, each having paid the one-strip fee for holding on to the pole. "*You're* the one who doesn't have a sense of history, my friend. Ferengi history is a long and noble one, and one that doesn't include females earning profit—or wearing clothes. It doesn't include benefits for workers, either."

The aircar lurched, forcing Bindu to grip the pole more tightly. It wasn't that windy out, and Bindu wondered if it was a different driver today. The aircar company kept the drivers out of sight of the passengers, as it kept their insurance rates down.

"I don't see you complaining about getting to take a vacation," Bindu said as the aircar took another lurch.

"Of course not—I *need* a vacation from the supervisor. He hates giving us breaks, hates having to pay overtime, and takes it out on us. It's been miserable at work since the reforms came in."

"Really?" This genuinely surprised Bindu. "But my office has been wonderful. Productivity is up, profits are up—and yes, wages are down overall since we have to pay income tax, but it's looking very likely that we'll get a higher-than-usual salary bump next year."

Joq looked at Bindu like he was crazy—which was fitting,

since that was how Bindu also saw Joq. "That's madness. How can work be improved?"

"Well, everyone wants to go to work now that it's a pleasant place to be. Makes us all want to do better for the boss. And you know what? It's working! Soon I'll have saved enough to buy that house in the suburbs."

"Why would you want to do that?" Joq asked.

Bindu pretended to think about it, counting off notions on his fingers. "Well, let's see, I'd have more space than I have now. I'd actually get a seat on the aircar." Then he opened a third finger and looked right at Joq. "And I won't have to talk to you every day."

"Laugh all you want, but mark my words—this is the end of Ferenginar as we know it. Rom will run us into ruin!"

Before Bindu could reply, the aircar lurched again. *Definitely a different driver.* His grip on the pole became white-knuckled. He looked out the window to see the Tower of Commerce, glowing in the gloom of the day in the center of the capital city, its spire climbing into the cumulus clouds like a lightning rod, a beacon of hope to Ferengi everywhere. *Maybe if I get that promotion, I'll get the office with the view of the Tower. Got to remember to check the account I've been saving up the bribe money in.*

As the vehicle began its descent, the final ad of the ride appeared in a holographic display projected over everyone's heads from the ceiling. It was always the same set of ads every day, and Bindu had long since learned to tune them out, but this last one was different. He'd never heard the music before, but it was a rather catchy jingle.

A very honest-looking Ferengi asked, *"Tired of the same old same old? You should be. It's time for something new. So wipe that green slime off your lips and go for today's soda: Eelwasser."*

The image switched to another Ferengi that looked familiar to Bindu. He was holding a bottle of Eelwasser.

"I'm Congressman Brunt. When I joined the FCA, I drank Slug-O-Cola, but now I know better. Like any good member of the Economic Congress of Advisors, I go with what works

now—*and that means Eelwasser.*" He took a long sip of the liquid, then wiped his lips with a sleeve. "*Ah, refreshing. When I'm Grand Nagus—which I hope, for the sake of Ferenginar, will be soon—I'll make Eelwasser the official drink of the nagal residence, because I believe in doing what's right.*"

Brunt was replaced with the Eelwasser logo. A voice said, "*Sponsored by Chek Pharmaceuticals on behalf of the Brunt for Grand Nagus Campaign.*" Then the logo and the jingle, which had been playing in the background the entire time, faded.

Bindu frowned. "We already have a Grand Nagus."

"If we're lucky, this Brunt fella will take over," Joq said. "You heard him, he used to be FCA. *They* understand *real* Ferengi ways."

"I don't want a Grand Nagus who drinks Eelwasser. That stuff is vile."

The aircar came in for a landing, though the driver apparently was having a hard time coordinating the braking thrusters with the ground. Bindu felt the half-digested arachnids he'd swallowed for breakfast creeping back up his throat, and was grateful that the ride was over.

As they milled with the crowd toward the aircar's exit, Joq said, "Who cares what he drinks? As long as he isn't Rom. Besides, you heard who's backing him—Chek Pharmaceuticals. They're a good business, and don't have any connections to politics. They're not insiders like Slug-O-Cola."

"What do you mean, 'insiders'?" Bindu asked, thinking that Joq was crazier even than usual this morning.

"Nilva, the head of Slug-O, is on the Congress."

This was the craziest argument Bindu had ever heard, and he'd been arguing with Joq for years. "So's Brunt."

"Yes, but he was only just appointed a few days ago. He's an outsider who'll bring Ferenginar back to the old ways, before Rom and his cronies got control of it."

They exited the aircar. Bindu pulled out the three strips he'd need to pay to use the tunnel from the aircar terminal to his office building. Joq went in a different direction, as he preferred to walk in the rain to the Zalp Building.

"Whatever you say, Joq." That was what Bindu always said when they went their separate ways. "See you tomorrow."

"Assuming Ferenginar's still standing tomorrow."

Bindu went off to work. As he paid the three strips to enter the tunnel, he found himself whistling the jingle to the Eelwasser ad he'd just seen.

6

Never make fun of a Ferengi's mother....

—RULE OF ACQUISITION #31

"Ow!"

For the sixth time in as many minutes, Nog hit his head on the ceiling of the crawlspace. The bellow of pain allowed the penlight to fall out of his mouth, where he'd clenched it between his teeth.

The tunnel wasn't this small the last time I was here, he thought irritably, as he resisted the urge to rub his crown. Instead, he picked up the penlight, put it back between his molars, and forced himself to soldier onward.

It had seemed like a good idea at the time. Nog recalled from his youth on Ferenginar that Grandfather's house had a secret crawlway that led to an equally secret hatchway buried in the Gleb Jungle. Nog had found out about it from one of Grandfather's servants, who explained that one of the house's previous owners had it built as a way of escaping his creditors in case of bad times. The servant was also fairly sure that Grandfather didn't know a thing about it.

Mindful of Grandmoogie's words from yesterday, Nog had taken care to use this old crawlspace, in which he used to hide regularly as a boy whenever he wanted to get away from Grandfather—which was fairly often—so he would not be seen. It had been slower going than Nog had anticipated, mainly because he didn't realize how much he had grown since he was five. Nog was short even by Ferengi standards, and he wondered as he made his slow-but-sure way down the tunnel how the previous owner ever thought this would make a good getaway method.

I get the feeling that, when Jake and Korena talked me into seeing Mother, this wasn't what they had in mind. . . .

For perhaps the first time ever, Nog was grateful for his artificial leg. The biosynthetic limb, lost during the Dominion War at AR-558, had mostly served as an unpleasant reminder of the horrors of combat. Today, though, Nog was thankful that only one of his legs was cramping up from the confined space.

Just a little bit farther. The doorway into Grandfather's basement was coming into view in the beam of his penlight. *I just hope that Grandfather never found out about this tunnel. Or if he did, that he didn't seal it.* It had taken half an hour to crawl all the way here from the jungle hatch—after spending the better part of the day searching for the hatch while slogging waist-deep through the sludge. The Gleb Jungle had remained undeveloped only because several attempts to build on the swampland had served only to make matters worse. The last three owners of the land had foreclosed on it after financially disastrous construction attempts, and it now lay untouched and overgrown, considered a huge bad-luck charm. So Nog was not surprised to find that the hatch was still there. It had taken only a moment to bypass the locking mechanism. *Few locks can stand up to Ferengi ingenuity and Starfleet training,* Nog thought with pride.

Finally, he reached the end of the line, an occasion he marked by hitting his head on the ceiling a seventh time. "Ow!"

This time, Nog did take a moment to rub his crown. He feared there'd be a bruise up there. *Times like this, I wish I was back on the station. Dr. Bashir doesn't charge to take a look at a head injury.*

The lock on the entrance to the basement was of the same manufacture as the one on the hatch, and it took Nog even less time to pick this one. He made a note of the manufacturer, and reminded himself to make a decision later—either sell his method of picking the lock to the manufacturer so they'd be able to account for it in later products, or sell it to the manufacturer's biggest competitor. *Or both*, he thought with a grin.

As soon as he opened the door, the lovely smell of rotting plants wafted across his nostrils. *I see Grandfather still has the mold farm.* Nog wondered if his grandfather had finally, after twenty years, figured out a way to turn a profit on the thing.

Grateful he'd remained in uniform, Nog jumped from the doorway into the ankle-high swampwater. The lower half of his uniform was already a mess from wading around in the jungle all day. His Starfleet uniform was better insulated—and easier to clean—than any of his civilian clothes, which would have been ruined or necessitated an exorbitant cleaning fee.

The basement was dark—the mold didn't do well in the light—so Nog shined his penlight around looking for a switch before he'd take the risk of speaking out loud. *Not that I'm being all that stealthy wading through swampwater,* he thought with annoyance. Few houses on Ferenginar had basements, and those that did were usually blessed with plenty of swampwater. Grandfather had tried to take advantage of this inevitability by breeding mold, with limited success.

"Oh, it's you."

Nog whirled around toward the voice, which came from the top of the staircase. He saw a middle-aged Ferengi with ears that were starting to droop, bags under the eyes, and puffed-out cheeks: Dav, father to Prinadora, grandfather to Nog.

"What're you doing here, boy?"

Noticing that Grandfather was holding a several-decades-old Starfleet-issue phaser on his grandson, Nog didn't move. Not that the old Ferengi needed the weapon. All of Nog's memories of Dav were of an old man who was constantly yelling, hitting, screaming, and punching, and those memories were burbling up to the fore right now.

"Uh, I came here to see my mother."

"So you came in through the basement?"

"I didn't want to be seen. How did you know I was here, Grandfather?"

Snorting, the old man lowered the phaser. "Don't go calling me that, boy. Your father made it clear that I wasn't family anymore."

"The way I remember it," Nog said tersely, "that was *your* idea." Nog also noticed that Grandfather—that Dav—hadn't answered the question. Nog hadn't detected any alarms, but he could have missed something.

"Look," Dav said, "it didn't matter none when your father was a failure, working for his brother on some Cardassian space station in the middle of nowhere. Even after they found that wormhole, your father was nothing. But now? Grand Nagus? That's just wrong."

This didn't sound like the old man who loved to intimidate Nog so much that he drove the youth to hide in crawlspaces. *Then again, it has been a long time.*

"My father hasn't done *anything* wrong."

Dav raised the weapon again. "You're kidding, right? He married someone else—he's having another kid. He *broke the contract.*"

A thought occurred to Nog. "So did she!"

"What're you talking about?"

"Father told me that Mother remarried after you swindled him out of everything he owned."

"I didn't swindle anybody!"

Now Dav's menacing tone of yore was coming back, and Nog was sorry he'd provoked him. He tried to keep his biological leg from shaking. Intellectually, he knew that he was an adult now, a war veteran with Starfleet combat training, and Dav was no longer the intimidating giant that he was to the five-year-old Nog. *But old habits die hard—especially when the other guy's also holding a phaser on me. . . .*

Dav continued. "And your mother never remarried. She spent time with another man, but they never married. She wanted to—*I* wanted her to—but we weren't about to break a contract. We ain't that kind of Ferengi."

A likely story. Nog didn't buy any of this, but he wasn't the one holding the phaser. Instead, he tried a more diplomatic tack. "Look, we can argue about this all day, but—I just want to see my mother."

"Too bad. 'Cause she doesn't want to see you."

Nog was aghast. "I'm her *son*."

"So? All you'll do is remind her of pain. She didn't mind being separated from Rom before, but now? Going all over the planet with that Bajoran hussy? Having their *child*? You know, all anyone can talk about is that damn kid. I won't tolerate it, and I won't tolerate you in my house upsetting my daughter. Get out."

Dammit, Nog thought. Ever since Jake and Korena encouraged him, he found that he was really looking forward to seeing Prinadora again.

He thought about Jake, losing his mother to the Borg when he was only a little bit older than Nog had been when he and Father left for Terok Nor. He thought about Shar, and the tremendous impact his *zhavey* had had on his life. He thought about Prynn and her obsessive quest to find her mother, leading to such a tragic end in the Gamma Quadrant, one that drove a wedge between her and her father, Commander Vaughn. And he thought about Father and Uncle Quark, and what they—along with Nog himself—went through to rescue Grandmoogie from the Dominion two years ago.

All he knew of his mother was a vague recollection from when he was too young to realize that they'd be the only memories he'd have.

Yes, he wanted to help Father and stop Brunt from his latest attempt to destroy their family. *But I also want to see my mother.*

However, it was quite obvious that Dav wasn't going to let that happen.

"All right, I'll leave." He started sloshing through the swampwater toward the staircase.

"Hold it right there." Dav was waving the phaser toward the door to the tunnel. "You can go back the way you came, boy. I don't want you tracking swampwater in my house."

Nog looked at the door he'd broken through. *Great, I'm only just getting full feeling back in my leg.* His hip was starting to ache, too.

Bowing to the inevitable, and now very sorry he hadn't brought a phaser of his own with him—or borrowed Ro's before coming here—he sloshed over to the entry.

He took one look back at his grandfather. "Will you at least tell her I was here?"

"I *said* get out, boy!"

Turning back toward the doorway, he climbed up, put the penlight once again between his teeth, and started his slow crawl back to the jungle.

It's official, Ro thought, *I'm sick of Ferengi.*

She wasn't sure what it was that put her over the edge. She'd spent two days alone in a transport with three Ferengi—Quark, Nog, and the pilot. She'd spent two more days on Ferenginar. If they had any offworld tourist industry, it wasn't visible in the nagal residence or in the Tower of Commerce. Aside from the Bolian in the spaceport, the Vulcan at the aircar kiosk, and two Gallamites standing outside the Tower gazing up at it from ground level, Ro hadn't seen a single non-Ferengi since leaving Deep Space 9.

It wasn't even that she minded their company—much. Most of the people she'd been dealing with were, in fact, very solicitous. Given that they were the nagal serving staff, who were more than happy to provide her with anything she needed and more than she wanted, that didn't surprise her. Even with the cloud currently hanging over Rom, he was still the Grand Nagus and Ro was still his guest.

Unfortunately, the one thing the servants could not provide was a way of proving that the contract Brunt had produced was a fake. She had brought all of her skills to bear, many of which she learned during Starfleet advanced tactical training, particularly a decryption course that left her wondering how anything was ever kept secure on a computer.

Driven both by a need to talk to someone—anyone—who wasn't a Ferengi, and also by the fact that she was, technically, still on duty, she put a call through to Deep Space 9, charging it to the Grand Nagus's account. *I'll pay Rom back later if I have to.*

Kira's face appeared on the viewer. Ro still did a double take every time she saw her in Starfleet colors. On the one hand, she'd associated Kira with the red Bajoran Militia uniform she'd worn for the first six months or so that Ro had served on the station. On the other hand, the new uniform suited her.

"Ro," the colonel—or, rather, captain—said. *"Good to see you. Status report?"*

"The ambassador's safe and sound—but I'm not sure I can say the same for his brother." Quickly, she filled Kira in on the situation.

Kira looked dubious. *"I can't believe Rom'd be capable of something like that. Almost any other Ferengi, maybe, but not Rom."*

"That's what Quark said. We're looking into it."

"Good. Rom's doing some real good over there, I'd hate to see some of those trolls ruin it."

Chuckling, Ro said, "You really don't like Ferengi much, do you?"

"What was your first clue?" Kira also chuckled. *"I don't think I could ever stand to visit their homeworld. Do you know, the first time I met Zek, he hit on me?"*

"Somehow that doesn't surprise me."

"You'll be okay there?"

"Actually, it's not that bad," she said, her words belying her feelings of only a few minutes before. "Being here has actually put a lot of Quark's personality into focus."

Again the dubious expression. *"And that's a good thing?"*

Ro considered her words. "Useful data, if nothing else." She didn't want to get into how she felt about Quark with the captain—especially since she herself wasn't a hundred percent sure how she felt about Quark. Changing the subject, Ro asked, "What's happening on the station?"

That query prompted a quick rundown of the station's status—which was unusually quiet. *"Oh,"* Kira added, *"and tell Quark that Treir's doing a fine job running the bar."*

"I'm not sure he'll be happy to hear that."

Kira grinned. *"Why do you think I want you to tell him?"* Then her expression grew more professional. *"All right—keep me posted about what's happening, Lieutenant. Any change in power on Ferenginar is going to have an impact on the rest of the quadrant."* She seemed to consider her words for a moment, then added, *"I'm not sure how big, but definitely some kind of impact."*

Nodding, Ro said, "Don't worry, Captain. I'll update you every twenty-six hours."

"Good. Kira out."

Kira's face faded from the viewer, replaced with a display of a receipt telling Ro the cost of the communiqué, and asking Ro to acknowledge it. She did so with the touch of a control, at which point the view switched to a still image of a well-dressed Ferengi man watching a naked Ferengi woman chew food.

"Do you miss the good old days, when males were real males and females were naked and quiet?"

As the voice spoke, the woman spit out her food and handed it to the man, who hungrily ate the masticated bugs. Ro had to swallow down the bitter bile that welled up in her throat at the sight of it. The image switched to the same Ferengi man punching something into a padd, then holding it up to the camera. The words TRANSACTION CONCLUDED were visible in the Ferengi language on the padd's display.

"When Ferengi businessmen were free to earn profit without worrying about ridiculous tax burdens, or unwanted competition?"

The image switched to Rom, looking even more befuddled than normal. *"The Grand Nagus is trying to spit in the face of Ferengi tradition—and Ferengi values. Ferenginar doesn't need a Grand Nagus who breaks a contract and destroys the Ferengi family by interbreeding with aliens. Ferenginar needs—"*

Rom's face faded, replaced by the smiling face of Brunt, which actually served to make Ro more nauseous than watching a woman pre-chew her husband's food.

"—Brunt. He understands what made Ferenginar great. Sponsored by Chek Pharmaceuticals on behalf of the Brunt for Grand Nagus Campaign."

Well, Ro thought, *they're certainly laying it on thick.* Several attempts to end the commercial had failed, as the unit apparently could not shut down until the ad was complete.

As she tried to banish thoughts of herself sitting naked next to Quark chewing an assortment of worms for him—a mental image she would go to her grave never sharing with Quark—Ro realized that talking to Kira over a comm line wasn't enough. She still felt overwhelmed by the general Ferenginess around her, and needed a stronger palliative.

After a moment, she realized that the Brunt commercial had provided her with the answer.

Within a few minutes, one of the toadying servants was able to secure her a transport that would take her to the hospital where Leeta was being treated.

En route, she saw several more advertisements, including a bunch for Eelwasser soda, all of which involved Brunt, and all of them sponsored by Chek Pharmaceuticals. *These are people who have it in for Rom. Okay, so maybe the contract is a dead end, but there are routes to pursue in the other direction. We know Brunt has a motive to stop Rom—maybe Chek's involvement goes beyond sponsorship?* She wasn't sure where this would lead, but she also hadn't started digging yet.

Something to take on after visiting the pregnant lady.

As expected, Ro had to pay a fee to enter the waiting room of the hospital, another to visit Leeta, and yet another to be allowed to stay more than a minute, since it wasn't official visiting hours.

The hospital itself was like none Ro had ever seen. She'd been in treatment centers, infirmaries, sickbays, medical units, and hospitals all over the quadrant, and most of them shared a certain antiseptic feel. More to the point, all of them had that distinct chemical smell that came of storing large quantities of medicine. Even the most pristine Starfleet sickbay had at least a mild whiff in the air.

But not this place. With décor as tacky as the décor everywhere else on this planet, the only thing Ro smelled here was the metallic tinge of gold-pressed latinum. She saw no evidence of medical equipment in the waiting room or the hallways. The staff was dressed in the multicolored jackets, shirts, and vests that most Ferengi favored; if the sign outside the building hadn't specified that it was a hospital, Ro would have assumed herself to have entered an ordinary office building.

It just figures, she thought. *Human doctors take an oath*

that says "First, do no harm." The Ferengi doctors' oath is
probably more like "First, take their money."

Leeta's room was not the one listed at the front desk, a fact
not revealed to Ro until a staffer had escorted her to the corner
room listed in the computer. The door slid open to reveal a
huge room containing plush carpeting, a window with a view
of the Tower of Commerce, curtains of what looked like Tho-
lian silk, and several comfortable guest chairs. The large
biobed at the center looked more comfortable than any biobed
Ro had ever seen, and was also the first thing she had seen in
the entire hospital that looked even vaguely medical. As it was,
the display unit over the bed was framed in something that was
at least plated gold.

The biobed was, however, empty.

When the staffer double-checked his padd, his eyes
widened. "Oh, dear. I'm *so* sorry, but it appears that the Grand
Nagus's wife has been moved to smaller accommodations. It's
coincidental with the change in her billing cycle."

Having already gotten the lay of the land, Ro didn't even
ask the next question until after she'd handed a strip of latinum
to the staffer. "What change?"

Pocketing the latinum, the staffer started leading Ro back
down the corridor. "Her billing cycle actually almost ended.
Dr. Orpax prefers not to treat customers who break contracts.
However, the Grand Nagus convinced him to keep his wife on
as a customer—for a price." The staffer leaned closer to Ro.
"He'd better hope he comes out of this okay, because Orpax is
charging *double* his usual fee, and if he's ousted as Grand
Nagus, he won't have a strip to his name."

Ro looked at the staffer in shock as they turned a corner.
"You mean to say that if Rom hadn't paid up, Orpax would've
kicked Leeta out?"

The staffer, in turn, looked at Ro in even more shock. "Of
course. What else *could* he do? Dr. Orpax is a professional,
who spent years in very costly training to become a medical
practitioner. Do you really expect him to just *give* away his
services? Where's the logic in that?"

Ro found she couldn't come up with a good answer to
that—and was relieved of the need to do so by their arrival at a

door in the middle of one of the back corridors. The door slid open to reveal a tiny room in which there was barely enough space for a much more standard-looking biobed, with a display unit over it that was as utilitarian as any seen on a Starfleet ship. There was only one chair, and no window.

Both bed and chair were occupied by sleeping forms—Leeta in the former, her belly swollen with the child she carried; Rom in the latter, curled up with his nagal staff in his lap. Leeta awoke at Ro's entrance. Rom, though, didn't budge.

"If you need anything," the staffer said, "simply come to the front desk and drop a slip of latinum into the box." With a bow, he then departed.

Ro had checked over Leeta's security file before leaving the station, more out of curiosity than anything else. There wasn't much there. The only specific security-related items in her file involved the formation of a union among Quark's employees and her incarceration—along with Kira, Rom, and Jake Sisko—as part of a resistance movement on the station when the Dominion had taken it over during the early days of the war. The only other information consisted of her relationships with both Dr. Bashir and Rom and a few pictures.

She looked like none of those pictures now, of course. Her red hair was uncombed and unstyled, splayed out on the pillow of the biobed, she was pale, her eyes watery, her skin blotchy in spots, and she had that puffy look that pregnant women tended to get.

"Hi," Leeta said in a sleepy voice. "You must be Lieutenant Ro. Rom said you came with Quark and Nog."

"Yeah, yeah, I did." Ro gave an encouraging smile. "We met briefly at the signing ceremony. I just wanted to check up on you, see how you were doing."

"Honestly, I've been better. Pregnancy's supposed to be a wonderful time—you're creating new life. But this has just been awful. I've been sick, I've been tired, and then this whole thing with Rom . . ." Her voice trailed off. Then she started coughing, and Ro went and grabbed the glass from the sideboard, assuming it to be filled with water. However, it was empty. A quick perusal of the sideboard revealed a spigot with a strip slot next to it. Sighing, Ro dropped a strip of latinum into the slot and put the glass under the spigot. As soon as the strip fell into the receptacle with a hollow clunk, the spigot released the water.

Gratefully taking the glass, Leeta said, "Thanks," in a hoarse voice, then drank three-quarters of the glass's contents. "Still," she continued, her voice strengthened by the water, "it's worth it. Rom and I are having a baby." She looked over at Rom, still sleeping soundly. Ro thought she heard a bit of a snore coming from the chair.

"Can I ask you something?" Ro said after a moment.

"Sure."

Ro hesitated. "How can you stand to live here? I mean, it's been an—interesting visit, to say the least, but I think I'd go crazy if I had to stay here."

"It's not that easy," Leeta said, lowering her eyes. "Nobody here really *likes* me. I mean, Rom's servants are all *nice* to me, but they just see me as the Grand Nagus's wife. And that's kinda nice, really, but—honestly, I don't have any real friends. Rom's mother doesn't approve of me, and there's nobody else here to talk to." She sighed. "And there's nothing for me to *do*, either. Yes, I'm the Grand Nagus's wife, but there's no real job that comes with that. And since I'm not a Ferengi, there's not much I can do here except look pretty standing next to Rom." She smiled. "It's kind of ironic, really."

"How do you mean?" Ro asked.

Leeta took another sip of water. "I don't know if you know this, but I'm an orphan." Ro had assumed as much, based on the lack of a family name in her file. "When I was really young, I went to work as a serving girl in the home of a rich Cardassian named Gallek. He thought I was a nice little girl, and he always used to sneak me treats. Then, when I got older, he"—she hesitated—"he became attracted to me."

A flush of anger suffused Ro, as she knew exactly what happened to Bajoran women who were deemed attractive by Cardassian men.

Quickly, Leeta said, "But he never did anything to me! That's the weird part—I kept expecting him to. The head of the serving staff kept warning me that he might—she'd been raped when she was a girl by a different Cardassian, and she lived in fear of it—but Gallek never touched me. He treated me well, he was always nice to me, and he always told me how—how beautiful I was, but it never went past that." Her lips twisted in an expression that was, oddly, part smile and part frown. "So I used it. Gallek's servants were all treated much better than most Bajoran servants, mainly because I asked him to. He could never say no to me—at least, he mostly couldn't. It wasn't much—better food, nicer clothes, no beatings—but it made everyone's life easier. And everyone was happier. Maybe not happy, but you took what you could get."

Ro shook her head. She'd left Bajor behind during the Occupation, after living in a succession of offworld refugee camps, because she refused to live among a defeated people. "So you gilded your cage a little," she said in perhaps more snide a tone than she'd wanted.

"What else was I supposed to do? I didn't know anything about the Resistance—I'd heard rumors, but most of us thought the Resistance was just a myth that Bajorans perpetuated as a way of keeping up hope. I was an orphan with nowhere to go. The one thing I had going for me was that the head of the house was fond of me. So I used it to make my life easier." She finished off her water. "Gallek died of a heart attack about a week before the Cardassians pulled out of Bajor. Suddenly, we had nowhere to go—the Cardassians torched his house before they withdrew—so I took the money I had saved over the years. Eventually, I came up to the space station. I already knew how to use my looks to influence people, so I went to Quark." Leeta smiled. "He never treated me as nicely as Gallek, but he also paid me better. And I was free, which was the important part."

Again, Ro shook her head. Leeta wasn't entirely what she'd expected. "Can I ask you something?"

"Sure."

"You're free, like you said. You're not Gallek's servant anymore—in essence, you *are* Gallek."

"I know—that's why I thought it was ironic."

"So why stay here if you don't like it?"

"I never said I didn't like it." She looked over at Rom, whose snores had gotten a bit louder, and suddenly, she was beaming. The paleness, the puffiness, the blemishes on her skin, all of them seemed to recede as she gazed longingly at her husband. "I'm happier than I've ever been in my life—because I'm with him."

From what Ro had seen, she wasn't sure that that was worth it. *Then again, I dropped everything to come visit Quark's homeworld and to spend time with him, so who the hell am I to judge?*

"Can I ask *you* something?" Leeta said in a small voice.

"Of course."

"You really seem to like Quark."

Here it comes. "Yeah—yeah, I do."

Leeta shook her head. "*Why?*"

Unable to help herself, Ro burst out laughing, as did Leeta a moment later. "Honestly, there are times when I have no idea. But he's so—so *sincere*."

Giving Ro an incredulous look, Leeta said, "He's the most insincere man I've ever met!"

"Yeah, I know, but he's so sincere in his lack of sincerity. I mean, yes, he's totally full of it, but he's completely up-front about how full of it he is. It's kind of—well, endearing."

"If you say so." Leeta didn't sound convinced.

"He's really not a bad person," Ro said. "For all his bluster, he's as compassionate in his own way as Rom is."

Leeta grinned. "I can tell *you* never worked for him."

"True. And he's certainly capable of being a conniving bastard, but—there's more to him than that. Besides, he and I have a lot in common."

That seemed to surprise Leeta. "Like what?"

Choosing her words carefully, Ro said, "Neither of us are entirely perfect fits with what our societies expect of us."

"I *did* notice that your earring's on the wrong ear."

At that, Ro laughed again. "Yeah, my little rebellion against the vedeks who kept grabbing my ear when I didn't want them to." She then gave Leeta a serious look, and decided, *Oh, the hell with it, I've been wanting to ask her this since I got here, may as well do it already.* "Mind if I ask a *really* personal question?"

Shrugging, Leeta said, "I guess."

"What's it like—being in bed with a Ferengi?"

This time it was Leeta's turn to laugh, though it turned quickly into another coughing fit. Ro immediately dashed over to the water spigot, tossed what she hoped was only a strip into the receptacle, and poured her some more water.

After gulping down half the glass, Leeta said, "I'm sorry, I just—I guess I assumed that you and Quark—I mean, knowing Quark, I can't believe he'd hold *back*, and—"

Ro held up a hand. "It's all right. We've actually been taking it pretty slow."

"That's not Quark's usual style."

"Don't be so sure of that. He's got a romantic streak in him. He mostly tries to hit it over the head and keep it tied up in a corner, but it does exist."

"Hmp." Leeta took a smaller sip of water. "I guess the best way to describe it is—enthusiastic. But I don't know how much of that is Rom and how much of that is normal for Ferengi. He's certainly a lot different from Julian."

Before Ro could even try to scrape off the mental image that last sentence was leaving in her brain, a beep emitted from her tricorder. She opened it up to see the words PROGRAM COMPLETE on the display. She entered two commands, and then muttered, "Damn."

"What is it?"

"Something involving the investigation." Ro didn't want to get into specifics—especially since the news wasn't good. Leeta was having enough problems without adding the stress of bad news regarding Rom's travails. "I need to get back to the nagal residence."

"Of course. Thanks for coming by."

"No problem." She turned to leave.

"I mean it, Lieutenant—apart from Rom and Nog, you're the only person who's visited me."

Turning back, Ro gave Leeta an encouraging smile. "Call me Laren. And like I said, it's no problem."

"It's just nice—nice to have a friend to talk to."

Ro blinked. She really only just met Leeta, and wasn't entirely sure the word *friend* applied. Hell, if they hadn't been thrown together by this circumstance, she doubted she'd have more than two words to say to the woman.

Then she looked at Rom's sleeping form, and thought back on Quark.

"Well," Ro finally said, "we do have a lot in common. I'll talk to you later, okay?"

Leeta nodded and yawned. "I think I need to get some more sleep."

Waving good-bye, Ro turned and left the room.

As soon as she did, she frowned and stared down at the tricorder. Her latest attempt to expose the forgery had failed. Every trick she knew indicated that this contract was wholly genuine.

Which meant that Leeta's days as the Grand Nagus's wife were likely to be numbered. . . .

7

Trust is the biggest liability of all.

—RULE OF ACQUISITION #99

Brunt stepped out of his favorite *tongo* parlor, having just left the table three bricks richer than when he came in. Of course, his fellow players thought he was five bricks ahead, but they didn't know about the two-brick bribe to the dealer that guaranteed his continuous victory. The owner turned a blind eye to Brunt's actions, mainly because he got a good percentage of the two bricks. That was why it was Brunt's favorite parlor.

It was only *melnering* today, so Brunt didn't feel the need to hire an aircar to take him to the Tower of Commerce. Instead, he walked, the refreshing drizzle cascading on his face.

It won't be long now, he thought with glee. *That idiot will be ousted and I at last will attain the nagushood—permanently this time.* He'd dreamed of the day when he took his rightful place as nagus, a dream that had only become more intense since he had oh-so-maddeningly-briefly held the title of Acting Grand Nagus. Zek was on the way out for his ludicrous reforms—but Ishka and her loathsome family had managed to weasel out of that, convincing Nilva to back Zek, leaving Brunt in ruin.

But Brunt was never one to let defeat keep him down. He fought his way back to prominence, putting aside his distaste in order to aid Quark in his rescue of Ishka from the Dominion, for which Zek—the fool—was so grateful that he restored Brunt to his old position of FCA liquidator, thus setting in motion the chain of events that now put him only a step away from the nagal staff's being in his grasp once again.

He entered the Tower of Commerce just as a familiar form was exiting.

"Well well well," Brunt said with a wide grin. "If it isn't Quark."

Quark looked up absentmindedly, then, upon recognizing the congressman, stopped in his tracks. "Brunt."

"That's right." Brunt continued into the Tower's massive, latinum-walled lobby. Quark followed him. "It's been a long time."

"Only about a year—about three centuries less than I'd have preferred, to be honest."

"I have to admit to being surprised to see you here, Quark. When Chek told me he was recruiting you, I warned him that you would probably be recalcitrant."

Quark had been holding a padd, but he put it in his inner jacket pocket as he replied. "You told him that, did you? Based on your close personal relationship with me?"

Brunt sneered. "What a disgusting notion. No, I simply told him that you were all talk and no action."

As expected, that brought Quark up short. "What're you talking about?"

"Please—I remember that grand speech you gave when Zek handed the nagal staff over to your idiot brother. You called that dreary bar of yours the last outpost of what made Ferenginar great—a declaration that lasted right up until Bajor entered the Federation. Filed your tax returns on time this quarter?" And he meant that last question to sting.

"I don't have to justify myself to you, Brunt."

Shrugging, Brunt said, "Maybe not. But you know what the best part is?"

"I'll give you five strips of latinum if you *don't* tell me."

Brunt hesitated at the offer, then decided that, as nice as the five strips would've been, the gloating was just more *fun*. "The best part, Quark, is that no matter what happens, you lose. Either you help Chek and me destroy your brother completely—or you help him maintain a Ferenginar you hate." He leaned in close to Quark and whispered, "And a day when you lose is a good day for me."

With that, Brunt laughed loudly in Quark's ear, causing the latter to wince in pain, then straightened, turned on his heel, and continued through the Tower lobby. He didn't bother to look behind him to see what Quark would do.

It's a good day to be me, Brunt thought with glee.

"Nagus?"

Zek squinted at the Ferengi sitting perpendicular to him in the—*Where am I, anyhow?* Then he remembered—the beach house on Risa.

So who is this guy, anyhow? He definitely isn't Ishka, and he's certainly not Maihar'du. He decided to take the direct approach. "Who are you, again?"

The Ferengi, who had small, beady eyes, a bulbous nose, and a round mouth, said, "For the fourth time, I'm Gaila—Ishka's nephew."

"Ishka? She's not here. She went back to Ferenginar." He frowned. *Why did she go back, again?* "I think it was to help out my no-good son. No, wait! *My* no-good son is helping her. But I know she's got a son somewhere. . . ."

"You mean Rom."

"Right! Rom! Nice boy. He's doing well for himself on that space station."

"Actually," Gaila said slowly, "Rom is the Grand Nagus now—and that's what I wanted to talk to you about."

"Talk to me? What for? I'm not Grand Nagus anymore. I gave it to that son of Ishka's—what's his name? Rom!"

"I have to say, Nagus—"

"I'm not the nagus anymore," Zek said irritably. He hated people who didn't keep up with current events. "I retired. Call me Zek."

Gaila smiled, an expression that, in Zek's opinion, his face was ill suited toward and that he rather wished he'd stop. "Very well—Zek. I have to say, I find your generosity quite surprising."

"Generosity?" Zek had trouble even *saying* the word. "I didn't let you into my house so you could insult me!"

Holding up his hands, Gaila said, "No insult was intended, Zek. I simply wanted to express how impressed I am at the sacrifices you're willing to make for Ferenginar."

"Sacrifices? What sacrifices? What're you talking about? Ferengi don't make sacrifices. There's a Rule about that, I'm sure of it." Zek racked his brain, but the only Rule he could remember was the one about money.

Even as Zek thought, Gaila continued nattering on. "I'm talking about the way you're willing to let Ishka go for so long in order for her to help Rom with his nagal duties. That you're willing to give up the happiness and bliss of your retirement for the betterment of Ferenginar . . ." Gaila shook his head. "I'm in awe, Zek. I truly am in awe."

"Awe? Of what? Who are you, anyhow? Why did Maihar'du let you in here?"

The person in the chair perpendicular to Zek's couch said, "I'm Gaila—Ishka's nephew."

It came back to Zek. "Right, right, of course. What brings you to the nagal residence?"

"This isn't the nagal residence, Zek, it's—"

Pointing a gnarled finger at Gaila, Zek barked, "Hah! Thought the old man was losing it, didn't you? Well, I fooled you! There's nothing wrong with *these* lobes, let me tell you— I'm as sharp as I *ever* was!"

"I'm sorry I ever doubted you, Zek."

"Good." Zek paused, then stared at the man. "Who are you, again?"

"I'm—"

Then it came back to him. "Gaila! You're Ishka's nephew." He frowned. "Where *is* Ishka, anyhow?"

"On Ferenginar, Zek, remember? She's helping Grand Nagus Rom. And I was telling you how noble it was for you to make this sacrifice—being away from Ishka for so long, just so she can assist my cousin Rom in his endeavor to be a decent Grand Nagus."

"Decent?" Zek didn't like the sound of that. Rom was Zek's handpicked successor, after all. "He's better than decent!"

Gaila winced a bit. "Not much better, I'm afraid, Zek." Leaning forward, Gaila whispered, "Between you and me, my cousin isn't doing such a good job of it."

Zek leaned forward also. "Why are we whispering? There's no one else here."

"The walls have ears, Zek—you can't be too careful."

That phrase sounded familiar to Zek. He'd heard it somewhere before. . . .

Gaila continued. "And with this latest revelation . . ."

"What revelation?" Zek hadn't heard anything about a revelation. If there had been a revelation, then by Gint, he should have heard about it.

"Well, nothing's proven, of course, but there's an accusation against him of violating his marriage contract to his first wife when he married that Bajoran woman."

Zek smiled. "I met a Bajoran woman once. She had lovely red hair. I'm trying to remember her name—she was on that space station near the wormhole. . . ."

"The point is, Zek, that Rom is having trouble. It's not like it was in the good old days when you ran things."

"Trouble?" Zek didn't like the sound of that. "What kind of trouble?"

Gaila leaned forward again. "He's accused of violating his marriage contract. It's why Ishka's still on Ferenginar when she should be here with you. It's why he's destroying your legacy at the same time as he's ruining your retirement."

Zek was outraged. In fact, he was so outraged that he stood up. "How dare he! Nobody ruins my retirement and gets away with it!"

Also standing up, Gaila asked, "What do you intend to do, Zek?"

"Do? I'll tell you what I'm going to do!" Then he realized he had no idea. Looking blankly at Gaila he asked, "What *am* I going to do?"

Putting up his hands, Gaila said, "Well, I wouldn't presume to give you advice."

"Presume!" Zek said. "My Ishka's been taken from me, and I need to know what to do about it!"

Gaila rubbed his chin. "Well, if it were me, I would go back to Ferenginar and do everything in my power to get Ishka back."

Zek nodded. "That's what I'd do if I were me, too."

"You *are* you, Zek, I think—"

Then, finally, he remembered. "Kira!"

"I beg your pardon?"

"The redhead on Deep Space 9," Zek said, wondering why Gaila was being so obtuse.

"Of course, Zek. My apologies."

"Well, you *should* apologize. Honestly, what are the youth of today *coming* to, anyhow?"

"I couldn't say, Zek."

"Of course you can't. It's pitiful, that's what it is." Then he looked at the other Ferengi in confusion. "What were we talking about?"

"Your return to Ferenginar to bring Ishka back and stop Rom from destroying the entire Fererngi Alliance."

"Right!" Zek couldn't believe he'd forgotten that. He'd thought of little else besides bringing Rom home and stopping Ishka—or, rather, the other way around—for weeks now. "So what're we standing around here for? Let's get back to Ferenginar!"

"As it happens, I have a ship waiting." The younger Ferengi gestured toward the door. "If you'll come this way, Zek, we can be under way within half an hour."

"Excellent!" Zek liked this young Ferengi—he was efficient. "I'll just get Maihar'du to pack a few things."

"Already taken care of, Zek."

Even more efficient than I thought. That's what I like about the youth of today, they're on the ball.

"All right, then," Zek said, "just one more thing, then."

"What's that?"

"Who are you, again?"

Nog sat in the common room of the nagal residence. He had FCN on—he always found that it made excellent background noise. Ever since Father ascended to the nagushood, Nog had been able to get FCN broadcast in his quarters on Deep Space 9 for free, which had been a great boon. Prior to that, the fee for subscribing to the news network was far more than he could afford, given his limited profit-making opportunities as a Starfleet officer.

I wonder if I'll still have that privilege by the time I'm back on DS9.

In the two days since the emergency session of the congress, the market had gone down two hundred and fifty points. Sales of chances in the birth raffle had slowed to a trickle—though that endeavor was already in the black, so it would be profitable no matter what. *If we're not careful, the raffle will be the only profit Father has left.*

On top of that, Brunt's face was now *everywhere*. Eelwasser had unleashed a massive ad campaign with Brunt as their spokesperson. Sales of Eelwasser were up, sales of Slug-O-Cola were flattening out for the first time in years, and Brunt's public profile was almost as high as Quoop's, and Quoop had just released his most popular recording six months ago.

Grandmother and Krax had been working to put out ads of their own, with sponsorship from Lakwa Clothiers. They were more than happy to support Rom, as the new reforms had turned Lakwa from a minor emporium to the most popular place to buy clothes in the Alliance, all thanks to the legalization of clad females.

Speaking of which, Nog thought as he looked up at the newsfeed to see that they had gone to a commercial. The screen showed the image of a female, naked and looking depressed. *"Females of Ferenginar—do you miss the 'good old days'?"* The female sneezed. *"Always getting colds . . ."* The female started to talk, but then a male appeared next to her and clamped a hand over her mouth. *"Never being allowed to speak . . ."* The male handed the female some tube grubs, which the female proceeded to chew dolefully. *"Having to chew men's food for them . . ."* A bar of latinum appeared in the female's hand, only to have the male yank it away from her and put it in his pocket. *"Not being permitted to earn profit . . ."* Now a close-up of the female, with a deep frown on her face. *"Of course you don't! Why should you? Why should you be denied the warmth of clothing?"* The female now wore a very fashionable dress. *"The right to speak?"* The female was now in the middle of a conversation with several Ferengi of both genders. *"And most important, the right to earn profit."* Another bar of latinum appeared in her hands, but this time she put it in her *own* pocket. *"And for you males out there, why would you want to keep half your household from earning profit for your entire family? Sure, you may think you earn enough now, but doesn't the Ninety-Seventh Rule of Acquisition state that enough is never enough?"* Now the male and the female were seated at a table, jointly counting their latinum. *"The new Ferenginar—giving all Ferengi a chance to be true Ferengi. Sponsored by Lakwa Clothiers, on behalf of Grand Nagus Rom and his supporters."*

"Not bad," said a voice from behind Nog. He turned to see Ro standing in the doorway. "Certainly better than looking at Brunt's smile for the ninety-third time."

Nog chuckled. "You're lucky—you've never had to deal with him in person."

"Weren't you going to the hospital?" Ro asked.

Sighing, Nog said, "Unfortunately, Dr. Orpax called. He said Leeta is too weak to have visitors. She's getting worse."

"Damn." Ro shook her head. "I hope this Orpax guy is as good as you all say he is."

"He couldn't get away with charging as much as he does without being as good as he is. If he wasn't worth the money, there are enough other doctors on Ferenginar who would get his business. But they don't, because Dr. Orpax provides results, which leads to good word-of-mouth."

"I guess so."

From years of practice, Nog knew he had to be patient with non-Ferengi—especially ones like Ro who had lived most of their lives in the Federation, and therefore had been insulated from the realities of finance. To help seal the deal for her, Nog said, "Leeta will be fine. I'm as confident in him as I would be if she were in the infirmary with Dr. Bashir."

Ro blew out a breath and walked over to the replicator. "I hope you're right." She dropped a slip of latinum into the slot and said, "Tarkalian tea, iced, and a *jumja* stick."

Nog was about to point out that a Ferengi replicator wasn't likely to be able to fulfill such a request, when the requested items appeared with a small glow.

Then he remembered—a Bajoran lived in this house, so of course the replicator would have been reprogrammed to accommodate Bajoran tastes.

Taking a sip of her tea, Ro moved over to join Nog on the couch. "I just finished talking with Kira."

"How're things on the station?"

"Pretty quiet, actually."

"That's a change."

"Yeah." Ro took a bite of *jumja*.

Nog hesitated briefly. He didn't want to ask the question, in part because he could guess the answer based on the fact that Ro hadn't said anything about it, but he still wanted confirmation as to the status of DS9's science officer. "Has there been any word from Shar?"

Ro shook her head. "Not since we left the station. He's still on Andor, and no clue as to when he's coming back."

Sighing, Nog said, "I hope he's all right. Prynn told me he's doing what he wants to be doing, but—well, I miss him."

"Me, too." Ro took a sip of her tea. "I can't imagine what he's going through right now."

A voice from behind Nog said, "Do you know how ridiculous the two of you sound?"

Turning around, Nog saw Uncle Quark enter the sitting room. "We're worried about Shar, Uncle," Nog said in an annoyed voice.

"Fine, worry about him. Nothing wrong with that. I like the guy, too—gotta love someone who's always looking to try new and expensive drinks. But don't talk like he's going through something unimaginably bizarre. Nog, you were less than three years out of your Attainment Ceremony when you went into combat—which eventually led to your leg being blown off. Laren, you watched Cardassians torture and kill your father when you were a kid." At those words, Nog shot a look at Ro. He hadn't known that about the security chief. Uncle Quark continued: "You're trying to tell me that, with all that, you can't imagine what *Shar's* going through?" Before Nog could say anything, his uncle went on: "Have you proven that the contract's a fake, yet?"

Ro shook her head. "No. I think we're going to have to check it against the archive."

Nog frowned. "I read the report from Investigator Rwogo. She verified it against the archive."

At that, Ro smiled. "Did she?" Setting down her *jumja* stick and tea on the side table, she pulled out a padd. "I've been doing a little checking into this Rwogo woman."

Uncle Quark's eyes widened. "She's a female?"

Giving him a withering look, Ro asked, "You have a problem with female investigators, Quark?"

Opening his mouth, then closing it, Uncle Quark then said, "There's no way I can answer that question without getting in trouble, is there?"

"Not really, no," Ro said with a grin. "In any case, Rwogo's financial portfolio turned up some interesting transactions. She's come into possession of about two dozen shares in Chek Pharmaceuticals. Prior to being hired as an investigator, she was doing odd jobs for the past year and a half, and hadn't saved up enough to pay for this—and she's only been an investigator for a week, and payday isn't for another three weeks."

Uncle Quark frowned. "So how'd she pay for the shares?"

"That's a really good question. I haven't been able to track that down."

Nog leaned forward on the couch. "Chek is the company sponsoring all those Eelwasser ads with Brunt. This is starting to look like a conspiracy."

"Why would Chek want to bring Rom down?" Ro asked.

"I don't know," Uncle Quark said, "but he does. Trust me."

Nog shot his uncle a look. As far as he knew, Uncle Quark didn't have any connections with Chek—pharmaceuticals weren't really his line. "How do you know that?"

"I hear things."

Ro stood up. "Where did you hear this?"

"What difference does it make?" Uncle Quark now sounded defensive.

He started to say something else, but Ro grabbed her *jumja* off the side table and said, "So help me, Quark, if you quote the Seventh Rule at me, I'm going to shove this *jumja* stick in your ear."

"Hey, look, I *do* keep my ears open." As Uncle Quark said

the words, he backed slowly away from Ro. "The point is, we need to check the archive ourselves."

"I don't see how," Nog said. "Only authorized personnel are allowed into the archive."

"Who's authorized?" Ro asked.

"Only two people," Nog said. "Glat, the owner of the company that provides the computer that houses the archive, and Torf, the programmer who maintains it. It's got the best security of any place in the Alliance."

"State-of-the-art systems?" Ro asked.

Nog nodded. "That's part of it, yes."

Uncle Quark added, "Glat is also one of the three or four richest Ferengi in the galaxy, and he pays Torf an obscene salary. Nobody can afford to bribe either of them."

"Not that anyone really would," Nog said. "That archive is the ultimate preservation of the Seventeenth Rule."

"Of course *somebody* would," Uncle Quark said in a derogatory tone. "Don't be so naïve."

Before Nog could reply to the slander, Ro said, "Is there any way we can get access to it?"

Shaking his head, Nog said, "Only the FCA and the investigators can check the archives, and they have to do it by special request to Glat. If anyone else wants to, they have to submit an application and token bribe to Glat and then expect at least a two-month wait."

"We don't have two months," Ro said dolefully.

Uncle Quark then got the wide-eyed, openmouthed look on his face that usually meant he had an idea that he, at least, thought was brilliant. "No, but we have something better. I'll need to make a call."

Nog hadn't really been paying close attention to the FCN broadcast on the wall viewer, but the words *"former Grand Nagus Zek"* caught his attention, and he turned toward the screen.

What he saw made his lobes shrivel. "What's Gaila doing here?"

Ro and Uncle Quark followed Nog's gaze to the screen. It showed Zek slowly walking through the corridors of the space-port, Maihar'du keeping the crowds at bay. Walking behind

Zek was the unmistakably smarmy face of Nog's second cousin.

Nog said, "Computer, raise volume."

"*—ival at Fram Memorial Spaceport this morning in the company of his Hupyrian servant and another Ferengi described as 'an old family friend,' but whom the FCN has identified as Gaila, a weapons merchant. When asked why he had returned to Ferenginar from his retirement on Risa, Zek had this to say.*"

The image switched to a close-up of Zek's wrinkled face. "*I'm here because the Ferengi Alliance is in trouble. Throughout my reign as Grand Nagus, I always made sure that Ferenginar was a beacon of hope to entrepreneurs across the galaxy. What I see now is a Ferenginar that shines a dim light indeed. I'm here to support Chek Pharmaceuticals' efforts to bring glory back to Ferenginar—and to stop Grand Nagus Rom before he ruins this great alliance!*"

Zek was then replaced by the image of the newscaster. "*We'll return for an analysis of Zek's statement after these advertisements.*"

As soon as Nog heard the first note of the Eelwasser jingle, he cried, "Computer, disengage FCN!"

The screen went blank.

The three of them stood and looked at each other for several seconds.

Then, finally, Ro spoke. "This may be a problem."

"Understatement number nine hundred and twelve," Uncle Quark muttered. "Someone has to tell Mother."

Nog looked at his uncle. So did Ro.

Putting his hands to his chest, Uncle Quark asked, "Why are you looking at me?"

"She's *your* mother," Ro said.

"How is that *my* fault?"

Before his uncle could whine further, Nog said, "It's all right—*I'll* tell her."

"Good. Besides, like I said, I have a call to make." He looked at the now-blank viewer. "And it looks like I need to make it sooner instead of later."

The riskier the road, the greater the profit.

—RULE OF ACQUISITION #62

Clad in his state-of-the-art bog suit, Eliminator Leck swam through the muck of the Mayak Swamp. The heads-up display on the visor of his helmet gave him a sensor reading that indicated that the Glat Archive was only a few more minutes away, if he kept swimming at his current pace.

The HUD beeped a warning that a swamp eel was moving toward him. Leck unholstered his phaser and fired. The beam sliced through the mud and plant life—as well as several muck-encrusted items of refuse—and vaporized the eel.

Swamp eels were, of course, completely harmless, but Leck didn't see that as a good enough reason to pass up the chance to shoot something.

Leck had been grateful for Quark's call. An eliminator of many years' standing, Leck rarely found himself challenged. Mostly, he just eliminated people. At first it was fun, especially since his targets were often under some kind of protection. Getting through a Starfleet security system or Nausicaan bodyguards was great fun. But after a while, it just got too *easy*. He was up on all the latest security technology, and Leck had never had any trouble getting past bodyguards of any species. True, the profit margin was high, but latinum was never Leck's primary concern. He'd made more money than he could possibly spend in three lifetimes after his first year as an eliminator.

No, what Leck wanted was a *challenge*.

Quark understood that. Leck had first met the bartender when the eliminator was doing a job in Cardassian territory, one that had taken him to a Cardassian space station in orbit of Bajor called Terok Nor. After the job was done, he'd gone to Quark's bar for some recreation, and found it in spades. Quark had a Deltan holosuite program that Leck had been trying to track down for *years*.

They'd stayed in contact over the next decade or so. Quark had sent some business his way, including some of his most interesting clients.

One was Quark himself, only a couple of years ago. When Quark's mother had been taken by the Dominion, Quark hired him to help in the rescue operation. The operation certainly needed his help, since the rest of the team consisted of a down-on-his-luck weapons dealer, an equally down-on-his-luck ex-liquidator, two engineers, and Quark. It was slipshod, amateurish, poorly planned, pathetically executed, and more fun than Leck had had since his last trip to the Badlands.

The HUD beeped again. He was only a few meters from his target.

The Glat Archive had been formed a little over a century ago, the final authority on the veracity of a contract. Copies of all contracts were backed up here, and their records were sacrosanct. The primary security for the facility was natural. The archive was, basically, a big metal box containing one very large computer. Once it was constructed, it was dropped into the Mayak Swamp, the deepest, murkiest, filthiest, most garbage-filled swamp on the entire planet. Direct exposure to the swamp's toxic waters pretty much guaranteed an early grave.

Leck set the bog suit's scanners to look for entrances. He found three. One was big enough to accommodate a ship, which Leck dismissed. That entrance would allow only a ship to gain ingress. The second was one that was at the top of the structure, and would provide the easiest access to someone coming straight down through the Mayak Swamp. Leck, not being a fool, had taken a more curcuitous route through the swamp. He dismissed that entrance as well: it was the obvious place to go, which meant Leck knew to avoid it at all costs.

Only two people in the galaxy were authorized to enter the Glat Archive. On the one hand, that meant security was fairly straightforward: anyone who wasn't Glat or Torf wasn't allowed in. On the other hand, it also meant that, if you could fool the security system into thinking you were one of those two, you'd be free and clear.

Quark was lucky that he called when he did. Had it been three months earlier, Leck would have had a much harder time breaking into the archive. But two and a half months ago, Leck had been hired by Janx Outerwear to eliminate a member of the research-and-development team of their chief competition, Sorv Spacesuits 'N' Things. Janx had apparently stolen the design for the very bog suit Leck was now wearing from Sorv. The Sorv employee who facilitated the deal was threatening to go public if he didn't get more money than Janx was willing to pay. Fearing that this employee would continue to blackmail them for years on end, the president of Janx felt it would be more cost-effective all around if he instead just had the employee eliminated.

In lieu of a fee, Leck requested as payment one of the bog suits, which not only enabled the wearer to move freely about in the densest swamp on Ferenginar, but also provided camouflage, which was handy in avoiding the various swamp-dwelling life-forms that were somewhat more dangerous than the eels.

In the course of his elimination of the employee, Leck learned that Janx sold two suits to Glat, and also that the bog suits could be used to mask the wearer's life signs. After all, sometimes the predators in swamps weren't natural.

After Quark's call, it was a simple matter for Leck to determine the biosignature of Torf and program it into his bog suit.

But Leck also knew it wouldn't be this simple. Which was why he did not use either of the first two entrances he found.

The third entrance was on the underside of the structure, buried underneath a ton of algae and piles of refuse.

Leck didn't think like most Ferengi, but he still knew how

most Ferengi thought. He also knew the Eighty-eighth Rule of Acquisition: "It ain't over till it's over." Most would assume that it would be enough to put the archive in the swamp and equip the entrances with bioscanners. They wouldn't realize that that wasn't the end of it, and would then be stopped by the additional security precautions at the other entrances.

Secure in the knowledge that the entrance on the top of the archive was designed to keep *everybody* out, Leck avoided it and spent the extra time plowing through the foliage and waste that blocked the entrance on the underside.

Once his phaser made short work of the impediments, he double-checked his HUD to make sure it was giving off Torf's biosigns, down to the DNA level. In addition, he double-checked the optical camouflage he'd placed in his eyes. Salvaged off the body of a Tal Shiar operative he'd eliminated a year ago, they would fool any optical scanner into thinking he was Torf. He even wore a holomask that, if he took off the bog suit, would make him look like Torf.

Confident that all his equipment was functioning as it should, Leck then activated his Orion Codebreaker, which he'd taken as payment for eliminating someone on behalf of the Orion Syndicate. It could tell you the proper sequence for any code lock in the quadrant. By itself, it wouldn't be enough to get in, but the code, combined with his assorted camouflages, would do the trick.

Or so he thought. To his surprise, the Codebreaker revealed that there were *two* codes that would open the door.

Of course, Leck realized after a moment. *One code for Glat, one for Torf. The question is, which is which?*

What made this entire operation more difficult—a factor that just made it more appealing to Leck—was that the bog suit had a limited power supply. In order to maintain the sensors, the camouflage, and protection from the toxicity of the swamp while limiting the energy leakage, it had to eat up a great deal of power.

That also meant the more time he spent trying to figure out which was the right code to use, the less time he would have inside to find Rom's original marriage contract, make a copy of it, and get back to the surface without being discovered.

He stared at the Codebreaker's readout. *Which do I choose? Fifty-fifty odds—that's better than most of my jobs.*

The codes were numeric. One was 58128, the other 31954. Since Glat was the owner, and Torf a mere programmer, Leck decided that Glat would give himself the higher number.

If I'm wrong, those Klingon disruptor emplacements the suit is picking up around the door will reduce me to my component atoms.

Leck had imagined his own death on numerous occasions, and each one of them had involved combat of some sort. To die at the bottom of the Mayak Swamp during a simple break-and-enter would just be embarrassing.

He entered 31954.

The door opened.

It was an airlock, of course. Leck went limp as the swampwater poured into the open chamber, and let himself be carried inside.

A moment later, the outer door closed, and Leck heard the sound of the ventilation system. The swampwater was being sucked into a drain in the corner of the airlock. Within a minute, the room was dry and the inner door opened.

While waiting for the airlock to cycle, Leck had checked the bog suit's power supply. It took twenty-five minutes to swim from the surface to the archive, and thirty-five minutes of power remained. That left him with only ten minutes to do what he came here to do. *Perhaps fifteen if I swim very fast.*

The airlock opened to a tiny room with a small desk at its center; on the desk was a terminal. There was no other way in or out of the room. Leck assumed the rest of the structure had the actual computer. Briefly, he wondered how the physical maintenance of the computer was performed, then decided that he didn't really care all that much.

He activated the terminal.

It asked for his access code.

Leck consulted the Codebreaker.

This time there was only one code. Leck was about to enter it when the Codebreaker's display changed to a different code.

Leck frowned. *Which is it?*

The display didn't change. Then he checked the bog suit's

chronometer. The code had changed right at the top of the hour. *The code changes on the hour—or maybe on the half- or quarter-hour. Either way, this code should be fine now.*

He entered the new code, then touched the tab marked SE-LECT.

The terminal's display then read: WELCOME, TORF. PLEASE ENTER YOUR REQUEST.

Leck grinned. *I love it when a plan comes together.*

It took only a few minutes to call up Rom's marriage contract. Then he removed the padd from one of the sealed pockets in the bog suit and instructed the computer to copy the contract to his padd.

The computer's response: ENTER ACCESS CODE AND PRESS SELECT.

Rolling his eyes—or, given the optical camouflage, rolling Torf's—Leck activated the Codebreaker once again.

To his shock, the display indicated that there was no code. *How is this possible?*

Leck was starting to get angry. Based on the bog suit's chronometer, he had only a few more minutes before he needed to head back to the surface. In all his years as an eliminator, he'd never failed in a job—except that once, but it was a long time ago, and nobody was left alive who knew about it, so it didn't really count. He wasn't about to start now, especially at a job that would help the Grand Nagus. The last thing Leck wanted was a return to the old ways. Since females started going into business, Leck had been busier than ever. Years of oppression had made females ruthless and creative, and being forced to do business with females had had a similar effect on many males. This kept the need for Leck's services at an all-time high. The last thing he wanted was Brunt and his cronies turning back the clock.

But if there's no code, then . . .

Then he laughed. *Brilliant! Absolutely brilliant!*

The Codebreaker couldn't find a code because there *was* no code. Mindful not only of the Eighty-Eighth Rule, but also the Two Thirty-Ninth—"Never be afraid to mislabel a product"—Glat and Torf had added another layer of security. If someone managed to penetrate this far, and obtain their access codes, they would be caught at this point when they entered an access code that was unnecessary. No doubt, had Leck obtained the access codes through other means, a false code for this stage would have been part of the intelligence he gained. But computers couldn't lie—only their programmers could—so Leck was able to see through the deception.

Without entering a code, he simply pressed SELECT.

The contract started copying.

Leck smiled.

Ten seconds later, the transfer was complete. Leck put the padd back into the sealed pocket, shut down the terminal, and took his leave of the archive with one minute to spare.

As he swam back toward the surface, he wondered if there were any more eels around he could shoot. *That'll make the trip complete. . . .*

Nik threw a strip of latinum into the pot as it rotated. "Acquire," he said, and took another card.

Naturally, the card didn't help his hand any. It had been a miserable night at the *tongo* wheel. *Then again, it's the perfect ending to a perfect week,* he thought angrily as the player next to him—a female—tossed three strips in and said, "Confront."

Muttering a Klingon curse, Nik showed his hand, which was, of course, woefully inadequate. His only consolation was that the female who confronted didn't win, either—her hand was worth the risk, but Helk had a slightly better hand, and took the entire pot.

Across the table, another female asked Helk, "Why didn't you confront sooner?"

Helk snorted. "With this hand? I wanted a bigger pot than this. Not," he added with a gap-toothed grin at the female who confronted, "that I mind taking this one."

The female smiled right back. "The night is young, Helk."

Nik said nothing, but fumed quietly. He couldn't even enjoy a good *tongo* game without females being involved. It wasn't enough that they were gallivanting around the streets with clothes on, but they also had to come and invade the *tongo* parlors.

In the old days, Nik would unwind after a hard week at the

Tower of Commerce with a few rounds of *tongo*. The back room of Geln's *Tongo* Parlor was one of the most exclusive *tongo* games on Ferenginar—you had to pay two bricks a month just to be allowed into the back room—and Nik had been a proud regular for over a decade.

Now, though, Nik wasn't sure why he bothered, since unwinding was the last thing he could do while being forced to share a *tongo* table with two clothed females. *Tongo* was a male's game, and letting females into it just ruined everything.

Of course, so did letting females into the business world. And letting idiots hold the Grand Nagus's staff. We're all going to the Vault of Eternal Destitution in a muckraker, I can tell you that.

Nik couldn't entirely blame Geln for letting females in— after all, if they had the two bricks a month, who was Geln to argue? Their latinum was as good as anyone else's, and besides, to exclude females would just put the parlor on the Grand Nagus's sensor screen and, even with the current scandal, that wasn't a place any Ferengi wanted to be.

But it still irked Nik.

As the dealer gave each of them a new hand, Nik took some solace in the fact that he was still making a dishonest living, which was the most any Ferengi could truly ask out of life. His skills as a stockbroker were well known in certain circles, along with his ability to be discreet. After all, some transactions were best done in private, away from the prying eyes of the securities exchange—or the FCA.

Just as Nik took his final card, the door to the front of the parlor opened to reveal Geln. "Hey Nik," he said, "there's someone here to see you."

Nik was about to tell Geln that he was busy, but he knew Geln wouldn't have even admitted that the back room existed, much less come back to pass on this message, if the person in question hadn't provided a hefty bribe. Anyone who had that kind of money was probably someone it was worth Nik's while to talk to.

Though it meant sacrificing his opening fee, Nik put his cards down and said, "Divest."

He went out to the front room, which included a bar, three

restaurant-style booths, and a dozen low-stakes public *tongo* wheels, to see the usual assortment of Ferengi, a few aliens here and there—

—and a Bajoran female in a Starfleet uniform sitting in one of the booths. Geln pointed to the booth and said, "Her."

This can't be right, Nik thought. Starfleet officers rarely carried money. *How could she have bribed Geln? I wonder if he's in trouble with Starfleet.*

His enthusiasm for the meeting having dimmed considerably, Nik walked over to the booth. "Can I help you?"

Standing up, the Bajoran said, "Assuming you're Nik, yes, you probably can. I understand you quietly sold some shares in Chek Pharmaceuticals."

Perhaps she does *have cash. It would take considerable bribe money to find that out.* Nik was filled with both respect and apprehension, and he wondered why Starfleet was involved in this. *I thought they didn't interfere in other planets' affairs.* Then again, the woman's collar was gold, which either meant engineering or security—and, all things considered, the latter seemed the most likely.

"What makes you say that?" Nik said evasively.

The Bajoran started to say something, then smiled. "You know, Nik, it's been a *very* long day. I've been trying to track down these stock transactions, and it's taken me all over the capital city. I know that some of them went to an investigator named Rwogo, but the number of shares sold doesn't match what's in her portfolio. So I've bribed, I've offered *oo-mox*, I've bribed some more, and I've even offered privileged information."

That surprised Nik. "Privileged information? I didn't think you Starfleeters did that sort of thing."

Again, she smiled. "It wasn't like I was giving away access codes or anything. Someone wanted to know the erogenous zones on a Vulcan."

Nik's eyes widened, and his right hand brushed over the middle part of his right lobe. "You know the erogenous zones on a Vulcan?"

Now the Bajoran looked at Nik as if he were insane. "Of course not. I just made something up. My only regret is that I won't get to see the look on his face when he tries it out on the next Vulcan woman he meets."

Despite himself, Nik was impressed. This female knew how to deal with Ferengi. "So what is it you want from me?"

"I thought I said that already. I want to know who those shares of Chek stock were sold to."

Nik laughed. "My dear—" He peered at her gold collar, saw two solid pips, then continued. "—Lieutenant, even if I did have such information, why would I give it to you?" She wasn't likely to offer information, given what she just revealed about her Vulcan deception, and that meant either latinum or *oo-mox*, either of which suited Nik fine.

"Well, like I said, I've done all sorts of things to get the information, and I'm tired of it. There are times that call for the direct approach."

Grinning, Nik thought, Oo-mox *it is, then*, even as the female reached for his ear.

Then a sharp pain shot through Nik's head, and went all the way down to his toes. The Bajoran might not have known the erogenous zones on a Vulcan, but she knew the precise location of the most sensitive part of a Ferengi male's lobes, and how hard to grip it in order to induce the most agonizing pain.

"Tell me who you sold the shares to, please."

Nik hadn't felt agony this intense since he was a boy and his left ear got caught in his father's old-fashioned latinum counter. It had taken an hour just to pry his head out of the machine's gears.

"I'm waiting," the Bajoran said, even as Nik's knees buckled. To his dismay, that action did not cause the Bajoran's grip to ease up.

"What do you think you're—" That was Geln's voice, but it was cut off by the Bajoran's using her free hand to unholster a phaser.

"I'm talking to my friend here, something I paid you quite handsomely for the privilege of doing, so back off."

Putting up his hands, Geln backed off. The rest of the bar grew quiet; at least, Nik thought it did. It was possible that his hearing was impaired. Certainly, his sight was getting there.

Spots were dancing in front of his eyes, and his legs felt as if someone were sticking several pins into them.

The Bajoran tightened her grip yet again, revealing to Nik precisely what a phaser drill through his skull would feel like.

"All right!" he cried.

She let go.

Nik fell to the floor, unable to make his legs work.

He looked up to see the Bajoran standing with one hand on her hip, the other still holding the phaser. "I'm waiting."

"I sold the other shares to someone named Gash."

"He's a Ferengi?" the female asked.

Nik nodded, then regretted the action, as it just caused his head to swim more. He added, "I can give you his account number."

The female produced a padd. Nik forced himself to stand up, even as the phaser drill continued its work on his skull. He took the padd, entered Gash's account number into it, then handed it back, putting his other hand to his mangled lobe.

"Anything else?" he asked in a voice that was much shakier than he wanted it to be.

"It'll do for now." She turned to Geln, who was keeping his distance but still watching the tableau. "Sorry for the disruption."

With that, she turned and left.

Nik gently massaged his sore lobe. *So much for unwinding in the* tongo *parlor. Maybe I should take up dom-jot. . . .*

Never allow family to stand in the way of opportunity.

—RULE OF ACQUISITION #6

"Ow!"

The novelty of hitting his head on the top of the tunnel that ran from Grandfather's house to the Gleb Jungle had long since worn off for Nog. But it would be worth getting the bumps on his head to finally get to talk to his mother.

Nog was better prepared for this trip than he had been for his last one. For one thing, he wore an oversuit that protected his uniform from the muck of the Gleb, not to mention the swampwater in Grandfather's basement, so he'd get to talk to his mother in a clean uniform.

He also came with a scrambler, which would negate the alarm Grandfather had placed on the tunnel entrance. Nog had also installed a recording device near the front entrance of the house that would inform him of Dav's comings and goings. *It's good to be an engineer and have the Grand Nagus's resources at your disposal,* he had thought with a smile.

When the device told him that Grandfather had left—taking an aircar—Nog quickly arranged transport to the Gleb Jungle, and from there he made his way back to the house.

So far, so good, he thought as he entered the basement. Sloshing through the swampwater, and avoiding disturbing the mold farm, Nog went to the staircase—this time without incident.

Leaving the muck-covered oversuit at the top of the stairs, he entered the house.

The place was pretty much the way Nog remembered it. Grandfather had been an avid collector of *yorra* beads, and they were *everywhere*—even draped over the furniture, the lamps, and the wall hangings. In the latter case, it was just as well, since Grandfather's taste in art had actually gotten worse over the years, which Nog would not have believed possible.

"Is someone there?"

I know that voice, Nog thought. He didn't remember much about Prinadora, but he remembered what she looked like, and most of all, he remembered her voice. It was a very pretty voice, and from the sounds of it, it hadn't changed in twenty years.

"It's—it's Nog," he said as he turned toward the voice.

He saw a female standing naked in the doorway. "Nog? I know that name. Oh, but I shouldn't be talking to you. But my father isn't home—are you a friend of his?"

Nog couldn't believe what he was hearing. "Moogie, it's *me*—Nog. Your *son*."

"Son? Oh, yes, I do believe I had a son once. I think. It was *such* a long time ago."

Prinadora stepped into the room. She was as beautiful as Nog remembered—small, delicate lobes, large brown eyes, a small nose, and perfectly sharpened teeth. She had a few more wrinkles in her skin, but nothing too bad. He could see why Father fell in love with her.

"I'm being rude—can I get you anything?"

"I'm fine, really, Moogie, I—" His brain could barely process this. "You don't remember me at all?"

She shrugged. "As I said, you look vaguely familiar. I'm sorry, I don't remember things very well. Father says it's because I'm a female. We don't have lobes as well developed as males, which is why we have to remain at home and not wear clothes. That is a privilege for males only."

Prinadora spoke by rote, as if repeating something she'd been told many times, but didn't entirely understand. Seeing her reminded him of what Father saw in her, but now Nog started to wonder if there was anything to her beyond those looks.

"Don't you remember my father at all? Rom? You used to be married?"

Frowning, she asked, "Isn't Rom the Grand Nagus now?"

"Yes."

She nodded. "Right, of course. I remember now—Father reminded me, he and I were married once."

Nog's mind was reeling. "Don't you remember him, either?"

"I think so." Her face scrunched up a bit. "Yes—it was a long time ago, but I seem to remember that he was a very nice fellow. He had a good heart. I was sorry when he left. He had a boy with him—I think I was the mother." Suddenly, her brown eyes grew wider. "Oh! That would be you, wouldn't it?"

"Uh, yes—yes, that was me." Nog struggled to find the right words to say. "Do—do you remember *anything* about what happened when you and my father ended your marriage?"

"Not really. Father told me recently that we were still married, but I don't remember the details. That's male business, after all, and as a female it isn't my place to question or discuss such things."

Again with the rote talking. Nog had grown up being taught that this very behavior was how Ferengi females were supposed to act. But it had also been years since he was exposed to a female who behaved like this. In fact, most of the females he had lived and worked with since he and Father left Ferenginar to go to Terok Nor were the diametric opposite of Prinadora. After years of exposure to the likes of Kira Nerys, Jadzia and Ezri Dax, Kasidy Yates, Prynn Tenmei, Keiko O'Brien, Ro Laren, and even Korena, he found he could no longer simply accept a "proper" Ferengi female.

His mother continued: "I do know that it makes Father very upset. For the last few weeks, he keeps meeting with people, and talking about how they're going to bring down the Grand Nagus for what he's done." She looked at Nog. "But I'm still being rude. Is there anything I can get you? We have some lovely tube grubs that are fresh from the garden—I can chew them for you."

"No, thank you." His joking with Korena notwithstanding,

Nog had long since lost his taste for pre-chewed food. "I really can't stay that long. I just—I just wanted to see you again."

She smiled. "Well, that is very sweet of you—Nog, isn't it? That's a lovely name. What's that outfit you're wearing? I don't recall anyone wearing anything so—well, drab."

"I'm a Starfleet officer."

"Starfleet? Is that related to the FCA?"

Briefly, Nog considered trying to explain what Starfleet was, then decided it wasn't worth the effort. *Even if I did, I'm not sure she'd understand it,* he thought.

"You look sad," Prinadora said. "What's wrong?"

"Nothing's wrong," Nog lied. *How can I tell her that she's not at all what I expected when I decided to have a reunion with my moogie?* Besides, something she had said reminded Nog of the other reason why he wanted to talk to Prinadora. "May I ask you something?"

"Of course."

"You said that your father has been meeting with people about bringing the Grand Nagus down."

Prinadora nodded.

"Do you know *who* he's been meeting with?"

Shaking her head, Prinadora said, "Not by name, no. I could describe them for you, if you wish."

"That would be great, thank you." Nog wanted to be able to salvage *something* from this trip.

"One of them I remember very well, because he smelled *horrible....*"

Rom stared at the sleeping form of his pregnant wife. According to Dr. Orpax, she was in a coma, though she didn't look any different from the way she looked when she was asleep. On the other hand, she had been asleep for over a day, and that wasn't normal, Rom knew that.

I don't know what to do.

"How's she doing?"

Rom turned to see Quark standing in the doorway to the hospital room. "Not good," he said to his brother. "Dr. Orpax says he's going to wait three more hours to see if she goes into labor naturally."

"And if she doesn't?"

"Then," Rom said, stretching the word out in order to avoid what he had to say next, "he'll have to operate."

"So what's the problem?" Quark asked as he entered the room and stood on the other side of the bed from Rom.

"Her immune system may not be able to handle the surgery! She could *die*!"

Quark put his hands on the bed. "Listen to me, Rom—Dr. Orpax is the best there is. And Leeta's a tough customer. She'll be fine—and so will your child."

Rom knew that Quark had no way of knowing that for sure, but he appreciated the rare gesture, so he simply said, "Thank you, Brother," in a quiet voice.

"Now that we've got that out of the way—we need to talk."

"What about?"

"I think you know."

Scratching his head, Rom said, "I really don't, Brother."

Quark rubbed his forehead with his right hand. "I'm talking about the marriage contract to Prinadora that Brunt showed to the congress."

"What about it?" Rom said evasively.

Holding up one finger, Quark said, "It's a *fake*!"

"Okay."

"It took us *days* to figure out that it was fake—you know why? The forgery was done by Gash."

"Oh. He's very good."

"I know he's very good, Rom." Quark glowered at his brother, and Rom shrunk from his gaze. "Why do you think I keep hiring him? He's the best there is—and his forgery was so good, nobody could crack it."

"So how'd you find out it was a fake?" Rom's voice was so quiet, even he could barely hear it.

"I got Leck to break into the contract archive to find the original contract."

Rom's eyes went wide. He knew Leck was insane, but this was on a whole new level. "Leck broke into the archive? And survived? And didn't get caught?"

"Yes, yes, and yes."

Impressed, Rom said, "That's amazing."

" 'That's amazing'? Is that all you can say?"

"What do you mean, Brother?"

Quark gripped the side of the bed. "Why did we have to go through all that trouble to find out what you could have told us in three seconds? Why didn't you say that Brunt's contract was a fake?"

Rom had been hoping it wouldn't come to this, even though he knew full well it was going to eventually. Sighing, he said, "Because I didn't know."

"What do you mean, you didn't know?" Quark was now yelling so loud, Rom half expected his voice to awaken Leeta from her coma. "You signed the contract, didn't you?"

"Signed, yes." Rom found he couldn't look his brother in the face. "Read—no."

Quark's mouth fell open. "You didn't *read* the contract? How big an idiot *are* you?" Before Rom could speak, Quark said, "Don't answer that."

Rom shrugged. "I didn't remember any of the details of the contract, just what Dav told me when we separated. For all I knew, Brunt was telling the truth."

Looking at Rom like he had grown a third ear, Quark asked, "Why would he start now?" He shook his head. "It's amazing. Your entire life has been one insane decision after another."

"No, it hasn't." Rom knew he sounded miserable, but didn't care. "That's just it—I never made *any* decisions." He looked at the beautiful sleeping female lying between Rom and his brother. "Until I met her, anyhow."

"That's the most ridiculous thing I've ever heard you say." Quark pointed at Rom. "And considering all the things I've heard you say over the years, you know I'm not saying that lightly."

"It's true!" Rom stared at his brother. "You know what I was like before I met her. Always letting people push me around and make decisions for me. And then I met Leeta." He looked at her sleeping form again, and just watching her filled him with joy. "You know why I formed that union in the bar? For her. And that led me to become an engineer on the station, because I knew that it would make me a better match for her, especially if we weren't coworkers anymore."

"Great. Someone *else* you're in love with who's making you be an even bigger idiot." Quark shook his head. "I should never have done it."

Rom frowned. "Done what?"

"Taken you in! You know what the best years of my life were? After I left home and before you showed up at Terok Nor begging for a place to live and work because Dav cleaned you out."

Rom still didn't get it. "You think the best years of your life were when you were a cook on that freighter?"

Quark's eyes widened. "Yes! And you know why? *You weren't there!* Leaving home was the smartest thing I ever did, because it got me away from my family." Quark threw up his hands and started pacing the room—as best he could in the small space, anyhow. "Away from Father and his failures, away from Mother and her radical notions, and away from you and your abject stupidity! But then you show up with your little kid begging me to take you in. Did I listen to the Sixth Rule? Of *course* I didn't!" He looked at Rom. "And now look where it's gotten me! My entire life is disintegrating before my eyes because *you didn't read a contract!* The most *basic* tenet of Ferengi life, and you can't even manage that."

Rom lowered his head, ashamed. "I'm sorry, Brother."

"Oh, well, wonderful. That makes all the difference. You're *sorry*. Rom, I don't want you to be Grand Nagus because I think you and our mother are destroying the Ferengi Alliance—but I *have* to do everything I can to keep you in power because if I don't, I lose the bar and *Brunt* becomes nagus, and that way lies destitution." He walked around to the other side of the bed. "Which means you're coming with me right now."

"I can't."

"Yes you can. You're going to call an emergency session of the congress and we're going to present the evidence that Laren, Nog, and I have spent the last few days gathering." Quark grabbed Rom by the arm, but he stood his ground.

"No, Brother, I'm not." He yanked his arm out from Quark's grip, and turned to look at Leeta. "I'm not leaving her side until this is all over."

Clenching his fists and holding them in front of his chest, Quark cried, "Rom, you could lose the nagushood!"

"I could lose *Leeta*—and that's more important than anything. Even the nagushood." He turned his back on his brother and sat back in the guest chair. "When Leeta and the baby are okay, then I'll leave. But I'm not setting foot outside this hospital until then."

Quark shook his head. "A lifetime of being an idiot—why stop now? Fine, do whatever you want. Destroy the entire Ferengi Alliance, ruin everything you and Mother and Zek have built."

"I thought you didn't approve of what we're doing," Rom said, confused.

"I don't, but that doesn't change what you've accomplished." Quark shook his head and laughed ruefully. "Rom, you've changed the course of *history*! You've probably had more of an impact on Ferengi society than any nagus since Gint, and you've only been at the job a year! That's an *amazing* accomplishment!" Now he turned his back. "I can't believe you're throwing it away for a female—again."

"I *love* her, Quark."

"Just like you loved Prinadora? You've already destroyed your life once because of love. Don't do it again."

As Quark approached the door, Rom blurted, "Wouldn't you do the same for Lieutenant Ro?"

Quark froze in the doorway. "What's she got to do with this?"

"I see the way you look at her, Brother, so don't bother denying it. You have feelings for her."

Turning to look back at Rom, Quark said, "Maybe I do. But to answer your question: No. No female is worth that."

Then he left.

Sighing, Rom slumped in the guest chair and stared at his comatose wife.

I hope everything comes out okay.

10

Whisper your way to success.

—RULE OF ACQUISITION #168

Quark nearly jumped out of his lobes when he saw the second person in the nagal aircar that was waiting for him in the hospital's garage. Before he could even register who the intruder was, he cried, "What're *you* doing here?"

Even as he spoke, and tried to get his breathing under control, he recognized the person in the aircar's passenger seat across from him: Chek. That also explained how he got in— Chek certainly had the cash to offer a sufficient bribe to the chauffeur.

Said chauffeur closed the door and started to pilot the aircar out of the garage. He didn't wait for Quark's fee, nor did Quark have any intention of giving him one, seeing as how he let Chek in without permission.

"I'm here to reiterate my offer to you, Quark. You've been on Ferenginar for several days—you've had more than adequate opportunity to see what a failure your brother is."

Quark smiled. "I already knew all about my brother before I came here, and nothing I've seen has changed my opinion."

Chek leaned back in the seat and picked up a drink that Quark hadn't noticed. It probably came from the aircar's well-stocked bar. As he sipped, Quark recognized it as a fungus fizz.

"That's excellent news," Chek said, putting the drink down and wiping the slime from his lips. "Then we can count on your support in our campaign to oust Rom."

Shaking his head, Quark said, "Not a chance."

The shock Quark got from Chek's invasion of the aircar was more than made up for by the stunned look on Chek's face now. "But—but—you said you were on our side!"

"When did I say that?"

Pointing an accusatory finger, Chek said, "You said you wanted to restore the Ferengi Alliance to the old ways!"

"When did I say that?"

Chek's wide eyes squinted. "You can't fool me, Quark. I know you—you're on our side in this."

Quark laughed. "Chek, don't tell me you've forgotten Rule of Acquisition Number Two Hundred: 'A Ferengi chooses no side but his own.' I freely admit that I would prefer a Ferenginar I could be proud of, a return to the good old days of full-fledged greed and exploitation. But let's look at it from my perspective. If things stay the way they are, I'm the Ferengi Ambassador to Bajor, and I have a thriving bar on one of the most important ports of call in the quadrant. Ever since Bajor joined the Federation, the place has been lousy with tourists who want to visit famous war sites or wallow in what passes for beauty on Bajor."

"But—"

Quark refused to let Chek interrupt him when he was on a roll. "On the other hand, if I throw in with you, I support Brunt. He's a *liquidator,* and I can assure you that he wouldn't think twice about revoking my diplomatic post. Brunt's dedicated his life to making *my* life miserable, and it would take a lot more latinum than you've got to convince me to help *him* become Grand Nagus. Not to mention the fact that your entire campaign is based on slander against my brother."

Chek's mouth hung open in shock. "You yourself keep calling him an idiot!"

"That's not slander, that's fact. But a contract-breaker? Not even my brother would do that—he's an idiot, he's not a moron."

Snorting, Chek asked, "There's a difference?"

"Yes, there is." Quark leaned forward. "Even the most lobe-less Ferengi doesn't break a contract without good reason, and Rom had no good reason to break this one."

"The evidence—"

"Is completely false." Quark grinned. "And I have the proof." A lurch in Quark's stomach indicated that the aircar was descending toward the nagal residence.

Chek took another drink of his fizz. "Your so-called proof won't withstand scrutiny."

"Oh, I know how good a forger Gash is, and I'm sure he did his best work—but my proof comes straight from the Glat Archive."

Sputtering in his fizz, Chek said, "That's impossible!" He grabbed the rain towel from its shelf and wiped the fungus off his jacket. "The investigator checked it against the archive."

"Apparently not." As the aircar landed, Quark called out to the chauffeur. "Please take Chek wherever it is he wants to go—as long as it's far from here."

The door opened as the aircar landed in the enclosed entry-way to the nagal residence. "What I have to wonder," Quark said as he exited the vehicle, "is if you're in on the scam—or if you really believe Brunt's 'evidence.' 'Cause I gotta tell you, if you did believe Brunt, you're a bigger idiot than my brother ever could be."

Whistling the Slug-O-Cola jingle, Quark entered the nagal residence. Behind him, he heard the whine of the aircar's engines taking Chek away.

Ro Laren held her breath as she, Quark, and the rest of their entourage approached the room where the Economic Congress of Advisors met. They had called another emergency session, this time to vote on whether or not to oust Rom as Grand Nagus. Rom himself refused to leave the hospital—Leeta was about to undergo surgery to retrieve the baby—so Krax came along to act as his proxy, which the first clerk was apparently empowered to do in these circumstances. Ishka was also present, as was Nog.

However, Ro was holding her breath because of the sixth member of their little party: a Ferengi named Gash, who had apparently last bathed some time prior to when Zek was born. Ro couldn't even get a good look at the forger's face, as a miasma seemed to surround his entire body—plus, every time she looked at him, her eyes watered.

Ishka and Gash stayed behind—for which Ro was grateful, as the congress met in an enclosed room, and she didn't want to think about what his stench would be like in there—with the remaining four entering the meeting room.

Like every other space on Ferenginar, the room was tacky as all get-out. Ro was starting to think that there wasn't a place on this planet that wasn't a decorator's nightmare. It wasn't so much that the décor was so hideous—though much of it was—but that it so obviously represented conspicuous consumption. Everyone wanted to show off how much money they had, whether they had it or not. Of course, Ro would expect it in places like the nagal residence and here at the Tower of Commerce, but after her whistlestop tour of the capital city, culminating in her interrogation of that stock buyer at the *tongo* parlor, she had come to the conclusion that this entire planet was full of people who wanted everyone to think they were rich to the point where it was downright wearying.

Ro found her eyes drawn to the tapestry of Grand Nagus Gint on the far wall. Quark had told her when they came here last that it was sewn in latinum.

Instinctively, Ro wondered what that tapestry's market value was, and how useful it might have been to the Bajorans during the seven years that they were rebuilding after the Occupation. Then she pushed the thought aside. *That way lies madness.*

Sitting or standing around the table were fourteen Ferengi. One of them, seated at the far end, was as old as any Ferengi Ro had ever seen. Another was the instantly recognizable face of Brunt, whose smiling face had seared itself on Ro's brain despite her best efforts.

The biggest surprise, though, was the identity of the fourteenth Ferengi in the room: Zek. He was standing in a corner mumbling to himself. She leaned over to Quark and whispered, "What's he doing here?"

Quark whispered back, "I don't know. Mother's been trying to talk to him since he arrived, but he won't see her."

Brunt stood up from his chair upon their arrival. "This is a *closed* congress. Krax is entitled to be here as the nagus's proxy, but the rest of you must leave." Brunt looked at Ro with revulsion, which matched how she looked at him. *"Especially that clothed female!"*

"If she takes her clothes off, can she stay?" Quark asked.

"That isn't funny, Quark," Brunt said.

"Damn right it isn't," Ro muttered.

The person seated to the right of the nagus's chair—who, if Ro remembered correctly, was Fal, the president of the congress—said, "Actually, Krax is entitled to bring assistants to aid in testimony. They will have to leave when the vote is taken, but they are allowed to participate in the prior deliberations."

"What a ridiculous notion," Brunt said. "I'll have to remember to abolish that when I'm Grand Nagus."

"I wouldn't get so overconfident if I were you," Nog said. "Remember what happened the last time you thought you were Grand Nagus."

Brunt sneered at Nog. "Don't think that uniform entitles you to anything, child." He looked at Ro, and the revulsed look came back. "Or you either, female. Starfleet has no jurisdiction here."

"Perhaps not," Krax said as he took his seat, "but they have aided in the nagus's investigation into the slanderous accusations that have been made against him."

Brunt also sat down, as did the other congressmen. Zek remained in his corner; Ro, Quark, and Nog took up position just behind Krax, who, Ro thought, looked distressingly comfortable in the nagal seat.

"What investigation is there to be made?" one of the congressmen asked. "The contract was verified by Investigator Rwogo."

"We only have her word for that," Krax said.

"Enough!" Brunt said. "There's nothing to debate. I have presented incontrovertible evidence that Rom broke his marriage contract to Prinadora. He should be removed from the nagushood immediately, at which point the new Grand Nagus should instruct the FCA to have him banned."

"We have evidence—" Krax started, but Brunt interrupted and pointed to the old Ferengi in the corner.

"I have even had the esteemed former Grand Nagus brought back from his peaceful retirement on Risa, because he is so outraged at the behavior of his handpicked successor. Isn't that right, Grand Nagus?"

Zek looked up from his mumbling. "Eh? What? Oh yes. Outraged. Very outraged." He frowned. "What are we talking about, again?"

Ro winced. *How the mighty have fallen.*

The old man at the end of the table said, "We're talking about Grand Nagus Rom, you senile old *gree* worm! He's accused of breaking a contract!"

"Well, he shouldn't *do* that," Zek said. "In my day, we'd never tolerate a Ferengi who would do that."

Brunt smiled. As always when he did so, Ro felt the need for a shower. "Quite right. And we still don't, even in this so-called enlightened age."

"But Rom didn't break a contract," Krax said calmly. "Father, even you can agree that a forged contract is no evidence of anything."

"Well, of course it isn't!" Zek snapped. Then he squinted and asked, "Isn't it?"

Krax held up a hand, and Quark handed over the padd Leck had provided. "I have in my hands the actual marriage contract between Rom and Prinadora, as retrieved from the contract archive." Krax touched a control that sent the contract to all the terminals in front of each congressman. "If you turn to clause 47, paragraph 22, you'll see that, in fact, the marriage extension had a limited term, and that the marriage is *over*. There was no violation of the clause when the Grand Nagus married again."

One congressman asked, "How do we know this is not a fake?"

Nog said, "It was retrieved from the *archive*."

"How? No order was made to Glat to retrieve it, except the one on record made by Investigator Rwogo."

"That," Quark said, "would be the same Rwogo who received a portion of a set of shares in Chek Pharmaceuticals right before she produced this contract?"

Brunt scowled. "Females are allowed to buy stocks now. Perhaps she did the same."

Ro spoke up. "This job with the investigator's office is the first one Rwogo has had that allowed her to support herself beyond room and board, and she hasn't even reached her first payday yet. She doesn't have the money to buy these shares. Besides, the stock buyer who negotiated the purchase, a gentleman named Nik, has already admitted to giving the shares to her on behalf of a third party."

At the mention of that name, several congressmen squirmed. Ro suspected that several of them had made use of Nik's discreet services in the past.

One congressman—whom Ro recognized from various advertisements as Nilva, the head of Slug-O-Cola—said, "What did you mean by 'a portion of a set of shares'?"

On the one hand, Ro was impressed that Nilva had the sense to ask the question. On the other hand, it meant that they were reaching the moment she—and her nose—had been dreading. She looked down at Nog and gave him a nod.

Returning the nod, the young officer went to the door, opened it, and said, "Grandmoogie—bring him in."

As Ro held her breath, Ishka came in with Gash.

Her arrival got Zek's attention. "Sweetie-foot?"

Before Ishka could reply to that, Brunt, now with an embroidered handkerchief over his nose, asked, "What is *that* doing here?"

Quark smiled. "His name is Gash. He's probably the best forger in the galaxy—and he's confessed to being hired by Prinadora's father Dav on behalf of Chek Pharmaceuticals, Eelwasser, and their Brunt for Grand Nagus Campaign to forge a marriage contract."

Ro gave Quark a look of annoyance. Gash was willing to cop to the forgery only if Ro was willing to look the other way regarding Quark's Grisellan totem icon scam—which Gash had been sure to mention as soon as Nog tracked him down and brought him to the nagal residence. True, they already had Prinadora's description of Gash going to Dav's house, not to mention Nik's admission that he gave shares of Chek stock to Gash, but neither of those would be as convincing as a direct confession.

"That's right," Gash said. "Pretty damn complicated job, if'n y'ask me, but that Dav fella, he paid me in Chek stocks—good'uns, too. Went on about how it was for a noble cause an' all, but I didn't give two slips 'bout that—just a job well done. And I gotta say, I done right well on that one."

Nilva was now looking straight at Brunt, though he addressed Gash. "So you're saying that the contract Brunt gave this congress—"

"—is a damn fine piece'a my work, youbetcha."

Brunt stood up. Ro noticed that he avoided making eye contact with Nilva. "This is outrageous! Are we to believe the words of a female, a bartender, two Starfleet officers, and this filthy creature over a liquidator in good standing of the Ferengi Commerce Authority?"

The old man at the end started to speak, then suffered a coughing fit. After a moment—during which Ro swore he placed the handkerchief he coughed into inside a specimen case—he spoke: "The phrase 'liquidator in good standing' is a contradiction in terms."

"The point is," Brunt said, "we are Ferengi businessmen. Do we base our decisions on"—he gestured dismissively at Krax and those standing around him—"*these* types of people? A Ferengi contract has been violated!"

Suddenly, a thought occurred to Ro. She was, at once, pleased with herself for thinking of it and angry at herself for not thinking of it sooner. "No, one hasn't."

"Females have no place in this—"

Fal cut Brunt off. "What is it you wish to say, Lieutenant?"

"Let's, just for a second, ignore the fact that we have a confession from the forger, corroborated by the man who provided his payment, and that a copy of the original contract was retrieved from the contract archive. Let's say you all dismiss this overwhelming evidence for a second, and believe that Brunt here showed you the real copy of Rom and Prinadora's marriage contract. Rom still didn't violate it."

Several mutters went around the table, many expressing dismay at the inability of non-Ferengi females to understand finance. Even Quark and Ishka were looking at her as if she were insane.

"Hear me out," she said. "Rom didn't break this contract, and the resason I know this is because I know your Rules of Acquisition—specifically the seventeenth one. More specifically, the clause you guys like to leave out when you're dealing with offworlders. 'A contract is a contract is a contract—but only between Ferengi.' "

Brunt rolled his eyes. "What does this—?"

"It has to do with Rom's second marriage. If that marriage contract is in violation of the first contract, then you really should produce the contract for the second marriage to prove it, right?"

The congressmen all looked at each other in confusion.

Ro pressed her point home. "But you don't have one on file, do you—because Rom's second marriage was *Bajoran*, performed on a Bajoran space station, presided over by the Bajoran Emissary. And by your very own Rules, that's not a legitimate contract, because it *isn't* between Ferengi."

One of the congressmen said, "She has a point."

"Nonsense!" another congressman said. "I doubt that that was the true intent of Grand Nagus Gint when he framed the Rules."

"Who are we to presume what Gint meant?"

"I believe—"

Leaping to his feet, Brunt cried, "It doesn't matter! The Grand Nagus has lost the faith of the Ferengi people! He must be removed from office immediately! And where is the Grand Nagus, anyhow? Why does he not come here to defend himself? Why does he send these lackeys to speak for him? I'll tell you why—he's a sham!" He pointed to Zek. "That man has been stuck on Risa, being miserable because the female he thought he was retiring with has been back here, doing the Grand Nagus's work *for* him! He relies on females, children, and aliens to help him, but he himself is nowhere to be found! Why?"

"Uhhh—I was busy."

Ro whirled around to see Rom standing in the doorway to the meeting room. His shoulders were slumped, and Ro feared the worst. Before she could ask, though, Brunt spoke. "Oh, so now you're here. What do you have to say for yourself, contract-breaker?"

"Well, for one thing, that I'm not a contract-breaker." Rom slowly entered the room. "I loved Prinadora very much, and I allowed myself to sign an agreement that gave Dav all my worldly possessions—all I had left was my son." He looked at Nog and gave him a smile. Then he turned back to the congressmen. "When I took over as Grand Nagus it was in order to lead Ferenginar to a new era. Because the old Ferenginar wasn't any good anymore. The Ferengi are the joke of the galaxy. Even Klingons treat their females better than we do. People see us as caricatures—worthy of making fun of, and maybe, *maybe,* doing business with, but only if there's no other choice, because they know that we're going to exploit them.

"Well, maybe that was good enough before, but not anymore. Times are different now. This quadrant almost fell to the Dominion because the governments were all divided. But the Klingons, the Federation, the Romulans, they all came together and won the war. The Cardassians and the Breen didn't, and look where they are now. If the Ferengi are gonna keep surviving, if we're gonna be an important part of the galactic community—then *that's* what we have to be, a *part* of it, not just its exploiters. And I believe we can do it. I believe that we can still earn a profit, but not do it at the expense of others. I believe that we can lead Ferenginar into a new age of prosperity."

Rom's posture had improved with each sentence he spoke. But now, his shoulders slumped again. "Anyway, that's all I have to say. I guess you're gonna vote now."

Fal turned to Krax. "I'm afraid you're all going to have to leave while the congress votes."

Krax nodded. "Of course."

As Ro exited the meeting room, she noticed that no one was looking at Brunt—except Zek, who said, "Wait a minute— you're the one who tried to have me removed as Grand Nagus. Twice! Who let you on my congress?"

Nervously, Fal said, "Uh, Grand Nagus—I'm afraid you'll have to leave, too. The congress's votes are done in private. If you wish to view them afterward, recordings are made available for a small fe—"

Zek hobbled over to where Fal was sitting. "I know they'll be on sale tomorrow—don't teach your grandfather how to cheat Vulcans!"

As soon as they all went outside and the door shut behind them, Ishka ran to the former Grand Nagus. "Zekkie, what're you doing here?"

"Hm? Uh, well, I was going to the beach when this nice young man named Gaila came by—said he was your nephew. Said that Rom was doing a lousy job and that it was up to me to stop him."

"Zekkie, Rom's doing a *fine* job."

"But he violated a contract!" Then Zek's mouth fell open and he squinted again. "No, wait, that female just said he didn't. I'm confused—sweetie-foot, I *need* you to help me focus."

Ishka stroked Zek's ears, an image Ro feared she'd never be able to get out of her head. "I know, Zekkie, I know. I promise, I'll come back to Risa with you, and this time I'll stay, so nobody can confuse you anymore."

"Good."

Nog looked at Ro. "I wonder what happened to Leeta and the baby."

The door to the meeting room opened. "We're about to find out," Ro said.

Rom was the first one out, and he had a huge smile on his face. "Hello, Brother! Hi, Nog! Hello, Moogie!"

"You're in a good mood," Quark said.

"Why shouldn't I be? I'm the Grand Nagus!"

Nog pumped a fist. "Yes!"

Ishka put a hand on Rom's shoulder. "That's *great* news, Rom."

Zek said, "I'm proud of you, son. I'm sorry about what I said in there—and back at the spaceport. But I thought—"

"It's okay, Grand Nagus."

"Hey—*you're* nagus. I'm just Zek."

"Uhh, well, then, it's okay, *Zek*. You had every reason to think it."

"What about the baby?" Nog asked.

Rom's smile, which Ro thought was as wide as possible on a Ferengi mouth, actually grew wider. "She's just fine."

"Damn," Quark muttered.

"Quark!" Ishka snapped.

"I'm sorry, Mother, it's just—I had a boy in the raffle."

Ro laughed. "Well, I'm happy for both of you, Rom."

"Thank you. Leeta's resting in the hospital, and so's our little girl."

Krax let out a breath. "Thank the Divine Exchequer."

"What he said." Quark indicated the first clerk with a wave of his head. "We were all a little worried."

"I don't know why," Rom said. "Dr. Orpax *is* the most expensive doctor on Ferenginar."

"What time was the baby born?" Krax asked. "For the raffle."

After Rom gave the exact time of birth, Ishka asked, "What about Brunt?"

"He's being voted out right now. I abstained from voting, but I don't think it matters very much. He's finished with the congress, I'm sure of that."

Krax was consulting a padd. "Well, he'll have some small consolation."

Ro turned to the first clerk. "What do you mean?"

Holding the padd display-out, Krax said, "Brunt won the baby raffle. He guessed a girl, today, only two minutes off from the right time."

A silence fell over the waiting area.

Ro was the first to break it by bursting out laughing.

Within seconds, everyone else followed suit.

Opportunity plus instinct equals profit.

—Rule of Acquisition #9

Krax entered his home in a fairly good mood, right up until the point where he felt the sharp edge of a knife blade on his neck.

"If you move," said a deep voice from behind him, "I'll slice open your throat." A pause. "Well, start moving, already! I haven't killed anyone in *days.*"

Another voice came from in front of him. "Oh, don't kill him yet, Leck. He has a few questions to answer first." *That's Quark,* Krax thought.

This thought was confirmed a moment later when the lights went on, and Krax saw Quark and that Bajoran Starfleeter he'd brought with him.

Leck's presence also answered the question of how they got into his private residence. After all, if Leck could penetrate the Glat Archive, getting into Krax's home, which was secure, but no more or less so than the average Ferengi citizen's house, would be child's play.

"I've been suspicious of you from the start, Krax. Remember what happened eight years ago on the station? You tried to blow me out an airlock!"

"Th-that was a long t-time ago, Quark." Krax didn't want to

sound quite so craven, but that was difficult when a psychopath had a knife at your throat.

"And yet, you haven't changed a bit. You're still trying to destroy the Grand Nagus. Then it was me—now it's my brother."

"You—you've got me all wr-wrong!"

"I don't think so. You see, we've been looking into the 'Brunt for Grand Nagus Campaign,' and imagine my surprise when the trail led right to you." Quark pointed an accusatory finger at Krax. "You were the one who arranged with Nik to have the Chek stocks given to Rwogo and Gash."

"I—"

Quark wasn't done. "Furthermore, Nog talked to his mother. She described the two men who came to Dav's house to plot the contract-forging scam. One of them was Gash—the other one was *you*."

"I—"

"You *introduced* Gash to Dav! You set my brother up!"

"Yes!" Krax blurted out. "I set him up to *win!*"

Quark and the Bajoran exchanged confused looks, then both regarded Krax. "What?"

"Yes, I set this whole plan in motion, so Rom would come out *on top*."

Frowning, Quark said, "Once more, with clarity."

"C-could you get this lunatic off my throat first?"

"No." Quark smiled. Leck then tightened his grip.

"O-okay, okay—he can stay, that—that's fine."

"I'm waiting." Quark folded his arms.

Krax took as deep a breath as he could while in Leck's duranium grip. "Dav has been trying to bring Rom down ever since he became Grand Nagus. He's invested hundreds of bars of latinum into Chek during its hard times."

"I didn't know Dav *had* hundreds of bars."

Trying and failing to shrug, Krax said, "It was a good year for mold. Anyhow, Dav was the one who spearheaded Chek's little meeting of businessmen in your embassy, he's the one who brought Chek and Brunt together, and he's the one who sent your cousin to bring Zek back here—he figured that Gaila's family connection to Ishka would do the trick, and he was right."

"Nice way to fob the blame off on someone else. But we have—"

"I'm not finished!" Krax cried, worried that Quark would tell Leck to slice him open. "I found out about what Dav was doing. It was a long-term plan, one that would give Dav and Chek and Brunt plenty of time to undermine Rom. They'd slowly build support and gradually sway people away from Rom's camp. That's when I brought myself to Dav's attention—myself *and* Gash."

The Bajoran frowned. "I don't understand."

Quark nodded. "I do. You gave them Gash and the idea of the broken marriage contract."

Grateful that Quark understood, Krax said, "Exactly! Instead of going long-term, I gave them this scheme which would necessitate accelerating their plan—not taking the time to build the support, but going for one big play. By doing that, their attack would be more intense, but also wouldn't have the time to take root. So when Gash's existence was revealed before the entire congress, they would be discredited in one fell swoop, and all their support would go away."

The Starfleet female held up a hand. "Hold on a minute—you mean that Gash's confessing to the forgery was part of the plan all along?"

"Yes."

"Did Gash know this?"

"Of course! He didn't care—he just wanted the challenge of forging a contract."

From behind him, Krax heard a wistful sigh from Leck. "So nice to see another artist who takes pride in his work."

Giving Quark a very nasty look that scared Krax almost as much as the knife at his throat, the Bajoran female said, "We're going to have a long talk about that deal we made with Gash, Quark."

Waving her off, Quark said, "Later. So tell me, Krax, when were you planning to share this little scheme?"

"There—there was no need to! It worked out a lot differently than I expected—I didn't think you and this female and your nephew would find out so much on your own—or that you'd get someone to break into the archive. I didn't even think that was *possible!*"

"Thank you," Leck said.

"You're—you're welcome." Krax felt odd exchanging pleasantries with someone about to kill him, but anything to appease the lunatic was worth it. "But the end result is the same—Brunt, Chek, and Dav have been discredited, Rom's position as Grand Nagus is stronger than ever, and the market's even gone back up fifty points, and it'll probably go up again tomorrow." Another thought occurred. "And—and—and as an added bonus, Eelwasser will probably take a huge hit, which will make Nilva happy, since Slug-O-Cola's sales will go up! He's a good ally to have."

Quark stood rubbing his chin. The Bajoran was still staring daggers at Quark. Leck's grip has loosened a bit. Krax's left leg was starting to cramp.

Leck finally spoke. "Can I kill him now, please?"

"No," Quark said, causing Krax to let out the breath he hadn't even realized he'd been holding. "Not yet, anyhow."

The knife came away from Krax's throat, the grip on his torso released, and Krax stumbled forward into his sitting room. Holding a hand to his throat, he asked, "What—what do you mean, 'not yet'?"

"We're going to leave now. I'll even make sure Rom doesn't know what you almost did to him. But let's just say there'll be a price."

"What will that be?" Krax asked with a nervous glance at Leck.

Quark smiled. "Someday, I'll let you know."

12

There is no substitute for success.

—RULE OF ACQUISITION #58

Ro decided that she liked Leeta's other hospital room better.

The fancy room—the one she'd been mistakenly taken to when she first visited Leeta, and to which Leeta had been returned after Rom's nagushood was reaffirmed—didn't look any better when it was crowded, and it was certainly packed to the proverbial gills. Zek, Ishka, and Krax all stood on one side of the bed, the latter giving Quark and Ro nervous looks. On the opposite side, Ro stood with Quark on one side of her and Nog on the other. Everyone was smiling, but nobody as widely as Rom was, standing to Quark's left.

Everyone's eyes, of course, were focused on the occupants of the bed: Leeta and the new baby.

Objectively, Leeta did not look better than she did when Ro saw her last—her face was still puffy and splotchy, and she looked even paler—but the huge smile on her face made it impossible to be objective.

She said she was happy before—now she's positively glowing.

"What's her name?" Ishka asked.

"Bena," Leeta said. "We sort of named her after the Emissary."

"And," Ro added, "the word means 'joy' in Bajoran."

Ishka's smile was so wide, the corners of her lips were encroaching on her neckframe. "It fits."

Quark turned to stare at his brother. "The word means 'underflooring' in Ferengi."

"Uhhh," Rom drew the syllable out a bit, then paused. "Well, it, uh, symbolizes how children are always getting underfoot!"

Nog laughed. "Nice save, Father."

"Anyway, she's a beautiful child," Ishka said.

"Thanks." Leeta looked down at the child, bundled in a latinum-lined blanket (of course).

Ro wasn't entirely sure that *beautiful* was the first word that would come to mind when looking at little Bena. Admittedly, in Ro's opinion, all newborns looked hideous—Bajoran babies looked like *kava* fruit, and human infants looked like stewed prunes—and this hybrid looked even worse than usual. Leaving aside the wrinkles and the scrunched-up face common to mammals newly arrived in the galaxy, Bena had ears that were too big for a Bajoran but too small for even a female Ferengi, a Ferengi-shaped head (that was expected, given what Dr. Orpax had said about Leeta's difficulties during the pregnancy), a nose that combined the wideness of a Ferengi nose with the wrinkles of a Bajoran's, and—most peculiar of all on a Ferengi-shaped head—a tuft of brown hair on top of her crown. *That kid's gonna hate being out in the rain.*

Then she squirmed in her incredibly expensive blanket and curled closer to Leeta's chest. Ro couldn't help but find that sight—even on this baby—to be nothing short of adorable.

"Today is a great day," Rom said. "My wife and child are healthy, we came out ten bars ahead in the baby raffle, the market's back up another fifty points, Brunt isn't on the congress anymore—"

Quark took a breath. "Can't really complain about any of that."

"—and I'm still Grand Nagus!"

"*That*, on the other hand . . ."

Ishka reached across the biobed to smack Quark's hand. "That's enough, Quark. You're not going to spoil this day."

Shaking his head, Quark said, "Whatever you say, Moogie."

Nog said, "I just feel sorry for anyone invested in Chek Pharmaceuticals or Eelwasser—they've both taken *huge* financial hits ever since it was revealed that they sponsored someone who forged a Ferengi contract."

Ro was amused that Nog specified a Ferengi contract, remembering once again that extra clause in the Seventeenth Rule. . . .

Ishka smiled. "I bet Nilva's happy as a grub in dirt, though."

Leeta said, "I'm just glad everything worked out okay."

"Me, too," Ishka said, then turned to Zek. "I'm especially glad you went on FCN and recanted your condemnation of Rom."

Zek shrugged. "It was the least I could do."

Quark muttered only loud enough for Ro to hear: "Never let it be said that Zek didn't do the least he could do." It was all Ro could do to control her reaction.

"Besides," Zek continued, turning to Ishka, "it means I'm getting my sweetie-foot back."

The pair of them pressed their noses together in the traditional Ferengi show of affection.

"You bet, Zekkie," Ishka said. "I promise, I won't leave your side ever again." She then turned to Rom. "And don't worry—I trust Krax to do a fine job as first clerk."

Quark put a hand on Rom's shoulder. "Actually, so do I."

Rom whirled on his brother and fixed him with a befuddled expression. "You, uhh—you do?"

With a significant look at Krax, Quark said, "Yes, I do."

Krax swallowed. Again, Ro had to control her reaction.

Holding hands with Zek, Ishka said, "We're going to be heading back to Risa first thing tomorrow morning. Rom, if there's anything you need—ask someone else. We're *both* retired."

Grinning, Rom said, "Don't worry, Moogie. I'll be fine."

"And I'll make sure he stays fine," Krax said. "Father, can I talk to you for a second?"

Krax and Zek moved to a corner of the room. Rom then asked, "What about Gaila? Does anyone know what happened to him?"

Nog shook his head. "He hasn't been seen since Zek came to Ferenginar."

"He probably was just hired to convince Zekkie to come here." Ishka shook her head. "Just grabbed the opportunity and left—Gaila always did have good lobes."

He betrays everyone and they admire him for it—I have got to get off this planet. Ro focused her attention on little Bena, who was now nestled into Leeta's chest and fast asleep.

"By the way," Rom said slowly, "I went to see Prinadora."

Leeta sat up straighter. "You *what?*" That woke the baby up, and she started crying. "Oh no, Bena, Mommy's sorry." She started rocking the girl slowly back and forth. "I didn't mean to wake you, my sweet baby."

Then Leeta started to softly sing a Bajoran lullaby that Ro hadn't heard since she was a girl herself.

While Leeta sang, Quark asked, "What did you go and do that for?"

"After what Nog told me about how she acted, I wanted to see if it was true."

"You didn't believe your own son?"

"No! It's just—"

Ro came to his rescue. "You wanted to see for yourself?"

Nodding, Rom said, "I just needed to know if she really—if she—that she honestly—"

Quark looked to the ceiling in supplication. "Rom, spit it out, already!"

Slumping his shoulder, Rom said, "She never loved me. She barely even *remembered* me. I think if I hadn't become nagus, she'd've forgotten me completely." He took a deep breath. "She acted the way she did so I would fall in love with her—and she did it because Dav told her to."

"Everything she *ever* did was because Dav told her to," Nog said.

"Well, that won't last," Ishka said. Ro shot her a look at that, as did everyone else—even Leeta, who cut herself off in mid-lullaby. "Rom's not the only one who went to see her. Dav's not going to be able to afford to feed her—he's barely going to be able to afford to feed himself—and it's long past time she got herself her own job."

"What did you do, Mother?" Quark asked with a wince.

Ishka grinned. "I hired her. She'll be my personal assistant. I'll be taking her back to Risa with me, teaching her to read and do math. When she's ready, she'll be able to handle my affairs so I can spend more time with my Zekkie."

Rom gave his mother a smile. "Thank you, Moogie."

Quark turned to Ro. "Can we go home now?"

Now it was Ishka's turn to look to the ceiling. "Can't you wish your brother well just once, Quark? After all, you went to the trouble of helping him keep his position as nagus."

"That's because, as bad a Grand Nagus as Rom is, Brunt would've been a million times worse." Quark sighed. "At least I can take some solace in the fact that Brunt's destitute and out of a job. And a day when Brunt loses is a good day for me."

"The FCA will never take him back now—I made sure of that." Rom spoke with a sadistic glee Ro hadn't credited him with prior to that.

A thought occurred to Ro. *What if Dav, Chek, and their little cabal hadn't recruited Brunt? What if they went for someone who had less of a personal grudge against Rom and Quark and Ishka? Would Quark have been on Rom's side, or would he have been leading the charge to depose his own brother?*

Ro wasn't entirely sure she liked the answer that seemed most probable.

Zek wondered what it was that his son wanted to say to him that couldn't be said in front of Ishka and Rom. *Then again, maybe it's one of those father-son talks. We haven't had one of those in—* He thought a moment. *Come to think of it, we've never had one of those.*

"What is it, Krax?" Zek asked.

"I just wanted to say, Father, that I took your advice, and I hope you can see that."

Zek frowned in confusion. "What are you *talking* about?"

"Back when you first tested me to see if I was ready to assume power, you told me I failed the test because I didn't worm my way inside—I didn't become the power behind the throne. Well, now I think I've done it."

This surprised Zek. "You have?"

Krax then went into a lengthy explanation of a rather complicated plan he hatched that would force Rom's enemies to play their hands sooner than expected, thus allowing Krax to expose and discredit them. Zek followed only about a quarter of it, but it sounded like a good plan—mainly because it worked, which was really the only criterion by which one could judge a plan.

"Best of all," Krax said, "I've invested heavily in Doremil Drugs—Chek's chief competitor. Their stocks are going through the clouds!"

That Zek was able to follow. "Good work, son. You've made yourself valuable to the Grand Nagus *and* improved your portfolio!" He put a fatherly hand on Krax's shoulder. "I'm proud of you, my boy. I always knew that someday you'd learn your lesson."

Krax's beady eyes widened. "Really, Father?"

Zek laughed. "No, not really, but I'm glad you did it anyhow."

Leading his son back to the biobed, he saw that Quark, Nog, and the Bajoran female were getting ready to leave.

Quark was, as usual, babbling. "Either way, we've done our bit to make Ferenginar safe for democracy—may the Divine Exchequer have mercy on us all—and I for one would like to get back to my bar."

"Actually," the Bajoran female said, "much as I hate to say it, Quark's right—we all should get back. I have a security division to run." Like that redhead back at the space station and Rom's wife, this Bajoran was quite delectable to Zek. *I need to get me one of them*, he thought. Then he looked at Ishka, and thought better of it. *Then again, there's all kinds of pleasures to be found on Risa. . . .*

Nog added, "And I need to get back before Ensign Senkowsky takes over."

The Bajoran looked at Nog and smiled. "I thought you trusted him?" Nog started to say something, but the female cut him off. "No, wait, don't tell me—'Hear all, trust nothing.' That's, what, Rule One-Twenty?"

"One-Ninety, actually," Nog said with a grin.

"Feel free to come back anytime, Brother," Rom said. "After all, my house—is *your* house."

Quark put his head in his hands. "And yet another Ferengi tradition bites the dust during the Rom regime."

Zek laughed and clapped Quark on the shoulder. "I couldn't have said it better myself, my boy. Now come on, let's leave the happy parents to be with their little girl."

A Ferengi without profit is no Ferengi at all.

—RULE OF ACQUISITION #18

"Dabo!"

Quark smiled as he came down the stairs from the upper level. Having just finished conducting a most profitable transaction with Captain Rionoj—a lovely Boslic woman with whom he had done good business and about whom he'd had many good fantasies over the years—he now watched Treir in action.

The winner of this dabo spin was a Kobheerian who was almost out of the game. Winning this spin won him three bars, which meant he would likely stay in for at least another hour. Since he'd been drinking like a fish, and had expensive tastes, this also meant he'd be buying more—in fact, he was signaling Frool for another Tzartak aperitif, the most expensive drink on the menu.

Life, Quark thought, *is good.*

He also noticed that the other players were shifting uncomfortably in their seats, looking like they were going to leave.

Quark slid next to Treir, slipping an arm around her lovely torso, and asked, "How is everyone doing tonight?"

General affirmative noises came from around the table, most from the Kobheerian.

"Good! You'll all be happy to know that we have a special tonight—stay at the dabo table from now until 2100 hours, and you get the first half-hour of a holosuite program free." He leaned forward a bit, taking Treir with him, thus affording the players a better view of that cleavage of hers. "So if you stay for only half an hour, it's a free holosuite session. Can't beat that with a stick, can you?"

Several of the players looked pleased at that.

Looking up at Treir, Quark went on. "I'm sure our lovely Treir will see to your every need, won't you?"

"Of course." Treir's voice was in full-on purr mode, and Quark's lobes just tingled.

Slowly extracting his arm, Quark said, "Enjoy yourselves, folks—we're here to make sure you have a good time."

As he worked his way back to the bar, he nodded at assorted customers. He saw Bashir, Tarses, and the rest of the medical staff all sharing a drink. In one corner, Nog was eating a spore pie while conversing with his assistant, the ensign with the unnecessarily long last name, and who looked more than a little nauseated by Nog's dinner choice. *Humans*, Quark thought with amusement. *No sense of good cuisine, and no idea how to keep nomenclature simple, like Ferengi. I mean, really, who wants to conduct business with someone where it takes half an hour just to say their name?*

At the bar, he saw that Frool was making a *targ*'s ear of the aperitif. "You lobeless idiot," he said to the waiter. "That mixture is for a Lisspeian. Tzartak aperitifs are tailored to the body temperature of the drinker, and a Kobheerian's body temperature is five degrees warmer than a Lisspeian's."

"Sorry," Frool muttered, and remixed the drink.

"The cost of the bad drink is coming out of your salary," Quark said, then moved on to see if anyone sitting at the bar needed another drink. Predictably, Morn wanted another ale, which Quark dutifully provided, making a notation on the Lurian's rather lengthy tab.

Everything seemed under control, so Quark reached into his pocket, pulled out his padd, entered the security code, then called up his two favorite files.

One was his own current financial profile, which wasn't as

high as he'd have liked, but still not bad. Although the Yridians' bidding was sufficiently fierce for the forged Grisellan totem icons that the profit margin on that scam was huge, his token investment in Chek Pharmaceuticals—made as a gesture after Chek arranged the meeting in the bar weeks ago—had tanked, the syrup of squill shipment wound up being more expensive than expected thanks to Balancar's new prime minister's imposing higher tariffs on exports, and both *kanar* and *yamok* sauce had gone up in price *again*, thanks to the new government, such as it was, on Cardassia. On the other hand, Quark had heard that the new government on Mizar intended to revoke all tariffs, which meant that he'd be able to obtain Mizarian nuggets—a delicacy favored by Klingons, of which there were still an appalling number coming through the station these days. Nuggets were difficult to obtain within the Empire because the High Council refused to trade with a planet that was conquered so often—which Quark thought was just typical of Klingons.

The other file Quark called up was Brunt's financial profile. The only latinum the ex-liquidator had to his name were the ten bars he won in the baby raffle. He had no other assets, having been banned by the FCA for publicly falsifying a contract.

Quark took an incredible amount of glee from that bit of irony.

He put the padd back in his jacket pocket. Ezri Dax walked in, and joined Nog and his assistant at their table. His right hand brushing against his lobe, Quark recalled that Dax and Bashir had ended their relationship during that nonsense on Trill, which meant that Dax was single again.

"Oh, barkeep? A tarkalian tea, please?"

Turning, Quark saw that Ro was sitting at the bar, and he wondered how long she'd been there without his noticing. Odo used to do that all the time, too—just appear in the bar like a ship decloaking—but he'd chalked that up to his shapeshifting. *Maybe it's something they teach you at security school.*

"Coming right up," he said with a smile.

As he prepared the beverage, Ro said, "Quark, we need to talk."

"Let me just get the drink—"

"Forget the drink," she said. "Take a walk with me a minute."

This sounds serious. Quark didn't like it when females wanted to have serious talks. They almost always ended badly for the male on the other end of the conversation.

Ro said nothing until they reached the security office. They entered, Ro moving around to her side of the desk and sitting down in her chair while closing the door. "Have a seat," she said.

"Is this an interrogation?" he asked, not actually sitting down yet.

"I think I figured out why you left Ferenginar, Quark."

"I thought you liked it there."

Snorting, Ro said, "No, I just got used to it. Barely. Well, okay, I got used to the humidity, but that's about it. But I can see why you left. On Ferenginar, it's just Ferengi trying to screw each other. You're not like that."

Putting his hands on the back of the guest chair, Quark said, "I don't have to stand here and be insulted."

"It's not an insult. It's not that you're not eager for profit—in that, you're the perfect Ferengi—but you don't generally screw people over. Or, at least, not in ways that cause permanent harm. I mean, antiquities fraud and price gouging aren't exactly victimless crimes, but the harm is comparatively minor."

Now Quark was confused. "What're you getting at, Laren?"

Ro took a breath. "In a lot of ways, you're the perfect embodiment of Rom's new Ferenginar—earning a profit without actually hurting anyone." Holding up a hand before Quark could interrupt her, Ro said, "Before you interrupt me and say I'm insulting you again, I'm not, really. The main reason why I think you left Ferenginar is that there you're just another Ferengi. You were never going to be someone like Chek or Nilva or Kain—but out here, in the Bajoran sector, you're unique. You provide things no one else can."

Finally, Quark did take a seat, just because he needed to sit in order to conserve energy so he could devote his entire brain to figuring out where the hell Ro was going with this. "Laren—"

"I don't think that you and I are going to work, Quark."

Quark felt like he'd been punched in the stomach. "What?"

"I saw your little meeting with that Boslic woman. I saw you putting your arm around Treir. And I saw the way you were looking at Ezri." She smiled. "When Ezri and Julian broke up, the first thought in your head was how you could get Ezri into the holosuite with you."

"That's not true!"

Ro stared at Quark.

"Entirely," Quark added reluctantly. "Look, I'm a male with active lobes, I can't help—"

"I know you can't, Quark. It's the way you are. You're incapable of committing to one person because you're incapable of committing to one of anything. How many dozens of scams do you have going at any given time?"

Quark wasn't about to answer that definitively, but the fact that he didn't say anything was probably enough for Ro.

"Oh, by the way," she said, holding up a padd, "Balancar *didn't* raise their tariffs, and the next time you tell someone you raised the price for squill because of it, I'm busting you for fraud."

This stomach-punch wasn't quite as bad as the previous one, but it was close. "Laren, I had no idea—truly," he said, trying desperately to sound sincere. "I was going on second-hand information." *And*, he thought suddenly, *I can use that. Tell the distributor that I know what he's trying to pull, and my good friend the DS9 security chief will lock him up on my say-so, so he'd better lower the price.* "I'll take care of it, don't worry."

Shaking her head and sighing, Ro said, "I knew it."

"Knew what?" Quark now was even more confused.

"I just gave you a perfect opportunity to turn in your distributor for those fraud charges. But instead you decided to hold that information to yourself, and wait until it was the best time for you to take advantage of it, secure in the knowledge that the security chief is a friend of yours."

"I—" Quark found he couldn't say anything. *I love a woman who's so far ahead of me.*

"Quark, I can't do this. You're always going to be going

after the next big score, whether it's financial or sexual. It's the way you are."

"I can change." Quark was pleading now. This thing he had with Ro was good, and he liked it, and he didn't want to lose it.

"No, Quark, you really can't. And what's more, I don't *want* you to. If you change, if you become wholly monogamous, you won't be Quark anymore, and I *like* Quark. I was willing to go off with you to find our fortune when Bajor joined the Federation, and I don't regret that decision, even though my commission and your diplomatic post solved the problem instead." She fixed him with her beautiful *seola* gem-colored eyes. "But here, now, with me as security chief and you as the bartender, I think I'm better off sticking with Quark as a friend and occasional pain in my ass—and that's it. You okay with that?"

"Do I have a choice?"

"Actually—yes."

Quark blinked. This wasn't at all what he was expecting. He'd been turned down by females before—he'd practically made a career out of it, mostly by going after females he knew he had absolutely no chance with. Ro actually responded, which was a situation he was almost totally unfamiliar with. Only Natima Lang and Grilka had responded the same way, but those relationships were doomed from the start.

As is this, apparently. Third time's definitely not the charm. Besides, everything she said is exactly right.

"Then I choose—for us to be friends. If that's okay with you."

At last, Quark was favored with Ro's wonderful, wide smile. "Definitely."

Smiling back, Quark got up. "How about a celebratory dinner between friends tonight? I've got some fresh *hasperat* just in from Bajor."

Ro also stood up. "It's not 'in' yet, Quark—the shipmaster of the *Fortra* hasn't kept all her licenses current, and until she straightens it out, her cargo doesn't get unloaded."

"I don't suppose I could call upon my *friend* to—"

"No."

Quark grinned. "Didn't think so." Ro opened the door and

Quark turned to head back to the bar. He hesitated as he crossed the threshold. *Wait for it. . . .*

"Oh, Quark?"

I knew it. He stopped and turned back around. "Yes?"

"If Gash sets foot on this station again, I'm posting a guard on him, understood?"

Making a mental note to put a call in to Gash telling him that they'd have to meet off-station from now on, Quark said, "Understood."

With that, he went back to his bar. He had a business to run—

—and a dinner date to plan. After all, just because Ro wanted to keep their relationship platonic didn't mean Quark had to stop *trying* for more. . . .

"And stay out!"

Brunt stumbled forward onto the wet streets of the capital city, having been physically thrown out of his favorite *tongo* parlor by the owner—brandishing a rare Minosian rifle— owing to his being banned by the FCA. Rain pelted onto his head, water seeping into his lobes and eyes and nose.

For years, I banned people—never knew how miserable it was for the person being banned. But then, why should he have cared? He was a liquidator, and liquidators only cared about the marketplace, not the people.

That sounds a lot better when you're the liquidator and not the victim.

Chek and Dav had sold him out to the FCA, saying that all of this was Brunt's idea. Never mind the fact that Dav was the one who brought in that forger, never mind the fact that Chek was the one who recommended Brunt come in—the truth didn't matter to these people. They just wanted someone to blame, a scapegoat, so they could try to salvage their precious profits.

Well, there's more to life than profits!

Getting up off the wet ground, Brunt thought, *Did I really just think that? By the Divine Exchequer, I think this ban has addled my brain.*

He had been spending the last two days trying to find a simple job, but no place would hire him. No bar would hire him as a waiter, no aircar service would hire him as a driver, no rich household would hire him as a servant. He thought he had it made when he read about the waste-disposal business that needed someone who could drive a Federation Sporak—apparently, they bought one with money they claimed to have received directly from the Klingon chancellor himself. Brunt's first job after his Attainment Ceremony involved driving a Sporak, so he thought that those rare skills would supersede his FCA ban, even if the idea that the Sporak came from Chancellor Martok was patently absurd.

But even the waste-disposal people turned him down.

All wasn't completely lost. He still had ten bars of latinum. The Grand Nagus, in his infinite stupidity, gave him special dispensation to keep it.

How I hate him. This is all his fault—him and that misbegotten family. Oh, how I long for the good old days of Zek's rule, when Ferengi were feared and respected. Now we're a joke, thanks to that wicked woman pouring lies into Zek's drooping ears, leaving us with her idiot son as a Grand Nagus. Not to mention the rest of them—Quark and his ridiculous bar, Nog and his Starfleet commission. Starfleet! The very idea!

"Down on your luck, Brunt?"

Brunt peered through the *frippering* at an overhang, which was where the deep voice had come from.

After a moment, he made out the face through the forcefield that kept the area under the overhang completely dry.

Gaila. *Another member of that tiresome family.*

"What do you want, Gaila?"

"To talk."

"I have nothing to say to you."

"Oh, I think you do." He reached into his pocket and pulled out a strip of latinum. He tossed it through the semipermeable forcefield, and it landed in the muck at Brunt's feet. "Come on in."

Brunt bent over to pick up the slip without thinking. Even as he did so, he considered just taking the slip and continuing on his merry way. *What could I possibly have to say to him?*

Then he remembered that Gaila had worked on behalf of

Chek and Dav also—he was the one who brought Zek back from Risa. And unlike Chek or Dav, Gaila was actually speaking to him.

I'm willing to at least hear him out.

He put the slip in the receptacle next to the overhang. The forcefield went down for a moment, and Brunt stepped in.

As the forcefield reactivated, Brunt pulled his handkerchief out of his jacket—or, rather, he pulled out the handkerchief he'd snuck into his jacket pocket when the FCA came to take all his assets away—and wiped his head and eyes. "I'm listening. Now what could the cousin of the Grand Nagus possibly have to say to me?"

"Believe me, Brunt, I've got no love for my cousin—either of them. But I'm not a part of their insanity. When we first met, you referred to me as a failure—but that's only because I was foolish enough to bring Quark into my weapons business. Up until then, I was doing so well I was considering retirement." He smiled. "Now, it seems, *you're* the failure—but you don't have to be."

Brunt rolled his eyes. "Is this what that slip you gave me buys? Your life story followed by insults?"

"You know the Rules, Brunt—'A wise man can hear profit in the wind.' "

"Well, you're certainly creating a lot of it," Brunt muttered.

Gaila smiled. "I'll get right to the point, then. I don't have any connection to Chek or Dav. They just hired me to bring Zek back from Risa. I took the job because they paid me handsomely. Between that, the investments I made after we rescued Ishka, and the fee from some negotiating I did for a race called the Petraw, I'm starting to rebuild my portfolio. And I've still got plenty of contacts—but I could use a new partner. There are plenty of opportunities out there—ones that could use an ex-liquidator's assistance."

Obviously Gaila suffered from the same mental deficiency as the others in his wretched family. "I've been banned by the FCA. You can't do business with me."

Gaila shook his head and laughed. "The FCA's reach doesn't extend very far beyond the Alliance's boundaries. And believe me, my business takes me very far beyond the Alliance's boundaries."

Brunt stared at Gaila's tiny eyes and large nose, and thought back to his perusals of the financial records relating to Ishka and her family back when he first investigated her five years earlier. He remembered then that Gaila was a highly successful weapons dealer, working with a now-dead human named Hagath. He wasn't a close enough relation to gain Brunt's notice then, nor the other times he investigated Quark and his family of lunatics.

From the sound of it, Gaila has about as much use for Quark and his close relatives as I do. No reason to let his family stand in the way of my opportunity. "Tell me more," Brunt said.

"Of course—but not here. Let's go into that *tongo* parlor—have a few drinks, play a few rounds, and speak as businessmen."

Brunt's face fell. "I can't—the owner just kicked me out."

"For me, he'll let you in." Hitting Brunt a little too hard on the shoulder, Gaila grinned. "Who do you think sold him that Minosian rifle?"

At that, Brunt found himself forced to smile. Then he grinned. Then he laughed.

So did Gaila.

They exited the dryness of the overhang and headed straight for the *tongo* parlor, Gaila's arm around Brunt's shoulder even as they stepped out into the rain.

"Gaila," Brunt said as the *frippering* once again got into his eyes, "this could be the beginning of a beautiful friendship."

SELECTIONS FROM THE FERENGI RULES OF ACQUISITION
by Grand Nagus Gint

These are excerpts from *The Ferengi Rules of Acquisition*, published centuries ago by the first Grand Nagus, Gint. A more complete list is available in the book *The Ferengi Rules of Acquisition* by Quark, as dictated to Ira Steven Behr, and a list with commentary can be found in *Legends of the Ferengi*, also by Quark, as dictated to Behr & Robert Hewitt Wolfe, both available at finer merchants everywhere.

Each Rule comes with a citation for the chronicles in which the Rule was quoted. "[DS9]" indicates an episode of *Star Trek: Deep Space Nine*, "[VOY]" indicates an episode of *Star Trek: Voyager*.

1. Once you have their money, you never give it back. ("The Nagus" [DS9])

6. Never allow family to stand in the way of opportunity. ("The Nagus" [DS9])

7. Keep your ears open. ("In the Hands of the Prophets" [DS9])

9. Opportunity plus instinct equals profit. ("The Storyteller" [DS9])

16. A deal is a deal—until a better one comes along. ("Melora" [DS9], *The Ferengi Rules of Acquisition*)

17. A contract is a contract is a contract—but only between Ferengi. ("Body Parts" [DS9])

18. A Ferengi without profit is no Ferengi at all. ("Heart of Stone" [DS9], "Ferengi Love Songs" [DS9])

19. Satisfaction is not guaranteed. *(The Ferengi Rules of Acquisition)*

20. He who dives under the table today lives to profit tomorrow. *(Worlds of Star Trek: Deep Space Nine Volume Three—Ferenginar: Satisfaction Is Not Guaranteed)*

22. A wise man can hear profit in the wind. ("Rules of Acquisition" [DS9], "False Profits" [VOY])

25. You pay for it, it's your idea. *(Worlds of Star Trek: Deep Space Nine Volume Three—Ferenginar: Satisfaction Is Not Guaranteed)*

31. Never make fun of a Ferengi's mother—insult something he cares about instead. ("The Siege" [DS9], *The Ferengi Rules of Acquisition*)

33. It never hurts to suck up to the boss. ("Rules of Acquisition" [DS9])

53. Never trust anybody taller than you. *(Mission: Gamma Book 1: Twilight)*

58. There is no substitute for success. *(The Ferengi Rules of Acquisition)*

62. The riskier the road, the greater the profit. ("Rules of Acquisition" [DS9], "Little Green Men" [DS9], "Business As Usual" [DS9])

75. Home is where the heart is—but the stars are made of latinum. ("Civil Defense" [DS9])

88. It ain't over till it's over. *(Worlds of Star Trek: Deep Space Nine Volume Three—Ferenginar: Satisfaction Is Not Guaranteed)*

94. Females and finances don't mix. *(The Ferengi Rules of Acquisition*, "Ferengi Love Songs" [DS9], "Profit and Lace" [DS9])

95. Expand or die. ("False Profits" [VOY])

97. Enough is never enough. *(The Ferengi Rules of Acquisition)*

99. Trust is the biggest liability of all. *(The Ferengi Rules of Acquisition)*

139. Wives serve; brothers inherit. ("Necessary Evil" [DS9])

168. Whisper your way to success. ("Treachery, Faith, and the Great River" [DS9])

190. Hear all, trust nothing. ("Call to Arms" [DS9])

200. A Ferengi chooses no side but his own. *(Worlds of Star Trek: Deep Space Nine Volume Three—Ferenginar: Satisfaction Is Not Guaranteed)*

208. Sometimes the only thing more dangerous than a question is an answer. ("Ferengi Love Songs" [DS9])

218. Always know what you're buying. *(The Ferengi Rules of Acquisition)*

239. Never be afraid to mislabel a product. ("Body Parts" [DS9])

280. If it ain't broke, don't fix it. *(Worlds of Star Trek: Deep Space Nine Volume Three—Ferenginar: Satisfaction Is Not Guaranteed)*

285. No good deed ever goes unpunished. ("The Collaborator" [DS9], "The Sound of Her Voice" [DS9])

THE DOMINION

Olympus Descending

David R. George III

ABOUT THE AUTHOR

David R. George III has returned to the ongoing *Deep Space Nine* saga with *Olympus Descending*. He previously visited DS9 in the novels *The 34th Rule,* set during the timeframe of the series, and *Twilight,* set after the finale. His other *Star Trek* contributions include a first-season *Voyager* episode, "Prime Factors," and one of the *Lost Era* books, *Serpents Among the Ruins,* featuring Captain John Harriman and his executive officer, Commander Demora Sulu. David will revisit the latter character in a story to be published in the upcoming *Tales from the Captain's Table* anthology. And 2006 will see the release of an original series trilogy he will pen as part of the celebration of the fortieth anniversary of *Star Trek.*

In his almost-nonexistent spare time, David enjoys trying his hand at new experiences, from skydiving to auditioning—with his lovely wife Karen—for *The New Newlywed Game,* from hiking a glacier in Alaska to belly dancing in Tunisia, from ocean kayaking in Mexico to having dinner at an actual captain's table somewhere in the Pacific Ocean. Recently, he performed his first wedding ceremony—which he and Karen also wrote—marrying their friends Jennifer Rasmussen and Ryan Van Riper. David believes that the world is a wide, wondrous place, with exciting adventures waiting around just about every corner.

He remains free on his own recognizance.

To
David R. George
and
John M. Walenista

Two men, both larger than life,
who taught me in ways they knew
and in ways they didn't,
and who brought me joys
that will remain with me always

ACKNOWLEDGMENTS

My thanks must begin with Marco Palmieri. Not only did he invite me to the dance, but he invited me *back*. Working with him ranks for me as a privilege, both because of the passion and creativity he brings to the table, and because of the professionalism and artistry with which he edits. I am grateful to him for reasons too numerous to detail, not the least of which is that he always improves my writing. Readers of the novels upon which Marco works—myself among those readers—are well served by his efforts.

I wish to acknowledge and thank Elizabeth Knezo Ragan, who after nearly a century, still left us too soon. In my mind, she will forever remain a strong, vibrant woman, the undisputed matriarch of her family. I can never adequately convey how much the love and support she lavished on Karen meant to me. Baba's caring and influence can easily be seen in succeeding generations, and will doubtless continue for generations to come.

Thanks as well to Barry J. Berman, who also left the field of play too soon. With the organization of the first Bakersfield baseball tournament, and of all the events that followed from there, Barry impacted my life in amazing ways that neither of us ever could have anticipated. Later, he welcomed me to town with unparalleled magnanimity. On the diamond, his range might never have exceeded his reach, but off the field, among his friends and fellow ballplayers, his reach exceeded everybody's expectations. I will always remember Barry, as well as the strength and caring of Barry's love, Kay Lewis.

I also want to thank Steven H. Pilchik, who always believed. Ever since he read a pair of hastily written one-act plays back in the day, his enthusiasm and support have continually encouraged me. I've always felt us kindred spirits, from those very first days in the basement of Hood Hall (wildebeests along the way and all), and I treasure his friendship. I am fortunate indeed to know Steve, his lovely wife Cheryl, and their boys Brian and Joshua.

Thanks too to Jason and Lia Costello for their love and encouragement. Their wonderful friendship shines like a beacon in the darkness to me, and their own loving relationship is a delight to behold. Resolute and supportive, they are also bighearted and fun, and I always enjoy the time I spend with them.

I always seem to be thanking Armin Shimerman for something, and in this case, it's not only for his friendship and support (and that of his fabulous wife, Kitty Swink), but for the loan of a laptop computer in desperate and difficult circumstances. Armin and Kitty possess a generosity of spirit that constantly warms my heart. The quality of their many talents is surpassed only by the kindness of their souls.

No matter how many times I do it, I can never thank Anita Smith enough. Always there, always supportive, she is a kind and loving person like no other. I admire her courage, strength, and determination, and her presence in my life is a gift.

I can also never thank Jennifer George enough, or laud her enough. A fine woman, filled with bravery and heart, intelligence and wit, and with talents aplenty, she continually impresses me. I could not be more proud of her. Her love and support lift me up.

I also don't have enough words for Patricia Walenista. She remains the source of all things good in me. Friend, confidante, role model, and more, she provides clarity, wisdom, a moral compass, support, and above all, love. And she's pretty fun to be around too.

Finally, as always, I want to thank Karen Ann Ragan-George for all that she does and for all that she is. My constant light, my delicate flower, wellspring of belly laughs and of the very best kinds of tears, she is everything to me. Like poetry, Karen is complex, beautiful in form and content, filled with vivid meaning and hidden depths, and on occasion, she even rhymes. Not only would I not want to do any of this without her, but I could not do it without her. I have always loved her, and I always will.

HISTORIAN'S NOTE

This story is set primarily in December, 2376 (Old Calendar), ending approximately thirteen weeks after the conclusion of the *Star Trek: Deep Space Nine* novel *Unity*.

PREAMBLE

The sky had changed.

Odo peered at the irregular burst of light looming unexpectedly above the nameless world of the Founders. Thoughts of Nerys—reminiscences of the past weeks with her, contemplations of their future together—fled as anxiety rose within him, along with the certainty that in his absence some awful event had befallen his people. He stood on the bridge that sat at the core of the Jem'Hadar attack vessel, the monocular headset he wore providing him with a view of surrounding space. As the ship approached the planet, the relentless beat of the impulse drive fell heavily within the compact control center, saturating it without surcease. The voices and movements of the small crew joined the tableau like hasty postscripts, thrown in at the last, to little effect. Odo's body hummed with the rhythms of the engines, his ever-malleable cells in constant agitation as they reflexively sought to adjust—to *quiesce*—in response to the proximate activity.

On his headset monitor—a few centimeters wide and half as tall, with two corners on one side of the otherwise rectangular flat "sliced off"—the brilliant addition to the starscape dominated the scene. Surmising—and hoping—that what he saw might simply be a display error, Odo swung his head left. The image on his viewer slewed to port, roving across another section of the firmament, but when he looked back again at the

Founders' world, the luminous patch remained. To the left and above the planet from this vantage, the glowing, blurry-edged circle drew his gaze to it, shining as it did more brightly than any other celestial object in sight . . . and because it hadn't been there when last he had been immersed in the Great Link.

"Weyoun," Odo called, focusing past the translucent eyepiece and across the bridge, to where the Vorta stood amid several Jem'Hadar, most of them operating various stations. Weyoun turned at once from Seventh Rotan'talag, to whom he'd been speaking, and paced quickly over. As he did so, he reached up and flipped his own flickering monitor away from his eye.

"Yes, Founder," he said, bowing his head for a moment, his hands parting in a patent gesture of subservience. He wore auburn pants, and a darker, patterned jacket atop a sulfur-colored shirt. "How may I be of service to you?"

"I want to know if my people are all right," Odo said, with more force than he'd intended. His disquiet felt surprisingly strong, and seemed to spring more from intuition than observation.

"They are perfectly fine," Weyoun said calmly, and Odo's thoughts veered toward relief. "I scanned the surface of the planet myself as soon as we were within sensor range. The Great Link is as you left it." The tight line of the Vorta's lips widened and curled upward slightly at the ends, a familiar smile that readily conveyed a desire to serve, along with a fear of being unable to do so adequately. All of the Weyoun clones Odo had known had worn similar expressions at one time or another, save for perhaps one of them.

"What is that bright object above the planet?" Odo asked, even as he recalled the exception among this Weyoun's predecessors. The sixth clone to bear the name, who during the war had defected to the Federation, had speculated aloud about whether he'd been faulty, but never had he wavered from the apparent surety of his ability to attend Odo. His death by his own hand—an action taken to prevent Odo from being killed—had been heroic, but not more so than his decision to abscond from the Dominion in an attempt to rescue it from itself.

"An observant question, Founder," Weyoun said, obsequious as ever. Odo still felt uncomfortable being addressed as "Founder," but he no longer reproached Weyoun or anybody else for doing so. How could he, when he'd left behind his life in the Alpha Quadrant more than ten months ago, and had come here to live with his people? He'd counted himself among their number ever since, even despite having been away from them for the past fifteen weeks.

"I noticed the object myself," Weyoun went on. "The seventh"—he never referred to any of the Jem'Hadar by name, at least not in Odo's presence—"reports that it is likely a distant nova, and that it poses no threat to the Great Link."

"If Rotan'talag isn't certain what it is," Odo questioned, "then how can he conclude that it isn't a threat?" For some reason, the unanticipated appearance of the intensely shining object stirred a depth of emotion in him that he could not readily identify, feelings that seemed more complicated than mere concern for his people.

"Quite right," Weyoun agreed without hesitation, as though he had been about to make the same point. "Which is why I've ordered the seventh to continue gathering and analyzing readings, so that he can make a complete and accurate report. I'm also going to contact my colleagues on other vessels and speak to them about their observations." Numerous other ships regularly patrolled the region of space about the Founders' planet, all crewed by Jem'Hadar soldiers and commanded by Vorta overseers.

"Very good," Odo said, nodding curtly as he glanced once more at the image on his personal viewer. The rough circle of light burned there like the malevolent eye of some massive spaceborne creature, lying in wait just beyond the planet. "Keep me informed."

"Of course," Weyoun said, again bowing his head. He withdrew across the center of the bridge, taking a couple of steps backward before rounding on his heel and walking back over to Rotan'talag. The two conversed briefly, then turned to a nearby console.

Odo watched them through his headset monitor, the duo visible through a glittering sweep of the planet where starlight touched the amorphous form of the Great Link. Both Weyoun and Rotan'talag had served him well these past months, he reflected, though neither had shown any indication yet of growing beyond the bounds established for their respective species by the Founders. He still believed that they could, though, especially given their unusual personal circumstances.

Rotan'talag, during a systematic search of the Dominion ordered by Odo, had been discovered to be one of only four Jem'Hadar not dependent on ketracel-white. He'd been too young—three years old at the time, four now—and too inexperienced to send to the Alpha Quadrant on the mission that Taran'atar had instead taken on, but Odo had chosen to keep him close. Years ago, back on Deep Space 9, Odo had failed to guide a newborn Jem'Hadar away from the martial purpose for which he'd been bred, but that unnamed fighter had been reliant on the white. And while Taran'atar—like Rotan'talag, free of the chemical dependency—appeared to be fulfilling his assigned task of observing and living among the denizens of the Alpha Quadrant, his mindset about himself and his place in the universe hadn't changed in any significant way. Odo hoped that it would one day be different for Taran'atar, but in the meantime, he would use another tack—frequent personal contact—to try to foster Rotan'talag's development.

As the nova—or whatever it turned out to be—stared down on his eyepiece at the Founders' world, Odo's thoughts shifted to the Vorta who had effectively become his deputy. On Cardassia Prime at the end of the war, the eighth Weyoun had been shot dead by Garak, and the Founder leader had declared him the last in the line—probably because she hadn't expected anybody to retrieve his transcoder implant so that his knowledge and memories could be downloaded into a subsequent clone. But Odo *had* recovered the device, aware of its existence and purpose from Dr. Bashir's autopsy of the Weyoun defector. The implant the doctor had removed had self-destructed when Chief O'Brien had attempted to dump its data, but its function had been evident: it continuously recorded the thoughts and experiences of the clone into whom it had been embedded, automatically uploading it for more secure storage whenever in range of either the Dominion wide-area communications network or a sufficiently equipped vessel.

Knowing that he would return to live with his people in the Gamma Quadrant, and foreseeing that he would strive to transform the bellicose nature of the Dominion, Odo had gone back and removed the transcorder from the corpse of Weyoun Eight. A new clone, he'd reasoned, might develop as the sixth had, with a yearning for peace and a willingness to act on that desire. And as would be the case with Rotan'talag, Odo had intended to do whatever he could to influence the personal growth of the next Weyoun.

Across the bridge, a monitor set into the far bulkhead blinked to life, the face of a woman appearing on it. Odo recognized her as Vannis, one of the Vorta who assisted Weyoun and others in carrying out the will of the Founders. She possessed sharp, angular features, and long, dark locks framed her face. Her pallid complexion contrasted dramatically with both her hair and her vibrant indigo eyes. The jacket she wore matched her eye color, and covered an ivory blouse. As Odo looked on, she opened her mouth and spoke, and Weyoun responded, their voices low, their words indistinct, swallowed up by the cadences of the impulse engines. The Jem'Hadar seventh paid no apparent heed to the conversation, keeping his head down as he worked at an adjacent console.

Odo had arranged for the assignments of Weyoun and Rotan'talag to this ship. Known simply as Jem'Hadar Attack Vessel 971, it was initially stationed in orbit about the Founders' planet, one of those delegated to safeguard the Great Link. Not long after Odo first left the Alpha Quadrant and rejoined his people, he started spending brief periods away from them, on the tiny island where he'd said his good-byes to Nerys. He needed separation so that he could consider things in the manner to which he'd become accustomed, and also so that he could mark time, the experience of which felt very different within the Link.

Shortly after that, Odo had begun transporting up to the ship, weekly at first, and then daily. Wanting to more fully understand the forces that defined and drove the Dominion, he studied the security reports continually compiled by the numerous Vorta acting as agents of the Founders. Once he posted

Weyoun to the ship, and then Rotan'talag, the repeated visits also allowed him to maintain regular contact with them.

Although no attempt had been made to stop him in those endeavors, a sense of disapproval permeated the Link. Odo's ongoing interest in the minutiae of life among the solids was deemed an unhealthy fixation. The Founders, he quickly learned, did not concern themselves with everyday events beyond their world. The genetically programmed fealty of the Vorta and the Jem'Hadar had long ago obviated the need for the changelings to involve themselves directly in such matters. The Founders ruled by proxy, and unless they felt endangered, essentially isolated themselves from the rest of the galaxy. Consequently, they regarded Odo's attention to security reports, his recurring contact with Vorta and Jem'Hadar, and his particular interest in Weyoun and Rotan'talag, as efforts to cling to the life he'd led in the Alpha Quadrant, among solids. Although he had abandoned that life and returned to the Link, they believed him unwilling to free himself completely from an existence that, in their collective judgment, defined his infancy.

For Odo, such opinions betrayed the intransigence of his people. The irony did not escape him that a species so physically fluid could also be so mentally and emotionally inflexible. Back on Bajor and DS9, he had himself endured characterizations of his own rigidity, his own obduracy. Seeing the same traits reflected in the amber ocean of his own kind was sobering. He tried to help the Link see that their refusal to consider themselves connected to other, non-changeling lifeforms, and their rejection of the possibilities afforded by amity rather than distrust, should be regarded as antithetical to a species that exulted in self-change. The Founders seemed capable of any transformation, he maintained, but in their own view of the universe.

Odo peered over again at Weyoun and Rotan'talag. The image of the female Vorta winked off of the monitor there, replaced an instant later by the green-and-purple symbol that represented the Dominion. Weyoun turned and addressed Rotan'talag, who looked up from the console he'd been working. As Odo watched them, he wondered if he would ever succeed in altering anyone's perspectives here. Perhaps he had set himself impossible tasks: bringing tolerance and openness to the Great Link; setting the Vorta and Jem'Hadar onto different paths that would lead them away from their genetic encoding; reshaping the often brutal policies and actions of the Dominion into something benign. Even working from within, how could he realistically expect to foment such radical alterations in such well-defined and long-standing cultures?

Still, even during the relatively short span he'd spent back among his people, change had occurred. Over time, the Founders' concerns about Odo's trips up to the Jem'Hadar vessel had abated. They remained unconvinced of the wisdom of his actions and intentions, but they at least stopped summarily dismissing what he did and thought. His people seemed now to take in what he tried to communicate to them, and perhaps even to consider the merits of his convictions. That marked a beginning, Odo thought, one upon which he hoped to build once he transported down to the planet and slipped back into the Great Link.

And yet he also felt compelled to admit that, in some ways, the Founders had been right. Not about their resistance to peaceful relations with non-changelings, but about Odo's daily scrutiny of Dominion security reports, about his regular contact with Weyoun and Rotan'talag. Whatever his asserted aims, Odo had found himself enjoying the routine, one not all that far removed from how he'd spent his days back on DS9. More than that, he had allowed his curiosity and his predilection for investigation to lead him away from his people.

Nearly four months ago, Odo had set out in Attack Vessel 971 for the open port of Ee, so that he could explore rumors of a healer and theologue whose adherents supposedly included a number of Ennis. The descriptions of this religious figure and her followers had entwined with memories of stories that Nerys had related to him through the years, and had brought him to the possibility that the healer might somehow be Opaka Sulan, former kai of Bajor. However unlikely a prospect it might have been, Odo had needed to find out for sure.

There had also been another reason he'd wanted to locate the healer: she'd purportedly had contact with a member of the

Ascendants, a mysterious nomadic species long absent from the region of the galaxy now occupied by the Dominion. The Ascendants' time in this part of space antedated the rise of the Founders' empire, and few details remained of their society. Vague, sometimes contradictory accounts painted them as fanatically pious crusaders, merciless zealots who had ravaged entire worlds on a quest to join with their gods. The fossil records on several planets in the Gamma Quadrant revealed mass extinctions that had taken place around the time the Ascendants had allegedly swarmed through this area of space, but evidence of such catastrophes existed even in the other quadrants of the galaxy, and had been ascribed to numerous other causes. Still, if the Ascendants had not died out, and if the possibility of their return existed, Odo wanted to know about it.

In truth, though, Odo had doubted that he would find evidence of either Opaka or the Ascendants. But the mere possibility, however remote, of reconnecting with some aspect of Nerys's life had provided him with an irresistible motivation. In the end, he'd done just that—reconnected with her—in ways that he had never anticipated.

Disguised as a Trelian, Odo had unexpectedly encountered Jake Sisko on Ee, and then they'd found the healer, who had indeed turned out to be Opaka. Together, the three had traveled with acquaintances of Jake's to the Idran system—they'd been on hand for the shocking developments there—and then the trio had continued on to Deep Space 9. Odo had maintained the fiction of his Trelian identity during the parasite crisis on the station, ultimately making his true presence known when Nerys had needed assistance in combating the invaders.

After the situation had been resolved, Odo had prepared to return immediately to the Great Link. Weyoun had shadowed him aboard Attack Vessel 971, waiting by the Gamma Quadrant terminus of the wormhole to ferry him back to the Dominion. But Odo's first hours alone with Nerys had brought him a peace and happiness that he hadn't known since he'd bid her farewell almost a year ago. He hadn't realized until then just how much he'd missed her presence in his life. He'd allowed their time together to stretch into days, and then into weeks. He'd rationalized his sojourn in the Alpha Quadrant by accepting an invitation from First Minister Asarem to represent the Dominion at the ceremony in which Bajor would formally join the Federation. Even after the ceremony, though, he'd stayed a couple of days more, unwilling to part with Nerys just yet.

While Odo would not have characterized his actions as clinging to the life he'd lived among solids, did such a distinction really matter? His people believed that he hadn't yet given himself over to them completely, and though he denied that charge, he could not deny that he'd found reasons to leave them, if only temporarily. When Odo had first joined with the Great Link, it had fulfilled him in ways that he never could have imagined, and that he thought could never be surpassed. And yet if that were true, he had to ask himself, then how could he have left, and how could he have stayed away for so long?

Movement caught Odo's attention, pulling him from his thoughts. Weyoun marched toward him, a smile decorating his features, a smile different from the partially fearful countenance he'd worn earlier. His lips had parted, his squarish white teeth visible between them, the corners of his eyes wrinkling slightly. His eyepiece monitor still sat swung upward and away from his face.

"Founder," he said as he stopped before Odo. "I've received a report on the object from a Vorta aboard another vessel, and the seventh has now independently confirmed the information I was given." He paused expectantly, looking up at Odo as though wanting encouragement or validation before continuing.

"Go on," Odo said simply, not wishing to buttress the Vorta's insecurities.

"The object is indeed a nova," Weyoun said. "It became visible in the sky here just three days ago, increasing steadily in brightness during that time. But it is located at a far enough remove from the Founders' world that it will not cause any danger to the Great Link."

Odo felt himself relax, the tension he'd been feeling dissolving away like ice under a hot sun. "Very good," he said, relieved that his concerns had been misplaced. "How long before we're in transporter range?"

Weyoun raised his hand to his viewer and repositioned it in front of his eye. After a moment, he said, "Less than three minutes from now."

Odo nodded once and said, "I'd like to beam down as soon as possible." He pulled off his headset and held it out toward Weyoun.

"Of course," the Vorta said, taking the headset. "It is always a pleasure to serve you."

Odo moved off to the right, a quarter of the way around the bridge, to where an alcove sat tucked into a bulkhead. He stepped inside, onto a transporter pad. Weyoun followed, and stood before a neighboring control panel. They waited in silence as the ship neared the Founders' world.

Finally, Weyoun announced, "We are within range." He worked the transporter controls, which responded with clicks and muted tones. Before he finished, though, Odo stopped him with a question.

"How far, Weyoun?" he asked. "How far away is the nova?"

Weyoun reported the distance, and then added, "It lies just beyond the edge of the Omarion Nebula."

The information jolted Odo, as though a surge of electricity had passed through his body. "The Omarion Nebula?" he echoed, a note of wonder slipping into his voice as he pronounced the name of the place the Founders had formerly called home. Years ago, Odo had been drawn to the nebula when he'd first seen it, a response fixed in him—in all of the Hundred—by his people, so that he—and the others—would one day return to them. Now, faced with his original reaction to the nova, juxtaposed with the revelation of its location near the Omarion Nebula, Odo's thoughts swirled as he attempted to make sense of it all.

"Founder?" Weyoun said into the ensuing silence.

"Yes," Odo said absently, and then he looked up and gestured for Weyoun to continue working the panel. Seconds later, a hum rose in the alcove. Odo's vision clouded for an instant, as though a draft of opaque smoke had wafted past his eyes. Then, just as quickly as the whirr of the transporter had escalated, it diminished.

The Jem'Hadar ship had gone, replaced underfoot by a sea-girt islet. All around spread the brassy, swelling surface of the Great Link. Odo paced forward, then lifted his head and gazed into the dusky sky. Seeing nothing but the normal stars, he slowly turned in a circle where he stood, until just past the pair of peaked, ten-meter-high rock formations that ascended on one side of the islet, he spied the nova. It appeared larger than any of the other lights adorning the empyrean, and shined with an intensity far greater.

Suddenly, Odo understood that he'd mistaken feelings of awe for those of concern. Now, something far more powerful replaced his ebbing fears: hope. The brilliant, flaring star captured his psyche in much the same way the Omarion Nebula once had. All at once, the nova seemed a harbinger of a bright future for his people, an augury of peace and joy for the Founders in the days ahead.

Only later, when Odo stood here again, in the same spot, and stared out over the planet's cold, empty landscape, would he recall this moment and realize how wrong he had been.

The strange beast descended on vast gossamer wings, coasting gracefully down through the atmosphere as though deciding whether or not to allow gravity to take hold of it. Its simple, relatively small body—no larger than a runabout—appeared little more than a cytoplasm-filled pouch. The primitive mass hung from the juncture of the membranous extremities, dwarfed by them as they blanketed the twilit sky with their filmy reach.

Odo perceived the unfamiliar creature not by way of his own senses, but via those of the Great Link. He drifted through the changeling deep not unlike the way the unusual being floated through the air. Odo's metamorphic body, protracted into countless planes and tendrils, many only a single cell through, stretched through the commingled volume of his people, a part of the whole. Connections formed and dissolved with contact and separation, passed from one to another, from one to many, from many to one. Fluid shapes arose sporadically in the living ocean like silhouettes in a lightless room, then slipped away, shadows uniting with the dark.

Communication occurred among the changelings as both control and reflex. Discourse and dialogue took place, willfully directed, while the experience of form flowed involuntarily from one to another, a spontaneous response of tangency. Emotion and perception fell somewhere in between. Odo sensed the mammoth creature through his interface with other Founders. Those whose cells blended to fashion the surface of the Link conveyed their observations of the winged being as it glided downward through the sky.

Odo withdrew into himself, away from the joining. He moved, fluttering the wisps of his body and propelling himself upward through the liquid assemblage of his people. As he did so, he felt their communal unease, which seemed now to grow. When Odo had returned to the Great Link a month ago, he'd been welcomed back eagerly, but in addition to that enthusiasm, he'd also distinguished an undercurrent of restiveness. He'd attributed it at first to his homecoming after having been away for so long, but as time had passed and the Founders' anxiety hadn't lessened, he'd eventually concluded that some other impulse drove their collective state of mind. He had just begun to explore what that might be when he'd become aware of the huge, diaphanous beast dropping toward the planet.

A sliver of Odo's body reached the upper limit of the Link and touched the air above it. His transitory form possessed no humanoid sensory organs at the moment, and so he did not see or hear, smell or taste. And yet he experienced *sensation,* comprehensive sensation, and with it, an awareness, a perception of the external universe.

Odo regarded the skies, and now identified not just one bulbous projection depending from the center of the creature, but three. He also discerned that it had decreased overall in size; its quartet of wings, which had initially extended almost from horizon to horizon, now traversed less than half that area. As the creature dropped, the diminution continued, its aerial appendages rippling in patches as they contracted, the sheer, delicate flesh shimmering a metallic-golden color there. Abruptly, Odo recognized the being.

Gathering his body, Odo set off through the Great Link, a finned, undulating missile traveling at speed. As he raced toward the two-peaked islet that rose out of the glistening changeling sea, he noted the mixture of anticipation and concern building higher in his people. But while he could understand their expectancy, and felt excited himself at the return of another Founder—and perhaps *three* other Founders—he felt disappointed and isolated that they had not divulged to him the original source of their disquiet.

He slid swiftly along, images from those at the surface of the Link confirming what he'd foreseen: that the trajectory of the arriving changeling would bring it down onto the islet. As Odo approached the same location, he slowed and looked inward. In his mind, he called up visions of tides, rolling waters embodying motion, progressing inexorably through time and space. Within the tides, he summoned the circular movements of vortices, and within the vortices, their unseen but quantifiable derivatives: points without length or depth or breadth, measuring instantaneous rates of change.

Odo began to alter as he visualized what he would become. He saw with precision the contours of the body he would inhabit, felt the exact limits of the physical frame he would take. The path to change had not always been like this for him, so clearly definable. For a long time, he had pictured a result he lacked the capability to fully assess. His cells would adjust and shift, but not as he'd wanted, not entirely, and in the end, his form would be left only a close approximation of his conception. But now, after months of guidance from his people, what he envisioned, he became.

Odo's body mutated, spinning into a contained whirlpool, swirling in upon itself, and upward, counter to gravity. He hurled himself free of the Great Link and into the open air, and then over, in that direction, toward the scrap of land, and down, onto the ragged rock. He felt the mercurial potential of his physical being, and strived to construct reality out of mere possibility.

And so: the transformation, proprioception made conscious thought, surging through the process in reverse, from the fluxion of the dimensionless instant, through vortex upon vortex, wheeling in retrograde eddies, incorporating into the internal current, growing focused, and so: the transformation.

He became the humanoid Odo.

Standing on the small island, he looked skyward, just in time to see the returning changelings' wings fold in on themselves in an iridescent rush. The three teardrop-shaped pouches, deprived of their means of flight, dropped the twenty or so meters onto the center of the islet. Each less than a quarter the size of a runabout now, their pliant bodies spread on the bottom as they landed, absorbing the impact. Odo expected all of them to morph immediately into other forms, but only the one in the center did so. It climbed upward, straightened and narrowed in a coruscation of orange-gold, then solidified into a humanoid figure with a broad chest and wide shoulders: Laas.

"Welcome—" Odo started, and then hesitated. He'd been about to say "Welcome home," but found himself choking back the second word. He nodded, and began again. "Welcome back," he said.

Laas paced forward until he stood directly in front of Odo, making no move to link with him. Though having proven adept at learning from the Great Link the practice of perfectly mimicking other life-forms, Laas still took on the approximate, somewhat unfinished appearance that he'd worn during his two centuries with the Varalans. When Odo shapeshifted into humanoid form, as he just had, he did likewise, choosing to manifest not precisely as a Bajoran, but with the same smooth features he'd established during his years among them.

" 'Welcome,' " Laas responded, practically spitting the word. His deep-set eyes narrowed beneath the fleshy ridges that ran across his brow. Odo, several centimeters shorter, peered up and studied his features: the slight, V-shaped bulge of his forehead; the pronounced cheekbones; the mouth curling downward at its edges; the flanges of skin connecting his nostrils to his face. He wore an expression of unmistakable anger. "I do not want to be welcomed," he declared. "I want to know why the Hundred were sent out. I want to know why we were sent *away*."

Odo met Laas's stare for a long moment, unimpressed by the vehemence with which he'd delivered his words. As chief of security aboard Deep Space 9, Odo had often been confronted with belligerence, and he'd always tended to react to it impassively. He did so now, stepping casually to the side and around Laas. "It's good to see you as well," he said.

"I have no quarrel with you, Odo," Laas said, turning toward him. "You are one of the Hundred. You are one of *us*." He gestured past Odo, at the other two changelings. Laas, who'd had no knowledge of the Founders prior to meeting Odo in the Alpha Quadrant almost a year and a half ago, had joined the Great Link after the end of the war. The Founders had cured him of the slow-acting disease engineered by Section 31, but he'd stayed only a few months before leaving on a personal quest to locate more of the Hundred.

"You know why we were sent out," Odo said. "I told you about it when we first met."

"I know what you *told* me," Laas snapped. "Now I want to know the truth." He stalked past Odo, heading toward one of the other changelings.

"I've told you the truth," Odo insisted.

"Have you?" Laas challenged him, spinning to face him. "Do you even know the truth?" Holding Odo's gaze, he stepped backward to the center of the islet, into the space between the two amorphous changelings. "Tell me again then. Tell me why the Great Link sent out a hundred of their own—a hundred *innocents*—to endure loneliness, and suffering, and death."

"What are you talking about?" Odo asked. He looked at one of the unformed shapeshifters, and then at the other. Only then did he spy the small mound of ashes sitting between the two, the grainy, charcoal-gray substance difficult to see against the dark rock. Laas must have carried the material with him, depositing it on the islet when he'd landed. Odo had seen such a sight just once previously—nearly five years ago, aboard *Defiant*—but he knew it at once as the remains of a dead changeling.

"Yes," Laas said, apparently noting Odo's recognition of the unmoving ashes. "That's what I'm talking about." His heated tones filled the islet. "So tell me again: why were we exiled from our people? For what good purpose did this happen?"

And suddenly, staring at the desiccated reliquiae of a fellow changeling, Odo no longer had an answer.

Taran'atar opened his eyes in darkness. His body tensed immediately, his instincts readying him to spring into action. He reached for the *kar'takin* sheathed on his back, pleased to find the ax still in its place as his hand wrapped around its perfectly balanced, perfectly proportioned haft. He focused his concentration, preparing to shroud, to bring down around him, through force of will, a cloak of invisibility.

But first, seeking to take the measure of his situation, Taran'atar examined the input of his senses. His gray, pebbled flesh registered the tight circulation of air, as though within an enclosed space, and the slight flexing of his muscles revealed no restraints about him. His empty hand confirmed the cushioned seat beneath him, and though he detected no one in the room with him now, the scents that reached his nose told him that others had been here recently. Underscoring it all, a muted vibration suffused his environs, accompanied by a low, steady rumble.

Warp engines, Taran'atar thought. He gauged the pitch, loudness, and timbre of the sound, and distinguished the drive as that of a Federation runabout. In an instant, he recalled his location—aboard *Rio Grande*—and his circumstances: crewing a nonmilitary mission with Captain Kira, Lieutenant Bowers, and Ensign Aleco.

Taran'atar bolted up out of his chair in the lightless compartment, drawing his blade in the same motion. Rage coursed through his body like ketracel-white, feeding him, *driving* him. "Victory is life," he hissed through clenched teeth, attempting to control his anger and deal with the failure he'd just borne. For him to be unaware of his surroundings, even for a moment, represented an unacceptable defect in his abilities.

"Computer," he said, working to keep his voice even, "lights." Two short tones acknowledged his command, and the darkness receded beneath the rising glow of the overhead panels. Taran'atar peered around the runabout's aft compartment. As his gaze took in the design and engineering style characteristic of Starfleet vessels, he felt his fury anew.

He had come to abhor this place. Not just the runabout, or the space station, or Bajor, but the whole of the Alpha Quadrant. And he had come to abhor the beings who populated it. He held a degree of respect for some of those he'd encountered—such as Kira and Vaughn—and managed a tolerance for others—Ro, Bashir—but that did not mitigate his general contempt for the species and individuals here. He stayed for one reason only, for the same reason he'd come here to begin with: because the Founder had issued him those orders. But months after leaving the Gamma Quadrant for this undertaking, he still did not really understand the purpose he'd been assigned. Given that, and despite the words of encouragement Odo had offered during his visit to Deep Space 9 two months ago, Taran'atar believed that success had completely eluded him here, and always would. Worse, he realized that his time on this mission was not simply futile, but also detrimental to his effectiveness as a soldier of the Dominion.

Taran'atar glanced down at his hand, at the ax clutched before him in a posture of attack. How often had he wielded such a blade against a foe? He remembered vividly sending his *kar'takin* slicing through the face of the Hirogen he'd fought in the Delta Quadrant, and before that, burying it in the chest of one of Locken's misbegotten Jem'Hadar on Sindorin. Flashes of memory from back in the Dominion played through his mind: his steel tasting the blood of the Ourentia as his phalanx put down their reckless uprising; a well-thrown knife delivering relief from a power-mad Vorta whose unchecked ambitions threatened the life of a Founder; under orders from his first, cutting through the rugged hide of the ninth and removing his still-warm hearts, an example to the other Jem'Hadar of the consequences of disobeying an order during combat. Taran'atar's blades had carved through the flesh of scores of different species, killing hundreds, perhaps thousands. For his twenty-two years, he had served the Founders, had defended their empire in uncounted campaigns. But now he felt useless to his gods.

In his hand, the thin blade of the *kar'takin* reflected the overhead lighting. Taran'atar looked at it, the urge to use it to fight his way back to Dominion space a strong one. Instead, he struggled to suppress his wrath. He returned the ax to its scabbard. No weapon, no matter its utility or lethality, would aid him in vanquishing his newfound enemy: sleep.

"Computer," he said in a low growl, "time." An automated voice responded, and Taran'atar calculated that he had slept approximately one hour, forty-seven minutes. His hands squeezed into fists.

Taran'atar's need for slumber—several hours, a couple of times per week—had developed not long ago, just prior to Bajor's official admission into the Federation. Deeply concerned about his new vulnerability, he'd gone to Odo for assistance. The Founder had instructed him to allow a medical examination by Dr. Bashir, who'd determined his sleeping to be a consequence of no longer ingesting ketracel-white. The amalgam in the white's carrier solution of enzyme and nutrients, coupled with the delivery method, somehow forestalled the necessity for a Jem'Hadar to rest. Unable to reproduce the effect by other means, Bashir had offered no solutions. Taran'atar had then appealed to Odo to sanction his return to the Dominion, but the Founder had denied the request, and had even suggested that being more like the people he'd been sent to live among might provide him a fresh perspective from which to learn about them.

Taran'atar had acquiesced—he had no choice but to do as one of his gods commanded—but in the weeks since, his dissatisfaction with his own capacity to function well as a Jem'Hadar soldier had grown. He had obeyed the will of the Founders his entire life, and he always would, but how could he serve them on Deep Space 9, by living among Bajorans and humans, Andorians and Trill and Ferengi? And of what use could he be to them, how effective could he be, if he continued to require sleep?

No use, he thought now. It had been that realization that had set him on his present course of action.

To his left, the door to the aft compartment slid open, followed by the sound of somebody stepping inside. Taran'atar turned to see Captain Kira standing there, the central corridor of the runabout visible behind her. She looked different to him now than when he'd first come aboard the space station. Back then, she'd worn the ocherous uniform of the Bajoran Militia; now, she clad herself in the black-and-gray of Starfleet. Like him, he thought, she'd been forced from her world and into the insidious influences of the Federation.

"Taran'atar," she said, "I just wanted to let you know that we're only an hour out from the *Mjolnir*."

He looked at her face, and though she'd conducted herself

competently during the time he'd spent in the Alpha Quadrant, his ire built within him once more. Quickly reining it in, he said, "Acknowledged."

"Would you like to join us up front?" she asked, hiking her thumb back over her shoulder.

"No. I prefer to be alone at the moment," he told her. "Unless you are ordering me . . ." Odo had instructed him to follow Kira's commands.

"No, not at all," Kira said. "I just thought . . . well, never mind." She took one step out of the room, then peered back at him. "Are you all right?"

"Yes," Taran'atar said. Then, not wanting his terseness to invite additional questions, he added, "I'm fine, thank you, Captain." Kira nodded and offered a half-smile, clearly not convinced, but she headed back toward the front of the ship. The door eased closed behind her.

It will not be long, Taran'atar thought, looking at the spot where Kira had been. One hour until the rendezvous with *Mjolnir,* where Bowers and Aleco would disembark *Rio Grande.* With Kira, he'd travel the next leg of his journey, and then . . . and then maybe he could finally bring his time away from the Dominion to an end.

Odo stared at the ashes of the fallen changeling. Anguish washed over him like a cold and bitter wind. He stood motionless, arms at his sides, feeling as though he'd been assaulted.

Perhaps this explained the combination of rising anticipation and upset in the Great Link, he thought. The Founders had espied Laas and the other two changelings descending through the sky, but also must have perceived the inert mass of the fourth. From his own experience, Odo understood the devastating impact that the loss of one of his people had on the rest. Difficult as the death of a cherished family member or loved one might be for a humanoid, the demise of a Founder meant that and more; the Link lost not only an individual, but a literal piece of the whole as well. Odo had suffered the grief of personally witnessing the deaths of two changelings, and after the first of these, he'd also experienced the terrible sorrow that subsequently had come to pervade the Great Link.

Laas paced back across the islet, his soft footfalls a lonely sound in the still setting. Around them, the silently rolling changeling sea mirrored the coppery gloaming. "Why?" Laas asked again as he came abreast of Odo, his voice much quieter now. "Why did our people send out the Hundred?"

Odo searched for an answer different from the one he had been told, different from the one he had some time ago recited for Laas, but he could not find one. "You know why," he repeated. His gaze still rested on the gritty, leaden remnants of the lifeless changeling.

"No," Laas insisted, though gently. "I really don't know. Please tell me."

At last, Odo looked up. He sighed, a quick burst of air from his mouth, a habit he'd developed long ago, during his years on Bajor with Dr. Mora. "Our people sent out a hundred of us to learn about the galaxy," he explained, "and then to return that knowledge to them."

"But why send newly formed changelings?" Laas asked. His inflection implied a genuine lack of comprehension.

"Because the Great Link felt the need to hide," Odo said. He looked around, past the margins of the islet, and out across the expanse of their people. "They used to travel the stars, discovering all they could about the universe, meeting other species, but . . ."

"But," Laas echoed, his tone clearly expressing not a question, but a prompt.

"But they were feared by solids," Odo continued, recollecting the tale he'd been told when, after being drawn to the Omarion Nebula, he'd established contact with the Founders. The changeling leader—she did not actually lead the Great Link, but had taken the mantle, first, of communicating with Odo in his humanoid form, and later, of directing the Dominion's war machine against the residents of the Alpha Quadrant—the changeling leader had welcomed Odo back, and had shared the reasons for the seclusion of their people, as well as the reasons for the Hundred. "Some solids were suspicious of their ability to shapeshift, and changelings were hunted and sometimes killed. For reasons of self-preservation, the Great Link isolated itself from others."

"But they still wanted to expand their knowledge of the galaxy," Laas offered. "And to gather intelligence about the dangers that awaited the Link."

"Yes," Odo agreed. "So they sent us out, with a genetically imprinted drive to return."

Laas did not respond immediately, and after more than a few seconds, Odo turned from peering out across the Link and back toward his compatriot. Laas raised his hands and gripped Odo firmly about the upper arms. Slowly, he said, "That does not make sense."

"What doesn't make sense?" Odo asked.

"Sending newly formed changelings—*infants*—on charges of exploration and intelligence," Laas said. "Why attempt to gather information in such an unstructured, uncertain manner? How could they abandon a hundred waifs in unfamiliar space, with no tools or instructions, with no life experience whatsoever, and expect them to execute a successful mission?"

Odo listened to Laas's questions, and found himself unable to provide reasonable responses. He peered over at the pair of other, living changelings, and saw them spilling across the islet toward the Link. He wondered where Laas had located the two, whom he inferred belonged to the Hundred. As Odo considered what Laas had said, he had to admit that the justification he'd been given for seeding him and the others throughout the galaxy did not seem to bear up under scrutiny.

"And if the Founders were so concerned about the constant threat posed by monoforms," Laas went on, employing the term he used to describe non-changelings, "then how could they deliver infants from the Link into their midst, with no guidance and no protection?"

Odo looked back at Laas. "Solids are not inherently a danger to changelings," he argued.

"No?" Laas said, his voice rising again in obvious agitation. He raised an arm and pointed toward the pile of flinty remains. On either side of the ashes, Odo saw, the other two changelings had slipped from the islet and rejoined the Great Link. "This Founder," Laas said, stalking back toward it, "died by the hand of a humanoid, killed for no other reason than the ability to alter form at will." He locked eyes with Odo from the center of the islet, the brace of jagged peaks behind him a dramatic backdrop. "Have you so quickly forgotten the Federation's attempted genocide of our people?"

"That was an action undertaken by a small subset of the Federation, a few individuals," Odo protested. "And even that came only after the Founders had already launched the war."

"Odo," Laas said, shaking his head from side to side, "you have no sense of objectivity in these matters. Your love for a monoform blinds you to their bigotry."

Odo felt the return of an old inclination: to deny his feelings for Nerys, as he had done for so long. But denial, he knew, would convince Laas of nothing but Odo's unwillingness to be honest. Ever since his return to the Great Link after the end of the war, Odo had determined not only to be honest in communicating with his people, but to be open as well. He knew that his efforts to convince the Founders to join in peaceful relationships with others beyond their world would require them to trust in both him and his motives.

"I love Kira," he told Laas. "But my emotions for her do not alter facts . . . facts like my overriding feelings for the Link, which are evidenced by my continued presence in it."

"Your 'continued presence'?" Laas questioned. "According to Vannis, you've recently come back after being away for more than three months, much of it spent in the Alpha Quadrant." Before arriving on the planet, Laas must have had contact with the ship Vannis commanded. "So much for your commitment to our people."

"I left to track a potential threat to the Great Link," Odo claimed truthfully, thinking of the rumors of an Ascendant. He knew that he would also have to detail investigating the rumors that eventually led him to Opaka Sulan, as well as to admit his time with Nerys. Laas had clearly learned of his travels, and so revealing anything less would doubtless be perceived as subterfuge, undermining his words. But before Odo could say more, Laas spoke again.

"Did you find any Ascendants on Deep Space 9 or on Bajor?" he said. He took a step forward, in Odo's direction. "Or perhaps in Kira's bed?"

Odo shook his head as he folded his arms across his chest.

"Is that intended to provoke me?" he asked. Odo had contended with enough criminals—Quark came to mind—to know when somebody baited him. "The Founders know the reasons for my time away from here, including my time in the Alpha Quadrant," he said calmly. "They also know that I'm here now, that I didn't remain with Kira." But just mentioning the prospect of staying with Nerys, just the notion of making a life with her, sent a thrill through him.

"Your presence here is for the purpose of swaying the Great Link to your views of monoforms," Laas said. "Do not deny it. Your goal is not to help the Founders, but to change their way of thinking. Once you've done that . . . or maybe even if you don't . . . ultimately, you will return to her."

Laas took another step forward, and suddenly, his body quivered. Golden ripples emanated from the center of his torso outward, like the influence of a stone dropped into sun-drenched waters. Odo watched as the ripples of light spread, quickly encompassing Laas's entire form. His body shortened and contracted, but retained a basic humanoid shape.

Odo waited until the effulgence retreated, congealing into definite colors and textures. When the effect finished, Laas no longer mimicked the shape and characteristics of a Varalan. His form had metamorphosed into something else, Odo saw. Into some*body* else.

It was Nerys.

The face of the Dominion spread across the floor of the transporter platform. Vannis stood on the Jem'Hadar bridge, just outside the alcove, peering in at the shapeless, gelatinous form of the Founder. Its face was no face at all, a glistening orange-gold surface devoid of features. Vannis recognized it as *a* changeling, but not as any *particular* changeling. This could have been the same shapeshifter who last month had issued her orders about the revolt on Rintanna, or it could have been one whom she had never before met.

Whatever the case, it mattered little to her. A Founder was still a Founder, and the Founders were gods. They spoke only rarely to her—to any Vorta or Jem'Hadar or other humanoid, as far as she knew—so when they did, she listened. She knew that she served the Founders well, but she strived to serve them better than any other Vorta did, than any other Vorta ever had.

After securing the transporter console, Vannis turned fully toward the Founder. The shining mass stirred here and there, pushing outward, pulling inward, rising and falling, almost as though breathing. The urge to ask how she could serve the Founder nearly overwhelmed her, but she fought down the impulse. Too often she had witnessed the sycophancy of her people—had even practiced it herself—only to see a Founder respond with loathing and contempt. Over time, she had come to understand such reactions to be a by-product of Vorta behavior and demeanor, and not simply of the Vorta themselves. Since that realization, Vannis had labored to modify her own conduct in order to avoid incurring the disdain of her gods.

And so now she waited.

Before long, the Founder shifted, a small portion of it drawing upward near its center. Its flesh then moved again there, and developed into the shape of a mouth—not into eyes or a nose or any other facial characteristics, but only into a mouth, which immediately spoke. "What is the situation with the Overne?" the Founder asked, its voice high enough to be categorized as traditionally female.

Vannis stepped over to the center of the threshold dividing the transporter alcove from the rest of the bridge. "The agricultural plague on Overne III has been eradicated," she reported. "But foodstuffs are low and, even rationed, might not last through the winter in the northern hemisphere." The Overne served an important role within the Dominion, manufacturing both ships and weapons for the Jem'Hadar. They operated facilities in several systems, but their primary drive production and starship assembly took place in plants on and around their home planet. Recently, a mutant virus had destroyed crops worldwide there, threatening the population with famine.

"The foodstuffs *might* not last the winter?" the Founder said, her tone impatient. "When will you know with certainty?"

"Within the next two to three weeks," Vannis said. Then she realized that in answering the Founder's question directly, she had failed to provide other important and relevant information. She quickly added, "But we have a solution ready."

"And what is that solution?" the Founder demanded. Although Vannis had seen the effect before, the faceless mouth unnerved her a bit as it formed words.

"We have brought another world, Rindamil III, into the Dominion," she answered. The planet had been located just beyond the perimeter of Dominion space, and now marked its outer boundary. The Rindamil themselves lacked warp capabilities—although they did possess rudimentary transporter technology—and had not yet ventured past their moon, but she had personally introduced them to life beyond their world. "If necessary," Vannis further explained, "this new Dominion planet will provide food for the Overne."

"Why are you waiting to see if it will be necessary?" the Founder asked.

"Because the Rindamil foodstuffs cannot fully support the populations of both worlds," Vannis said.

"They don't have to," the Founder asserted. "They only have to support the Overne. The starships and weaponry needed to protect the Dominion are the priority."

"I understand," Vannis said. "Shall I commence transfer of the foodstuffs at once?"

To her surprise, the Founder did not reply right away, and Vannis had to suppress a compulsion to fill the hush that followed with her own voice and words. She wanted to make sure that she had not angered the changeling, or failed her in some way. But she knew that seeking such assurances would only serve to infuriate the Founder.

And so again she waited.

At last, the Founder said, "You will wait two weeks only to assess the severity of the Overne winter and its impact on the food supply. If there is any possibility of a shortfall, begin shipments from Rindamil III at once."

"Acknowledged," Vannis said. She peered over at the transporter console and took note of the time. She would follow the orders precisely.

"Before then," the Founder continued, "I want you to take a ship to a moon orbiting a world near the Anomaly." She listed the Dominion designation and coordinates of the planet, which Vannis also committed to memory. "A tribe called the Sen

Ennis resides there. A Founder was told by a former inhabitant of the moon that a member of a race calling themselves the Ascendants spent some time there when its ship crashed, although it has since departed." Vannis assumed the Founder referred to Odo, whose recent travels she had learned about from Weyoun. "I want you to go there and determine whatever details you can about the incident, about the Ascendants themselves, about their return to this region of space, about their technology . . . whatever you can learn."

"Acknowledged," Vannis said again.

"Do you have anything to report?" the Founder then asked.

A number of items passed through Vannis's mind—the new trade agreement with the Alorex, the construction of the education center on Karemma, the resumption of subspace-relay operations on Callinon VII—but she knew that since none of those issues bore directly on the security of the Great Link, the Founder would have no interest in any of them. "No," she said. "I have nothing else to report."

"Then send me home," the Founder said. After the last word, the lips that formed her mouth sealed and blended back into her changeling body.

Vannis quickly returned to her position before the transporter console, specified the appropriate settings, and beamed the Founder back to the planet below, to one of the numerous small islands scattered throughout the extent of the Great Link. Then she turned to the rest of the bridge, quickly scanning the Jem'Hadar that worked at various stations and picking out the ranking soldier. "First," she said, and when he looked over at her, "prepare to break orbit." She enumerated the details of their destination, as provided by the Founder. "Best possible speed."

The Jem'Hadar first acknowledged the order and set his crew to work. As the impulse drive came alive and sent a familiar vibration through the bridge, Vannis crossed to a console and operated the controls there. She searched the Dominion databases for any information she could find on the Ascendants, as well as for the available data on Rindamil III and its people. In order to learn what she could about the Ascendants, it might help to be familiar with whatever body of knowledge about them already existed. She would also plan her own part in the Jem'Hadar assault on the Rindamil, should it be needed.

It would be a busy month.

Odo reacted to the provocation without thinking. He started toward Laas, intent on forcing him to surrender the guise of Nerys he'd perversely assumed. Odo imagined himself melting into his native, liquid state, hurtling forward, driving into Laas, and wrenching him out of his inflammatory appearance. But after two quick strides, he stopped, regaining control of his emotions just before he reached Laas.

Odo looked across the short distance that separated him from the counterfeit figure of Nerys. The very idea of Laas— or anybody—appropriating her form filled him with revulsion and anger. As he regarded the pretender, though, he saw that not all details had been accurately reproduced: six horizontal ridges, instead of five, decorated the bridge of this Nerys's nose; the hair, pulled across the top of the head and arcing down the side, fell a couple of centimeters longer than it had the last time Odo had seen her; and the auburn uniform designated the real Nerys's former position in the Bajoran Militia, and not her current captaincy in Starfleet. Laas obviously remembered his time aboard Deep Space 9 inexactly, some of the knowledge he did retain now out of date.

"Are you going to attack me?" he asked in a voice that closely approximated that of Nerys, though not quite with her true intonation. "How like a monoform you are."

Odo did not rise to the taunt. "Why are you doing this?" he said. "Why are you acting like this? I'm not your enemy." Uncomfortable conversing with a simulacrum of the woman he loved, he recalled a time when the changeling leader had enacted a similar masquerade. Odo hadn't known it at the time, owing to the precision of the impersonation. Now, though, he focused on the inaccuracies that differentiated this fraudulent version of Nerys from the real one.

"At this moment, I consider the entire Great Link an enemy of the Hundred," Laas vowed. He indicated the dead changeling. "This one adrift, alone for centuries, then found by humanoids, experimented on, and finally killed in a paranoid frenzy. Me—" He pointed a finger at himself, tapping the chest of the imitation Nerys. "—living among monoforms for two hundred years, tormented, miserable. The same story for the other two." He motioned to either side of the islet, evidently to include the other two changelings he'd brought with him, though they'd already glided back into the Link. "For what?" Laas concluded, in a way that did not invite an answer. But Odo volunteered one anyway.

"For knowledge," he said flatly, again reiterating the justification he'd been given for the Hundred. But as with Laas, he found that he could no longer countenance that explanation. Right now, he wondered why he had never questioned it.

"How can you say that?" Laas asked sharply, and the rebuke abruptly took Odo back to Deep Space 9, to a time when the Dominion had occupied the station. Odo had plotted with Nerys, Jake, and Rom to thwart the Cardassians in their efforts to destroy the Federation minefield obstructing the Alpha Quadrant entrance to the wormhole; the mines provided a vital function, preventing the Jem'Hadar from sending reinforcements for the war. Instead of doing as he'd promised, though, Odo had linked with the changeling leader. As a result, Rom's attempted sabotage had been discovered, and Rom arrested and sentenced to death. Nerys had understandably demanded an explanation of Odo, and when he'd told her that he'd been linking with the Founder, and that the war really had nothing to do with him, she'd asked the same thing Laas—utilizing her face and voice—just had: *How can you say that?*

"I don't know," Odo confessed now to Laas. "It's what I was told. I had no reason to disbelieve it."

"Don't you see," Laas said, "that we have *every* reason to disbelieve it?"

"That may be," Odo allowed, "but *I* never lied to you. You don't have to fight me."

Laas stepped forward and looked up with Nerys's eyes. "You've lied to yourself, Odo," he said, "and that means you've lied to me as well." He circled around and headed for the edge of the islet. "And the Founders have lied to us both," he called back.

Odo turned in time to see him descend from the rock surface and into the golden flow of the Link. Laas did not morph immediately, but strode out into the great assembly of changelings. "What are you going to do?" Odo called after him.

Laas stopped and looked back. "I'm going to learn the truth," he said. Odo watched as his form—Nerys's form—began to sink into the living swells, merging with them. In seconds, only the Great Link remained.

Sadness beset Odo . . . not for Laas, but for Nerys. Even with the distress and woe he already felt for the deceased changeling, this fresh emotion touched him in a deeper, more personal way. Witnessing the facsimile of Nerys disappear into the gleaming ocean of the Founders reminded him of when he'd done the same, leaving her alone on this undersized chunk of rock. He'd known that it must have been difficult for her, but not until now had he understood it in such a visceral way. It troubled him to think that, just recently, he'd forsaken her again.

How can I keep doing that to her? he asked himself, because those had not been the only times he'd abandoned her. He recalled again his betrayal of their resistance cell during the Dominion occupation of Deep Space 9, which had led to Rom's arrest. Although Odo had later helped to rescue Rom, that action still did not justify his disloyalty. Even after Starfleet had expelled the Dominion forces from DS9 and retaken the station, his friendship with Nerys had not immediately revived. For weeks, their working relationship had been horribly strained, their personal association nonexistent.

For Odo, the memory of that time felt raw, as though it had only just occurred. These days, he shouldered the weight of his separation from her, knowing that their love persisted despite the distance between them, but back then, loving her from afar, his estrangement from her had been almost unbearable. Nevertheless, it had been Nerys's strength that had allowed them finally to talk, and ultimately to reconcile. Looking back at that long night of conversation, of tears and laughter, of resentment and forgiveness, he realized that it had been then that they had cemented the foundation for their eventual romance.

As Odo stood looking out over the rise and fall of the surface of the Great Link, he knew that Laas had been right: he would go back to Nerys, and sooner rather than later. In the months since he'd last seen her, he had reconnected with his people, had endeavored once more to learn from them, to teach them in turn, and to understand the agitation they'd exhibited since he'd rejoined the Link. Now, he'd also welcomed Laas back, witnessed the return of two more of the Hundred, and learned of the death of another.

And yet what filled his mind most was Nerys.

Odo raised his head and peered up at the sky, past the brilliant flare of the nova, and toward the formation of stars he knew lay in the direction of the Bajoran wormhole. He stood like that for a long time, as though he could see into the Alpha Quadrant, to Deep Space 9, and to his future with Nerys.

But what he saw in his mind was the past.

2

Odo heard the source of the complaints as he arrived at the doors, two of his deputies accompanying him on either flank. He nodded to the junior security officer, Hava, and the young man reached up and tapped at the panel set into the bulkhead. Odo waited only an instant before moving forward, though, suspecting that the rapid drumbeat originating in the cabin beyond would preclude anybody within from hearing the visitor signal.

The doors parted to reveal Dax's quarters, and Odo stepped inside. People filled the living area, most clad in colorful and decidedly civilian raiment, though a few did wear Bajoran Militia or Starfleet uniforms. Some sat, some stood, some danced, their laughter and conversation joining with the bass rhythms to create a clamor that, to judge by the grievances that had reached the security office, traveled readily through the bulkheads.

Odo peered to his right, and saw Leeta capering atop a table. She wore a multihued outfit that looked like something Quark might have selected for her—

He felt Kira's presence before he saw her, and before he could even consider what to do, he peered left. She stood there, just inside the doorway, just ahead of him. They made eye contact, then looked quickly away from each other, as they'd been doing in the weeks since the Dominion had left the station.

They had attended meetings of Captain Sisko's senior staff and had conducted themselves professionally, had even spoken to each other when their duties had required it of them. But while they'd managed to conceal their rift from their crewmates, the tension between them had only increased with time, and they avoided contact with each other whenever possible. Now, though, with Kira beside him, he felt that he could not simply walk away without saying anything.

"I've been getting complaints about the noise," he told her. In front of him, Nog jumped about in place, his legs and arms spread, dancing in that peculiarly Ferengi way. Across the room, a brawny, bare-chested man—Lieutenant Atoa, of the *Sutherland,* Odo recognized—pounded on a drum, and wore what appeared to be a grass skirt and a necklace composed of teeth. Between Nog and Atoa, Morn—ever the life of the party—gamboled about with a Bolian, the two punctuating their movements by throwing themselves at each other and butting their upper torsos together. The rambunctious behavior reminded him of another complaint. "Someone even mentioned something about a fight," he added.

"Oh, there was scuffle between Morn and one of the Bolians," she said, and Odo risked a glance in her direction. "But they worked it out," she concluded with a small laugh. She continued looking into the room and away from Odo.

"How long will this—" He gestured at Nog, still bounding about to the percussive music. "—party continue?" Odo would discharge his duty here, he decided, and exit as soon as possible. Dax had invited him here to help celebrate her upcoming wedding to Worf, but he had demurred specifically so that he could avoid any awkward interaction with Kira.

"This party will continue until further notice," Kira said, in a way that Odo found difficult to read. She appeared to be enjoying herself, he thought, but there also seemed an undercurrent of pique beneath her words. Obviously uncomfortable, she nervously wrapped the fingers of one hand around the thumb of the other. "On the personal authority of the station's first officer," she went on, "who just happens to be me." She turned to him for a moment, wearing a close-mouthed smile that could have been forced or genuine.

"You're in a good mood," he said, choosing to believe her good humor to be real. She wore a sleeveless, bright-red dress, he saw, with red leggings and high, black shoes, an outfit that softened and flattered her. Thinking that perhaps they could finally begin to find their way past the troubles in their friendship, he realized that he had come here now with just that possibility in mind. He'd intentionally not attended Dax's celebration, but he could have sent any of his deputies here to deal with the noise. Instead, he'd elected to come himself.

"Aah, well, it's a good party," she said with a laugh, but in a way that seemed somehow to distance her from him. She reveled in these festivities for Dax, while he had come to deliver news of complaints, just another of the divides between them. As quickly as he had thought to use this chance to try to begin mending his problems with Kira, he now realized that the time still was not right.

"Well," he said, and he turned, starting for the doors. He would return to the security office and—

"Odo," Kira said, her tone plaintive. He turned back to her. "Odo," she said again, and they at last looked at each other, *really* looked at each other. "I think we have a lot to talk about."

"I agree," he said, and though they had yet to have that conversation, he felt immediate relief that the necessity for it had finally been voiced.

"So let's talk," Kira said.

"Now?" Odo questioned, surprised at the suggestion.

"Don't you think we've put it off long enough?" she asked.

They had, of course, Odo agreed, but he had no desire to talk on such a personal level in so public a setting. He knew Kira, though, and understood that she also would not want to have a private discussion amid so many people. Trusting her, he motioned to his deputies, waving them forward. "Enjoy yourselves," he said, and the two men wasted no time in moving into the party.

Kira looked around the room. "Let's, um, find someplace a little quieter," she said, placing a hand around Odo's upper arm. She pulled him deeper into the room, and over to the door that connected the living area of Dax's quarters with her bedroom. The panel slid open before them, and Kira pulled him inside. She let go of his arm, walked farther into the room, and turned to face him. The door closed behind Odo, and the sounds of the party, though still audible, diminished considerably. "There," Kira said. "That's better."

"I'm not sure where to start," Odo said haltingly. He had spent long hours and days imagining this conversation, searching for the words that would bring about his rapprochement with Kira, but he had yet to find anything satisfactory.

"I think we need to start where all of this began," Kira said. "With you and the female changeling."

The gender-specific description of the Founder leader had always seemed strange to Odo, though he used it himself. Even though he had joined with her several times now, and with the Great Link itself, he still had no deeper understanding of their physiology than what he had learned from Dr. Bashir; he did not even know how they reproduced, or if analogues of male and female truly applied in any meaningful way to changelings. But they had to refer to her in some manner, and when Odo had asked her name, she had claimed not to have one.

"You're right, of course," he said. He could have expected Kira to open their discussion by addressing the heart of the matter. He had always appreciated her directness.

"How could you have allowed her to keep you from fulfilling your promise to our resistance cell?" she asked.

Odo listened to the question, noting that Kira had already shifted some of the responsibility for his betrayal from him to the Founder leader. Although it would be hard, he knew that he would have admit to her that he alone had been to blame for his actions. "I don't want—" he began, but stopped as he noted the cessation of the drums in the other room. "I don't want to make—" he said, but then stopped again. "Did you hear that?" he asked Kira. "It sounded like a woman threatening to cut off somebody's head."

Kira crossed the room back over to Odo. "Probably just somebody responding to one of Quark's ridiculous advances," she said. "Don't worry. I'm sure your deputies can handle it." She took Odo by the arm once more, leading him over to another set of doors. They opened, and Kira walked into Dax's 'fresher. She reached into the closet section of the small area and dragged a storage bin from it, then sat down on the short stool that stood in front of the vanity. She gestured toward the container, clearly inviting Odo to sit down opposite her.

"Do you think the lieutenant will take exception to our being here?" he asked. "I mean, this is . . . personal."

"Jadzia's not exactly a private person," Kira said. "I don't think she'd even mind if we tried on her clothing." She paused, and then added, "Well, I don't think she'd mind if *I* did." Odo looked at her, and knew from the expression on her face that she was picturing him in one of Dax's fashionable dresses. Suddenly, Kira burst into laughter. Odo watched her for a moment, and then couldn't contain his own throaty expulsion of breath; the unexpected release felt good, in particular because he shared it with Kira.

As the welcome moment continued, he moved into the small room with her and dropped down onto the bin. As their laughter subsided, Kira leaned forward and worked a control pad beside the doors, and they glided closed, completely cutting off the sounds from the living area. Odo opted to utilize the moment to pick up the conversation they had only just started. "Nerys," he said, "it wasn't the female Founder's fault that I didn't run the security diagnostic when I said I would." Their plan had been for Odo to execute the procedure at a specified time, disabling various alarms so that Rom would be able to carry out his sabotage. But Odo hadn't done that.

"I'm glad you accept responsibility for your actions," Kira said seriously, leaning forward, resting her elbows on her knees, the smile that had accompanied her chortles now gone from her face. She looked down at the floor, seeming to struggle to find what she wanted to say. At last, she lifted her gaze. "I don't understand how you could abandon your friends like that."

"It had nothing to do with my friends," Odo tried to explain. "It had only to do with me. I had an opportunity to learn about my people, to learn about the Great Link itself."

Kira's features hardened, and she sat back up, pulling away from Odo. "By joining with the female changeling?" she said, more statement than question. The contempt in her tone left no doubt about her disapproval of such an action.

"Yes," he said.

"What about the promises you made to our resistance cell?" she asked. "To the people who care about you?"

"My people care about me too," he said. It startled him a bit to hear in his voice an edge of indignation.

"I'm sure that they do," Kira said, though she sounded less than convinced of the point. "But the war isn't about you. It's about *them*." She paused, and peered around the room—to her right, into the closet area, and left, toward the shower stall—as though she might find the next thing to say hidden among Dax's things. Finally, she looked back at him and asked, "Did you have to link with her then, right at the time that we needed you?"

"It just . . . happened," Odo said, wanting to provide a better explanation than that, but unable to do so. "I didn't plan it."

"I know *you* didn't," Kira said, her indictment of the Founder leader plain.

"She didn't either," Odo avowed. "I was pressing her for information about our people and about the Great Link. I had so many questions. . . . I *still* have so many questions."

"You've had them for a long time," Kira observed. "Couldn't you have waited to ask them just a little bit later?"

Odo shook his head from side to side. "The time just seemed right," he said, not expecting Kira to understand. "It just happened. I'm not defending my choice. I'm simply telling you what took place. We linked because I asked questions, and words were insufficient to answer them. We linked, and everything else lost importance to me."

"And you don't think that was *her* doing?" Kira asked, anger lacing her voice.

"I know it wasn't," Odo said. "She didn't force me to pose the questions I did. She didn't force me to link with her."

Kira raised her hands from her knees and brought them back down with a slap. "Then how could *you* have done it?" she demanded.

"And broken the promise I made to you?" he said. Kira had extracted a pledge from him that he would not link with the changeling leader again until after the end of the war.

She looked at him, but did not answer.

"I shouldn't have done it," he told her.

"I'm glad you see that," she said. "Communicating on that level with the enemy—"

"No," Odo interrupted. "I mean that I shouldn't have made that promise to you."

"What?" Kira said. Her eyes widened in obvious incredulity. "How can you say that?"

"Imagine if somebody tried to keep you from a natural relationship with your people," he said, trying to make her see why she should never have asked of him what she had.

"The Bajorans aren't trying to destroy the inhabitants of the Alpha Quadrant," she argued, her voice loud in the enclosed area. She waited for a moment, seeming to try to calm herself, then continued with a more modulated tenor. "Odo," she said, "I wasn't trying to keep you away from your people. I was trying to protect you and me and everybody the Founders are trying to kill."

"My linking with the female changeling didn't expose the Federation and the Alpha Quadrant to danger," Odo said. "Not to that sort of danger. The Link is not about exchanging information."

"I know you say that, but it doesn't make sense to me," Kira said. "Didn't you just say that you were going to get answers to your questions through linking?"

"Yes," Odo said, "But the delivery of that sort of information—intellectual, and not emotional or sensory—has to be deliberate. In some ways, it's almost like talking. You can speak with somebody about something without revealing confidential data you know."

"It's more intimate than talking," Kira said.

"Yes," Odo acknowledged. "But the point I wanted to convey was that linking with the female Founder didn't mean that she had access to everything I knew. Nor was I compelled to reveal anything to her that I did not choose to reveal. As I've told you, linking is not about the communication of information. It's about the fusion of the thought and form, the union of idea and sensation."

Kira's head dropped. "I don't understand what that means," she said quietly.

Odo tried to find a way to describe the experience. "It's like—"

"Don't bother," Kira stopped him, sounding resigned. "I know I'll never understand what it means to link, because I'm not a changeling."

"I don't agree," Odo said. Kira looked back up at him. "Of course you're not a changeling. Of course you can't experience the Link the way I can. But I don't think that means that you can't come to understand it. I just need to determine how best to explain it to you, and maybe how to simulate the experience for you."

"Simulate it?" Kira said, clearly skeptical. "Even if you could figure out how to do that, it wouldn't be the same thing."

"Not the same thing, no," Odo said. "But it could go a long way to helping us understand one another better."

"I don't know."

"I do," Odo said. "I'm not a humanoid, but I've spent a great deal of my life in the form of a Bajoran, and so I was able to demonstrate what that means to the female Founder."

"What do you mean?" Kira asked.

"I'm not a humanoid, she's not a humanoid, so we can't experience things in the same way that humanoids do," Odo said. "We can take humanoid form, though, and I took it a step further for the female changeling and approximated the humanoid form of linking with her."

Kira's jaw fell. "What are you saying?" she asked, clearly aghast.

"I wanted to show her—"

She bolted to her feet, her presence seeming to fill the small room. "Are you saying that, in addition to linking with her, you slept with her?"

"Well . . . yes," Odo said, feeling somewhat offended by Kira's reaction. "But it wasn't—" He stopped as Kira reached for the control panel beside the doors. An instant later, they slid open. "Nerys," he said, trying to keep her from leaving. She didn't respond, but rushed past him, her right leg brushing against his left as she did so.

As he turned to watch her stride across the bedroom, he realized that things between them would never be the same again.

3

Odo sat on the speck of land, his back against one of the rock spires. He had raised his eyes to the dim sky, but he no longer saw the stars as he recalled that night in Dax's closet with Kira. Those hours with her seemed so far away, the events of their lives intervening between then and now like a broad chasm that forever separated yesterday from today. He could peer across the gulf and see what had come before, but he could never return there.

Even awash in his memories, Odo felt the passage of time in a way he did not within the Great Link. He'd come to understand that he needed that, needed to measure the hours and days, the weeks and months as they elapsed. If there was to be change in the Founders, if he was to help guide them from their past of suspicion, fear, and violence, to a future of acceptance, understanding, and peace, it would take time. The Link seemed slow to change, but not impervious to it.

When he'd first rejoined his changeling family after the war, Odo had found his people mired in unrest. As individual Founders came back to the Link, bringing with them reports of the continuing outcome of their defeat to the powers of the Alpha Quadrant, the turmoil increased. Odo hoped that his own return would calm their communal emotion, but the reverse was true. His rejoining prompted both excitement and agitation, the Link joyous to have back one of the Hundred, but

troubled at the ideas he brought back with him. Indeed, his notions of peaceful coexistence with solids, and nonviolent resolution to disturbances within the Dominion, were met not only
with skepticism, but with defiance. The Founders reacted
swiftly and severely to rebellions kindled on some of their subject worlds by the Alpha Quadrant's victory in the war, sending
in Vorta with Jem'Hadar troops to restore order.

Eventually, though, Odo had perceived a change. The Link
seemed to settle down, and resistance to his ideas diminished,
if only slightly. But then he left to pursue the rumors of an Ascendant, and the reports that had led him to Opaka. When he
came back this time, he expected to find his people in much
the same emotional state as when he'd left them. Instead, he
encountered tremendous agitation, which had only increased
in the weeks that followed. Now, as he pulled his gaze from the
heavens and peered out over the Great Link, he saw that its
surface had grown choppy, and he knew that the return of Laas
had stirred even greater emotion in the Founders.

Ahead of Odo, a whine suddenly grew out of the silence, as
though emanating from the surface of the islet. He quickly
stood, not comfortable being seen in such a relaxed position. A
moment later, the air seemed to solidify, glints of light flashing
and then thickening to a mass of color. When the transport had
completed, it had deposited Weyoun there.

"Founder," he said, and this time, Odo felt a look of annoyance cross his features before he could stop it. "Odo," Weyoun
corrected himself. "I noted your prolonged presence here, and
I wanted to see if you required anything."

"No, Weyoun, I don't," Odo said. "But thank you." Most of
the islands sprinkled throughout the changeling sea—including this one—had communications equipment cached on them
so that a Founder could contact any of the Jem'Hadar vessels
in orbit. But the Vorta also monitored the planet, an added precaution against interlopers, and a means of anticipating the
needs of the Great Link.

Weyoun inclined his head slightly. "It is always my pleasure to serve," he said. He took a couple of paces toward Odo.
"Will you be transporting up to—"

"Weyoun," Odo said sharply, holding the flat of his hand

out. The Vorta stopped walking, just as a grinding sound emerged from beneath his feet. He had stepped into the remains of the dead changeling.

"Odo?" he asked, peering down at the gray ashes. He backed up quickly, then looked up with an expression that appeared equal parts disbelief and dismay. Odo did not know if Weyoun had ever seen the dusty vestiges of a dead Founder, or if he reacted simply from intuition. It seemed apparent, though, that he at least suspected the nature of what lay before him.

"It is a dead changeling," Odo confirmed. "Laas brought it back with him."

Weyoun's mouth opened soundlessly as he regarded the mass of ashes, the look on his face transformed now into one of horror. Odo went to him, striding across the islet until he stood beside him. He reached out and took hold of Weyoun's upper arms, forcing the Vorta to turn and face him. "Weyoun, it's all right," he intoned. "It's—" He paused, wondering about the truth of his own words. How could the death of a Founder ever be all right? And yet, the universe would not end, the life of the Great Link would not stop. Odo still had responsibilities, still had duties to perform, chief among them right now, learning the Great Link's reaction to Laas and then dealing with it accordingly.

"It's all right," he told Weyoun once more. "Go back to the ship. I'll probably beam up later."

Weyoun nodded vacantly, then stepped back and reached for the transporter control wrapped about his wrist. Before he could trigger it, Odo said, "Keep this to yourself for now." Though he did not necessarily agree, he knew that the Founders would be reluctant to allow news of the death of one of their own to disseminate through their empire. Weyoun nodded again, and then activated the transporter. Odo watched as his body dematerialized amid a quick shimmering of light.

Alone again on the islet, he considered what to do with the remains of the lost changeling. He realized that he did not know if his people practiced funerary customs. When the Founder who'd infiltrated *Defiant* had been killed—accidentally pushed by Odo against the containment field surrounding the warp core—Starfleet had taken possession of the remains. And when the unformed changeling that had been brought to DS9 and nurtured by Odo had died, it had somehow infused itself into Odo's body. The latter event caused him to wonder now if incorporating the remains of the dead back into the Great Link might be what the Founders normally did. He would need to find out.

Odo walked to the edge of the land, where he turned his mind's eye inward, to the flows and eddies of his changeling anatomy. He felt his cells quicken, and his body gelled into an inchoate mass. He reached out over the Link and down, into its wavering collective.

Beneath the surface, the Great Link roiled. Living currents rushed past his shapeless though still gathered form. Thoughts and feelings inundated him as he let himself go. His body extended outward, spreading into flats and gyres, wisps and strands. He came into contact with more and more of his people, and through them, with the rest.

The immense sea of changelings churned in a frenzy, driven, Odo perceived, by the trauma of a dead Founder brought home to them, and by Laas's demand for answers. Flashes of great sorrow buffeted Odo, interspersed with bolts of anger and opposition. Echoes of Laas's pleas reached him, repeating the questions that Laas had asked him earlier.

And there's something else, Odo thought. Something that perched on the edge of discernment, segregated by the high emotions flooding the Link. He reached for it, attuning his cells to it, sending the filaments of his body into closer contact with those Founders from whom he sensed—

Unease. Expectation.

For a month now, since his return to the Great Link after his travels to Ee and Deep Space 9, that combination of anxiety and eagerness among his people had persisted. When the havoc caused by Laas had subsided, Odo would have to resume his pursuit of an explanation. For now, though, he wanted to communicate with his fellow member of the Hundred.

He concentrated, searching through the innumerable connections he shared with other changelings, seeking Laas. Around Odo, beside him, against him, figures morphed into and out of existence, transient shapes embodying thought and sensation. He sought Laas in every contact, and beyond. He heard echoes of his questions—*When were the Hundred sent out? Why did you send us? How could you abandon us like that?*—but could not locate the mind that had originally posed them.

Within the flaxen deep, Odo felt a Founder attempt to bond with him, and he opened himself up to it. Their connection grew as more and more of the other changeling's cells interwove with his own. A tranquillity exuded through their junction, a stillness that diverged from the furor infusing the rest of the Great Link. Odo sensed a long arc of time, and of purpose, and wondered why this Founder wanted to join with him.

The other changeling shifted, the range of its body contracting, drawing into an embryonic hulk beside Odo. The serenity it radiated receded then, as it spun into definition, spawning limbs and features and colors. Finally, Odo found the thin, papery structures of his own body wrapped about the humanoid form of Laas.

The *form* of Laas, but not the real Laas. Just as it had not been the real Nerys.

Odo understood what had happened—he had been sought out by this changeling, just as he had sought out Laas—but not why. In response, the figure of Laas dissolved in a whirl of movement, replaced an instant later by a Bajoran. In his present amorphous state, Odo possessed no eyes, but his changeling senses nevertheless allowed him a clear image of the man. He searched his memory, but could not identify him.

Who is this? Odo asked, sending the question through his link with the other changeling. At once, the man's face changed, but continued to be unrecognizable. And then it changed again, and again, and several times more, revealing to Odo a series of Bajoran strangers. Odo studied the visage of the final man in the sequence. Like the others, it bore the effects of a life lived over many years: deep crags lined the face, the flesh of the jawline and neck sagged as though gravity had begun to assert itself over it, and frail, colorless hair hung down limply.

Time, Odo thought. He was aware of time, a long stretch of time, and he realized that he had just been presented something like that, etched in the series of old Bajoran men paraded past him. Again, he took meaning from the forms: not time, but *age*. Age, and experience. This Founder who communicated with Odo had been around for centuries, perhaps millennia.

Through their link came confirmation of that conclusion. But the ancient changeling conveyed more than merely an introduction of itself. This also articulated an answer to one of Laas's questions: *When were the Hundred sent out?*

Long ago, Odo now understood. Seemingly further in the past than he had thought. But could that truly be? He himself had been found adrift in the Denorios Belt decades ago, not *centuries* ago.

Odo visualized the internal currents of his changeling body, and moved, pulling his malleable cells into himself. He pictured the humanoid form he took, and then altered the familiar image. When he finished shapeshifting, he floated next to the old changeling as the humanoid Odo, but aged, as though he'd lived centuries as a Bajoran.

Beside him, the ancient Founder transformed again. As Odo awaited the end result of the shift, the word *indurane* occurred to him—Bajoran for *ancient*—and he decided to apply it to this changeling. Although the Founders generally eschewed the use of names, Odo did not. In fact, over the years, he had found it not only inconvenient to have to refer to the changeling leader without any sort of proper appellation, but often felt insulted by terms such as *the female Founder,* as though only one such individual existed. He had often invoked such terms himself, but did not like doing so.

The aged Founder—Indurane—completed his alterations, this time becoming the double of the wizened Odo, a clear confirmation that Odo had lived far more than the four decades since he'd been found. He'd considered this possibility before, when back on DS9, Laas had revealed that he'd begun his own life among the Varalans two hundred years earlier. But Odo had concluded that Laas must simply have been sent out a century and a half prior to Odo. Now, though, he was being told something different, something that seemed not to make sense. For when Odo had been discovered by the Bajorans, he'd been unformed and unknowing, a shapeless mass that lacked the knowledge and ability to modify its own form into anything definite.

Floating in the changeling deep, Odo asked the question of Indurane by changing form once more. Odo gave up his face and limbs, and all his humanoid traits, collapsing into a nebulous sac of metaplasm. He surrendered control of his body, and permitted himself to tumble down through the changeling tide. He existed as when he had been found: unformed, unable, an infant.

The old Founder followed Odo down, still linked with him, still in the semblance of a wrinkled, humanoid Odo. Time passed, and they neared the surface of the planet, the lower bound of the Great Link. Odo noted with appreciation, as he always did, the complex shapes that decorated the nether landscape. Although they had only inhabited this world for five years, the Founders had already modified vast tracts of this land, carving into the rock, sculpting it to fit their needs and desires. Odo recalled the structures he had installed in his quarters on DS9, and the pleasure he had taken assuming their myriad forms. But his small menagerie of shape and texture paled in comparison to the massive and diverse collection below. A geometer's paradise, the topography held all manner of figures, including cylinders and spheres, planes and polyhedra. Surfaces varied from smooth to rough, hard to soft, and every grain and durity in between. Indescribable manifolds abutted tunnels and ridges, hills and chasms. Odo had spent days down there himself, and had never emulated the same shape twice.

He came to rest beside a hexagrammic antiprism, Indurane settling beside him. Odo waited for an answer to his question—*How can I be centuries old when I was an infant just decades ago?*—and Indurane answered with another change to his shape. The aged Odo-form disappeared, shrinking into an unformed changeling infant.

Not an infant, came a thought directed to Odo through the link with Indurane. Beside him, the indistinct structure seemed to fade away, and Odo understood that Indurane had shifted his cells to match those of the Founders surrounding them in the Great Link in order to produce the effect.

I don't understand, Odo communicated, even as he thought he did. In response, Indurane formed an infant changeling once more, only to then dissolve its form, as though it had never existed.

I don't understand, Odo thought again, and again, Indurane became the image of an infant changeling, and then disintegrated into seeming nothingness. Odo resisted the apparent meaning in the transformation, gleaning the unacceptable implications of the message before he even acknowledged its veracity. He refused to—

There are no changeling infants, Indurane told him.

Odo scoffed at the claim, even as he dreaded that it might be true.

There are no changeling infants, Indurane repeated, *because changelings cannot procreate.*

The large, interlacing metal doors separated with a sharp clang, then hummed smoothly apart. Kira walked into the sizable shuttlebay of the Starfleet vessel *Mjolnir,* its commanding officer at her side. The two women walked between the numerous and varied support craft housed aboard the Norway-class starship, wending their way through work bees, support modules, maintenance platforms, shuttlepods, and short- and long-range shuttles.

"I'm actually a little disappointed in the numbers," Kira said, holding out a personal access display device for Captain Hoku to see. "My chief engineer was told that the upgraded waveguides on the new runabouts would provide a significant increase in warp velocity." Kira pointed to a section on the padd detailing performance expectations and field-trial results of the new craft. While both sets of figures represented improvements over the capabilities of Deep Space 9's current complement of runabouts, the differences amounted to only marginal advances.

"If you study the final specifications, I suspect you'll find that no new waveguides were installed," Hoku said. "My guess is that they haven't even been manufactured yet. The shipyards are still overburdened just trying to replenish the fleet."

"I know," Kira agreed. "Believe me, I know." She felt that

she appreciated as well as anybody the staggering cost to Starfleet—in both matériel and personnel—of the Dominion War. She had witnessed firsthand enough ships being blasted to nothingness in the unforgiving vacuum of space, had read enough names on the rolls of the dead and wounded.

Checking the production log at the top left of the padd display, Kira saw that the new runabout had been constructed at the Antares Fleet Yards. Many of the more powerful starships had been built there, she knew, and such vessels composed a priority for the Federation these days, given the loss of defenses incurred during the war. She supposed that she should consider the station fortunate to be getting a new runabout at all.

Kira deactivated the padd with a touch and dropped it to her side. Not wishing to dwell on remembrances of the war, she thanked Hoku for her hospitality. In the ninety minutes since *Rio Grande* had touched down in *Mjolnir*'s shuttlebay, the two captains had spent most of that time in Hoku's quarters, first completing the formalities of transferring responsibility for the new runabout to Deep Space 9, and then catching each other up on their lives. During *Defiant*'s recent three-month exploration of the Gamma Quadrant, *Mjolnir* had initially been scheduled to stand in at the station, but Starfleet Command had then altered those plans. The ship had arrived at DS9 weeks early, and had spent just enough time there to allow Admiral Akaar to meet with Kira. She and Hoku had been able to speak only briefly, and only in their official Starfleet capacities.

Today, though, the two friends had at last been able to visit. For her part, Hoku had asked about Kira's captaincy, Bajor's entry into the Federation, and the new first minister. In turn, Kira had wanted to discuss the hearsay intimating an impending promotion for Hoku to rear admiral, but it ended up that the *Mjolnir* captain had heard fewer rumors about it than she had.

As the two women came abreast of a work bee, Kira spied their reflections in one of its wide viewing ports. Each wearing a Starfleet captain's uniform and standing approximately the same height, they might have looked a great deal alike, but did not. Although cropped short, Hoku's blond hair had something of a wild appearance about it, and her brilliant blue-green eyes peered out of a milky, delicate complexion. Most distinctively, she carried herself with an elegance and confidence that almost suggested royalty.

As for Kira's own aspect, even more than two months after her being commissioned as a Starfleet captain, it still occasionally startled her to see herself in anything but a Bajoran Militia uniform. Just when she thought she'd become accustomed to her new habiliments, she would find herself surprised by an inadvertent glance at her likeness in a mirror or, as in this case, a viewport. The same thing had occurred during the final weeks of the war, when she'd gone to Cardassia as a Starfleet commander.

Rounding the pointed bow of a type-ten shuttle, Kira and Hoku arrived at the bay's landing pad. The new runabout sat directly ahead of them, its forward hatch on the port side swung open, its interior lights shining out onto the decking. To the left, *Rio Grande* appeared dark, its hatches closed. Past the runabouts, in the direction the craft faced, the shuttlebay doors stood open. Through them, the sable sprawl of the universe, sprinkled with countless specks of stars, provided an impressive backdrop. A thin, electric-blue strip of light bordered the wide aperture, signaling the operation of the force field that prevented the atmosphere in the bay from boiling off into space. Beyond the opening, the inner hulls of *Mjolnir*'s nacelle struts stretched away on both the port and starboard sides, extending outward in shades of gray and white.

As Kira and Hoku approached the new runabout, Lieutenant Bowers exited down its steps. "Captain Hoku," he acknowledged, then addressed Kira. "Captain, we've completed our diagnostics and the preflight checks, and we're all set to go." He pointed toward the forward side of the craft, and added, "Specialist Lynn finished with the name." When Kira and her crew had arrived here to take possession of the new runabout, the craft had already been adorned with its Starfleet registry—NCC-75353—but its name had not been applied, as the privilege for selecting that designation fell to DS9's commander. Once *Rio Grande* had touched down, Captain Hoku had assigned one of her crew to add to the hull the name Kira had chosen.

"Yolja," Hoku read now. "I know that Starfleet runabouts are all dedicated for *Earth* rivers, like *Rio Grande—"* She nodded her head in the direction of the other runabout. "—But there's no terrestrial waterway called Yolja that I'm aware of," she finished, a knowing look in her eye.

"It's on Bajor," Kira verified. "In Kendra Province."

"That's right," Hoku said.

"This is the first one we've given a Bajoran name," Kira said, pleased with her selection.

Hoku smiled. "Now seems an appropriate time," she offered.

"I thought so too," Kira said, nodding in agreement.

Hoku glanced inside *Yolja*—young Ensign Aleco had appeared in the hatchway, Kira saw—and then looked over her shoulder, her gaze coming to rest on *Rio Grande,* its systems clearly powered down. "Where is Taran'atar?" Hoku asked. Kira noted her conspicuously conversational demeanor, which displayed no hint of concern, nor even of real curiosity. She'd also observed that the *Mjolnir* captain hadn't posted security outside the shuttlebay, though Kira suspected that the ship's internal sensors had been trained on this location since *Rio Grande*'s arrival. No matter that Taran'atar had lived aboard DS9 for more than half a year now; as a Jem'Hadar and a formerly active soldier of the Dominion, he would continue to be monitored closely by Starfleet.

Particularly where we're going, Kira thought, and a knot of tension tightened in her abdomen.

"He's still aboard *Rio Grande,*" Bowers reported of the Jem'Hadar. When Kira and her crew had set down aboard *Mjolnir,* they'd been greeted by Captain Hoku. Kira had introduced Taran'atar—as well as Bowers and Aleco—and then she'd followed the captain to her quarters for their meeting. During their discussions, Hoku had expressed a desire to speak at greater length with the Jem'Hadar. Kira had explained Taran'atar's discomfort with social situations, and had suggested that such an interaction might be better at a later date. Hoku had understood, and so Kira believed that her query now about his whereabouts concerned her wish, not to talk with him, but to confirm that a well-trained and potentially dangerous Dominion soldier did not currently roam the corridors of her ship.

"Well, please convey my satisfaction in meeting him," Hoku said.

"I will," Kira told her. Then, to Bowers and Aleco, she said, "Lieutenant, Ensign, it's time we departed."

"Yes, sir," Bowers said. He mounted the steps up into *Yolja*, Aleco moving into the cockpit ahead of him. The two men would take the new runabout back to Deep Space 9, while Kira and Taran'atar headed for a different destination.

As *Yolja*'s hatchway folded closed, Kira turned back to Hoku. "It was great to finally see you again, Kalena," she said, making reference to the missed opportunity at DS9 a few months back. Kira held out her right hand, and Hoku took it in her own.

"And you, Nerys," the captain responded. "I'll have to see if *Mjolnir* can put in for some R and R at Bajor one of these days."

"Maybe when you're an admiral," Kira joked.

"Maybe," Hoku said with a chuckle.

They parted, Hoku heading back toward the doors through which they'd entered the bay, and Kira for *Rio Grande*. She quickly accessed the controls behind a small panel in the hull, triggered the hatch open, and climbed into the runabout. Inside, the lights came up, increasing the dim illumination already coming into the cabin through the bow viewports. Seated at a forward station, Taran'atar said nothing as Kira boarded the craft. Taking the chair beside him, she said, "I see you're anxious for us to be on our way."

"I am merely prepared for the journey ahead," he said stonily, "and for anything that is required of me."

Again, Kira felt a twist of anxiety. *I am prepared . . . for anything that is required of me.* What did that mean, exactly? What did he think would be required of him, and by whom?

Nearly a month ago, when Taran'atar had first made his request to visit Ananke Alpha, Kira hadn't known what to make of it; in truth, she still didn't. She'd neither supported nor hindered his petition, instead taking the matter directly to Admiral Ross. Knowing the principals involved, and wanting to forge whatever good will he could with Taran'atar—as well as with the legion of Jem'Hadar, and ultimately with the Dominion itself—the admiral had consented to the appeal. Although not sure that Ross had made the right decision, Kira had chosen to trust Taran'atar. She'd agreed to escort him on his journey, and the scheduled rendezvous with *Mjolnir* had provided an opportunity to do so without drawing unwanted attention.

She leaned forward in her chair and worked the runabout's primary station, cycling *Rio Grande* up to full power. For a few moments, only the beat of the engines and the electronic chirps of the controls dressed the cabin, until she opened a comm channel to *Yolja*. With Bowers, she coordinated the launches of the two runabouts, and obtained clearance from *Mjolnir*'s bridge, currently under the watch of the ship's first officer. A minute later, Kira watched through *Rio Grande*'s viewports as *Yolja* glided forward just a couple of meters above the decking. It reached the force field and punched through, a flash of bright, blue pinpoints sparking about the hull as it flew out into space. The new runabout immediately assumed a downward trajectory in order to clear the wing structures that supported *Mjolnir*'s warp nacelles.

After confirming that *Yolja* had reached a safe distance, Kira worked the flight controls. "Prepare for launch," she said automatically, her fingers skipping in practiced movements across the main panel, extracting from it the measured tones that accompanied its operation. The runabout lifted from the deck, its antigravs engaged, then followed *Yolja*'s path, first off of the ship, and then down and away from *Mjolnir*'s nacelle supports. "Setting course for Ananke Alpha," she announced as she set *Rio Grande*'s navigational parameters. Around them, the thrum of the drive rose and then evened out as it took the small ship to warp.

Kira studied the readouts for a few moments more, verifying the runabout's route, velocity, and overall performance. Satisfied, she leaned back and peered over at Taran'atar. He still sat stiffly in his chair, facing forward. She opened her mouth to say something, but closed it again when she could not determine how to start.

Although Taran'atar could never have been accurately described as social, Kira had perceived an increased iciness in him of late. He'd been more reticent, less approachable, and had not seemed as inclined as previously to spend time observing life among the residents of the station, the task Odo had set him. Kira knew that Taran'atar had recently found it necessary to sleep a few times a week, an aberration for his species. She'd assumed that had been troubling him, and that the changes she'd perceived in him had been the result. Still, perhaps more than at any time since he'd arrived at DS9, she felt intensely aware of him being a Jem'Hadar, along with all that implied: the physical prowess, the extensive military training and experience, and the determination bred into him to follow and serve the Founders. And that last fact concerned Kira more than anything else right now: Taran'atar's devotion to his gods. After all, what would she not do herself in order to satisfy the will of a Prophet?

"Are you looking forward to this?" she asked him, the monotonous drone of the warp drive an undercurrent of sound in the cabin.

"I am doing what my duty dictates I do," he said, continuing to face forward.

"Right, I understand that," Kira said, although when Taran'atar had first made his request, he'd phrased it in a way that had implied his motivation to be more personal. "But I thought that you might still *want* to do this, apart from its being your duty." When he did not respond, she asked, "Is that the case?"

Taran'atar turned to look at her. His face bore no discernible expression, but the gaze of his dark eyes held her as surely as if he'd forcibly restrained her. "I am doing what my duty dictates I do," he said again. "That is all." He clearly did not appreciate being questioned, particularly about his motivations. Kira had recognized that in him a long time ago: he knew his purpose, and that purpose determined his actions; he considered questions irrelevant and a waste of time.

Kira nodded to Taran'atar, acknowledging his response, then looked back over at her station. In her peripheral vision, she saw him do the same. *I have to trust him,* she thought. During his stay at DS9, he'd given her no reason not to do so. He'd followed her orders without question, as Odo had instructed him to do, and he'd been instrumental in the successful resolution of a crisis on more than one occasion. More than that, the success of Taran'atar's visit to the Alpha Quadrant could influence the course of relations with the Dominion for some time to come. Kira therefore felt that she had to do everything she could to help him fulfill his mission. And right now, that meant trusting him.

She leaned forward and touched a control, then another, checking *Rio Grande*'s course. Then, with nothing else to do, she settled back in her chair, lacing her fingers together in her lap. She thought about getting a *raktajino,* but decided against it. Instead, she gazed through the viewport and out at the stars as the runabout flew on, headed for Ananke Alpha, the Federation prison facility where Taran'atar would soon visit the Founder leader.

Exhaustion and an unflagging ache enveloped Odo, like those times when, after holding form for an extended period, he was unable to return to his natural state. Anger welled within him, directed not at Indurane, but at the whole of the Great Link. Had his people hidden this information from him—information obviously essential to understanding them—or had they sent one of their number to lie to him now for some concealed purpose? They had done both in the past, but in this case, Odo simply could not credit what he had just been told.

You're lying, he told Indurane through their interface. Odo expected the charge to be met with denial, but instead, Indurane replied with a question.

Have you ever known a changeling infant? he asked.

I *was a changeling infant,* Odo responded. *Laas was a changeling infant.*

Indurane seemed to pause before answering. Around them, the Great Link continued to stir agitatedly. But Odo could not attend to those matters right now; he had to concentrate on his union with Indurane.

Were you an infant? the old changeling finally asked. *Was Laas?*

Odo wanted to answer affirmatively, definitively, but his career as an investigator told him that he needed to consider the evidence before he could reach a meaningful conclusion. He drew on the facts he had at hand, and found few that bore on Indurane's assertion. Odo knew that he had been discovered in the Bajoran system, in the Denorios Belt, decades ago. While he had only a vague memory of the event—merely an impression really—Bajoran and Cardassian records, as well as several Bajorans and Cardassians, provided support that it had actually occurred. Odo's own awareness had come later, along with the ability to consciously shapeshift. Laas had related a similar tale about his own life, although he had been found by the Varalans more than two centuries ago.

Little in either Odo's story or Laas's, but for their limited memories of their pasts, provided any sort of substantiation that they had both been infants at some point. Such a deduction relied more on assumption than actual fact. It seemed clear that both he and Laas had each been *unformed* at one time in their lives, but did it unavoidably follow that they had been infants?

Odo recalled the words of the changeling leader when he had first met her. He had been drawn to the world in the Omarion Nebula where the Founders had lived then, and had told her that he wished he could have remembered the place as his home. "It's understandable that you cannot," she'd explained. "You were still newly formed when you left us."

"Newly formed?" he had asked her. "You mean I was an infant?"

"An infant," she had replied, as though pondering a concept that did not entirely make sense to her—or perhaps to any changeling. She'd then finished by saying, "Yes," but Odo allowed now that the answer could have been a part of her calculations in dispensing limited information about the Founders to him. For later, when he'd questioned her about how long he had been away from the Great Link, she'd said, "A long time." Odo realized now that, if he had been away for, say, a century, then he had clearly not been an infant when he'd been found in the Bajor system just a few decades ago. And that implied that being an unformed changeling did not mean being an infant changeling.

But how can that be true? Odo wondered, still unable to believe that his people could not reproduce. He clung physically to Indurane, their cells meshing through their link, as he contemplated what he grasped of how species survived in the universe. Those that developed characteristics necessary and sufficient to their continued existence endured; those that did not met with extinction. And absolutely vital for a species to survive, it needed to be able to produce offspring. For without succeeding generations, how could the natural attrition caused by death be overcome? Unless . . . unless the Founders did not experience death.

Odo rejected the idea at once. *We are not immortal,* he offered, part declaration, part question. As fanciful as the notion of an unending lifetime seemed, it would at least provide some sort of justification for Indurane's contention that the Founders could not procreate.

Intertwined with Odo, Indurane modified his cells again, matching them to their surroundings so that it appeared as though he had vanished. The significance of the shift remained the same as earlier: nonexistence. Indurane concluded by affirming the idea that Odo had hesitantly proffered: *We are not immortal.*

But then how can the Founders lack the ability to reproduce? Odo questioned. *How could we have possibly evolved that way?*

The Founders did not evolve, Indurane averred, his cells adjusting to form a shapeless mass once more. *We are not some random event in space and time,* he continued, his contempt for such a concept manifest. *We are not the result of some fortuitous juxtaposition of matter and energy.*

But then how? Odo reiterated, even as Indurane's body grew, the volume of space he filled increasing radically. Left as a small body linked to the suddenly sizable changeling, Odo waited for Indurane's thoughts to reinforce the answer he had given by way of his form.

The Great Link was generated by design, he claimed. *The Founder population was created in its entirety by the Progenitor.*

Disconcerted, Odo thought of the Bajorans. His people were different from Kira's kind, he knew, this belief was different from theirs, and yet he could not fathom the reality of what Indurane had just revealed: a Founder god.

Kira looked up from her readouts as the tractor beam took hold of *Rio Grande*. Already she'd had to relinquish control of the runabout's weapons, and now its drive systems. The ship shuddered mildly, the inertial dampers disrupted briefly by the contact with the directed-energy field. Through the forward viewports, Kira spied the telltale blue luminescence that she knew now surrounded the runabout. Just visible past the glow, Ananke Alpha hung alone in space, a slim, crescent-shaped slice of the sphere illuminated by the planetless star that hosted it.

Located in a remote and untraveled region of Federation space, in a system that offered virtually nothing in either useful natural resources or interesting characteristics, the facility provided little likelihood for detection by even itinerant voyagers. The dark metal object measured less than a kilometer in diameter, and maintained a low sensor profile, emitting microwaves that mimicked the background radiation of the universe. A lightless speck that saw extremely few visitors, and whose few inhabitants practiced almost complete radio silence, Ananke Alpha would have been difficult to find without assistance. A small sensor-and-communications station tucked indiscernibly into an asteroid—one of several, Kira assumed—had passively scanned *Rio Grande* when it had approached the system, had authenticated its identity, and then guided it toward the facility. Now, Kira disengaged power to the engines so that the prison's tractor beam could bring the runabout in the rest of the way; had she not done so, the crew of Ananke Alpha would have fired upon the ship.

The procedures enforced here had been meticulously delineated for Kira by Admiral Ross. Until their meeting, Kira hadn't even been aware of the prison's existence, though she easily could have presupposed the necessity for something like it within the Federation. According to the admiral, it had been designed and constructed half a century ago, for the purpose of incarcerating a small number of criminals, those evaluated as the most dangerous and the most difficult to confine. After the end of the Dominion War, the few prisoners detained there had been transferred to other facilities, and the prison had been overhauled and modified so that it could safely and effectively hold its new, single inmate: the female changeling.

Kira peered again through the viewports—she could now make out the rest of the globe's shadowed body—and then over at Taran'atar. He'd said very little during their long journey, and only when Kira had spoken first. All of his responses had been terse, if not unfriendly. Since he'd arrived on Deep Space 9, he'd tended toward the laconic in his communications, but his taciturnity had peaked during this time aboard the runabout and the days leading up to it.

Why shouldn't he act that way? Kira thought. How would she feel, how would she behave, if presented with the prospect of a one-on-one meeting with a Prophet? While she did not consider the Founders to be gods—far from it—she knew that the Vorta and the Jem'Hadar did.

But he just spent weeks with Odo, she argued with herself. She'd observed some of their interactions, and although Taran'atar had been deferential to Odo, perhaps even reverential toward him, he hadn't been awed into near-silence. Now, though—

Admit it, she reproached herself. *Admit what's really concerning you.* Kira typically had little difficulty expressing her feelings, either to herself or to others. If anything, the reverse had been true, and she'd had to learn to be more diplomatic during her tenure on DS9.

"Taran'atar," she said.

"Yes?" He responded without looking at her. She said nothing more, waiting until at last he turned toward her. "Yes, Captain?" he said.

"Why do you want to visit the Founder?" she asked him.

"I've already told you my reasons," he said, turning back to face forward once more.

"I know that," Kira said, keeping her tone even. "I'm asking you to tell me again."

He did not answer right away, and for a moment, Kira thought that he might not reply at all. But in the months he'd been on the station, he had yet to disobey any order she'd given him. He did not do so now. "I wish to be of some small service to my gods," he said.

"How?" Kira persisted.

He looked at her again. "The Founder has been alone for a long time now, separated from the Great Link since shortly after the war started, and isolated from the entire Dominion since the end of hostilities," Taran'atar explained. "I hope to be able to offer some relief for that circumstance."

This had been the reason—the very *personal* reason, she thought—that Taran'atar had cited when he'd first come to her with his request. It sounded plausible to her, both then and now. Taran'atar had obviously convinced Admiral Ross of his motives as well. But regardless of the justification for the visit, just the fact that Taran'atar would be interacting with the female Founder concerned Kira. What if the changeling gave him new orders? Would the immediacy of those orders supersede Odo's directives to Taran'atar? And what if . . . what if—

"Are you going to attempt to free the Founder?" she asked bluntly. Like herself Kira knew Taran'atar appreciated candor. Still, his horned brow raised in apparent surprise at her question.

"No, I have no intention of breaking the Founder from her prison," he said. "For the sake of the Dominion, she has decided on this course, and I must respect that." In exchange for Odo saving the Great Link from extinction by providing the cure for the disease wracking their people, the female changeling had agreed to stand trial and accept responsibility for her actions with respect to the war. In the end, though, she'd waived her Federation right to a trial and had pled guilty to the numerous charges leveled against her. She had been sentenced to life imprisonment in a maximum-security facility, where she would be kept in isolation, both as part of her punishment, and as a safety precaution. Unsure of the ethics of interning for life such a long-lived being—the Founder had admitted to an existence that had lasted more than seven centuries already—the Federation had also decided to revisit the judgment every fifty years.

Kira considered what Taran'atar had told her, and realized that he hadn't entirely quelled her concerns. He had spoken of his intentions only, and not of his possible actions. "What if the Founder wants you to free her?" she asked.

"Captain Kira," Taran'atar said, "I have no doubt that if the Founder wished to escape her confinement, she could do so without my assistance."

Rio Grande was jarred slightly, and Kira recognized the sensation of the runabout passing through a forcefield. She looked again through the viewports, and saw that they had been towed close enough to Ananke Alpha now that she could make out features on its surface: weapons turrets, shield generators, and directly ahead, a single-paneled door opening to reveal a shuttlebay. "My question wasn't about your intentions, Taran'atar," she said, and looked over at him again. "What will you do if the Founder orders you to break her out? Would you disobey her, or do as she commanded?"

"Admiral Ross asked the same question," Taran'atar told her. "Captain, if you were asked to do something by one of your gods—by one of the Prophets—can you imagine a scenario in which you would not abide them?"

No, Kira thought at once, and did not like the answer. Taran'atar had implied an equivalence between her potential actions and his own, meaning that if asked to do so by the Founder, he would abet her attempt to flee her captivity. Kira did not believe they would succeed; Ross had described the facility as a fortress, essentially impossible to escape. He'd maintained that any effort to break out of Ananke Alpha would result in failure, with the death of the prisoner a possible outcome. And though it seemed clear to Kira that the death of the Founder would serve neither the Federation nor the Dominion—

Suddenly, as the runabout rumbled again—obviously passing through a second forcefield—Kira understood the point Taran'atar had been trying to make to her. "No, I can't imagine disobeying the Prophets," she said, "unless, by my doing as they say, they might come to harm."

"Then we are of like mind," Taran'atar said, "for I would not follow the Founder's instructions to help her escape her prison, not at the risk of her life."

Kira nodded, believing him. "Thank you," she said. "It's not that I don't trust you—"

"But it is," Taran'atar asserted. "You don't trust me. But that is of no concern to me." The light in the cabin increased as the tractor beam pulled *Rio Grande* into Ananke Alpha's brightly illuminated shuttlebay. "What I find . . . interesting," Taran'atar continued, "is that even though you do not trust me, you still asked me what I was going to do. If I had planned to break the Founder free of this prison, do you think I would have admitted that to you?"

"Yes," she said, and she could see again that she had startled Taran'atar with her response. "Yes, because of your dedication to the Founders. Odo directed you to follow my orders, and when I ask you a question, it's clear that I am expecting you to answer me honestly and completely. For you to do otherwise would be contrary to what Odo wanted you to do."

Kira felt the gentle impact as *Rio Grande* touched down. The sapphire radiance of the tractor beam fled as the energy field released the runabout. She stood up and moved toward the portside hatch.

"You are correct, of course," Taran'atar said as he got up from his chair and joined her. "And I have told you the truth."

"I know you have," Kira said. But as she reached for the controls that would open the hatch, she thought something different:

I'm about to find out.

Wearing his humanoid appearance, Odo paced across the islet, then back again, his thoughts a storm of confusion, doubt, and concern. After communing with Indurane, he'd retreated here, wanting time alone to process what he had learned—or at least what he had been told. Since then, he'd spent a considerable amount of time debating both the reality and the content of the ancient Founder's pronouncements. Although he had never even conjectured much of what the old changeling had communicated to him, Odo now found explained several questions he'd long contemplated. For him, though, the details proved far worse than any disappointments he'd suffered from not fully understanding his people.

Odo leaned against the rock spires situated at one end of the islet, the heel of one hand resting against each. He gazed between the two formations, out at the fluctuating mass of the Great Link. The notion of their population as one—a concept often advocated by the Founder leader—had never led Odo even to consider that the changelings did not multiply. But even as the idea readily explained the intense paranoia of his people—since each Founder death would move their species closer to extinction—it seemed almost impossible to credit, more likely a ridiculous lie than an implausible truth. He peered over his shoulder at the ashes of the dead changeling, and wondered again how a species could survive without the ability to produce succeeding generations. And yet . . . thinking back, Odo realized now that, within the Great Link, he had never perceived any gender among the Founders.

Pushing away from the twin spires, Odo began to walk along the edge of the islet. The strange silence that encompassed this world surrounded him as he walked, broken only by the crunch of his own footsteps on the rock surface, and the occasional lapping sounds of the changeling sea as it rubbed along the banks. Odo remembered the initial time he'd ever seen members of his own kind emerge from that golden soup and take humanoid forms. The first Founder to address him had been the individual who had come to be known in the Alpha Quadrant as the "female changeling," and her appearance did contain distinguishing sexual characteristics. But her distaff form could have been simply a component of her emulation, rather than reflecting a personal attribute. Odo himself had chosen his own Bajoran-like façade, during the time in which he'd learned to shapeshift, from that of the person he'd known best: the male doctor, Mora Pol.

Still, changelings did not necessarily require gender in order to breed. They conceivably might have been able to reproduce by fission, or via some other unusual means. Odo had told Indurane that, looking back, he'd always considered himself an infant at the time he'd been found in the Denorios Belt. Now, he recalled the undersized changeling Quark had once purchased from an Yridian—a changeling Odo had also believed newborn, based upon its mass and its inability to change its shape. But Indurane had ascribed such characteristics to inexperience, and not to infancy.

Trying and failing to make sense of what he knew of his people, and of what Indurane had told him, Odo felt his frustrations boil over. He reached the rock towers again, and brought his closed hands down hard against the surface of one of them. His fists flattened and spread against the dense material, absorbing the impact, but the sudden, violent movement did little to stanch his frustrations.

Indurane claimed that the Great Link hadn't evolved, but had been created in its entirety by a Being the changelings called the Progenitor. This supreme Being, Indurane asserted, had made the whole of the universe: energy, time, matter, life. Then, in the final stages of Its creation, It had gathered a population of solids and imbued their physicality with Its own awesome, changeable essence, making the Great Link after Its own image. Odo remembered questioning the changeling leader about whether the Founders had always been able to shapeshift, and her response that, eons ago, their people had been like the solids. Indurane's contentions did not contradict that.

According to the ancient Founder, the Great Link had been formless at first, possessing no knowledge and no understanding of shapeshifting. But as time had passed, some portions of the Link had separated from their collective mass, and with their changeling senses and intellect open to the universe and to their own selves, they'd learned about existence—about the world without, and the world within. Rejoining with their people, they'd shared their new knowledge and experience, and their civilization had developed.

During his time with the Founders, Odo had intuited the presence of unformed, unaware segments within the Great Link. He'd always thought of these as infants, but Indurane described them as those who had not yet divided from the Link, had not yet begun to learn. When eventually they did, they would be considered newly formed—just as Odo had been, prior to being sent out as one of the Hundred.

Behind him, Odo heard the familiar sound of a changeling varying its form. He stepped back from the rock formation, pulling his hands back into normal Bajoran shapes. He spun on his heel to see a glittering column swirling upward out of the Great Link. He watched as it arched forward over the surface of the islet and down. Its form tightened and coalesced, and Odo expected Laas's humanoid form to materialize from the biomimetic mass. Instead, an alien appeared, taller than Odo, taller even than Laas. An exoskeletal lamina covered its body and limbs—two legs, two arms—the hue and texture of the shell resembling a silvery, liquid metal. It had rounded, pearlescent features, and parallel grooves rimmed its large golden eyes, causing the orbs to look as though they were dissolving into its lustrous flesh. Odo identified the being from the data he'd collated from historical reports, as well as from Opaka's description of her own encounter with such a being: an Ascendant.

Although Odo knew the striking alien to be only a facsimile, its manifestation nevertheless chilled him. His recent confirmation of the continued existence of the Ascendants, and of their possible return to this region of space, concerned him greatly—particularly if, as Indurane had alleged, the Founders did believe in the Progenitor. Religious zealots on a quest to unite with their gods, the Ascendants destroyed any whom they believed worshipped falsely.

Indurane, Odo thought, sensing that the ancient Founder had followed him here. "You're the changeling I just linked with," Odo said, seeking verification.

In response, the Ascendant nodded slowly.

"Why are you here?" Odo demanded, but he thought he already knew: Indurane had come here to finish providing the information Odo had sought. For of all the questions he had just posed, one—Laas's question—remained unanswered: *Why were the Hundred sent out into the galaxy?*

"I am here for you," the old changeling said, its tone high-pitched and musical.

Odo studied the form of the Ascendant, looking for clues. He understood that, as had occurred within the Great Link, Indurane intended his shape to convey an idea. Thus, embodied in the image of the resolute and fearsome being, the historical disposition of the Founders revealed itself, the emotional context in which they'd sent out the Hundred: certain and fanatical.

Indurane shifted form again, the metallic covering of the Ascendant seeming briefly to melt before hardening into a figure resembling Odo's. The smooth-featured male Bajoran walked forward, to the center of the islet. He looked down, his mouth contorting into a rictus of grief. "This is one of the Hundred," he said, the words sounding almost as though they had been delivered by Odo's own rough, masculine voice. He looked up. "We failed you," he said.

Odo wanted to agree, wanted to tell Indurane that the circumstances that would have allowed him a complete life had been unfairly taken from him when he'd been sent away. He'd spent decades wondering about his people, yearning for them, and then when he'd found them, lamenting that he had no place among them. Except, for all of that, his life had improved immeasurably when Nerys had fallen in love with him, something that surely would never have happened had he not been sent out as he had.

"We failed the Hundred," Indurane said again before Odo could formulate a response. "But the Hundred did not fail the Great Link."

"What?" Odo asked. "What do you mean?"

"As the Great Link diminished over time," Indurane began, "persecuted by solids, decimated by wars, unable to reproduce, we sought completion of our lives . . . we sought to join with the Progenitor. But It had left us after creating the Great Link, back in the beginning of time. We had no idea where to search for It, or how. We had been met with suspicion, hatred, and violence by the solids we'd encountered, and fearing our metamorphic abilities, they hunted us, beat us, murdered us. We withdrew to a planet in the Omarion Nebula, where we made a home for ourselves in isolation. We wanted to seek the Progenitor, but dared not venture back out into the universe."

"So you sent out a hundred newly formed changelings," Odo said, angered at the blatant disregard for the well-being of the Hundred. "As bait."

"We'd hoped your lack of knowledge and experience would protect you from the solids," Indurane said. "Some argued against this, but the opinion ultimately prevailed."

"But how could you expect us to find the Progenitor," Odo asked, "when we didn't even know who we were, let alone of Its existence?"

"We did not expect you to find the Progenitor," Indurane said. "We hoped that It would find you."

"A hundred innocents lost in the universe," Odo said, understanding. "A hundred innocents, programmed to return to the Great Link."

"Yes. We hoped that you would attract Its attention, enjoy Its protection, and that It would ultimately be drawn back to the Great Link itself."

"It sounds preposterous," Odo said, even as he believed it. "Why did you keep this from me?"

"We did not expect any of the Hundred to return to the Great Link for hundreds of years," Indurane said. "We were not prepared, and we did not know when we could reveal it to you in such a way that you would not hate us. And your relationships with the solids . . . our quest was not for them to know, so that they could thwart us."

"Then why now?"

"Because Laas wanted to know," Indurane said. "And . . ."

"And?" Odo asked.

In response, Indurane lifted his head and gazed up into the sky. "And because the Progenitor has finally returned," he said, almost rapturously.

"What?" Odo said. Indurane continued peering up into the heavens, but behind him, a disruption began in the Great Link, its surface suddenly growing rough, its gently wavering form becoming wild and frenetic. Indurane turned just as a wave formed, a high wall of the changeling sea rising up just off of the islet. He turned back to Odo.

"There is much to decide," he said. As he rounded to face the wave again, the shining mass reached toward him, sending tendrils oscillating above the islet. Indurane reached up and joined with the filaments, his humanoid form losing shape and becoming one with the Link. In seconds, he was gone, the wave departing with him back into the golden flows.

Odo pondered what he had been told. The belief in the Progenitor struck Odo as almost religious, though he was sure that the Founders would have disagreed, claiming it to be a simple fact, rather than a matter of faith. But of course, a lack of doubt often defined faith. Odo thought of Nerys, of her great faith in the Prophets, and he remembered again their conversation in Dax's closet. They'd discussed faith then too.

Odo stared out over the Link, his thoughts wandering from Indurane to Nerys, from what he had just been told to what he recollected. After a few minutes, he pictured Indurane standing there, gazing upward. Odo turned and looked up, past the paired rock formations, and into the sky. And there glowed the nova he'd first seen when he'd returned from the Alpha Quadrant, a brilliant disk shining more brightly than anything else in the heavens.

A harbinger of a bright future for his people, he'd thought when he'd first seen it from the islet after beaming down.

Now he was not so sure.

4

Odo watched Kira stride across Dax's bedroom toward the closed door. As he stood up from the storage container, he recognized the set of her shoulders, the quickness of her movements. He knew that she intended more than simply to leave this room. She wanted to get away from him, and not for just right now.

"Nerys," he called after her a second time, the solitary word an earnest plea for her to stop. It seemed to have no effect on her as she reached for the panel in the bulkhead beside the door. But then she hesitated, her hand hovering before the control, poised to open her route of escape.

He waited. He didn't move, didn't speak, afraid that going to her or saying the wrong thing would fracture whatever delicate balance had been struck, would bring her hand down on the panel and send her fleeing from him. He stood motionless, gazing at her back, hoping that she would turn to him, hoping that they could put all that had happened behind them and resume their friendship.

Kira knew that he loved her, had known for months now. She did not reciprocate his feelings. Both facts had hung between them at times, awkward realities with which neither had seemed to know how to cope. For the most part, though, they had been able to ignore those emotions and continue on, as if the revelation of Odo's love had never taken place.

Yet as Odo waited now for Kira either to leave or stay, her reaction to his disclosure that he had slept with the Founder leader struck him as curious. Although Odo and Kira had never been romantically involved, she appeared hurt, her almost reflexive flight from him seeming like the response of a lover betrayed. He harbored no illusions that she had come to share his feelings—especially after the events on the station during the period of Dominion control—but he thought that perhaps it upset her to think that his love for her had been lessened by his actions with the Founder leader.

"Odo," Kira said, a multitude of emotions seeming to color her tones: frustration, disappointment, even yearning of a sort. She dropped her hand to her side and turned around. As she did, the hem of her dress flared outward momentarily, just above her red-stockinged knees, a graceful movement that somehow caused his deeper feelings for her to flare as well. "I'm sorry," she said. "I have no right . . ." She dropped her gaze to the floor, letting her words trail into silence.

"No, it's all right," Odo told her. "I want to explain it to you."

She looked up at him again. "No," she said, "that's not necessary."

"I don't know if it is or it isn't," he said, "but I *want* to explain." He gestured toward the vanity in the closet, toward the small stool she'd been perched upon during their conversation. "Please come sit back down," he said. She nodded, then walked back over and took a seat again. He leaned across the doorway and worked the controls beside it, sending the closet door sliding closed.

He turned to face her, but did not sit back down himself. "I . . ." he started, and searched for the easiest way to refer to his liaison with the Founder leader. He decided to employ Kira's own vernacular. "I . . . 'slept' . . . with the Founder," he stammered, uncomfortable even with the euphemism, "not so that she and I could grow closer, or share something special, but so that I could try to teach her about sol—" He hesitated, choosing to rephrase the end of his sentence. "About humanoids," he concluded.

"About *solids*," Kira said, emphasizing the word he had been about to utter.

Odo nodded, admitting to the term. "I don't mean it in a pejorative way," he said. "It's simply a means of distinguishing changelings from those who can't shapeshift."

"That's just it," Kira said. "I have no interest in distinguishing between us. You're my friend, and it's not important to me what species you are."

"I agree," Odo said. "And that's the sort of thing I was trying to convey to the Founder . . . my relationships with humanoids, my closeness to some of them. She didn't understand how I could sustain such feelings." Odo paused, wanting to isolate for Kira the words he would say next. "What I want you to know is that my . . . experience . . . with the Founder was not about intimacy, not with her. I wanted to bring her to an understanding of humanoid relationships, and to an appreciation of my feelings for some of them."

"I don't think it worked," Kira observed, a hint of sarcasm in her voice.

"No, it didn't," Odo agreed. "It only made her pity humanoids for their inability to link with each other, for the inherent isolation of their relationships. I think it also cemented her view of changelings as superior beings."

Kira laughed once, sharply and without humor. "I don't know why you expected anything different."

"But I did expect something different," Odo said at once. He sat down on the storage bin again. "I expected to be able to demonstrate to her the joys that humanoids can share among themselves, and that, even if not in quite the same way, we can still share in those joys as well." Although Odo had never had a romantic relationship with Kira, he had been involved with a woman named Arissa. "I wanted the Founder to know what . . . completed me . . . as an individual," he went on, "just as she showed me what helped to complete the lives of changelings. My relationships with humanoids . . . with you, for example . . . are important parts of my life, and something I need." He stopped, unsure if his words accurately expressed his feelings. He leaned forward, his hands on his knees. "Do you understand?" he asked Kira.

"I don't know if I do," she said.

"What is it that makes you whole?" he asked. "What is it

that helps to complete your life in a way that you could not do without?"

"I lived under the brutal oppression of the Cardassians for most of my life," she said. "I can do without a lot of things."

"I know you can," Odo acknowledged. He sat back up, automatically giving her space with her memories. "But what would you prefer not to do without?" he asked, knowing what Kira's response would be: her faith in the Prophets. Devout without being judgmental of those who did not share her beliefs, Kira attended Bajoran shrine services frequently, and prayed to her gods in private even more often.

But she surprised him with her answer. "For a time, it was Bareil," she said, obviously speaking of her romance with the Bajoran vedek, a romance that had ended with his death several years ago. "And then Shakaar," she said, naming the Bajoran first minister with whom she'd subsequently had a relationship.

Startled by the response, Odo felt an anxious surge of anticipation. He both dreaded and relished the opportunity to talk with Kira about love. While discussion of such personal matters had always been difficult for him, he also knew that it could be different with Kira—*he* could be different with her. But in addition to whatever normal risks attended addressing issues of the heart with Kira, doing so now could derail the reason they'd come together to talk in the first place: to deal with what had come between them, and still stood in the way of their friendship. He needed to explain to her why he'd done the things that had consequently caused the rift between them, and he could not do that by speaking of romance or the deeper feelings he had for her.

"I thought you would mention your faith in the Prophets," he told her.

"You asked what I would prefer not to live without," Kira said. "But my faith in the Prophets is something that couldn't possibly be taken away from me."

"What if you learned that the Prophets were not gods?" he asked. "That they were simply alien beings with an interest in the Bajoran people?"

Although he'd seen it displayed often, it still awed him to

witness Kira's sure knowledge of the divinity of the Prophets, and her unwavering belief that they would always take care of Bajor and its people. She had lived the first quarter-century of her life during a military occupation of her planet, had been robbed of a childhood, had seen family and friends tortured, maimed, and killed, and she now functioned as a soldier in the massive, devastating war with the Dominion. And yet through all of that, her trust and faith in the Prophets had not only endured, but flourished. She'd been right to contend that her beliefs could never be taken from her, but that also reinforced the point that he wanted to make: that her faith contributed to who she was, to what defined her, and to what made her life complete.

Odo did not share Kira's beliefs in the godhood of the aliens that existed within the Bajoran wormhole, but he surely recognized their influence on her life, and those of other Bajorans. And for the first time, he wondered why the Great Link had no such beliefs, and what it would mean to them if they did.

5

"And the Great Link sent out the Hundred," Odo said, "to lure the Progenitor to return."

Laas stared at him from across the islet, his face a mask of either confusion or disbelief, Odo could not tell which. "The Progenitor," Laas said, as though about to offer an observation, but then he peered down at the ground and said nothing more. The pervasive quiet of this world settled around them, the perpetually vesper sky enfolding them like a soft cloak.

Odo had just finished describing his encounters with Indurane, detailing all of the information that the ancient Founder had imparted to him. After Indurane had been carried from the islet by the changeling tide, Odo had returned to the Great Link himself to search for Laas. When he'd located him, the two had linked, and Odo had begun to share the knowledge he'd just been given. But Laas had before long broken their connection and come here. After two centuries of communicating via the spoken word, Laas sometimes still found it easier to assimilate information in that way; as Odo himself understood, joining with another changeling could be an overwhelming experience—physically, mentally, and emotionally—making it more difficult to process data newly learned.

Odo waited, allowing Laas time to consider what he'd been told. When finally he looked back up, his expression had transformed into one of disgust. "Belief in a First Cause is such a . . . monoform . . . concept," he said, his isolation of the word an obvious sign of his contempt for non-changeling life-forms. Despite Laas's prejudices, though, Odo had to agree with his conclusion.

"That's been my experience as well," he said, recalling his conversation with Nerys in Dax's closet, during which he'd for a moment conjectured to himself about what a Founder god or gods might be like, and about what such a concept might mean to his people. The notion had seemed fantastical at the time, even frivolous. If anything, the Great Link had set itself up as a collection of gods for many of its Dominion subjects—most notably for the Vorta and Jem'Hadar.

Still, Indurane's beliefs had seemed to be more than simply matters of faith. Odo said as much to Laas, and then elucidated his point. "Indurane actually conveyed recollections of the Progenitor," he said, "although his memories were old and indistinct. But I perceived his beliefs more as issues of fact than of conviction."

"Is that not always the way it is?" Laas asked. "Are not the so-called religious experiences of monoforms simply the result of certain electrochemical processes in their brains?"

Odo grunted, taking a look out at the constantly moving body of the Great Link. "Changelings don't have monoform brains," he said.

"That's not my point," Laas said, and he walked over to Odo, skirting the ashes of the dead Founder still piled in the center of the islet. "Isn't the belief in a god most often a reaction to the fear of death, a way for an individual to cope with the limitations of their life? And this ancient changeling told you that our people cannot reproduce. Even if we are long-lived by monoform standards, we are also not immortal. That means that not only will individual changelings die over time, but eventually, so too will the entire Great Link."

Odo looked at his fellow Founder, his fellow member of the Hundred, and tried to separate the reason in Laas's arguments from the contemptuous perspective from which he viewed humanoids. "You're suggesting that the Progenitor is not a matter of fact, but one of belief only, and essentially a means of coping with the ultimate extinction of the Founders?"

"I am saying that, yes," Laas confirmed.

"I don't know," Odo said. "Would the Great Link exile one hundred of its own kind, solely on the basis of belief?" The idea horrified him.

"The history of the Varalans is littered with barbarous episodes," Laas said, speaking of the humanoid civilization with whom he'd lived for two hundred years. "They often utilized their faith in the existence of an omnipotent, omniscient creator and savior as justification for heinous behavior, for cruel acts of savagery against even their own kind. The same story is true of many monoform races."

"But the Varalans and those other species are not changelings," Odo protested.

"No," Laas allowed, "and it pains me to think that our people can be compared to such inferior beings. And yet you've told me that the Founders sent out the Hundred based upon an absurd belief in a creator, a belief motivated by a fear of communal death."

"Indurane maintains that it is more than belief, more than faith," Odo said. "According to him, it's reality."

"That is what believers say," Laas contended.

"Except that Indurane thinks that the Great Link has succeeded," Odo said, divulging the final piece of information that the aged Founder had divulged to him.

"What?" Laas asked, clearly surprised. He took a step closer to Odo, almost coming into contact with him. Odo thought that Laas might reach out at any moment in order to link with him.

"The Great Link thinks that the scattering of the Hundred throughout the galaxy has brought about the result for which it was intended," Odo said. "They believe that the Progenitor has come back to them." He remembered the great anticipation and anxiety he'd perceived in his people recently, feelings which he'd ascribed to his own return from the Alpha Quadrant, and then to Laas's bringing home two more of the Hundred, and finally to the revelation of the death of a Founder. But he saw now that such collective emotions could also be explained by the belief that the Progenitor had returned.

"Why do they think that?" Laas wanted to know, a question

Odo had been asking himself ever since Indurane had revealed the information to him. "If that's true, then where is the Progenitor?"

"I don't know," Odo said slowly, and he visualized all of the shapes Indurane had become in response to his questions. But suddenly, his investigative experience and skills told him that he had been asking the wrong questions. Indurane had explained what the Great Link had done in sending out the Hundred, and why it had done so, and even when. But Odo understood now that he needed to know other things: *Where had they sent the Hundred, and to where did they think the Progenitor had returned?*

He looked back at Laas. "We need to contact Weyoun," he said.

As Taran'atar stood before *Rio Grande*'s port hatchway, waiting for Ananke Alpha's shuttlebay to finish pressurizing, a calm clarity overtook his mind, like the break of day enveloping a suddenly still battlefield. He felt as he often had on the cusp of military action. *I am dead,* he thought, reciting to himself the dictum of a Jem'Hadar first about to take his men into combat. He continued by altering the rest of the philosophy to fit the circumstances: *I go to visit the Founder to reclaim my life; I do this because I am Jem'Hadar.*

The litany, though skewed, seemed to Taran'atar as appropriate as ever—and perhaps even more apposite than usual. He hadn't felt in possession of his own life for some time now, ever since Odo had assigned him to reside alongside inhabitants of the Alpha Quadrant aboard Deep Space 9. Although in that time he'd employed his martial abilities on occasion, and although he'd filled much of the substantial downtime with numerous training exercises, it often felt as though his existence as a Jem'Hadar soldier had ended. The necessity for him to sleep—a feeble attribute shared by weaker species—underscored that characterization.

An indicator light beside the hatchway blinked from amber to green, signaling that the pressurization of the shuttlebay had completed. Taran'atar worked an adjoining control, and the hatch slid open. Before stepping forward, though, he glanced over his shoulder at Kira, who sat at *Rio Grande*'s primary console. Since no waiting rooms or guest quarters had been built into the prison, she would be required to remain aboard the runabout during his time inside.

Looking at her now, Taran'atar saw that in one hand she still held his *kar'takin*. After *Rio Grande* had set down aboard Ananke Alpha an hour ago, they'd prepared to disembark, but then had been instructed to wait while the facility's staff had utilized sensors to scrutinize the runabout and its passengers. During that period, Taran'atar and Kira had been apprised of the prison's rules and procedures, which had been few, specific, and strict. One regulation prohibited visitors from carrying anything inside, including not only weapons, but even equipment such as tricorders and medkits. Taran'atar had therefore disarmed himself, handing his blade over to Kira as he'd prepared to depart.

"Good luck," she said now, peering back at him from the bow of the runabout. "I hope you get what you came here for," she went on, though even the smile she offered could not camouflage her trepidation about his imminent visit to the Founder. Had it been her decision whether or not to allow such a meeting, he doubted that he would have been here right now. He had told her, and then told Admiral Ross, that he wished to call on the Founder in order to check on her well-being, and also because she'd been alone since the end of the war, segregated not only from the Great Link, but also from any members of the Dominion; he hoped that his presence might help relieve her isolation, however briefly. In truth, Taran'atar also sought his own relief, wanting the view of another Founder about the mission Odo had assigned him, as well as any assistance he could get about resisting his body's new requirement for sleep.

He stepped from the runabout and walked along a red line on the decking, as he'd been instructed. On the way, he noted several surveillance and sensor ports, as well as what appeared to be phaser emitters, security obviously considered a premium commodity here. He also assumed that the facility had been outfitted with transporter inhibitors. Following the guide line, he headed toward the lone door in the shuttlebay, located in the inner bulkhead. The solid panel retracted at his approach, and he continued on into a long corridor.

As the door closed behind him, another opened up ahead. He passed a closed door in the bulkhead to his left, and moved through the open doorway into a large, square room, perhaps ten meters on a side. Empty but for a small freestanding partition off to the right, the room possessed few other features: more surveillance, sensor, and weapons ports; the door through which he'd entered and one opposite; a continuation of the red line connecting the two; and a long window in the bulkhead to his left. He surmised the gray, metallic walls of the room to be constructed of rodinium or titanium. Through the window—which appeared to be a thick slab of transparent aluminum—he saw several monitors and control panels, and he counted five security officers, all clad in Starfleet uniforms. Two appeared to be human, one Vulcan, one Orion, and one Tellarite.

"Mr. Taran'atar," a female voice said via a comm system, the words coincident with the moving of the Vulcan officer's lips. He made eye contact with her as she spoke. *"I am Commander T'Kren. I am required by the United Federation of Planets to inform you that this facility has been deemed a no-hostage zone. In the event that you are taken captive by Ananke Alpha's prisoner, or by forces attacking this facility, Starfleet will not negotiate for your release. Do you understand and consent to these conditions for your visit?"*

"Yes," Taran'atar said.

"Then behind the screen to your right," she continued, *"you will find a Starfleet-issue coverall. Please step behind the screen, remove the apparel you are currently wearing, and dress in the Starfleet attire. Please do this with alacrity."*

Taran'atar would have removed his clothing immediately, but recalled an admonition he and Kira had been given aboard the runabout: while within the confines of Ananke Alpha, follow all instructions precisely, or be stunned with phaser fire into unconsciousness and removed from the facility. "Acknowledged," he said, and did as he'd been told, switching the black coverall he wore for the bright red one he found hanging behind the screen. He noted the closeness of the fit, and assumed that the outfit had been replicated for him after he and Kira had been scanned aboard the runabout.

He emerged from behind the screen less than twenty seconds after he'd moved behind it, leaving his black coverall on the decking. He saw only three security officers through the window now.

"Thank you," the Vulcan commander said, her politeness in this situation evocative of the unctuous nature of the Vorta. *"Please move to the approximate center of the room."* Once he had done so, she continued to issue instructions. *"In a moment, you will be joined by two security officers who will escort you to the cell housing the Founder. One will walk ahead of you, the other behind you. Please follow their instructions exactly. Do you understand?"*

"Yes," Taran'atar said, barely able to contain the contempt he felt for these people who dared to believe that they had the right to imprison a god.

"Once you have entered the Founder's cell, you will have one hour to visit with her," the Vulcan officer went on. *"At the end of that time, you will be escorted back here. Do you understand?"*

"Yes," Taran'atar said again, careful not to let the strong emotions he felt show on his face. He would do nothing to risk his meeting with the Founder.

The inner door opened, and two of the security officers he'd earlier seen through the window entered the room. One, an Orion male, moved quickly over to the outer door, now closed. He stood not even a meter and three quarters, with short, muscular legs, a wide chest and shoulders, and brawny arms. He had dark eyes and short black hair. The appearance of the other officer, a human female, contrasted significantly with that of the first; tall and lean, she had light coloring, shoulder-length blond hair, and narrow features. Both officers had small black pouches attached to their uniforms at the waists, and both held hand phasers at the ready.

"I'm Lieutenant Commander Matheson," the woman said from beside the inner door, which had closed behind her, "and this is Lieutenant Jenek." She pointed with her empty hand toward the Orion. "We are now going to walk with you to the

Founder's cell. At seven junctures along the way, either Lieutenant Jenek or I will ask you to stop. Please do so at once, and remain stationary until I ask you to proceed again."

"I understand," Taran'atar said, wanting nothing more at this point than to be on his way to the Founder.

"Good," Matheson said. "Please take a position between Lieutenant Jenek and me." Taran'atar did as directed. "Thank you," she said. "We'll now proceed."

As though Matheson had willed it, the inner door glided open. She walked from the room and into a corridor that ran to the left and right. She turned to the right, and Taran'atar followed. Out of Jenek's line of sight for just a moment, he quickly peered back the other way down the corridor, and saw a second door—closed—standing beside the first, doubtless leading to the control room crewed by the Vulcan commander and the other security officers.

Taran'atar looked forward again. Behind him, he heard Jenek exit the room, his footsteps falling heavily on the decking. Ahead, beyond Matheson, Taran'atar saw the corridor curving into the distance, its end lost from sight. Brightly lighted by panels in the center of the overhead, the enclosed space offered no adornments, the stark, gray bulkheads uninterrupted by anything but the ubiquitous surveillance, sensor, and weapons ports mounted high on their surfaces.

Just a few paces away, another corridor intersected the first, perpendicular to it and leading off to the left. Matheson turned into it, and Taran'atar did the same. The metronomic thumping of Jenek's boots clocking along the deck followed behind.

Up ahead, perhaps thirty meters away, a door reached across the corridor, impeding the way. As she reached it, Matheson turned and said, "Stop." Taran'atar complied immediately, and he heard Jenek do the same, the sounds of everybody's heels echoing for a few seconds before fading away.

Matheson faced the side bulkhead, holstered her phaser, and took hold of the pouch at her hip. She opened it and spilled its contents into her hand. She selected one of the long, thin, clear items she held, which looked like isolinear optical chips, though each had a serrated edge. After returning the others to

the pouch and then the pouch to her hip, she reached forward
and inserted the chip she'd chosen into a slot.

A physical key, Taran'atar realized. An added means of security, he reasoned, one which worked in concert with other
measures, but would by itself allow access and egress through
these passages should the facility's power systems fail.

Matheson turned the key, which produced an audible click,
then placed her hand against a plate inset into the bulkhead.
"Identify: Matheson, Lieutenant Commander Jacqueline," she
recited. "Requesting access."

A light beside the plate shifted from red to amber, not unlike how the external-atmosphere indicator aboard *Rio Grande*
had done earlier. As seconds passed in silence, Taran'atar detected movement, a vibration he perceived through the deck.
Beyond the closed door, he was sure, something moved—
something *big*.

Finally, the light blinked from amber to green, and the door
lumbered aside slowly, the panel at least ten centimeters
through. Matheson spun the chip, withdrew it from the slot,
and replaced it in the pouch, then drew her phaser once more.
"Let's continue," she said, and strode through the doorway.
Taran'atar started after her, and he heard Jenek follow behind
him.

As Taran'atar crossed the threshold, the lighting levels
seemed to decrease, and he detected a change in the texture of
the decking, from metallic to something less rigid. The sound
of his steps grew muffled, as did those of Matheson and Jenek.
He saw two narrow lines of blue running along the walkway,
along either edge. Forcefields obviously surrounded the deck
here.

Still, the claustrophobic feel of the corridor gave way to an
unexpected openness here. Taran'atar looked to both sides and
saw a cavernous area, extending outward, up and down, left
and right. The modified deck bridged the space, running to another doorway fifty meters ahead. At a remove from the walking surface, on either side, what appeared to be emitters of
some sort—large, silver cones—lined the distant bulkheads.

Radiation, Taran'atar thought. *A line of defense.* He
guessed that the security officers kept this zone constantly irra-

diated, protecting against unauthorized passage to and from the cell encased in the heart of the prison. Even if hostile forces penetrated the facility, or the Founder broke from her cell, even if closed doors could be forced open, the radiation would provide a barrier difficult to cross without ultimately sacrificing the lives of those who did—including that of the Founder.

They continued along the walkway to the far door. Shortly after Matheson did, Taran'atar passed through the second doorway and back into a corridor. They continued forward until Lieutenant Jenek spoke up behind them. "Stop," he said simply, just as Matheson had a few minutes ago. The lieutenant commander turned around to watch her colleague, and Taran'atar did the same. At the second doorway, Jenek performed the same series of tasks as Matheson had at the first—setting aside his phaser, retrieving a chip from his pouch, inserting the key into a slot, flattening his hand against a plate—but rather than requesting access, he asked for closure.

After the door had sealed behind them, Taran'atar continued on with the two security officers. Now, though, they encountered numerous intersections, and various corridors of differing lengths crossing each other at oblique angles. Matheson made several turns, seemingly at random. As they walked, Taran'atar saw a minuscule gap between the walls and the deck. He wondered at first if they might be part of a defensive system that could deliver debilitating gaseous agents into the corridors, but in light of the many junctions, turns, and odd angles behind them, he concluded that the bulkheads here moved. Walls would shift, new corridors would be created, old ones eliminated, with dead ends abounding and no obvious course through the maze. If Taran'atar ever returned to Ananke Alpha, he suspected that he would find gone the path that he followed this time to reach the Founder. He found it a clumsy but probably effective countermeasure to any escape attempts begun either inside or outside the prison.

Along the route, Matheson led the way through two more lines of defense, neither of them configured precisely as the radiation barrier had been. Taran'atar believed one of the zones to be kept heated beyond the endurance of most life-forms, and the other to be filled with a constant barrage of phaser fire. To be sure, the variegated fortifications would pose difficulties for anybody plotting to break into or out of the facility.

Which is why, he thought, *I would avoid altogether any attempt to breach the barriers.*

After Matheson had taken them through the third defensive zone, they traveled once more through a single corridor, the maze apparently behind them. At a T-shaped intersection, Matheson halted and addressed Taran'atar again. "Stop," she said, and he did so. "At the end of this corridor," she said, pointing to the right, "is the Founder's cell." She explained in detail the procedures for Taran'atar's entry into and exit from the cell, and then moved into the corridor off to the left. Taran'atar paced forward until he reached the junction, then turned right. Ten meters away stood a set of parallel doors, the first of the two transparent. As he approached the doors, he heard Jenek enter the corridor behind him.

Taran'atar looked over his shoulder and waited as Matheson used another of her keys and her handprint to request access to the Founder's cell. When the transparent door glided open, he entered the small antechamber. A moment later, that door closed behind him, and the inner one opened. He stepped forward into a long room, fifteen meters long and half as wide. A collection of seemingly unrelated items filled the space: a few plants of varying dimension and color, several regular and irregular geometric forms constructed of diverse materials, a tank of clear liquid, a box of sand, what appeared to be a crumpled piece of paper. He saw surveillance, sensor, and weapons ports here as well.

He did not see the Founder. At least not that he could identify.

"I am Taran'atar," he said as the inner door closed behind him, sealing him inside. "I am a Jem'Hadar first." He waited, but received no response. "I humbly seek to visit with you, Founder, to speak with you."

Still nothing.

Taran'atar waited, keenly aware from the moment he had first considered coming here that the Founder might not wish to see him. Merely a servant to her kind, he had little to offer her, and knew that, even if Admiral Ross had consented to this meeting, it remained to be seen whether the Founder would deign to speak with him.

"If you do not wish my visit, Founder," he said at last, "then I shall leave. It is of course your choice." He waited ten seconds, then ten more. When a full minute had passed, it became clear that the Founder did not want to see him.

Taran'atar began to turn, but as he did so, he saw movement in the room. Directly in front of him, the overhead seemed to slump down, as though melting, until the mass began to shimmer. It elongated until it touched the floor, spilled downward, then reached up into a humanoid figure. Color and texture appeared as though from nowhere, transforming the shining golden shape into a woman of medium height and build, her features smooth, like Odo's when he took Bajoran form.

Taran'atar had seen Founders shapeshift throughout his twenty-two-year lifespan, but it never ceased to produce in him a sense of awe. He stood motionless, waiting for the Founder to speak. He felt anticipation, pleased that he had managed this opportunity for himself.

The Founder took one stride forward and peered up into Taran'atar's eyes. Her lips formed a thin, straight line, almost hidden within the doughy flesh of her face. At last, she spoke:

"Why are you here?"

The two Founders waited behind him, their presence in his quarters a palpable, weighty thing, like a dense fog pushing in, unstoppable, suffocating. The bass drone of the ship's engines contributed to the onerous atmosphere. Weyoun attempted to concentrate on the readouts before him, on operating his companel, but could not prevent himself from stealing a look backward from time to time, hoping to verify that neither of his guests had yet lost their patience. Although Odo continued to pace anxiously back and forth across the room, the attitude of the other, motionless Founder—Laas—concerned Weyoun more. Like many changelings, Laas did not conceal his scorn for Vorta and other lower life-forms, but more than that, the intensity of his disgust appeared to cross the line into hatred. Weyoun doubted that any service he provided right now, no matter how helpful or beneficial to the Great Link, would gain him Laas's approbation.

At the same time, Odo represented a different challenge. Weyoun's memories, extending not only through his own brief existence, but through the lives of his predecessors, composed complex, often inconsistent portraits of the Founder. Odo had seemed to despise several of the Weyoun clones, but on an individual basis, and not because he judged Vorta to be intrinsically inferior to changelings—although of course they were. But after initially distrusting the motives of the sixth Weyoun—the *defective* Weyoun—Odo had come to show him sympathy, even tenderness. More difficult to fathom, the current relationship between Founder and Vorta had been marked by Odo's frequent attention. Although he still often displayed a stern manner, he regularly sought contact with Weyoun—as well as with the Jem'Hadar seventh—transporting up to the ship and engaging in lengthy conversations about a multitude of subjects. Such personal interaction delighted Weyoun, but it also disconcerted him a bit. Accustomed to striving constantly to serve the Founders to the best of his abilities and at all costs, he did not really know how to conduct himself with them in an alternate role.

"Weyoun," Odo said sharply from across the room, though he sounded more anxious than angry. "Are you making any progress?"

"I am," Weyoun responded, turning to face the Founder. Odo had stopped pacing and now stood beside the closed door that led out into the corridor. He had his arms folded across his chest. Laas leaned against the bulkhead in an adjacent corner. "I'm making significant progress," Weyoun said. As he peered from one Founder to the other, he became acutely aware of his many projects lying scattered about the room, spilling over just about every flat surface, including the deck. Vorta had no sense of aesthetics, but they did possess an intense curiosity. Many, including Weyoun, found satisfaction in studying and learning about almost anything, no matter how trivial or uninteresting such things might seem to others. He continually collected items from various places, bringing them here for later examination. Between his position at the companel and Odo, he saw shoes, coasters, bits of string, broken bottles, power cells, picture frames, and a chair leg. Knowing the changeling penchant for order, Weyoun felt embarrassed by the ragtag assortment of objects. Had he had any warning that Odo and Laas would visit him here, he would have packed away his academic olio.

"If you're making progress," Laas snapped, "then what's the delay?"

"My apologies, Founder," Weyoun said, folding his hands together and bowing his head. "I'm afraid that the information you're seeking is stored in numerous files, in different locations," he explained. "They're also encrypted in a variety of ways."

"But you do have the necessary clearances to access and decode the files?" Odo asked.

"Yes, I do, thanks to your foresight," Weyoun said. Prior to embarking on the task the two Founders had given him, Odo had increased Weyoun's already-high security authorization. "I've collected all of the files you asked for, and decoded most of them. I'm just waiting for the last few files to go through decryption, and then for the final collation of data."

"Is there no one who can do this faster?" Laas asked Odo.

Before Odo could respond, the companel emitted two quick tones, signaling the completion of the deciphering of the last files. Weyoun looked back to the readouts and verified the results. He told the Founders, then worked the console again for a few minutes, this time to bring the newly decoded data into the collection of the other files he'd already assembled. He touched one final control, which hummed at his touch, and then he turned back to Odo and Laas.

"Done," he announced, the smile on his face a gauge of the pleasure he felt in accomplishing a service for not one, but two of his gods.

"Then leave us," Laas said brusquely, pushing off of the bulkhead and standing up straight.

Weyoun felt his smile evaporate, sorry to be dismissed instead of being permitted to continue providing assistance. He hesitated for only an instant, though, before forcing a smile back onto his face, but Odo must have sensed his disappointment.

"If you don't mind," the Founder said. "It's just that Laas and I would like to discuss the contents of the files in private."

"Of course," Weyoun said. "I understand completely, and I'm more than happy to volunteer my home for you to work in." He padded across the room, sidestepping a large, green pyramidal object that he couldn't quite identify, although he recalled that the fifth Weyoun had retrieved it several years ago from Innerol V, during the repression of an insurgency against the Dominion. The door opened at his approach, and he passed Odo and started out into the corridor. Then he stopped and looked back at the two Founders. "As always, it is a pleasure to serve you."

"Thank you, Weyoun," Odo said. "Good work."

Weyoun could not prevent his smile from growing wider. "Thank you, Odo," he said, then he continued out into the corridor, the door closing behind him. As he headed for the bridge, he hoped that he had supplied Odo and Laas with what they needed. He felt privileged to have such close contact with Founders.

Most Vorta, Weyoun knew, were not so fortunate.

The cliffs rose high above a barren, meteorite-pocked plain. The dawning sun peeked over the arc of the horizon, throwing roughly curved shadows into the many craters strewn across the lunar surface. Still cool from the night, the air blew in a steady breeze here, occasionally gusting stronger. Above, a smattering of clouds scudded across the sky.

Vannis peered down from atop the cliffs and surveyed the unfriendly surroundings. She observed the steepness of the precipice, then turned toward the rocky hills rising just twenty-five meters away. "Are you certain this is the location?" she asked.

The middle of her three Jem'Hadar escorts stepped forward. "It is," First Rekan'ganar said. "Residual traces of a propulsion trail are scattered through the area, and ship's sensors detected small amounts of refined metals spread along this flat as well."

Vannis nodded. She looked behind her again, out over the cliff's edge, and considered the narrow strip of land upon which they stood, situated between the high, steep drop on one side and the hills on the other. "It must have been a crash or an emergency landing then," she said. No pilot would have intentionally chosen this place to put down, except in the case of a crisis. Such a conclusion supported the little information that the Founder had provided her—namely, that a former inhabitant of this moon reported that an Ascendant's ship had crashed here. "Find whatever you can learn," Vannis ordered the Jem'Hadar, quoting the Founder's instructions to her.

With a nod from Rekan'ganar, the Jem'Hadar fanned out immediately along the edge of the cliff, each operating a portable scanner. Vannis remained in her current location, and activated her own scanner. After a few minutes of scrutiny, she could find nothing of significance around her. She quickly looked about the area, then paced toward the hillside.

From the ship, sensors had identified a web of satellites in orbit about the planet. They appeared to encircle the moon, though they had all been deactivated. Their orbits had begun to decay, but the pattern they described seemed to indicate three satellites missing from the network. Scans substantiated that conclusion by revealing small pieces of irradiated metal near those locations, the remnant energy of weapons fire still detectable on them. Vannis had deduced a battle between the Ascendants' craft and the network, with both achieving measures of victory. She speculated that the trio of absent satellites had been destroyed by the Ascendant, and the remainder of the net ultimately deactivated, but not before it had forced the Ascendant's ship down.

As Vannis neared the hillside, a sound reached her sensitive ears from somewhere up ahead. It could have been a minor rockfall, but she also knew from ship's sensors both that the moon's small population resided nearby, and that a system of caves snaked through the hills. She continued her scans, but kept alert for additional sounds.

A few moments later, Vannis heard more noises, including a shuffling that might have been footsteps. She also detected a slight echo, suggesting a presence in one of the caves. Without altering her gait or posture, she reset the scanner to search for life signs. The device distinguished a single humanoid, just inside the mouth of the nearest cave. The individual appeared relatively small in stature, and carried no weapons of any kind.

Vannis considered calling back one of the Jem'Hadar, but didn't feel the need. Instead, she gradually altered her path toward the hills, until she ended up close to the cave entrance. Without looking in that direction, she said, "Hello there."

No response came, but neither did Vannis hear the individual fleeing. "Yes, I'm speaking to you," she said, and then she turned slowly toward the cave mouth, until she faced it from just a few meters away. "You, in the cave."

Vannis waited. If this was one of the local populace, she wanted to interrogate them about anything they might know regarding the crash or emergency landing of the Ascendant's ship. Just when she thought she might have to take different actions to accomplish this, she heard the shuffling sound again, and then somebody emerged from the cave.

The child, a young man, raised a hand before his face, obviously shielding his eyes from the morning sunlight shining in his direction. A patina of grime covered the swarthy skin of his hands and face, as though his travels had kicked up soil from the floors of the caves and deposited on him the resultant dust. Even through the layer of dirt, though, Vannis could see what appeared to be scars on his face, pale streaks slashed about his features. "Hello," he said excitedly, squinting in the bright dawn. "I was just playing and I saw you." Despite the remnants of injuries sustained, the boy behaved with a childlike bearing.

"I know," Vannis said. "What's your name?"

"Mine's Misja," the boy said. "What's yours?"

"I'm Vannis." She paused, then asked, "Do you live here?"

"In the village, yes," he said. "With my tribe."

"The Sen Ennis," Vannis ventured, sure of the fact, but wanting to verify it anyway.

"Ye-es," the boy said hesitantly.

"Oh, don't worry," Vannis told him. "I'm not here to hurt you or your tribe."

"Why are you here?" Misja asked, as Vannis had easily maneuvered him to do.

"I'm here to find a friend of mine," she said. "Quite tall,

and silvery." Vannis had gotten a description of the Ascendants from Dominion historical files.

"Raiq," the boy said eagerly.

"Yes, Raiq," Vannis said, guessing that to be the name of the Ascendant. "Is Raiq here?" she asked, knowing from the Founder that the Ascendant had already departed.

"No, she left a while ago, right after she healed," Misja said.

"Healed?" Vannis asked, feigning concern. "Was she injured?"

"She wasn't well, but Tadia and Sulan didn't know whether she was sick or got hurt when her ship crashed," Misja said.

"Her ship crashed? Oh no." Vannis asked. "Is it still here?"

"No," Misja said. "I guess it wasn't too badly damaged when she crashed." Then he pointed down along the hills, and provided Vannis the information she'd been hoping to glean from him. "She landed right over there. I saw it, and I told everybody about it."

"Would you show me?" she asked.

"Sure," Misja said, and he led her along the hillside. When finally he stopped, he said, "Right here," and pointed down at the ground. Vannis walked around him, peering downward, but she saw nothing to indicate that a ship might have even landed here, let alone crashed here. She bent down and surveyed the ground from that angle, and noticed only a slight depression in one spot, and several long, thin indentations in a couple of other places. If a ship had been responsible for these, its footprint must have been quite narrow, almost bladelike.

She was not convinced.

"Would you mind if I took some readings?" Vannis asked, standing back up. "I just want to make sure this was my friend's ship."

Misja shrugged. "Sure," he said.

Vannis operated the scanner. To her surprise, the boy's claims appeared to be accurate. She read a warp signature in the area, and while the Ascendant likely would not have utilized such propulsion to land or launch on the moon, the readings might indicate an active warp drive that simply hadn't been taken offline before the crash. She also discovered small pieces of refined metal buried all about, just below the surface.

To Misja, she said, "Yes, this is Raiq's ship." She smiled at the boy. "Thank you."

"You're welcome," Misja beamed. "Will you visit our tribe?"

"No, I don't think so," Vannis said. "I have to go. I need to find my friend."

"Okay," Misja said, though he seemed disappointed by her response.

"Well, if you go tell your tribe right now," Vannis said, wanting time alone here to continue her investigation, "people from your tribe can come visit me here before I leave."

"All right," the boy said with childish enthusiasm. "I'll go tell them right away."

"Good," she said. "Hurry."

Misja turned and darted for the cave. Once he'd entered it, Vannis waited a few seconds, then worked the scanner to ensure that he had actually gone. Once she'd verified that fact, she returned her attention to the surrounding area, where the Ascendant had apparently crashed.

Her scans revealed nothing more, but just as she had decided to recall the Jem'Hadar and return to the ship, she noted what seemed to be several metal fragments visible on the ground. Circular and a cloudy gray in color, they looked to her like bits of superheated metal that had dripped to the ground. Remembering the description of the Ascendants themselves, though, she switched the scanner to examine biological material. The device immediately identified the drops as containing organic substances from a living being.

Quickly, before Misja could return with members of his tribe, Vannis recorded all the information she could, including DNA-related data. She also dug around one of the spatters of what she believed to be Ascendant blood, and secured the entire specimen into a compartment in the scanner.

Then she stood up, smiling. She enjoyed nothing more than satisfying the needs of the Founders, not only to the best of her own abilities, but to the best of any Vorta's. She knew the members of the Great Link would be pleased with the information she had recovered here regarding the Ascendants.

This task at an end, she touched a control wrapped around

her wrist, summoning the three Jem'Hadar to head back to her position. Once they had returned, she would transport with them off of this moon. She would order the ship back to Dominion space, where she would then work to fulfill the other purpose that the Founder had set her: the Overne had to eat, and the Rindamil had enough food to allow that to happen.

Odo felt the swirl of his cells as he willed each of his hands to sprout two additional fingers. He wanted to examine with all possible haste the data that Weyoun had just amassed, and the extra digits would allow him to work the companel with greater dexterity and swiftness. He could shapeshift more than seven fingers onto each hand, or even fashion himself a third arm, but he'd found through experimentation over the years that with this particular combination he operated most deftly.

Studying the readouts and panel configuration, Odo sent his hands marching across the controls. He checked the new file in which Weyoun had aggregated all of the data, then modified the privileges on it so that it could be accessed only by a Founder. Then he opened the file and began to peruse its contents. Laas stood at his side, peering intently at the screen.

After Odo had informed Laas of what had been revealed to him about the Great Link, the Hundred, and the Progenitor, the two had transported up to Jem'Hadar Attack Vessel 971. According to Indurane, the intention of the Founders in sending out the Hundred had been to have them function essentially as lures and guideposts, attracting the attention of the Progenitor and pointing the way back to the Link. The ancient Founder had also claimed that the changeling god now *had* returned. Laas's ensuing question—*To where had the Progenitor returned?*—had raised other issues in Odo's mind, and had also hinted at a possible answer.

By Indurane's account, the Progenitor had abandoned the Great Link long ago, before the changeling population had settled on a world hidden in the interstellar gas and dust of the Omarion Nebula. The Founders had sent out the Hundred from that planet, though, a location they had wanted to remain secret. If the unformed changelings dispersed throughout the galaxy formed a map to a specific place, then surely the Great

Link would have wanted that place to be somewhere other than their own world. For if the Progenitor could follow the directions they had set out, then so too could others. Laas's question of where the Progenitor had returned therefore became a matter of determining the location to which the Hundred had pointed.

Once aboard the Jem'Hadar ship, Odo and Laas had found Weyoun in his quarters. That had suited Odo, as he'd wanted to enlist the Vorta's aid in private. He'd asked Weyoun to scour the Dominion databases to find out whether or not the Founders had kept any records of the Hundred, and the locations to which they had been dispersed. Weyoun had found numerous such files, scattered across the Dominion computer network, their data veiled by various encryption methodologies. It had taken some time, but Weyoun had eventually been able to decipher the data and collect it in a single file.

Now Odo set out to study that information. He sent his seven-fingered hands skittering across the companel. On the monitor, he brought up an image of the galaxy, the great disk comprising its spiral arms appearing edgewise and bulging at its center. "Here is Dominion space," he said to Laas as he continued to work the panel. The picture on the screen shifted, the point of view drawing in close on one section, where an irregularly shaped volume of space became highlighted in blue. "And here are all of the locations to which the Hundred were sent," he went on as he touched another series of controls. Small red circles began to appear beyond the borders of the Dominion, one after another, in a manner that looked haphazard. Odo noted several markers in the galaxy's other three quadrants, and one at the coordinates of the wormhole's Gamma terminus, obviously denoting the place to where he himself had been sent.

"They're not symmetrical," Laas observed. "They don't seem to be distributed in any pattern at all."

"No," Odo agreed.

"Where's the Omarion Nebula?" Laas asked. Odo knew that Laas had no memory of the area from which he and the rest of the Hundred had been sent away, but had learned about it from other Founders.

Odo tapped again at the panel, which accompanied his movements with quick, flat tones. Around a patch of blue on the screen, a yellow line appeared, demarcating the Omarion borders. "Here," Odo said, raising a hand and pointing at it. "And here's the planet formerly occupied by the Great Link." In response to his manual commands, a small yellow circle materialized within the confines of the nebula.

"It's not at the center of the distribution," Laas said.

"But Indurane told me that the Founders hoped that the Hundred would attract the attention of the Progenitor and draw it back to the Great Link," Odo said. "There must be some central locus here." Odo called up a mathematical catalogue from the ship's computer, and searched a list of numerical methods. He selected an interpolation subroutine, then executed it against the set of data points identifying the locations to which the Hundred had been sent. A series of equations scrolled up the right side of the screen, at the same time that thin red lines emerged from each of the red circles. As values adjusted rapidly in the formulae, the lines moved, shifting their direction, but remaining anchored to the original data points.

For several minutes, Odo and Laas watched in silence as the mathematical process unfolded. Some lines would intersect each other, while others traced a path nowhere near them. Finally, though, more and more of the lines began to converge, until at last they all passed through a condensed region. The values in the equations stabilized and then froze, as did the lines. The volume of space through which the lines all passed sat near to, but outside of, the Omarion Nebula.

"Are there planets there?" Laas asked, obviously assuming, as Odo did, that the Founders would have chosen a specific place to reunite with their Creator.

Odo keyed in a request for information about that area of space. "There's one star system there," he said, reading from the monitor. "Eleven planets around a—" Odo stopped, not sure what to make of what he saw.

Laas must have sensed his confusion, because he said, "What is it? What's wrong?"

"The only star in the area that the Hundred point to has

been the brightest object in the Great Link's sky for weeks now," Odo said. "It went nova."

Taran'atar was surprised when he found himself unable to answer the Founder. Just recently, he had spent a great deal of time with Odo, and throughout his life, he had interacted with a number of changelings. He had given all of them nothing but his obedience. Now, though, something more than his instinctive drive to serve took hold of him. The Founder that peered up at him from an expressionless face carried herself, more noticeably than any other changeling he had ever met, with a mien of power. He knew that she had led the Dominion war against the Alpha Quadrant, and if not for the traitorous Cardassians and cowardly Breen, would have bested all foes. Even at the end, when she had chosen to cease fighting and save the Great Link, she could have debilitated the Federation and its allies even in a Dominion defeat, had she chosen to do so. As she regarded him coldly, he sensed that she had lost none of that strength.

"I asked you a question," she said, and even though she spoke with an even tone, her words sounded to Taran'atar as if they held within them disapproval and an implicit threat. "Why are you here?" she asked again, and Taran'atar imagined that she had rarely had to repeat herself to subordinates. "Why are you in the Alpha Quadrant?"

Taran'atar blinked, hesitating still. He had thought that the Founder had wanted to know why he had chosen to come to visit her on Ananke Alpha, and not why he had left the Dominion. "I am in the Alpha Quadrant," he finally responded, "because three-quarters of a year ago, I was sent by a Founder to reside on Deep Space 9."

"Another Founder," she said, her inscrutable features seeming to tighten. "Odo?" she asked, although the single-word question conveyed the Founder's certainty about what the answer would be.

"Yes," Taran'atar confirmed. "Odo."

The Founder appeared to settle herself, then took a step backward and studied him. Taran'atar thought that he provided little to see: dressed in the simple Starfleet coverall, he carried no weapons or devices of any kind. Perhaps for that reason, since the Founder could focus on nothing but Taran'atar himself, her gaze felt penetrating to him. Finally, her scrutiny stopped at the left side of his neck. He felt the urge to reach up and cover the small slit in his flesh that marked where a delivery tube had for two decades entered his body. "You are free of the white," the Founder observed.

"I am," Taran'atar said carefully, uncomfortable admitting his difference from other Jem'Hadar. "My body synthesizes the enzyme it needs."

The Founder appeared to consider this for a moment, moving away from him and pacing deeper into the room. At the far end, near a tall, thin geometric sculpture with a rough-hewn surface, she stopped and turned back to face him. "Is your lack of dependence on ketracel-white a result of your advanced age?" she asked, obviously recognizing him as a Jem'Hadar elder.

"I do not know," Taran'atar said. "I do not think so. I believe that other, younger Jem'Hadar have been found with the same—" He had been about to utter the word *deficiency*, but did not want to show weakness to the Founder. "—the same characteristic," he finished.

"Others have been found?" she asked from across the room. "By whom?" Again, her appearance seemed to harden.

"By several Vorta," Taran'atar replied, "acting under the direction of Odo."

"Odo," she echoed. "He explicitly searched for Jem'Hadar without a dependence on ketracel-white? And then from that group selected you to live in the Alpha Quadrant?"

"Yes," Taran'atar said. Despite the fact that it had been Odo who had ordered both the identification of his defect and his assignment to the Alpha Quadrant, Taran'atar felt right now as though he had himself failed this Founder.

She walked back over and stared up at him with a piercing gaze. "Why did he take those actions?" she asked.

"I—I do not know," Taran'atar responded haltingly, unnerved at being asked to speak about a Founder's motives— even though he had fought such doubts and concerns himself during his months on DS9.

"He did not tell you?" she questioned him. "When Odo sent

you from the Dominion, he did not tell you what he wanted
you to accomplish?"

"He did, but I do not entirely understand," Taran'atar admitted. "I am to experience living among the species of the Alpha
Quadrant. I would never question the wisdom of a Founder,
but I do not understand why this is necessary, or why I—or any
Jem'Hadar—would be selected for such a mission. We were
bred for war."

"Yes, you were," she agreed. "Did Odo tell you for what period of time he would require you to stay in the Alpha Quadrant?"

"He did not," Taran'atar said. "But during his recent visit to
Deep Space—"

"His *recent* visit?" the Founder asked, her voice rising to
emphasize the middle word.

"Odo spent nearly four weeks on Deep Space 9 and Bajor,"
Taran'atar explained, "until he left to go back to the Great Link
almost three months ago."

"Why was he there?" she asked.

"Odo told me that he wanted to check on my progress,"
Taran'atar said. "He also accepted an invitation from the Bajorans to attend a ceremony in which they entered the Federation. I believe that he also wanted to see Kira."

"Of course," the Founder said. "His loyalties are still divided."

The assertion startled Taran'atar. Although he did not understand the reasons why he had been sent to live in the Alpha
Quadrant, and although he wished to return to the Dominion,
he had never mistrusted Odo. "I would not presume to evaluate
the loyalties of a Founder," he said. *Except . . .* he thought. *Except had he not come here to have this Founder give him new
orders—orders that would supersede Odo's?*

"Of course you wouldn't," the Founder said. "You are not
capable of doing so. But I am." Again, she turned and strode
away from him. "Odo lived for decades in the Alpha Quadrant,
among solids," she said, although Taran'atar could not tell
whether she meant her words for him or only for herself. "He
developed feelings for one of them, for Kira, and that emotion,
born in a life warped by exposure to solids and isolation from
his own kind, still drives him."

She stopped walking beside a small, potted tree, its short branches adorned with pentagonal leaves of various colors, from blue and violet on the lower branches, to red and yellow on the upper. Large thorns decorated its narrow trunk in parallel lines that swirled around it. As the Founder continued talking, she reached out and took hold of the trunk three-quarters of the way up.

"Odo seeks to change the Dominion, to change the Great Link itself, to alter the natural order of things." As she spoke, her hand began to display a flickering orange glow, and her fingers elongated, encircling the tree as her newly formed tendrils climbed upward and descended downward. "He foolishly wants to engender some sort of direct relationship between our people and the solids, so that he can unite his places in both worlds, and keep both the Great Link and Kira in his life."

The shining extensions of her hand now wrapping around the branches of the tree, the Founder looked back over her shoulder at Taran'atar. "But such efforts will never work," she said. "Even Odo, with his inexperience, will come to understand that one day."

Captured by her stare, Taran'atar felt compelled to respond. "As you say," he told her.

"And when he fails," she went on, as though Taran'atar had not spoken, "he will abandon the Great Link, and he will return to Kira. Not just for weeks, but for as long as Kira lives." A branch snapped beneath the entwining grip of the Founder's form, and then a second snapped as well. Taran'atar watched as the shimmering tendrils constricted, solidifying into milky white tentacles. Suddenly, the tree splintered, its trunk and limbs flying fragmented to the floor, its leaves fluttering down in a rainbow of movement. "Odo will flout the sacrifice I have made for our people," the Founder ended.

Taran'atar did not know how to react to what he took to be her show of anger. "Your sacrifice saved the Great Link," he said, understanding that her establishment of peace with the powers of the Alpha Quadrant had allowed Odo to bring a cure to the Founders when they had been assaulted by disease.

"It did," she said, raising her voice as she turned fully toward him. The pale appendages extending from her arm had fallen to the floor when the tree had broken beneath their clutches, and they remained there now, unmoving. "I agreed to end the war, to give myself over to my enemies . . ." She began walking toward Taran'atar, the extensions of her fingers trailing behind her, as though being dragged like something not a part of her own body. ". . . to relinquish my freedom at the hands of the lowly solids, all in order to save the Great Link . . . and to save Odo."

"To save Odo?" Taran'atar said, confused. The Founder's demeanor seemed odd to him, and he wondered if her isolation had affected her.

"He was one of the Hundred," she said. She abruptly stopped, looked upward, and threw her arms into the air. The tendrils contracted in an instant back into her hand, but then both of her arms wavered and separated into scores of slender filaments. They reached up toward the ceiling and curved back down at their tips, which ended in sparkling silver lights. The effect put Taran'atar in mind of a field of stars, somehow brought down from the sky to twinkle just a couple of meters overhead. "And I was one of those who decided to send him and the others away. But I wanted our people to survive and to be whole again. I had no choice but to send the Hundred away."

Taran'atar knew of the hundred changelings that had been seeded throughout space by the Great Link, but he did not understand the points the Founder appeared to be trying to make. He did not see how dividing the Great Link and sending individual changelings away could possibly help the Founders survive, or paradoxically, be whole. But he said nothing.

The Founder looked at him. "You know of the disease that struck my people," she said. She dropped her arms, and the filaments she had sent into the air fell to the floor with a strange, whispering sound, as though dozens of inaudible voices had spoken at once, combining to be heard. "My sacrifice in agreeing to come here, to be kept as a prisoner . . . my sacrifice saved Odo by seeing to it that he returned to the Great Link."

Taran'atar continued to say nothing, his muscles rigid as he stood motionless before the Founder.

"The Great Link," she said, repeating her own words, but

acting as though responding to somebody else. "Do you bring word of the Great Link?" she asked.

"I do not, Founder," he said, unable to ignore a direct question. "I can tell you that before Odo sent me to the Alpha Quadrant, he spoke of the Great Link being in turmoil, of having to deal with the loss in the war, and with rebellions that had arisen within the Dominion after that. But on his recent trip, Odo talked about the Link having calmed in recent months, and of the insurgencies quieting."

The Founder nodded absently, her eyes focusing past Taran'atar. With no warning, she raised her arms again, and the willowy strands projecting from them retracted. A moment later, they had formed into hands again. The Founder looked at him once more.

"Why are you here?" she asked, her tone reverting to its formerly measured tenor. "Why have you come to see me in this prison?"

"I am here—" he began, and thought, *because I am lost, because I do not belong in the Alpha Quadrant, because I want to go back to the Dominion, and to being a soldier.* But instead, he said, "—because I wish to be of whatever service I can be to you."

"I see," she said as she retreated back across the room, hands clasped behind her back. "And of what service do you expect to be?"

"I don't know," he said. "I thought that, since you've been away from the Dominion and the Great Link for so long now, I hoped that I might be able to offer some . . . relief . . . of that circumstance."

She spun sharply on her heel. "And you suppose that *your* presence here would do that for me, would allay the misery of my seclusion?"

"I don't know," Taran'atar said again, and he realized that what he had told Kira, what he had told himself, about wanting to ease the isolation of the Founder, had been nothing but a cover. He had kept from Kira his true motivation for wanting to come here, but he had lied to himself as well, professing a desire to help the Founder when he had known that he would be unable to do so. What sort of impact could a Jem'Hadar have on a Founder separated from the Great Link? No, the only reasons he had come here had been to get help for himself.

And now he would seek that help.

"I need your assistance, Founder," he said. "I am a Jem'Hadar soldier. I do not belong in the Alpha Quadrant. I do not belong without ketracel-white being fed into my body. I need guidance, but I have no means of contacting Odo."

"And so you thought to visit the only other Founder you could," she said.

"Yes."

"You seek my permission to leave the post to which Odo assigned you," she said.

"I would not defy the will of a god," Taran'atar said, "but Odo is not the only god."

"Nor am I," she said, her voice rising almost to a yell. "I am no god at all." Again, Taran'atar wondered if her captivity had impacted her emotional state, or even her mind. He dismissed the thought, even as he recalled the Jem'Hadar first on Sindorin, who had maintained that the Founders were not gods, and that the Jem'Hadar of the Dominion were no more than slaves. Taran'atar had denied both allegations because he'd believed them false, and he still did. This had been his life, and he had always known that until the day he died in battle defending the Founders, this would continue to be his life.

Except that Odo had changed all of that. And now this Founder stood before him and threatened to change it even more.

"Founder," he began, but she spoke before he could go on.

"The Founders are not gods," she said. "We developed the Jem'Hadar and the Vorta into what they are now, we are powerful and superior to all solids. But the one, true God—the Progenitor—created the Founders."

Taran'atar said nothing at first. The Founder needed his help, he realized, but he did not know what to do. As he'd told Kira, attempting to break the Founder out of this facility would put her life at risk. At the same time, her imprisonment had clearly had a deleterious effect on her.

"Let me serve you, Founder," he said at last, hoping that she would know what he could do to help her.

"Your servitude means nothing to me," she said. "You lost the war." Taran'atar immediately wanted to tell her that he had not fought for the Dominion against the forces of the Alpha Quadrant, but also understood that such information would likely not matter to her. "If you had been strong enough," she went on, "if the Jem'Hadar and the Vorta had been able to properly control the Cardassians and the Breen, then the Dominion would have conquered the Federation and the Klingons and the Romulans. And victory would have rendered my sacrifice unnecessary."

Taran'atar waited to see if she would say more. When it became clear that she would not, he quietly asked, "Founder, please, how can I serve you?"

"Leave me," she said.

Taran'atar stared at the Founder, feeling paralyzed. He did not wish to disobey her, nor did he wish to abandon her to this fate. He longed for the life he had once known, where he knew his place as a soldier and his responsibilities to the Founders, and where he understood how to fulfill his duties. Since Odo had sent him here to the Alpha Quadrant, though, he'd lost his way.

Taran'atar turned toward the inner door, preparing to go, but then he paused. How long would he have to live his life like this, he wondered, his soldier's duties past, his value to his gods incomprehensibly low? Perhaps the Jem'Hadar on Sindorin had been right after all: perhaps Taran'atar was only a slave, of no more worth to his creators than a cog in a machine.

He turned back around. "Founder," he said.

Odo's pliable cells spun as he joined hands with Laas. After studying aboard the Jem'Hadar vessel the records concerning the Hundred, they had transported back down to the Founders' world, intending to seek out Indurane to tell him what they'd learned. Now, to that end, they melded together and twisted up from the surface of the islet. Odo felt the familiar rush of his link with another changeling, the reactive unity defined by the marriage of idea—at the moment, the search for the ancient Founder—and sensation—the circular velocity of their entangled bodies as they spiraled upward. Pushing counter to gravity, they slowed and turned, arcing to the side and then down. As one, they plunged into the living sea formed by the union of their people.

Even before Odo reached out into the Great Link, he discerned the change in it. What he had sensed for the past month as a mixture of disquiet and enthusiasm had exploded into unrestrained excitement. More than he had ever experienced, the community of Founders seethed, its currents swirling into a massive maelstrom, a cauldron veritably boiling with movement. Figures took shape at a dizzying rate, solid forms blooming in the golden changeling deep like insects in amber, and then just as quickly dissolving back into the metamorphic essence from which they'd been sculpted. Odo perceived the untold shapes around him, along with a flood of thoughts, an effect not unlike the indistinguishable gesticulations and voices of a mob. He tried to attune his own mind to the scuttle of form and contemplation surrounding and inundating him, and could make out only one consistent concept: *the Progenitor.*

Odo quickly concluded that locating Indurane amid the turbulence of the Great Link would not be a simple matter. Still joined with him, Laas shared this thought and concurred with it. In the next moment, Odo felt the emptiness he always felt at the dissipation of a link with another Founder, as Laas separated from him. Odo reached out—first to Laas, and then to the rest of the changeling mass—sending his body scattering, but still intact, in all directions, like a pool of water dropped into an ocean. His perceptions expanded as his senses joined with those around him, and then spread again as his connections with those changelings extended through their own swarm of connections.

Laas, he thought, even as he identified his fellow member of the Hundred rocketing through the Great Link, a sleek, streamlined projectile slicing horizontally along, like a waterborne torpedo. His rapid motion meshed with the environment of elation all about them. Laas, initially troubled by the notion of a Founder god, had grown exhilarated as he and Odo had discussed the subject, and had wanted to urge Indurane and the Link to determine whether or not the Progenitor had indeed returned. Odo, intrigued but skeptical, had questions for Indurane.

Beneath the surface of the Link, Laas suddenly changed direction. His projectile form veered upward and broke through the top of the changeling sea, surging into the air. Through the communal senses of his people, Odo watched without eyes as Laas's flesh glistened, altering its contours. Thin, broad appendages appeared, stretching outward in a flash. The wings flapped once, twice, a third time, carrying Laas higher into the sky. Then he transformed again, rolling into a glowing sphere, almost too brilliant to view. The miniature sun hovered, and Odo marveled at Laas's abilities, wondering precisely how he had constituted his body to emulate a burning star and at the same time remain suspended in the air. Gradually, the fiery orb increased in brightness, until it became clear that Laas intended the faux nova to mimic the real thing that still dominated the sky of the Founders' world.

Around Odo, the Link grew more animated. He hunted for Indurane, and found his sensory pursuit directed back to the dual-peaked islet he frequented. There, a changeling climbed from the Great Link and onto land. It rose to a humanoid height, then shifted, most of its glowing orange façade darkening to the brown of the militia uniform Odo still simulated when he took Bajoran form, the rest of it lightening into the pale skin tones of a face and hands. When the alteration had completed, Odo saw a replica of himself standing there. He recognized the invitation to him, and knew Indurane to be the one offering it.

Odo drew his body into itself and hied toward the islet, until he lifted himself up onto land to face his own image. "You wanted to see me," Odo said, not asking a question, but stating a fact. "Laas and I wanted to see you."

As if in response, the changeling adjusted its form once more, the manifestation of Odo blurring momentarily, then clarifying into that of a male Bajoran, the same one that Indurane had previously taken. Beyond him, in the distance, the brilliant sphere Laas had become continued to increase in intensity. "You have information," Indurane said, also not phrasing his words as a question.

"I do," Odo said, and told him of the study of the Hundred that he and Laas had made, and their determination that if the placement of the array of unformed changelings throughout the galaxy had been intended as both a lure and a return map for the Progenitor, then it pointed directly to the region now containing the nova.

"We are aware of this," Indurane said, clearly speaking for all of the Great Link. "We have kept that area under observation, and we knew of the nova's existence when it first occurred, but it meant little to us until it appeared here, in our own sky. Since that moment, we have been drawn to it."

Odo suddenly remembered what he had felt when he'd first spied the nova seemingly looming above the Founders' world. His initial dread, motivated by a concern for his people, had given way to hopefulness once he'd transported down to the planet and viewed the star from that perspective. Apparently like Indurane and the rest of the Link, he'd also felt its pull on his awareness.

"We believe that the image of the starburst was implanted by the Progenitor in the minds of the Founders," Indurane said, as though explaining Odo's feelings, "just as we who sent out the Hundred implanted the image of the Omarion Nebula in their minds." The notion bolstered the belief that the changeling god had created the Great Link in its own image. Past Indurane, Laas's radiant form faded, then dropped back into the Link.

"And you believe that the Progenitor has returned there?" Odo asked, though the answer seemed clear.

"I do," Indurane said. "*We* do." He looked to the side, his gaze taking in the changeling deep surrounding the islet.

"What does the Link intend to do?" Odo wanted to know.

"We have contemplated that question for some time now," Indurane said. "At the first appearance of the nova, some of us—and soon many of us—believed that the Progenitor had returned. We anticipated it making the final leg of Its journey back to us, but as time passed and that did not happen, some of us proposed that we consider another action besides waiting."

Odo turned from Indurane and looked up into the twilight. The bright star stood out like an omen, and Odo wondered how much truth he faced here, and how much myth. Did the Progenitor exist in reality—had it ever?—or only as a figment in the history of the Founders? Odo didn't know, but the feelings of Indurane and the rest of the Great Link could not have been more plain. Their weeks of restlessness, building to the crescendo of excitement and activity he'd just witnessed moments ago, revealed genuine belief not only in a Creator, but in Its impending return to them.

To one side, Odo saw movement, and he looked in that direction to see another Founder reaching out of the Link and onto land. Quickly, it morphed into the Varalan form of Laas. He stood partway around the islet, between Odo and Indurane.

Odo waited for Laas to look his way, and then said, "They already know," explaining what Indurane had just told him.

Laas peered at Indurane. "What is the Great Link going to do?" he asked of the old Founder.

"We will travel to the region of the nova," Indurane said. "We will find the Progenitor."

Taran'atar disregarded the Founder's seemingly aberrant behavior, including most especially her claims that her people were not gods. If necessary, he would revisit all of that later. But for right now, he had no choice but to push all of that aside and execute the duty for which he—for which *all* Jem'Hadar—had been created.

As he exited the cell, Taran'atar concentrated deeply. He visualized the Founder reverting to her natural state behind him, her humanoid figure liquefying into a nebulous pool of biomimetic ichor. Vaguely aware of the inner door of the antechamber closing after him, he focused his thoughts intensely. In the facility's main control room, he presumed, at least one of the prison personnel would be surveying the monitors that allowed the cell to be kept under continuous surveillance. A picture of the Vulcan commander rose in his mind, and he quickly shifted his viewpoint in that mental scene to the image T'Kren saw on the security screen, namely that of the amorphous Founder.

Through the transparent outer door of the antechamber, Taran'atar saw Lieutenant Commander Matheson approaching. Lieutenant Jenek, the Orion, maintained a position behind her, fifteen meters away. Taran'atar noted the presence of the two Starfleet officers in a cursory way, at the periphery of his perceptions, but worked to ignore what his eyes witnessed, what his ears heard, what his skin felt, instead paying strict attention to the perfectly defined representation in his thoughts of the Founder's shapeless mass spread out on the floor of the cell. Even as the outer door wound open and Matheson invited him to follow her, and even as he did so, he continued to keep the Founder's gleaming form at the forefront of his consciousness.

Taran'atar took only passing notice as Matheson led him left at the T-shaped intersection, back down the corridor they'd taken when they'd walked here. As Jenek's footsteps began to fall behind him, the lieutenant obviously following just as he had earlier, Taran'atar listened reflexively to the rhythmic pace of his own boots marching along the deck. He let his legs carry him forward mechanically, tracking along after Matheson. He followed her back through Ananke Alpha's maze of corridors, his movements unthinking as he continued to envision the unformed changeling. He tramped back through two of the prison's defensive emplacements—the one armed with phasers, and the one with heat—until they neared the third line of defense.

As Taran'atar stopped at Matheson's order, he felt his mental grip on the image of the Founder begin to slip. Dimly aware of the door up ahead blocking the way, and of the lieutenant commander pushing a key into a slot in the bulkhead, he struggled to preserve his clear visualization of the Founder. He did not know how much longer he could sustain his efforts. Shrouding normally required a significant exertion of will, but far less, it turned out, than the task at hand. Taran'atar had never attempted what he did now, had not even known it possible until a few moments ago, having heard only unconfirmed rumors of Jem'Hadar who had utilized their shrouding capabilities for remote generation of images.

Activity up ahead penetrated his awareness. He plainly heard Matheson identify herself and request access to the defensive emplacement, distinctly felt vibrations through the decking as the door began to slide slowly into the bulkhead. *Too far,* he thought, intuitively understanding that his capacity to project a realistic image relied not only on his ability to concentrate, but also on his distance from the location to which he projected that image.

"Let's continue," Matheson called back to him, and she strode through the now-open doorway.

Taran'atar had almost reached the same point himself when a knot of pain tightened behind his forehead. Given the level of focus needed at his ever-increasing remove from the cell, the sensation became impossible to ignore. At the same time, he realized that he had moved beyond his range. Elsewhere in the prison, he knew, one or more security officers would see the glistering form of the Founder vanish from her cell. The instant before the red alert sliced through the corridor—and doubtless through the entire complex—Taran'atar knew that it would. It provided him just enough time to act.

He sprang forward, toward the doorway and, beyond it, Matheson. Then, as the klaxon sounded, he redirected his thoughts and shrouded, rendering himself invisible. He lunged to his right, to the side of the corridor, just in time to avoid the phaser blast that seared the air where he had just stood. He whirled around and sprinted along the bulkhead toward Jenek, while the security officer continued discharging his weapon, sweeping it left and right. Taran'atar had closed to within a couple of meters of his objective when the yellow-red beam swung toward him, chest high.

Desperate not only to break the Founder from captivity, but to protect her from harm in doing so—she currently blanketed the front his coverall, matching its texture and hue—he dove onto the deck. The powerful shaft of light streaked centimeters above him, its whine audible even over the sound of the red alert. Knowing that his shroud had dropped, he drove his boots against the decking and hurled himself forward. He struck Jenek below the knees, and the security officer toppled forward, his phaser shooting wildly for a second before his finger lost contact with its firing pad.

Taran'atar spun around and reached for the lieutenant's hand, pulling the phaser from his grasp. Then he sent an arm around the security officer's throat and quickly stood, dragging him upward. "Move," Taran'atar growled into Jenek's ear, "and I'll snap your neck." Towering over the stocky Orion, Taran'atar pulled him up off his feet, providing himself cover for his own upper body and head, and more importantly, for the Founder.

Almost at once, two phaser strikes surged past from behind him. Both narrowly missed Taran'atar, but Jenek cried out in obvious pain as one of them grazed his shoulder. Taran'atar looked back and immediately spotted some of the many weapons ports he'd seen on his way to the Founder's cell. He held Jenek up as a shield before those ports situated ahead of him, and fired at those situated behind him. In swift succession, one emitter after another erupted in a hail of sparks. Taran'atar then turned his phaser on all the rest, quickly disabling the weapons, as well as the surveillance and sensor ports.

When he'd finished, he glanced around Jenek, and saw Matheson racing back into the corridor from within the defensive emplacement. He'd hoped that she might have been caught in the lieutenant's phaser fire, but they had surely trained for events such as this, and that hadn't happened. Matheson fired her weapon twice, both shots high and to the left of Taran'atar and his captive. As he had so many times since coming to the Alpha Quadrant, he felt contempt for the weakness he continually observed here; Matheson had clearly targeted away from her colleague, unwilling to chance hitting Jenek, but at the risk of failing to fulfill her duties.

After firing, she turned to the control panel in the bulkhead beside the door. At the same time, Jenek launched an attack, kicking backward with both boots at Taran'atar's shins, sending an elbow into his gut, and biting down hard on the arm tightly circling his neck. Taran'atar felt the air rush from his lungs as the lieutenant reached backward and tried to wrestle the phaser from his hand. Gasping for air, Taran'atar let the weapon drop to the deck, then reached around Jenek's face with his empty hand, took hold of his ear, and pulled sharply. Even with the blare of the alarm klaxon, he could hear the Orion's neck break, the sound like wood crackling in a fire.

Taran'atar threw the inert body of the lieutenant to the side, where it struck the bulkhead. Unencumbered, he shrouded, took a deep breath, retrieved the phaser, then sped toward Matheson, who still worked at the panel. When the door beside her began to close, Taran'atar raised his weapon and fired, his shroud dropping in the process. The phaser shot struck Matheson squarely in the rib cage, and she crumpled.

Hurrying ahead, Taran'atar stepped over the body of the dead security officer, wisps of smoke rising from her blackened uniform. He examined the control panel. The indicator light there glowed amber, and the key that Matheson had used still sat in its slot. He reached for the key and turned it, producing a click, but the indicator light remained amber, and the door continued to glide closed. Taran'atar could still pass through this door, but he would never make it to the far side of the line of defense before the door there closed.

Quickly, he reached down, took hold of Matheson's arm, and pulled it toward the plate next to the control panel. He felt her shoulder give way beneath his efforts, her humerus ripping free of her scapula. As he thrust her hand down on the plate, her arm articulated in an unnatural way, her muscles and flesh seeming to hold her arm barely connected to her body.

The light flashed from amber to green. Beside Taran'atar, the door stopped moving, then reversed direction and began to open again. He let go of Matheson's arm, which flopped to the deck with a thud. Then he darted sidelong through the doorway.

Taran'atar looked to the other side of the defensive emplacement, his gaze following the blue forcefield lines on either side of the walkway that led there. Seeing the far door sliding open, he started forward, and felt again the slight give in the nonmetallic surface of the decking here. He ran with his head down, intent on reaching the next corridor. The alert klaxon echoed loudly here, though with a slightly tinny effect in the large space.

A third of the way across the span, Taran'atar saw the parallel lines of blue lighting darken, the forcefields obviously deactivated. A mechanical hum rose, a vibration more felt than heard. Ahead of him, a fissure seemed to carve through the walkway, and it split in two, the halves beginning to retract toward each of the doorways.

Taran'atar did not break stride. By the time he reached the

gap, the sections of the walkway had moved apart more than twelve meters. Timing his gait, he brought one foot down just short of the open space, then leaped. He knew immediately that he would not come down on the other section of walkway. Spreading his arms wide, he dropped the phaser and braced himself. His chest struck the edge of the other section, and he clamped his hands down onto its sides.

As he swung his legs up and around onto the bridge, he heard the phaser clattering somewhere below him. He gave brief thought to the Founder's safety—she still adhered to the fabric covering his torso—but knew that such a physical impact would have no effect on her. He clambered back up onto the walkway. The far door had begun to close, he saw, but he knew that he could cover the distance between here and there in time to make it through and into the corridor.

That was when the radiation emitters powered up.

The area brightened, and a heavy drone filled the air. Taran'atar crossed his arms over his chest, which slowed his pace, but he had to do whatever he could to protect the Founder. While a physical blow would not harm her, radiation certainly would.

Fifteen meters from the door, his body began to tingle, as though he had been enveloped by insects. Ten meters away, the sensation intensified, rapidly becoming painful, as though the insects had begun to devour his flesh. He soldiered forward, attempting to ignore the agony. At five meters, feeling as though he'd been set ablaze, he stopped, needing a moment to collect himself for the final part of his flight, even as he knew that his cells had begun to deteriorate, attacked without mercy by the radiation. But he'd lost Jenek's phaser, and he had to conclude that the Founder had not shapeshifted because she could not; Taran'atar had heard of fields that could prevent a changeling from altering form, and he reasoned that such a field had been activated within the prison once the Founder's escape had become known.

Pushing away the pain and refocusing his thoughts, Taran'atar shrouded once more, although not in invisibility. He took one more moment to assure himself of his concentration, then dashed forward. He flung himself through the almost-closed doorway and landed on the rigid decking of the corridor.

He waited for phaser blasts to slam into him. None came.

Slowly, he got to his feet, veiled in the likeness of Lieutenant Commander Matheson. He'd imagined her badly injured: one arm hanging limply at her side, a hand gripping the damaged shoulder, a wounded leg unable to carry her along without a limp, a charred, bloody hole in her side from an energy weapon. He mimicked the movements attendant with such injuries, leaning heavily against a bulkhead as he staggered along. His own pain simplified his efforts, making it easier for him to keep up the charade.

Lurching ahead, he let the clamor of the red-alert signal carry his concentration. At the end of the corridor, he stumbled around the corner and turned right. Just a few meters away, two doors stood closed in the left-hand bulkhead. The first led to the room where he'd donned the bright-red coverall, and the second, he felt certain, to the control room.

Aware that he'd likely been under observation since exiting the radiation emplacement, he continued to limp along. He passed the first door, and stopped at the second. A panel, similar to those that Matheson had operated on the way to and from the Founder's cell, sat in the bulkhead next to the door. Taran'atar reached for it, brushed his hand against one corner, then let his legs buckle. He tumbled heavily to the deck, and lay there, unmoving, his back against the bulkhead.

Only seconds passed before the door to the control room retracted. "Jackie," said the female Tellarite he'd seen earlier. She crouched down beside him, a phaser in one hand, and reached with two fingers of her empty hand toward what she clearly saw as Matheson's neck, evidently wanting to measure the security officer's pulse. When she'd come close enough, Taran'atar sent his arm flying upward, his shroud falling as his fingers wrapped around the Tellarite's thick, soft neck. He squeezed, and felt the cartilage of her larynx give way beneath his grip. She coughed once, feebly, spitting out mucus tinged with the lavender color of her blood. The phaser dropped from her hand.

In the control room, barely audible beneath the alarm,

Taran'atar heard commotion—voices and movements—and isolated the sounds to determine the presence of at least two other officers. His hand still around the neck of the sputtering Tellarite, Taran'atar swiped the phaser from the deck and jumped to his feet.

As soon as he stepped into the doorway, a phaser blast screamed in his direction, but struck the back of the dying security officer he held up before him. The scent of burning flesh filled the air. Taran'atar leveled his own weapon past the now-motionless Tellarite and returned fire. Across the room, the beam landed on a console, which exploded. The red-alert klaxon abruptly ceased here, though he could still here it in the distance. A flame reached almost to the overhead as smoke billowed upward.

Another shot rang out, seemingly louder now that the alarm had silenced within the room. A streak of phased energy scorched the air beside Taran'atar, then moved toward him. The beam caught him in the side before he could block it with the body of the Tellarite, and it felt as though a hole had been cut open along his rib cage. He ignored the pain, concerned only for the protection of the Founder and making good her flight from imprisonment. He fired his phaser again, and another console blew up beneath the assault. Thick smoke filled the room.

Taran'atar waited for the next phaser blast, then flung the body of the Tellarite hard in that direction. He threw himself to the side and onto the deck, his eyes and ears seeking a target through the murky, pungent smoke. He tried to shroud but could not; coupled with the damage done to his body by the radiation, the throbbing ache in his side would not allow him to concentrate enough to project his veil of invisibility.

Another phaser fired. The beam passed well above Taran'atar, but he tracked the yellow-red ray back to its source and discharged his own weapon. He heard the dull sound of a body as it thumped onto the deck.

A sudden calm seemed to overtake the scene, the only sounds that of his labored breathing and the occasional spark from one of the destroyed consoles, underscored by the far-off cry of the alarm. Although it was possible that his shots had incapacitated both of the officers here, he believed that one still opposed him. He waited, alert for any noise, any movement, and when none came, he tried again to shroud. As he did so, a blur flashed toward him from the side, and he felt something collide with his hand. The phaser he'd taken from the Tellarite flew from his grasp before he could act. He watched it land several meters away, then turned toward his enemy, who had already stepped back away from him.

"Where is the Founder?" the Vulcan woman, T'Kren, asked. She spoke with a level voice, even amid the chaos that had erupted in the control room. She carried her phaser in her left hand, its emitter trained on him.

Taran'atar did not bother to respond, instead calculating his best chance to overcome the Vulcan and depart Ananke Alpha. Any assault he launched now would easily be beaten back, particularly in his wounded condition. He peered down at his body, and saw that large patches of his rough, gray hide had blackened, some oozing a viscous, amber fluid, all doubtless a result of his exposure to the radiation. One of the shoulder straps of his coverall hung down loosely. Pieces of the garment had been torn away in places, and a hole opened where the phaser shot had punched into his side. He feared for the Founder, unsure if she remained spread across the fabric of the coverall, or if she had fallen away during the fight.

"I will ask you only once more," the Vulcan declared, and Taran'atar looked up at her. "Where is—"

Sudden movement interrupted her. She turned quickly, bringing her weapon around, but too late. The malleable, orange-gold strip, meters long and only centimeters wide, streaked from a place on the floor straight up to the Vulcan's phaser. The changeling twisted speedily around the fingers holding the weapon, preventing them from firing it.

Taran'atar scrambled up and across the room, to where T'Kren had knocked the phaser from his own hand. He picked it up, turned, and fired at the Vulcan. The beam struck her in the head and sent her reeling backward, out of the Founder's grasp, dead even before her body hit the bulkhead and crashed to the deck.

A moment later, the Founder stood before him, wearing the

guise of the smooth-faced humanoid he'd seen in her cell. "You're hurt," she said, the words seeming a statement more of fact than of concern. "Can you go on?" she asked.

"Victory is life," he told her. "I serve you for as long as I stand, and I will stand at least as long as it takes to return you to the Dominion."

"Then let us depart," she said.

"Yes, Founder," he replied, then hastened over to the consoles. Two had been completely destroyed, one of which had obviously controlled the field that had until now prevented the Founder from shapeshifting during their escape. Taran'atar made a fast study of the controls and readouts on the intact consoles, identifying all internal and external weapons systems, as well as Ananke Alpha's deflector screens. He deactivated all of them, then checked a map of the corridors, and worked to open the three doors between here and the shuttlebay, including the one opposite the door through which he'd entered the control room. When he finished, he turned back to the Founder. "I have a spacecraft waiting," he said.

"Lead the way," she ordered.

Taran'atar raced from the control room into a short corridor, which angled left to an open door and intersected with the first corridor he'd entered in the facility. He retraced his steps, noting in the center of the deck the red line he'd followed earlier. Finally, phaser drawn, he marched through another doorway and into the shuttlebay, the Founder right behind him.

Rio Grande sat in the same location and position as when it had landed, its forward port hatch open. Kira stood outside the runabout, clearly having just disembarked the ship. She carried no weapon.

Taran'atar stopped and looked at her, feeling the presence of the Founder beside him. Kira stared at him for a moment, then glanced at the Founder, and finally back at him again.

"Taran'atar," she said, her utterance of his name easily conveying her disappointment.

He did not respond.

"I'm ordering you to stand down," she continued, "and to return the Founder to her cell." She said nothing about Odo's directive to do as Kira commanded, but Taran'atar recalled well the parameters of the mission on which Odo had sent him. Disobeying Kira now would be the same as disobeying Odo—the same as disobeying a Founder. He had never done such a thing during the twenty-two years of his life.

"Kill her," said the Founder at his side. "Kill her, and let's get out of here."

Taran'atar's resolve wavered. He'd now essentially been giving conflicting orders by two different Founders, and he felt unsure how to proceed. He attempted to cover his indecision by examining the power level of the phaser, which he saw had been set to kill. He did not change it.

Hadn't he come here for this? he asked himself. Hadn't he wanted this Founder to issue him orders to return to the Dominion, orders that would contradict Odo's? And hadn't he intended to follow such orders? He had not thought that he would have to kill Captain Kira, but did that matter? He had believed that he would simply be able to leave her behind, but now he'd been given a different order.

"Kill her," the Founder said again.

Taran'atar raised the phaser—still set to kill—and aimed it at Kira. He looked at her face—*that* face—and finally found the sense of duty he needed to take action. He would do what he had to do, and then escape on the runabout with the Founder and return to the Dominion.

Taran'atar applied pressure to the triggering pad, and his weapon roared to life, its lethal beam springing from the emitter. The captain had no time to move. The shot struck her directly in the chest.

As Taran'atar watched, Kira collapsed to the deck of the shuttlebay, dead.

One of the changelings—not Laas or Indurane, but one of the three others in the small link with Odo—conveyed the impression of a pit. Flattening itself in a curved, irregular shape, it depressed the majority of its planar surface a few centimeters down from its raised outer border. From a macroscopic perspective, it would have taken on little meaning in terms of scale, but when observed from within, from a viewpoint of the infinitesimal, it took on grand proportions: soaring walls impossible to ascend, its floor vast, desolate, and in-escapable.

Surveying the gaping cavity, Odo wondered about its in-tended meaning. As he watched, something began to rise from the center of the barren plane, something changeable and strong, growing sizable enough to dominate its surroundings. Odo recognized the imagery even before the burning star formed beside it, and even before the star flared into a nova: the Progenitor, rising high to look beneficently down on the Founders, ready to save the Great Link from the abyss of their future extinction.

Most of the changelings present responded with movement, their unstructured bodies swaying frantically in jubilation. Odo himself shifted, but not as the others did. He seeped through them, until finally he rolled clear, his body curled into a tight golden sphere. He then weaved around the writhing mass toward a far corner of the large, empty cabin, settling near the intersection of two bulkheads. Exhausted by the frenzied ex-pectancy exhibited constantly by all of the Founders here—all of them but for Laas—he retained his round shape for a while, resting quietly as he attempted to distance himself from the tu-mult of their potent emotions.

Beside him, the gathering of changelings continued to un-dulate. Indurane and the three others had been selected by the Great Link to travel to the region of the nova, in search of the Progenitor, and Odo and Laas had chosen to accompany them. Once the decision had been made, Odo had suggested Jem'Hadar Attack Vessel 971, based upon his familiarity with its personnel, and there had been no objection. He'd trans-ported up to the ship first and prepared for the journey, inform-ing Weyoun of their destination, but keeping from him and the Jem'Hadar crew the reason for the undertaking. Odo had also secured individual quarters for himself and for Laas, since they both still broke from the Link on a recurrent basis, and would likely do so during their travels, even with the smaller link. Ad-ditionally, Odo had arranged this roomy cabin for the other four changelings, knowing that they would neither require nor want separate accommodations.

To this point, the voyage had been uneventful, though

hardly restful. Indurane and the other three Founders had joined together immediately upon arriving here, and none of them had since parted from the others. Laas had spent most of his time with them as well, Odo less so. Besides needing to keep his own counsel in his own manner, he had never before experienced such an arduous, draining connection with his people. The vigor and endurance with which Indurane and the others communed about the Progenitor—characteristics that echoed the current state of the Great Link—had driven Odo from them several times now. He found their manic, obsessive behavior difficult to deal with, and fundamentally incomprehensible.

Realizing that he would find no further respite, Odo reached upward, fracturing the perfect shape of the globe he had become. He adjusted his variable body, remaking himself into the imprecise Bajoran form he'd worn for decades. He peered down at the Founders joined together—the metaphorical gulf, the nova, and the Progenitor all lost now to their physical fluctuations—and felt very far from them, and from the rest of his people. Since his return to the Founders after the war, he'd frequently been at odds with them. He'd sought answers, presented arguments, and propounded suggestions about the future of the Great Link and its relationships with the rest of the galaxy, and often, he'd found himself a minority of one, his ideas disregarded and disdained, his motivations questioned. And yet despite that, he'd still felt united to them. Now, though, he did not. In this strange and unexpected circumstance, he felt far more at variance with them than ever he had before, felt . . . *distinct* . . . from them in a way he never had.

Odo had never favored the Dominion's war with the denizens of the Alpha Quadrant, of course, had never agreed with the Founders' opinion of their superiority over humanoids, but he'd at least understood the justifications for their isolationist and xenophobic practices. After all, throughout their history, they had been persecuted, hunted, and murdered by solids. But this conviction, not only that the Progenitor had returned, but that It even existed at all . . . that the Founders believed in a Creator, Whom they now also looked upon as their Savior . . . Odo had trouble crediting such a situation. He would have thought it all a lie, some sort of elaborate ruse meant to mislead him in order to fulfill some hidden agenda, if not for his own experience with the Link. Alongside their fervent hopes that the Progenitor had returned, Odo had felt their passionate certainty in Its existence. They had no doubts, and that concerned him.

As he gazed down again at the moving, twisting pool before him, a bitter emptiness seemed to imbue his body, as though he had shapeshifted himself into merely a shell. He had not yet really coped with the revelation that the Founders could not reproduce, and would therefore one day die out. Though he knew that individual changelings lived long lives—*very* long lives, by humanoid standards—it grieved him to know that his people would face not only each of their own deaths, but that of their entire species. It made more sense now than ever that the Great Link took so very seriously the death of even a single Founder. It also seemed quite reasonable that such an extreme and final reality could have given rise to the concept of the Progenitor, both as the beginning of the Great Link, and as its rescue from oblivion.

And yet the very rationalization for the belief in a Creator undermined the reality of a Creator. For while the fear of death—both individual and communal death—provided an easily understandable motivation for theism, it did not provide any evidence to reasonably justify it. Quite the opposite, it suggested that belief resulted from need and desire, and not from truth—that the Founders believed in a Creator because they *wanted* to believe, not because of any strong evidence. Even the Bajorans, staunch in their faith in the divinity of the Prophets, did not hold that their deities had created the universe or their people. Nor did they look upon the Prophets to save them, but simply to help and guide them through their lives. Given the intellect and strength of the Founders, and even considering their eventual extinction, it seemed inexplicable to Odo that they actually believed in a Deity—particularly their version of It. For what kind of a God abandons Its people for thousands of years, or longer?

More worrisome to him, though, was what the reaction of the Great Link would be when Indurane and the others did not locate the Progenitor. The Founders would doubtless continue the search for some time, but it would in due course become clear that they would find nothing. Would they conclude that they had been wrong about the Progenitor's return, or about Its existence? And how would they react in either case, whether to the notion that their God continued to disregard them, or to the realization that It did not really exist? With their current level of assurance and excitement, Odo could not imagine a positive outcome.

For the third time in recent days, he thought of his conversation with Nerys in Dax's closet. What he asked himself now about the Founders, he had essentially asked of Nerys that night. And while her response—denial—did not have repercussions for her people, he worried that the same would not be true of the Great Link.

Odo gazed down at Laas, Indurane, and the other three Founders moving together on the floor of the cabin, their shining bodies moving as one. Quick to draw conclusions, and even quicker to extreme action, they caused Odo to fear what might soon happen. With the promise of the Progenitor taken from them, how would they react? Would they withdraw even more from the rest of the galaxy, or would they choose to preemptively rid themselves of any threats to their existence, once more sending armies of Jem'Hadar out to eliminate any who could conceivably cause harm to the Great Link, and thereby hasten its demise? And how, Odo asked himself, could he act to prevent either course, or any other terrible turn of events that might occur?

"Weyoun to Odo," came the Vorta's voice over the comm system, interrupting Odo's thoughts.

"I'm here, Weyoun," he said. "Go ahead."

"You asked me to inform you when we approached the nova, Founder," Weyoun said. *"We have just closed to within sensor range of the system."*

"Thank you," Odo said. "I'll join you on the bridge." He started past the linked changelings and toward the door. As he did so, though, the pool of biomimetic cells quickly separated into five segments, like identically charged particles repelling each other. At different rates, the individual Founders expanded upward, each taking humanoid shape. Indurane and two of the others took on inexact Bajoran forms, while Laas and the remaining changeling approximated Varalans.

"I'll keep you informed," Odo told the group as the door opened before him. But they paid him no heed, and as he stepped into the corridor on his way to the bridge, all five changelings followed. Soon enough, Odo thought, he would find out how they would react to not finding the Progenitor.

He dreaded what that reaction would be.

6

"What if you learned that the Prophets were not gods?" Odo asked Kira. "That they were simply alien beings with an interest in the Bajoran people?"

She did not respond right away. For a few moments, she didn't even move, instead simply staring back at him. Finally, Odo added, "Or what if the Prophets abandoned Bajor?"

Kira furrowed her brow, then leaned back on the small stool, lifting an elbow and forearm up onto Dax's vanity. "Odo," she said, "I can't learn any of those things about the Prophets because none of them are true, or ever will be true."

"You believe that the Prophets care for the Bajorans, and guide them, and always will," he said. "Your people experienced such hardship and suffering under the Cardassian Occupation . . . you lost your mother and father, friends . . . and yet you still retained your faith through all of that."

"Yes," Kira said, her mouth widening to a smile that bespoke of the peace and joy delivered to her by her convictions.

Odo studied her expression, and struggled to decide how best to make his point to her. She'd reconfirmed her unwavering faith in the Prophets, and he needed to figure out how to effectively compare her faith in her gods to his faith in his own people. He knew that she would resist the analogy.

Leaning forward on the storage bin, Odo put his hands on his knees, his elbows akimbo. He glanced to his left as he tried to choose his next words, and noticed several articles of clothing and footwear heaped about the deck, as though they had been carelessly tossed aside. He noted a single Starfleet uniform lying beneath two dresses—one black, one with a floral print—and his investigative skills told him that, after her shift had ended today, Dax had tried on various items before settling on the purple outfit she now wore at the party.

Trying to focus his mind, Odo turned back toward Kira. "To me," he said, "your faith seems so . . . pure."

Kira laughed, and Odo felt himself buoyed by the spontaneous sounds of her delight. "I don't think I'd ever describe myself as 'pure,' " she said. Then, more seriously, she continued, "But my faith is *real,* and it will always be a significant part of who I am."

"I know," Odo said, then sat up straight, bracing himself for the point he wanted to make. "I've recently discovered that I also have faith." He paused as Kira's eyebrows rose on her forehead in obvious surprise at his claim. "Despite the torment they've endured throughout their history," he explained, "and despite the torment they've inflicted on others, I have faith in my people."

Kira's eyebrows crashed back down. She pulled her arm from atop the vanity and into her lap, as though unconsciously preparing to defend herself. "I'm sure you'll understand if I don't agree with comparing my beliefs in the Prophets to yours in the Founders." Her voice had turned cold.

"Nerys, please," Odo said. "I'm not trying to equate the Prophets and the Founders. But I am trying to relate what I've been thinking and feeling to what you think and feel. I want to explain why I made the decision to link with the female Founder when I did."

Kira looked down, then carefully folded her hands together. He could see the tension in her jaw. "I'm listening," she said.

Odo peered ahead at the path he thought he could take to get where he wanted to go, but he also knew that he might face pitfalls along the way. Still, if he didn't continue the conversation he'd already begun, he would never get there. As gently as he could, he asked, "Are the Prophets responsible for your actions?"

"No, of course not," Kira replied, still peering down at her hands. "The Prophets love me and guide me through life . . . offer a source of solace . . . provide a touchstone for prayer. But we all have freedom of will."

"The responsibilities for your actions are your own?" Odo asked.

"Always," Kira said.

"And have you been proud of every action you've ever taken?" Odo asked.

"What?" Kira said, her head snapping up, her hands parting and moving to her hips. "I don't see what that has to do with this. If you're going to compare what I did during the Occupation, what I *had* to do—"

"I know that you fought hard to free your people from the tyranny of the Cardassians," Odo interrupted her. "And I understand that. But I also know that you killed Vaatrick—"

"He was a collaborator," Kira roared, leaping to her feet.

Odo stayed calm, and looked up at Kira from his seat on the storage bin. "He was also a Bajoran," Odo said, "and I know that even though you felt you had to kill him, you didn't *want* to."

"No," Kira agreed. "I didn't."

"No more than you wanted to kill innocent Cardassians during the raids and other attacks you participated in during the Occupation."

"No," Kira said again, and she dropped back down onto the stool. "I'm not . . . I never wanted innocent people to die. But my people were at war. The Cardassians—"

"Nerys," Odo stopped her. "I'm not judging you. I was here during the Occupation. I understand what the Bajorans went through . . . what *you* went through." She looked down again, and Odo waited until her head tilted upward and they made eye contact again. Only then did he continue. "More importantly," he said, "I understand who you are, and what your values are. I could not be friends with you otherwise."

Kira seemed to think about this for a few seconds, and then slowly shook her head. "Yes," she said. "I know that."

"But that's why you're no longer sure about our friendship," Odo said. "You thought you understood who I was, and what my values were, but then I did something that contradicted that."

"That's right," Kira said.

"But in a way, that's our common ground," Odo said. "We've both made choices in our lives, and we've both made mistakes for the good of our people."

"This situation seems different," Kira said. "You didn't join with the Founder and abandon Rom in order to try and free your people from oppression."

"No," Odo admitted, "but we were each doing what we needed to do to make ourselves whole. For you, it involved doing whatever you had to do to help your people. And it was the same for me." Kira opened her mouth, apparently to protest the characterization of his impetus, but Odo held up his hand, and she allowed him to go on. "I know I wasn't attempting to save my people from the same horrible threat that yours faced, but I was trying to help them. And I still want to help them."

Kira's features seemed to soften. "To save them from themselves?" she asked.

"From themselves, from their history, yes," Odo said. "They're my people, and I want them to live in peace, not just for the sake of those they would oppose, but for their own sake. And in order to help them, I need to understand them."

Kira said nothing for a moment, but did not look away from him. "I can believe that," she finally said. "But I still have a hard time accepting that you allowed Rom to be arrested and sentenced to die."

"I didn't set out to do that," Odo said, "any more than you ever set out to kill Cardassian children. But yes, it happened because of me, because I desperately wanted to understand my people, so that I could become a fuller part of them, and help them from within. I don't want my people to wage war against anybody, but particularly not against my friends."

"Would that cause have been worth the sacrifice of Rom's life?" Kira asked. Although clearly a pointed question, she spoke the words quietly, apparently looking for an actual answer and not an argument.

"I don't know," Odo said honestly. "If I could have stopped

the war . . ." He let his words trail off, realizing that he had gotten caught up in his own argument.

"You had no expectation that you could put an end to the war by joining with the Founder then," Kira accused him.

"No, you're right," Odo said. "That was a longer-term goal. But I also did not expect that my actions would result in Rom's death. And in the end, they didn't."

"No," Kira said, and she actually smiled again, a slight, anxious expression. "I was so happy to see you walk into the cargo hold."

"I think I was even more happy to see you," Odo said. He remembered that day vividly, first learning from the Founder that Kira had been arrested and would be executed, later hearing that she and Rom and the others had escaped from their holding cells. He'd quickly assembled a team of his deputies and tracked the group's movements. Jake and Leeta had gone to hide, but Kira and Rom had already been discovered and pursued by Dominion forces. Outside cargo bay thirteen, Odo and his cadre had engaged the Jem'Hadar, ultimately dispatching them.

"You never did tell me why, though," Kira said to him. Just after Odo and his deputies had rescued Kira and Rom, she'd posed that very question. He'd told her there wasn't time, but also that she probably already knew.

"When I'd heard that you'd been arrested," he explained, "and that you would be put to death . . ." Again, he let his voice fade to silence. He knew that his decision to retreat from the Founder and his desire to assist Kira had begun to form even before he'd learned of Kira's incarceration. Although revealing that now would be difficult, he felt that he needed to be as open and honest as he could be. "Actually, when I—" He searched for delicate language, and again settled on employing Kira's equivoque. "—slept with the Founder, trying to teach her about solids, trying to demonstrate to her an important way in which they shared their love for one another . . . she didn't understand."

"I'm not sure of the point you're trying to make," Kira said slowly, not sounding comfortable with the subject.

"We . . . performed . . . the act," Odo said haltingly, "but I could not make the Founder feel or understand the sharing involved. I felt no warmth myself, and I realized that I never would be able to share with the Founder what I'd shared with Arissa." And though he did not say it, it seemed to Odo that his next thought—that he could never share with the Founder what he one day hoped to share with Nerys—hung in the air between them. If he had truly been a Bajoran, he knew that his face would have flushed red. Hurrying past the awkward moment, he said, "As much as I wanted to learn about my people, to help them, and become a part of them, I came to understand that those things would not make my life whole." He did not think it necessary to spell out for Kira what he believed would complete his life: her love.

"I don't know what to say," Kira told him.

"You don't have to say anything," Odo said. "I just hope that you understand better why I took the actions I did. I never wanted to turn my back on you, and I don't want to turn my back on my own people now. I still hope that the war will end peacefully, and that maybe someday I can return to them. But I want you to know that you can trust me, Nerys."

Kira looked away, turning her head toward the storage area of Dax's closet. "That might take some time," she said.

"I understand," Odo said. He peered down at his hands resting on his knees, and tried to hide his disappointment.

But then Kira's hands moved over his, her touch both intimate and electric. "It will take time," she said, "but it *will* happen. You've been a part of my life for a long time now, Odo, and I don't want that to change."

He looked up at her. "I don't want it to change either."

Stillness settled around them, comfortable and sweet. They sat that way for a few minutes, not moving or talking, but simply being together. It might still take some time, as Kira had said, but Odo believed at that moment that they had saved their friendship.

Finally, Kira withdrew her hands, and at the same time said, "Of course, just being a part of my life isn't enough. I mean, Quark's been in my life for a long time too, and I wouldn't mind if that changed."

Odo returned her smile with one of his own, even though he

knew she was only joking about Quark. Difficult as it was to believe, the scoundrel had actually been largely responsible for breaking Kira and the others from their holding cells. But the jest signaled a change in the direction of their conversation, in the tone of this time with each other.

They talked through the night and through much of the next morning like old friends who hadn't seen each other in a long time. They reminisced, laughed, and cemented in reality the reconciliation they'd just fashioned.

And at ten hundred hours, after Dax had found them still chatting away in her closet, and after they'd hastily left, parted, and rushed to their duty stations, Odo discovered that he'd fallen even deeper in love with Kira Nerys.

7

Taran'atar sat at the forward console in *Rio Grande,* piloting the runabout toward Deep Space 9. Beyond the station resided the Anomaly, he knew, and at a distance beyond that, the Dominion. Looking down at his hands resting beside the controls, he considered how physically easy it would be for him to reprogram the navigational computer and set a course back to the place he'd spent most of his life—and where he might finally reclaim that life from the consistently baffling mission on which Odo had sent him.

But as much as he wanted to do that, he could not. Taran'atar could not disobey the will of a Founder, even if he did not understand or agree with the orders he'd been given. In retrospect, his visit to Ananke Alpha had been ill conceived. He could justify seeking the Founder's guidance about his need to sleep, and he could even justify his pathetic desire to alleviate, if only briefly, her isolation. But he had also attempted to secure her permission—even her orders—for him to return to the Dominion. That hadn't happened, and he now felt relieved that it hadn't; had he succeeded in obtaining those orders, he would then have been forced to defy one Founder or another. As underutilized a soldier as he'd become in the Alpha Quadrant, he still did not wish to fail Odo.

In addition to all of that, the events that had transpired at the prison disturbed Taran'atar, and he knew that they would continue to do so. He could envision all too clearly his flight through the facility, putting the Founder at grave risk, dispatching the security officers, and then firing upon and killing Captain Kira. He felt no reservations about conceiving any of those actions, but it troubled him greatly to know that his body and mind had betrayed him further, delivering to him yet another new enemy, another new failing: dreams.

After his visit with the Founder in her cell, he'd returned without incident to *Rio Grande,* escorted by Matheson and Jenek, changing back into his black coverall on the way. While Kira had prepared for their return flight to Deep Space 9, and they'd awaited clearance from the prison personnel to depart, Taran'atar had sought refuge in the aft section of the runabout, wanting time to himself to consider the erratic behavior of the Founder. Unexpectedly, he'd fallen asleep.

He'd awoken confused, not only because of the initial moment of dislocation, but also because he'd quickly discovered memories of his own actions—the escape from Ananke Alpha, killing Kira—that he could not recall deciding to take, actions that he did not believe he *would* take. He'd also remembered impossible events; Jem'Hadar could not use their shrouding capabilities to project remote figures or disguise their appearance in anything but invisibility. On the heels of all those suspicious recollections came the contradictory images of his uneventful return through the prison to the runabout. He'd quickly risen and made his way to the forward section of *Rio Grande,* where he'd confirmed Kira's presence at the main console.

"Are you all right?" she'd asked him. He'd realized that there must have been something in his appearance that reflected his discomfiture, and he'd immediately reset his posture, his facial expression, wanting to dispel Kira's curiosity and preclude any additional questions.

"I am adequate," he'd told her, again seeing in his mind the phaser beam slamming into her body and dropping her lifeless to the deck. "I wanted to tell you that if you wished to rest, I would pilot the ship back to Deep Space 9."

Kira had demurred at first, but during the long flight, she had eventually grown fatigued. She'd retreated to the aft section to sleep, leaving Taran'atar alone at the main console. He sat there now, thinking again about the ease with which he could adjust the runabout's course and take it through the Anomaly, and then on to Dominion space.

And what reason do I have—what reason could there possibly be—for violating the command of a Founder? Self-interest hardly constituted sufficient justification, nor could he think of anything that would. He considered the merits of informing Odo about the seemingly aberrant behavior of the imprisoned Founder, but felt even that cause inadequate motivation for him to act in contravention of Odo's orders.

As he thought about his visit to the Founder in her cell, though, he also recalled her declaration that her people were not gods. Before he'd left her, he'd asked her to contradict what he thought she'd earlier said, believing—hoping—that the mistake had been his. "Founder," he'd said, turning back to her. "You are a god to the Jem'Hadar, are you not?"

"I am not," she'd said. "There is but one God: the Progenitor."

He'd left, thinking her assertion just another manifestation of the strange manner in which she'd acted. But did not her odd conduct actually support her blasphemous claim? For gods did not go mad.

Taran'atar reviewed the readouts on the control panel, automatically confirming the runabout's course, velocity, and nominal performance. Then he looked up and peered through a forward viewport. The panoply of stars recalled to him the sparkling lights the Founder had shapeshifted above him.

A tremendous sense of loss suddenly settled around Taran'atar, like water rising above his head, threatening to drown him. If his gods were not gods, then what did he have? And if they were, then had he not, by his attempt to circumvent Odo's wishes, thrown away the trust and responsibility that a god had commended to him? In either case, the very meaning of his existence seemed lost to him.

Taran'atar felt himself moving through his life without direction, more so now than at any other time since he had arrived in the Alpha Quadrant. His hatred for Bajorans and humans and all the other species here burned hotly within him, almost like a beacon he could use to illuminate and guide the course of his rudderless life. He had never wanted to live among these weak, ridiculous beings, and he resented all that had happened to him during the past year—his independence from the white, his forced role as observer, his need to sleep, his mind's conjuring dreams—all of which seemed to make him more like these species he abhorred.

Turning in his seat, he looked astern, as though he could peer through the bulkheads and espy Kira sleeping in the aft section. Whatever his regard for the captain, if his gods had abandoned him, or he them, he had no desire to continue following her orders. If he no longer had a relationship to the Founders, though, then neither could he return to the Dominion.

Perhaps I've lived too long, he thought. At nearly twenty-three years of age, he had outlasted every Jem'Hadar he'd ever known who'd been hatched before him. Although he could not be certain, he also thought that he might be the oldest Jem'Hadar who had ever lived. It occurred to him now that maybe a reason existed for that: maybe the Jem'Hadar brain had not been engineered to last much beyond two decades. Maybe he should be questioning not the godhood of the Founders, or his relationship to them, but his own sanity.

Taran'atar swung his chair back around to the console, and again checked the status of the runabout. Up ahead, unseen in its place in the Bajoran star system, hung Deep Space 9. Not knowing what else to do right now, he decided that he would return there with Kira.

But after that, he did not know what he would do.

Odo, in his Bajoran form, noted movement across the bridge of the Jem'Hadar vessel, and looked over in time to catch Weyoun glancing over his shoulder. Standing between Seventh Rotan'talag and another Jem'Hadar soldier, Weyoun immediately turned back to the console at which he worked, but not quickly enough to conceal the expression of anxiety on his face. Odo recognized the dismay of a Vorta failing a Founder—or in this case, half a dozen Founders.

Beside Odo, Laas and Indurane and the three other

changelings stood in a circle, their roughly humanoid figures glowing orange-gold. The group had followed Odo to the bridge, where he'd overseen the investigation of space surrounding the nova. As time had passed without result, the five changelings had faced each other and joined hands, re-forming their small link. The details of their humanoid forms had blurred, their bodies connected together via appendages that had earlier been arms.

Occasionally, Odo himself shapeshifted into their link. He wanted not only to update the Founders on the progress of their exploration of the region centered on the nova, but also to monitor their collective emotional state. The intensity of the group's anticipation and excitement remained extremely high. Even Laas had grown enthusiastic about the search, although his level of expectation paled in comparison to that of the others.

Now, seeing Weyoun's look of concern, Odo walked along the perimeter of the bridge, past numerous Jem'Hadar working at various stations. "Anything to report?" he asked as he stepped past Rotan'talag to stand behind Weyoun. Odo knew that there would be nothing to learn—if there had been, Weyoun already would have told him—but he asked the question in order to engage the Vorta in conversation.

"The radiation from the nova is interfering with some of our scans," said Weyoun, not looking up from his console. He paused, and then added, "It might help us to have some idea of what it is we're searching for." His demeanor and tone admitted traces of both frustration and impertinence. The latter surprised Odo, but also pleased him. In the months since he'd begun having regular contact with this Weyoun, the ninth in the line of clones, the Vorta had shown few character traits besides the expected efficiency, loyalty, and servility encoded into his genes and historically demanded of his position. Even this small display of mild disrespect heartened Odo, signaling at least the possibility that Weyoun and his fellow Vorta could escape their longtime mindset as ingratiating servants to the Founders.

For his part, Weyoun seemed suddenly to realize how he had just addressed Odo, and he retreated from the remark. "What I mean to say is, given the circumstances, I'm finding this a difficult task to accomplish quickly," he said, turning to face Odo. He wore a headset, but its small monitor had been swung up and away from his eye, deactivated. "I will endeavor to do better," he finished.

"I'm sure your efforts are more than satisfactory," Odo told him. Then, seeking to reassure him, he added, "In fact, I may have given you a task that will not yield any positive results."

"Founder," Weyoun began, and then peered left and right at the Jem'Hadar operating the adjoining consoles. "May I speak with you privately?" he asked, raising a hand and gesturing toward the center of the bridge.

Odo nodded once, and paced with Weyoun away from the Jem'Hadar. "What is it?" Odo asked once they'd stopped in the currently unoccupied middle of the bridge.

"I ask this only to aid me in my inspection of space around the nova, and because you made me privy to your research before we began this mission," Weyoun said, obviously referring to the files he had collected and decrypted for Odo and Laas. "Are we looking for one of the Hundred?"

Odo considered disclosing the truth, but decided not to do so. He could not be certain how Weyoun would react—how any individual would react—at learning those he worshipped as gods actually believed in the divinity of Another. Such news might contribute to the empowerment of the Vorta, possibly even to their flight from servitude, but it also might result in less desirable consequences, including violent revolt. Until Odo could deliberate at greater length about revealing such information, and until the Founders had completed their quest for the Progenitor and dealt with the impact of their failure to locate It, he opted to keep the Founders' goal for this mission from the ship's crew. "We're not looking for one of the Hundred," he answered Weyoun honestly. "But you would be well served if you conducted your search as if we were."

Weyoun cocked his head slightly to one side, a quizzical look appearing on his face. "Are you asking me to intentionally fail at the task you've assigned me, Founder?"

"No, I'm not," Odo said, understanding Weyoun's interpretation of what he'd just been told, that he should carry out his investigation by hunting for something—one of the Hundred—for which the Founders were not actually looking. "What I'm suggesting is that you direct your search by looking for changelings, but you should not expect to find any. The Founders here are—"

A pair of rapid, high-pitched electronic tones interrupted Odo. He peered over toward the source of the sounds, in the direction of the console at which Weyoun had just been working. Rotan'talag looked up from his own station and said, "Weyoun, I've found something."

"What is it?" Weyoun asked, striding over to the Jem'Hadar seventh. Odo followed behind him.

"Sensor sweeps in the neighborhood of the nova have detected an unusual object," Rotan'talag said, pointing to a diagram on his console that showed at its center the flaring white dwarf. "It is as massive as a planet." He detailed its size and its distance from the brilliant star.

"As 'massive' as a planet?" Weyoun asked. "Is it not a planet?"

"It is not an intact planet," Rotan'talag said, "though it may be the remnants of one. Its shape is that of a spherical cap, approximately twenty percent of the volume of what would have been the entire sphere." Odo imagined a huge, solid dome hanging in space, the lone portion remaining of a planet that had been destroyed by some cataclysmic event—perhaps by the impact of the ejecta of the nearby nova. "But if it is the surviving section of a planet, it is not obviously so," Rotan'talag continued. "Radiation in the immediate vicinity is interfering with sensors, and so I am able to scan only the surface of the object, but I detect no rock, mineral, or metallic substances there."

"What *do* you detect?" Odo asked.

"Biomimetic cells," Rotan'talag said.

As the implication of that information struck Odo, he saw Weyoun turn his head sharply toward him. He found the sudden movement accusatory. Only moments ago, he had told Weyoun that he should not expect to locate any changelings during the search, but to the Vorta, the veracity of that statement had obviously just been called into question. Wanting to maintain Weyoun's trust in him, Odo made a note to discuss the matter with him later. Right now, though, he needed to understand exactly what Rotan'talag had discovered.

"Are there changelings down there?" he asked the Jem'Hadar seventh.

"From the available readings, I would conclude that the biomimetic cells belong to a single shapeshifter, possibly a very large one," Rotan'talag said. "But I would also conclude that they do not belong to a Founder."

"What?" Odo said before he could stop himself.

"Through a few random breaks in the radiation interference, I have been able to isolate DNA sequences in the scans, although just a few," Rotan'talag explained. "The readings are consistent with shapeshifting abilities, but while the readings resemble those of a Founder, they do not match precisely."

Odo gazed past Weyoun and Rotan'talag at the console screen, at the golden circle to which the Jem'Hadar had pointed, and that represented the unusual, dome-shaped object. Though surprised by the scans of a shapeshifter on its surface, Odo had been prepared to believe that they had coincidentally run across a Founder, perhaps even one of the Hundred. And maybe finding one of the Hundred here would not constitute happenstance, but merely the outcome of traveling near the Omarion Nebula, to which all of the cast-out Founders had been internally directed. But if the changeling on the vestiges of the decimated planet was not a Founder, then could it be— could it *possibly* be—the Progenitor?

Odo peered across the bridge to where Laas and Indurane and the others stood linked with each other. They had become further enmeshed, Odo saw, their bodies having drawn closer together, although they had not yet dissolved into an indistinguishable mass. He would have to tell them what Rotan'talag had found, and he already knew how they would react: with certain conviction that they had located their God, with keen anticipation that they would soon reunite with It, and with the joy that would come from knowing that their people would soon be saved from eventual extinction.

Despite his own disbelief, Odo felt his own excitement rise

dramatically. He looked back to Weyoun, knowing what they would have to do next.

"Take us there," he said.

In the deep of night, hell descended upon the city. It arrived in the guise of soldiers, squadrons of them, who appeared in the streets, in homes, on outlying farms and in nearby processing plants, bringing with them agony and death. They loosed their well-muscled bodies in hand-to-hand attacks, inflicting pain, breaking limbs, fracturing necks. The steel of their knives, honed to a lethal edge and wielded with merciless skill, sliced through flesh as easily as though through water. The electric-blue bolts of their energy weapons flared and found their targets, searing clothing and charring the skin beneath. Blood spilled, thick as the cries in the darkness.

Vannis preceded all of this by a matter of minutes. She stood in the large, quiet bedroom, the reflected light of this world's moon stealing in through a casement and lending the surroundings a silvern cast. Remaining for a moment where the transporter had deposited her, she calmly surveyed her environs, alert for the unexpected. Though she squinted, her poor eyesight failed to allow her to make out much detail in the darkened room. Blockish shapes suggested furniture, and bulky hanging frames bordered what the inhabitants of this home no doubt considered art. A wide, flat screen set into the wall, along with a dimly illuminated control panel beside it, surely composed a computer or communications console.

A low sibilance, nearly a whistle, emanated from the far end of the room. Vannis studied the gentle sound for a moment, her keen audition verifying the slumbering presence of the two Rindamil who lived here. Unhurriedly, she started across the room, her shoes whispering quietly along the carpeted floor. Abreast of the wall monitor, she caught sight of her own reflection in it, blurred but recognizable enough. Even in the low light, her indigo eyes seemed to shine.

Moving past the monitor, Vannis stopped a meter or so from the raised, padded platform on which the two Rindamil slept. Before she spoke, she brought her hands together at her waist, preparing to activate the transporter recall affixed around one forearm. She likely would not need to employ its use, but she would sooner retreat than be captured or killed. Her transcorder implant, continuously recording her experiences and also uploading them to the Dominion subspace network, rendered her death, in some sense, impermanent. But she also knew from her previous demises—or more precisely, from those of her six predecessor clones—that dying carried with it anguish like no other. Whether the result of an accident, or murder, or even her own intentional use of her termination implant, the moments when life ended, leaving her to an incomprehensible nonexistence, had never failed to terrify her.

"Get up," she said, her mellifluous voice filling the still room, and belying her anxious thoughts. Her finger brushed along the side of the recall control as she awaited reaction. On the sleeping surface, both Rindamil stirred. "I said, get up," Vannis repeated, louder than before. This time, both of the aliens awoke, sitting up abruptly.

"What—?" asked the nearer of the two Rindamil. "Who—who's there?" His bass voice sounded gravelly. Beside him, his mate reached quickly toward the wall. Vannis braced herself, preparing to flee an attack, but scans had already shown the room to be free of any weapons. An instant later, overhead lighting panels flickered on, obviously triggered by the second Rindamil. Pastel-colored linens sat in disarray about the couple, the golden, semirigid plates that covered their stout bodies visible from their waists upward. The two appeared shocked and somehow small, hardly presenting the air of command to be expected from the viceroy and vicereine of a planet. The male blinked, once, twice, a third time, green nictitating membranes arcing slowly across his outsized, dark eyes. He seemed to struggle to come fully awake, and to make sense of what he saw, but then the four sections of his blunt beak parted in an expression of obvious recognition. "You," he said simply.

"Yes, me," Vannis agreed, elongating both words, almost singing them. "I'm delighted that you remember me, Teelent. I, of course, remember you." She watched for any indication that he might rush her, and saw none.

"Why wouldn't you remember us?" yelped Teelent's mate, Alsara, the dread in her voice plain. She jumped onto the floor on the other side of the sleeping platform, pulling a linen panel tightly about the lower half of her body. She stood about as tall as Vannis, not quite a meter and three-quarters, a full head shorter than Teelent. *"You* chose *us*. You came here uninvited and made demands of us, threatened us."

"On the contrary," Vannis said, injecting a note of offense into her tone, "when I first visited your world, I did so in order to welcome your people into the Dominion." She raised her arms and spread them wide, a gesture intended to underscore her words.

"To 'welcome' us?" Alsara said. Her voice rose with each word. "We never asked—we never *wanted*—to be in your Dominion. We told you—"

"How?" Teelent said softly, the single word quieting his mate in midsentence. "How did you get in here?"

"Why, I simply beamed in," Vannis said, knowing that the words, spoken truthfully, would have a chilling effect on the two Rindamil. Their society had developed technologically only to the point of visiting their world's moon, but they had somehow managed to construct and use elementary transporters. They had also consequently determined how to thwart such devices.

Or so they had thought.

"You *beamed* in?" Alsara echoed.

"But we . . ." Teelent began, and hesitated. Vannis suspected that he worried about revealing too much about his people's capabilities, but then he went on anyway. "We draped all of our cities in forcefields. And this very building. It should have been impossible for you to transport inside."

"And yet here I am," Vannis offered. She noted a change in Teelent's bearing. He seemed to deflate, and she grew less concerned that he would try to attack her.

"Why have you come back here?" Alsara demanded, her voice rising in volume again. She rounded the foot of the sleeping surface.

"She's here for our food," Teelent said quietly.

"It *has* been a particularly harsh winter in the northern hemisphere of Overne III," Vannis confirmed.

Alsara looked to her mate, then directly over at Vannis. "You can't take our food," she asserted.

"I'm afraid that I'm going to have to disagree about that," Vannis said. "When I welcomed you into the Dominion, I informed you of the responsibilities attendant with your membership."

"You can't just—" Alsara began, but Teelent raised a hand, signaling her to be quiet.

"Based upon your threats," he told Vannis, "we have done everything we could to increase food production. But crops are crops, and there's only so much arable land, only so many people to work that land."

"I'm sorry to hear that," Vannis said. "I thought I was quite clear about what would be expected of your people."

"Oh, you were," Teelent said, the parts of his beak clicking together twice in what Vannis took to be the Rindamil version of a sardonic laugh. "We can provide you all of our emergency stores," he continued. "They constitute—"

"No," Alsara interrupted, turning toward her mate. "We can't take that chance. Three of the last eight winters have been so severe that we've had to use our emergency stores."

"I know," Teelent responded, though he still looked at Vannis. "But what choice do we have?"

"No choice at all," Vannis agreed.

"Our emergency stores measure twelve percent of our entire stockpile. It is a significant amount, one I'm sure that will assist you combating the famine on the other world."

"I'm afraid that won't provide enough assistance," Vannis said. "As I already indicated, the northern winter on Overne III has been quite harsh. We'll require seventy-five percent of your foodstuffs."

"What!" Alsara shrieked, clearly staggered.

Teelent stepped forward, and Vannis reached for the controls around her forearm. But Teelent stopped after a single step. Rather than engaging the transporter recall, Vannis signaled the Jem'Hadar ship she commanded, currently in orbit about the planet. She needed to move this situation along.

"Seventy-five percent is excessively high," Teelent said. "Much of our own population would be unable to survive our own winter. Perhaps if we ration our food, we can increase the amount we can safely give to the people of Overne III. Perhaps we can part with as much as twenty percent . . . perhaps even twenty-two."

"I'm afraid you're not understanding me," Vannis said, although she knew that her voice contained no hint of sympathy. "The Dominion requires seventy-five percent of all food caches on the planet. Immediately."

"No," Alsara said again, but her voice had fallen to a mere whisper. Her eyes seemed no longer to focus.

"Yes," Vannis said. As though on cue, the sound of weapons fire reached Vannis's keenly tuned hearing. "This is not a request. We will take the stores we need." She motioned toward the window across the room, and Teelent and Alsara hurried over to it. One of them gasped when they arrived there, although Vannis could not tell which one. "Your only choice in this matter," Vannis said behind them, "is whether or not to cooperate. Jem'Hadar troops have transported down, not just here, but all over your world."

As more and more Jem'Hadar weapons fire screamed through the night, Alsara turned back toward Vannis. "How can you do this? Without enough food, hundreds of thousands of our citizens, maybe millions, will die over the next few months."

"If you choose not to cooperate," Vannis said, "then that number will die in the next few days."

For long moments, Alsara stared at Vannis, saying nothing, but obviously enraged. Behind her, Teelent continued to peer through the window at what Vannis knew to be Jem'Hadar soldiers giving his people no quarter. Finally, without turning, he said, "Take seventy-five percent of our food."

This time, Alsara said nothing.

"Excellent," Vannis said, and she touched another of the controls wrapped about her forearm. Shortly, she knew, her signal to her ship would be transmitted to all of the Jem'Hadar troops deployed on the planet. The attack would be halted, in favor of the collection of the Rindamil food needed for the Overne.

To Teelent and Alsara, she said, "Welcome to the Dominion." Then she activated her transporter recall and returned to her ship.

* * *

On Deep Space 9, Taran'atar stalked across his cabin, executing a complex series of small but difficult tactical movements. Wielding a short, two-pronged weapon that he had just replicated, he imagined an adversary at the ready before him: a Merakordi paladin, tall and well muscled, clad in traditional armor, brandishing a cutlass in one gloved hand and a spiked flail in the other. Taran'atar took one long stride, two, and lunged forward, then feinted to the right, toward where he envisioned the Merakordi's blade to be. He knew that his foe would be unable to bring the sword to bear at such close quarters, and would instead reach back with his other arm in order to swing the flail forward and down. As Taran'atar pictured the spiked metal ball arcing upward behind the paladin, he changed direction at speed, pitching his own weapon across more than a meter of open air, from his right hand to his left. In the same motion, he drove the weapon up beneath the bottom edge of the breastplate protecting his virtual opponent's torso. Recalling with precision the two battles in which he'd fought on Merakord II, he easily summoned to mind the sensation of the twin prongs penetrating through soft flesh and into vital organs, delivering rapid death to this nonexistent enemy.

Taran'atar froze, his muscles still tensed, his body beginning to admit fatigue after hours of these illusory combat exercises. Since Odo had first sent him here, he had little utilized these quarters that Kira had assigned to him, spending the majority of his time either observing station residents and transients throughout the starbase or training in one of the holosuites. While he'd also served on several missions with Kira and her crew, he'd used this personal space for little more than the storage of weapons he'd crafted for his military preparations. But in the three days since he and Captain Kira had returned to Deep Space 9 after his visit to the Founder in the Ananke Alpha prison, he had not left these quarters even once.

I'm failing Odo, he thought, not for the first time. Taran'atar had essentially abdicated the mission to which he had been assigned, limiting his contact with the station's inhabitants as much as possible, and thereby failing to continue the role of observer given him by Odo. He could change that, of course, simply by leaving this cabin and moving once more among Deep Space 9's population. But he did not want to do that—he had *never* wanted to do that—and he knew that he no longer would. *I'm failing Odo,* he thought again, and understood that he had grown increasingly comfortable with that reality.

He suddenly became aware of his left hand trembling. Moving only his head, he peered at his fingers wrapped tightly about the haft of his weapon. A tremendous rage boiled within him, and without thinking, he pivoted on his right foot, whipping his left arm down and hurling the weapon across the room. It struck the bulkhead beside the door that opened into the corridor, metal clanging loudly against metal. One of the dual prongs snapped off, spinning upward until it hit the overhead. Both the weapon and the broken tine fell to the carpeted deck with dull noises.

Taran'atar crossed the room and examined the bulkhead beside the door. Where the weapon had collided with it, a gouge had been scratched into its surface. It left him feeling . . . unsatisfied.

Whirling around, Taran'atar surveyed the cabin. Looking past the furniture—a sofa and several chairs, a number of tables and shelves of different sizes—he once again conceived of enemies standing close at hand. He saw the Ferengi worm with whom he had to deal when using the holosuites; he saw the two men who'd run the child-care center when he visited there; he saw the other puny Ferengi who functioned as the station's chief of operations; he saw the head of security, the chief medical officer, the executive officer. A multitude of people, Starfleet and civilian, surrounded him, standing with their backs against the bulkheads. He wondered if he might be dreaming again, and knew that not to be the case. He was not dreaming; he was furious.

Taran'atar shrouded and sprinted across the cabin, one hand sending a stuffed chair toppling over as he passed it. He ran directly at the genetically enhanced doctor, putting his shoulder down and throwing himself against the bulkhead. If Bashir had truly been there, his rib cage would have fractured and collapsed, crushing his heart in his chest. Taran'atar felt the bulkhead give, and when he stepped back, he saw that he had left a sizable dent in the hard, metal surface.

Spinning around again, he pictured the executive officer on the other side of the room, to his left. Again, he sped forward, this time kicking aside a low glass table as he crossed the center of the cabin. The table flew into the side of a companel and shattered, sending transparent shards flying in every direction. Almost all the way to his target, Taran'atar picked up a chair and raised it high above his head. As he reached the place he imagined Vaughn to be, he brought the piece of furniture down and thrust it against the bulkhead. In his mind, he saw Vaughn collapse to the deck, his midsection gored by a chair leg, his body ruined by the force of the impact.

Taran'atar continued his rampage. He visualized taking down Ro by splintering her neck, Nog by gutting his body, Quark by ripping off his limbs. His thoughts showed him Gavi and Joshua, the two men from the child-care facility, strangling beneath his grip, one man held in each of his clenching hands. He stormed back and forth across the room, battling the imaginary forms of the station's residents.

Finally, he paused, feeling the places on his hands and forearms where he had scraped his hide during his exertions. He calmed his breathing, which had grown heavy and ragged, and attempted to slow his hearts, both of which now beat quickly within him. After several minutes, he recovered his strength, though he felt exhausted.

Turning in place, Taran'atar inspected his surroundings. The cabin stood in ruins. Almost none of the furniture had survived his onslaught. Chairs, tables, shelves, the sofa, all had been strewn about, demolished, crushed, pieces of each lying about like lifeless soldiers. Motes of glass covered the deck, and flickered here and there through the air, like falling snow catching sunlight as it fell.

And still his wrath had not been sated.

Taran'atar looked across the room again, and this time brought to the forefront of his thoughts the image of Captain Kira. He saw her standing where Bashir had, and he studied her closely. The notion came to his mind that of all those he'd met in the Alpha Quadrant, Kira alone had drawn his greatest respect. But as he scrutinized her unreal form, the readiness of her stance, the strength of her frame, the tension in her face—

that face—whatever positive assessment he had made of Kira left him. A guttural roar escaped his throat, and he raced across the cabin, throwing himself feet first at his vision of the station's commanding officer.

He could almost feel her midsection give way beneath his attack, her internal organs bursting as he pinned her against the bulkhead, her death instantaneous. As he toppled to the deck, his sense of victory tempered by the lack of his foes' actual presence here, a loud report reached his ears, followed by a low-pitched alarm of some sort. He climbed to his feet, slivers of glass crunching beneath his weight.

Taran'atar examined the bulkhead where he had first struck Bashir, and where he'd just now slain Kira. The dent he'd made earlier had deepened, he saw, and several hairline cracks now emanated from it. He guessed that the alarm signaled the failure of the bulkhead, even though it had occurred in an internal structure, not in the hull, and therefore did not threaten the safety of the station. Ro's voice emerged from the comm system a moment later, confirming his suspicion.

"Ro to Taran'atar," she said. *"We're seeing an alarm down here originating in your quarters, a fracture in an internal bulkhead. Are you all right?"*

Taran'atar looked to his right, to the companel situated just a few paces from him. He could see himself tapping its controls and responding to Ro, but he had no intention of doing that. Instead, he waited, motionless.

"Taran'atar," came a second voice. *"This is Kira. What's going on down there?"*

Still, he said nothing.

"Taran'atar," Kira said again. *"Please respond."*

This time, he did respond. He paced quickly over to the companel and drove his right hand into its display screen. The slick, reflective surface ruptured, the circuitry behind it sparking. He withdrew his hand, then raised both fists above his head and brought them down onto the panel's controls. Again, the equipment could not withstand the power of his assault.

Taran'atar turned toward the door that led from these quarters and into the corridor. He had spent months failing to accomplish the task Odo had set him—a task he understood now that he should never have been given—and then over the past three days he'd tried to determine what actions he should next take. Now he found an answer.

As Laas and Indurane and the others stepped into the transporter alcove, Odo waited just outside of it. He watched Weyoun approach across the central section of the bridge. The Vorta carried in one hand a portable scanner, which Odo had requested prior to the six Founders beaming down to the planetary fragment, about which Jem'Hadar Attack Vessel 971 now circled. Despite their close proximity to the large, dome-shaped object, radiation continued to interfere with any but the coarsest scans made via ship's sensors. Even with the lesser power and range of a portable scanner, Odo hoped that actually being on the surface would allow him to overcome the interference and execute meaningful sweeps.

Weyoun handed him the device. "I hope you find what it is you're looking for," he said. He bowed his head and closed his eyes, then moved to the control panel beside the alcove.

"Thank you, Weyoun," Odo acknowledged before joining the other Founders on the transporter pad. He regarded his fellow changelings in their humanoid forms, and realized that even now he could sense from each of them—except for Laas—their profound anticipation. Since learning of the Progenitor from Indurane, Odo had come to believe It nothing more than a myth, and he'd worried about how his people would react once they'd discovered the truth. Now he wondered if they really would find the Progenitor on the planetary fragment below, and if they did, he wondered what would happen next. Would the Progenitor return to the Great Link and alleviate the Founders' slow slide toward extinction, as Indurane and the others expected? And how could that possibly happen? Could—and *would*—the Progenitor somehow grant the changelings the ability to procreate, or would It somehow bestow upon them immortality? Nothing seemed likely to Odo, and from his own, admittedly limited perspective, he still found it terribly difficult, if not impossible, to envision any positive outcome to the events currently unfolding. He'd had similar feelings during some of the investigations he'd made as chief of security aboard DS9. Rarely had his instincts proved wrong, but he hoped that would be the case this time.

To the other Founders, Odo said, "Prepare yourselves." Rotan'talag had pointed out to them the small gravitational force of the planetary fragment, and that its atmosphere had boiled off into space. Changelings could exist in such conditions, but needed to alter their physical composition accordingly. Odo himself made the necessary adjustments to his own makeup, then told Weyoun, "Begin transport."

Weyoun operated the transporter controls, which emitted clicks and soft tones beneath his touch. A whine grew in the alcove, and Odo's sight went dark. The hum of the transporter reached a climax, then drifted back down. Before Odo, his new location revealed itself as the materialization process completed.

In dim illumination, he stood on a vast, empty plain that stretched to the distant, curved horizon in shades of gray. Above, stars shined brightly, and patches of colored gases, doubtless ejected by the nova, spread like abstract artwork across the canvas of the ebon sky. The flaring star itself could not be seen, tucked out of sight somewhere beyond the edge of the partial world.

Odo looked around to make sure that the other changelings had materialized as expected. Already, Indurane and the three other Founders had come together. As Odo watched, they melted fully into each other, spilling downward into a shapeless mass and once more forming their small link. Laas stood apart from them, separate, an expression of curiosity on his imitation Varalan face. Other than the half dozen Founders, there appeared no indications of the presence of any other changelings.

As Laas started toward him, Odo lifted the scanner and peered at it, unable to see it clearly in the low light. He concentrated, shifting the composition of his eyes, adjusting the quantities and concentrations of rods and cones, until he could see the device through the night. Quickly, he worked its controls—the beeps and chirps of its operation absent in the missing atmosphere—and took readings of the immediate surroundings. He performed simple searches for movement and any objects visible on the surface—both of which provided negative results—then executed a scan for biomimetic substances.

The readout filled at once with information. He studied it for a moment, confused by what the scanner told him. According to the device, he currently stood atop a plain filled with changeling material.

Odo dropped the scanner to his side and looked all around, seeing nothing but the dull gray surface of this wounded world. Of course, a changeling could disguise itself as anything.

As Laas stepped up beside him, Odo bent and reached down toward the ground. He hesitated, leery of abruptly linking with an unknown shapeshifter—and perhaps even wary of finding himself connected to the Progenitor. But then he continued to move, pushing his hand downward. His fingers pushed through the surface, and Odo braced himself, prepared for the commingling of his thoughts and form with another.

Nothing happened.

Surprised, Odo closed his eyes and let his mind drift inward, into the spirals and circles of transformation. He wanted to reach out, and he did so, his fingers elongating and pushing forward through the insubstantial surface, attempting connections with whatever changeling life it encountered.

And still nothing happened.

He felt a touch at his side, and the distinctive pressure that came from a proffered link. Odo yielded at the point of contact, and then Laas was there with him. *Odo,* he called, and then offered the form of sand spilling downward, and the sensation of a fine mist landing on the body.

What? Odo thought, his mind reaching out to Laas, even as his fingers continued to reach out in search of changeling life here. Laas did not respond right away, and Odo's hunt turned up nothing.

And then Laas repeated the form of the sand, the sensation of the mist. Odo stopped the expansion of his body along—through—the surface, then pulled his flexible cells back into his Bajoran shape. He lifted his hand from beneath the surface of this strange place, and as he did so, delicate granules slipped from atop it and streamed back down to the ground.

Except it was not the ground.

Odo lurched to his feet, awkwardly pulling away from Laas, breaking their link. He stumbled forward, dragging his feet, and looking down to see them kicking up clouds of ash. He felt like screaming out the idea that rose in his mind, but instead dropped to his knees and slammed his fists into the powdery surface. They penetrated up to his wrists, and then to his forearms, and then to his elbows. Again, he looked inward, directed his cells into whorls as they changed their configuration, their shape. Half a meter beneath the surface, his arms extended, just as his fingers earlier had. Down and down, he reached into this world he suddenly knew was not a world, not even a portion of a world. He opened his mouth and screamed into the night, any sound that would have emerged lost in the nonexistent air.

Laas staggered up beside him, and once more touched him, putting his hand on Odo's shoulder, offering again to join with him. Odo peered up at him and saw a haggard, shocked look on his smooth face, an expression that seemed to mimic what Odo felt right now: realization, and awful sorrow. He could not imagine what Indurane and the others would feel when they made the discovery.

With the thought of the other Founders, Odo leaned his head to the side—arms and hands still buried in the ashes—and gazed over at the small link of the other four Founders. The entire mass quivered uncontrollably, and then portions of it reached upward, only to tumble back down. Even without being connected to his fellow changelings, Odo could feel their torment.

He felt pressure against his shoulder again, and he allowed Laas in. *Odo,* he called once more. But no words came after that, and he offered none, the shared silence a testament to all that existed around them.

Feeling small and lost, Odo gathered his body back into its normal Bajoran form, pulling the extensions of his arms back to their usual dimensions. Carefully, he withdrew his hands from beneath the surface, palms upward, sides pressed together, a cup filled with ashes. After a moment, Odo pulled his hands apart, and those gray grains sifted back down in silence.

He knew now that no planet had ever orbited here, torn to pieces when the star had gone nova. The ashes that stretched in all directions did not cover the rocky remnants of a destroyed world; they composed this spaceborne dome in its entirety. Here, all around and beneath Odo, lay the biomimetic cells of a single enormous changeling—perhaps even the Progenitor Itself.

But It was dead.

TERMINUS

Odo dropped the scanner, broke from Laas, and padded across the surface of this non-world, his feet kicking up the fine ashes of shapeshifter death. Laas followed, but Odo kept his eyes focused on Indurane. The three other changelings had parted from him, Odo saw, but the ancient Founder no longer moved at all. Then the others with whom he'd been linked departed, altering their forms in order to rise into the night. And still Indurane had remained motionless. Had Odo not sensed his profound anguish, he might have believed the old Founder as lifeless as the planet-sized corpse below them.

Odo stopped and turned to Laas, reaching for him. His hand touched Laas's upper arm, and amid the golden glitter of shifting flesh, they linked again. In just seconds, their two bodies became one, an amorphous column of moving cells.

Dead, came the singular concept from Laas, the texture of his body turning momentarily to powder where it mingled beside Odo's.

Dead, Odo confirmed, matching Laas's shapeshifting for an instant. As he did so, a terrible feeling of loss overcame him. The idea of a Founder god had only recently been made known to Odo, an idea he had at first considered a possibility, before finally concluding it nothing more than a myth. Even now, present atop the enormous mass of a deceased changeling, he hesitated to believe that they had found the Progenitor, or that the Progenitor existed—or *had* existed—at all.

Still, whatever the case, it did not diminish the ache he felt at the obvious death of a changeling life here. He also had no doubt that the pain suffered now by Indurane and the others, all believing the Progenitor dead, dwarfed his own. Odo could only imagine what they felt. Indurane seemed unable to move right now, and the others had found it impossible to remain here; Odo assumed that they would return to the ship, as an unassisted journey back to the Founders' world would last decades, perhaps even centuries.

Laas revised his structure again, forming the same shapes that one of the Founders had aboard ship during the voyage here: a deep, open plane representing space, with the Progenitor rising above it. *Their God?* Laas questioned, wondered. Our *God?*

I don't know, Odo responded, his body transitioning through several conversions, from an empty sphere to approximations of the other Founders that had accompanied them here. *But the others think so. Indurane thinks so.*

Indurane, Laas thought, briefly taking the ancient changeling's form. Odo understood and agreed that they needed to go to him.

Together, Odo and Laas bent toward the surface and pushed along through the lifeless shapeshifter dust. They approached the figure of Indurane, his unmoving body appearing lifeless in the low light. Odo let his thoughts drift inward, and he and Laas extended tendrils toward the old changeling. Their malleable cells flattened and came into contact with Indurane's, and—

—Odo fell through an endless void, darkness his only companion. He'd been plunging down from the beginning, he understood, and would continue to descend until swallowed up by the merciless maw of time. He saw nothing, heard nothing, sensed nothing about him but the hollowness of oblivion. Space had gone, and time, although the latter somehow waited to devour the end of his days, and him along with it. The external universe had ceased to exist. Soon so would he. So would they all.

He perceived the contradictions. Of his descent through nothingness, with nothingness as his destination. Of time destroyed, and yet time lingering, itself a destroyer. Of the eventuality of a solitary death, experienced with all of his people. And all of this with reality already no more than a memory. Light did not reach his eyes, sound did not reach his ears, no percepts of any kind reached any facet of his senses.

But still he could feel. Shock. Horror. Grief. And worst of all, a desolation that mirrored and magnified the infinite emptiness through which he plummeted.

The Progenitor was dead. Hope had perished with It. He would live alone now, they would all live alone now, and together, they would die alone. Extinction beckoned.

Odo witnessed himself falling, and accepted it, knew it useless to resist the inevitable. He observed the nebulous pool of his biomimetic material hurtling downward. Then, without warning, he saw himself alter his shape, taking on a form not his own. Rapt, he watched the new figure reach weakly forward with a newly formed hand, saw a mouth open and try to speak as—

—Indurane asked without words to go home. Odo pulled away from him, trying to break their link. But he remained connected to Laas, and Laas to Indurane, and so the feelings and thoughts of the ancient Founder continued to inundate him, although at a slightly lesser intensity.

Laas, Odo called, wanting not to locate and contact his mind, but to disconnect him from the devastated, forlorn mind of Indurane. *Laas,* he called again, and began to tug gently at his body, striving to pull him free of the unrelenting despair in which Odo himself had just been caught. Finally, Laas slipped his link with Indurane, leaving him joined only with Odo.

Death? Laas thought, but it came as a question, and Odo knew that the belief in the Progenitor, and that It no longer lived, had impacted Laas far less than it had Indurane, or apparently the others.

Before Odo could respond, a slight vibration reached him from nearby. Odo quickly sent a tendril out to where he had dropped the scanner, and found the device half buried in the ashes. He felt along its frame until he located the communicator attached there. As he brought it over to where he and Laas waited, he willed a cavity to form in the center of their joined bodies, fitting it with a gaseous medium able to conduct sound. He activated the communicator with a touch and pulled it through his metaplasm into the cavity, where he caused a mouth to take shape. "This is Odo," he said. "Go ahead."

"Founder, this is Weyoun," came the immediate reply, his voice clearly sounding concerned. *"I wanted to make certain that everything is all right. We just detected three Founders leaving the planet."*

"Everything is *not* all right," Odo said. "The changeling on this planet is no longer alive."

"We've just ascertained that as well," Weyoun said. *"And I think we know what happened to them."*

"I assume it was the radiation from the nova," Odo said.

"Yes, it was," Weyoun said, *"but I think we know what caused the nova."*

Odo sensed in Laas the same mixture of surprise and curiosity he felt himself. "Something *caused* the nova?" he asked. "Something other than natural forces."

"During our scans of the system," Weyoun said, *"we detected both warp signatures and the remnants of what appears to be the discharge of an isolytic subspace weapon of enormous power and range."*

Odo had difficulty believing what he heard. "Are you saying that a weapon launched from a ship *caused* the star to go nova?"

"That is what the evidence strongly suggests, Founder," Weyoun responded.

Laas seemed to consider this. *Was this intentional?* he asked Odo through their link, conveying to him the image of the lifeless shapeshifter.

"Weyoun," Odo said, recognizing that they needed an answer to Laas's question. "We have to try to determine who might have done this."

"Founder, we've already matched the warp signatures with those that Vannis recorded at the moon of the Sen Ennis," Weyoun said. *"This was done by the Ascendants."*

Odo felt himself tense. One of the reasons he'd gone in search of Opaka months ago had been to find out whether or not murmurs of her contact with an Ascendant had been true. And if she had experienced such an encounter, then he'd further wanted to determine whether the Ascendant's presence near Dominion space had been an isolated incident, or whether it presaged confrontations to come. Now he apparently had his answer.

"Weyoun," Odo said, "transport us up."

"Right away," Weyoun said. Odo closed the channel with another touch of a thin tendril to the communicator.

What are we going to do? Laas wanted to know.

We're going to go home, Odo said. *We're going to go home, and hope that the rest of the Great Link can handle the truth.*

And if they can't? Laas asked.

They're going to have to, because there's no longer just a possibility that the Ascendants are coming, Odo said. *They're already here.*

The walls of the horizontal shaft sped from left to right past the open front end of the turbolift. Kira watched as the bulkheads rushed by, but her thoughts had already leaped ahead to her destination. She'd come here with Lieutenant Ro directly from DS9's security office, where the two had been reviewing the latest communiqué from Gul Macet about possible leads in the matter of the Sidau massacre on Bajor, two months ago. They'd been interrupted by an alarm set off in the cabin belonging to Taran'atar. When he hadn't responded to their comm messages, they'd queried the computer about his location, confirming his presence in his quarters. While Ro had called for a backup security team to meet them there, Kira had procured phasers for the two of them from a weapons locker. She had no idea what had caused a failure in an interior bulkhead, but her intuition told her that something bad had happened.

Now, as the turbolift tracked through a crossover bridge toward the habitat ring, Ro said, "I don't think I've been to Taran'atar's quarters since we assigned them to him."

"Why would you?" Kira replied, glancing over at the security chief. "Until a few days ago, I don't think *he'd* been to his quarters since we'd assigned them." That might have been an exaggeration, but only slightly. Since he'd first arrived on Deep Space 9, Taran'atar had spent a significant amount of his time simply standing in ops and observing the actions of the crew. When not there, Kira knew, he could almost always be found training in a holosuite, battling anything from Capellan power cats to partial differential equations.

Except all of that had changed three days ago, when he'd returned with her to the station from Ananke Alpha.

The turbolift started to slow as it neared the habitat ring. The bulkheads stopped flying past as the car made the transition from its lateral motion to a descent. Soon the walls of a vertical shaft began moving by the front of the lift, alternating with doors as the car passed different decks.

"Do you think the Founder said something to Taran'atar at the prison?" Ro asked. "Something that might explain the change in his routine?" Although not strictly a secret, few people knew of the Jem'Hadar's visit to Ananke Alpha. But even though the event had taken place far from the station, Kira had thought it necessary to inform her security chief about it before the fact.

"I don't know," Kira answered Ro, though she'd considered that very possibility herself. During the journey aboard *Rio Grande* back to DS9, Taran'atar had been even less communicative than on the trip to the prison. On the first day back at the station, Kira had noticed when he'd failed to appear in ops at any time during her shift. She'd simply assumed at that point that he'd been in one of the holosuites, running through one of his numerous combat simulations, but when he hadn't shown up in ops the next day, she'd had the computer locate him for her. She'd been surprised to learn that he was in his quarters.

Yesterday, Kira had grown concerned when Taran'atar again hadn't appeared in ops and another check of the computer had revealed him still in his quarters. As Ro had just now, she'd wondered if, during his visit to the prison, he'd been affected in some way by something the Founder had said or done. Kira's complicated assessment of Taran'atar over the past months made evaluating the current situation difficult. Although wary of his training and role as a soldier of the Dominion, she also trusted Odo's judgment in sending the Jem'Hadar to DS9 in the first place, and Taran'atar himself had demonstrated his trustworthiness during his time here, following her orders as Odo had instructed him to do. But it occurred to her again that, at the prison, the Founder could have issued Taran'atar orders contrary to those he'd been given by Odo. If that had taken place, then Kira could not conclude with certainty what Taran'atar would do.

The turbolift slowed once more, coming to a stop before a set of doors, which parted. Kira and Ro exited the lift and turned to the right, in the direction of Taran'atar's quarters. "I'm trying to decide whether we should enter his cabin with phasers drawn," Ro said. "When we were on Sindorin, we wor—"

Ro stopped speaking in the middle of a word, a yelp escaping her mouth as though she'd had the air forced from her lungs. She flew backward, and Kira turned toward her in time to see the security chief land hard on her back, her head slamming into the deck. Her body immediately went limp, whether unconscious or dead, Kira could not tell.

At the same time, the air shimmered between Ro and Kira, and Taran'atar suddenly stood in the corridor. Kira reached for the phaser at her hip, and had actually wrapped her fingers around it when she saw the object in Taran'atar's hand. It appeared to be a weapon of some sort, though one she had never before seen. With a prong set off-center atop a handle, it looked peculiarly uneven.

As Kira drew her phaser, Taran'atar raised his arm and snapped it forward. Kira lunged right, still bringing her own weapon up and trying to aim it. But then she felt the object flung by Taran'atar breach her flesh and drive itself deep into the center of her chest. She fired once, the shot going high and wide, missing its target by a sizeable margin. Her shoulder crashed into a bulkhead, but that sensation seemed like something experienced secondhand, overwhelmed by the pain radiating from her midsection and screaming through her body. Her phaser slipped from her grasp as she folded up and fell to the deck.

Kira heard gasping sounds, and realized that they were coming from her. She looked down and saw the haft of Taran'atar's weapon jutting from her body. *A chest wound,* she thought, jumbled visions of her days in the Bajoran Resistance floating through her mind. *Difficult to survive without immediate medical attention,* she thought. *A quick death.*

The sound of the turbolift doors opening reached her, and she attempted to lift her head and look in that direction. As she did so, she saw splashes of crimson decorating the deck, and she understood that blood had gushed from her body. *Odo,* she thought wistfully as she rolled her eyes to one side and gazed toward the turbolift.

"Runabout pad A," she heard Taran'atar say.

Kira peered at him, tried to look him in the eyes, but the effort proved too much for her. *He's leaving,* she thought as she saw the air flicker about him. He vanished, shrouding again just before the doors to the turbolift closed. *He's leaving,* Kira thought again. *And so am I.*

Then she felt her own shroud accept her into its dark folds.

Odo stood on the world of the Founders, alone on the islet. He and Laas and Indurane had returned here aboard Jem'Hadar Attack Vessel 971 several days ago, although he could not be certain of the precise span of time. He had been in and out of the Great Link with such frequency that he'd been unable to track the hours and days outside of it. Normally he would have been able to synchronize his internal clock with that aboard the Jem'Hadar vessel, but although he'd been in contact with Weyoun, he hadn't gone up to the ship since he'd been back.

Within the Link, Odo had found it more difficult than usual to monitor external time. Since Indurane had rejoined the Founders, seemingly all of them had been attempting to cope with the news he had delivered. He'd informed them of the discovery of the enormous Changeling—the Progenitor, according to him—and that It had succumbed to the effects of the nova. Indurane had also divulged that the available evidence suggested that the Ascendants had returned to this region of space, and that they had been responsible for the star's going nova, and therefore for the death of the Progenitor.

For Odo, the latter information—that the Ascendants now roamed near the Dominion, and had enough power to ignite a star into a nova—held greater import. Even if he believed in the existence of the Progenitor, and even if he allowed that they'd found Its corpse hanging in space, the consequences seemed too far distant to be of any urgency. Assuming the death of the Progenitor and the loss of any chance for the barren Founders to be given the ability to procreate, the Great Link would one day die out, a tragic end for his people, to be sure, but one far in the future.

A zealous crusade through Dominion space by the Ascendants, though, could pose a significant and immediate threat, one that could endanger the continued existence of all changelings *right now*. But the Founders had almost completely ignored the news of the Ascendants, including the possibility that they had caused the death of the Progenitor. The same crushing levels of shock, horror, and grief that Odo had perceived in Indurane now pervaded the Great Link. In addition to Odo and Laas, a small number of other Founders seemed less distressed than the majority, but most appeared to suffer very deeply, unable to concentrate on anything but the death of their God and the loss of their anticipated salvation. Odo had trouble relating to his people with respect to this, but then he had not believed in the Progenitor, and awaited Its return, for millennia.

Odo paced along the edge of the islet. In every direction, the Great Link failed to shine with its characteristic golden glow. Instead, the barely moving surface appeared dull, almost lifeless. The languid, matte aspect of the changeling sea reminded Odo of how his people had looked when they'd been infected during the war with the disease intended by Section 31 to eliminate their entire species. In one respect, the current situation verged on becoming as bad as that; as horrible as the attempted genocide had been, the anguished Founders now appeared on the brink of mass suicide.

Over the past days, Odo had slipped often into the Great Link. At first, he sought to engage all of his people about the return of the Ascendants, but found his voice drowned out by the terrible sorrow permeating the Link. Amid the choking snarl of stunned disbelief and agonized mourning, even Odo reached the cusp of descending into the bitter pain. At those times, when compelled to battle the encompassing sadness, he took flight and escaped to the islet. There, he stabilized his emotions and regrouped, then reimmersed himself in the changeling deep, where he would try once more to convince his people to reorganize their priorities.

On the islet, Laas had occasionally joined him, but no other Founder had. Neither did any Vorta or Jem'Hadar appear, nor did Odo transport up to Attack Vessel 971, though he periodically contacted Weyoun. Odo had charged Weyoun with overseeing a Jem'Hadar task force, which would travel the Dominion and surrounding regions, seeking signs of the Ascendants. Odo did not desire another war, but he would not allow a race of religious zealots—he would not allow *anybody*—to attack his people or other members of the Dominion without launching an aggressive defense against them.

A thought occurred to Odo, and he stopped walking. He turned toward the center of the islet, to where the small pile of ashes still sat. For all the emotion over the death of the Progenitor, for all the dread of a coming Founder extinction, Odo still felt sharply the pain of losing a single changeling—and perhaps especially the pain of losing one of the Hundred.

Slowly, he stepped over to the patch of gray remains. He squatted down on his replica Bajoran haunches, then reached forward. He hesitated, halting his hand in midair, mindful of the numerous funerary customs he'd witnessed in the Alpha Quadrant. But this was not Deep Space 9 or Bajor, and this was not the cadaver of a humanoid.

As though demonstrating the latter fact to himself, Odo leaned down and pushed his cupped hand through the fine-grained powder. He lifted his hand to eye level, the ashes spilling down on either side of his palm and between his fingers. The remains of the shapeshifter fell dutifully to the ground, the biomimetic cells unable any longer to alter form, unable to flout gravity.

As Odo's hand emptied of the ashes, he saw something out beyond the edge of the islet. Far in the distance, a tall, narrow, funnel-shaped cloud reached from the dusky sky down to the Great Link. Odo stood up, his outstretched hand dropping to his side. Though he had never seen one in person, he had viewed recordings of cyclones sweeping across the lowland plains of Bajor, and thus realized the might of their destructive force. As he understood the phenomenon, though, the meteorological conditions required for its formation simply did not exist on this world.

But even as Odo thought this, another slender spire appeared, to the left of the first one, and much closer to the islet. It did not come into existence as he would have expected, though, and as he'd assumed the first one had. Rather than swirling down from the sky, it climbed up from the surface of the Great Link, like an enormous finger reaching for the heavens.

And then another formed. And another.

Odo turned in place. In every direction, the columns reached from sea to sky, with more sprouting up as he watched. He refused for a moment to accept the reality of the situation, even as it became clear to him that these were not cyclones.

These were Founders.

Above, the tips of the columns spread beyond their slim conic shape. Before long, they had flattened out into huge diaphanous planes. The effect put Odo in mind of Laas's form when he had returned here with the three members of the Hundred, floating down through the atmosphere on great, delicate wings.

Now the wings grew until they blanketed the sky, and then the vertical shafts connecting them with the Great Link withdrew upward, into them. Odo intuitively recognized the actions of his people. Although veiled from his view, he knew that above the planes of changeling flesh, more shifts in shape, mass, and internal pressure occurred. As the Founders climbed higher, to where the thinness of the atmosphere could no longer sustain their flight, they would alter their bodies, within and without, and do what they needed to in order to escape the planet's gravity.

To his left, Odo suddenly heard footsteps. So taken with the Founders' ascents had he been that he had not heard any of them shapeshift up onto the islet. He turned now to see Indurane, as a Bajoran, walking toward him. The ancient changeling stopped just a couple of paces from him, and without preamble said, "We have no direction. We have no hope."

"How can that be?" Odo asked him. "How can *this* be?" He gestured with both hands toward the rising masses of changelings all around them.

"For so long," Indurane said, "we have awaited—we have *sought*—the return of the Progenitor. It took millennia for us to settle on the plan of sending out the Hundred, and centuries more to implement that plan. And it worked. In the end, it worked. We saw the sign implanted in us, and we knew that the Progenitor had returned."

Odo saw in his mind the nova hanging in the sky, pictured himself plunging his arms deep into the massive changeling remains. He thought to ask Indurane how their people could be certain of the corpse's identity, but decided not to pose the question. Odo knew that whatever justification Indurane provided, it would not suffice to convince him. Nor, he surmised, would anything he said be sufficient to dissuade Indurane from his viewpoint.

"But why *this?*" Odo tried again, waving his hands once more in the general direction of the Founders pushing upward into the sky.

"Because there is no hope," Indurane said.

Indeed, Odo could sense from Indurane, and from all those around them, the bereavement of spirit of which the old changeling spoke. But he also perceived something else. "Do you feel guilty?" he asked. "Do many of the Founders?"

"I do," Indurane admitted. "We do. For those ill served when we sent out the Hundred. Like you. Like Laas." He raised an arm and pointed at Odo's feet, at the pile of ashes there. "Like this one," he said. "And like the Progenitor Itself."

"Is that what you're doing now?" Odo asked. "Dividing the Great Link and sending yourselves out into the universe that you believe is so hostile to shapeshifters, all as penance for what you did, as acts of contrition for your misdeeds?"

"We are guilty," Indurane said. "We abandoned pieces of ourselves, and in so doing, lured the Progenitor to Its death." He paused, and then with what seemed infinite sadness, he repeated the words with which he'd begun this conversation. "We have no direction. We have no hope."

"If you want to be whole," Odo said, "you make your own direction, your own hope."

"We do not," Indurane said flatly.

Odo considered what he might say to convince Indurane otherwise, but only ended up with more questions. "Are you relocating," he asked, "or dispersing?"

"Some may remain together in small links," Indurane said, "but most seek isolation, even from our own kind."

"What will *you* do?" Odo asked.

Indurane appeared to think for a few moments, his smooth Bajoran features expressionless and unreadable. Finally, predictably, he said, "I have no direction."

Before Odo could respond, Indurane's body began to shimmer, beginning at his head and moving swiftly down through his torso, waist, and legs, and then on to his feet. Then his form shot up into the sky, a huge spire emanating from the islet. Odo craned his neck and peered upward, in time to see the top of Indurane's new shape spread outward.

"Not everyone you encounter in the universe will be your enemy," Odo said, knowing that Indurane could still perceive his words. But then the base of the column Indurane had formed retracted upward, and was quickly lost to sight. Odo called after him anyway. "We all make our own direction," he said.

But Indurane was gone.

Odo watched for hours as column after column climbed into the sky and formed wings, which soon enough contracted and fled higher. Eventually, though, the number dwindled, and then at last, only a single column remained. When it too had gone, Odo lowered his eyes to look out at the barren world the Founders had once called home, and which they had now abandoned.

Stepping over to the edge of the islet—which, with the

changeling sea now gone, could best be described as the top of a rocky hill—Odo gazed out over the cold, empty landscape. Where the Great Link once had been, he now saw only the uneven planet surface. In some places off in the distance, Odo could see the features of a changeling world, the objects and structures fashioned by the Founders for their own satisfaction in emulating. Various natural characteristics separated those places: rolling hills off to the left; rocky, craggy terrain ahead; and cratered plains to the right.

Not that long ago, Odo reflected, he had stood here, on this islet, his mind filled with hope. Now he looked up over his shoulder at the brightly shining orb of the nova, which had so recently drawn his attention in the same way that the Omarion Nebula once had. Back then, after his return here from his trip to Deep Space 9, he'd thought the nova a harbinger of a bright future for his people, an augury of peace and joy for the Founders in the days ahead.

Odo realized now that he'd been wrong on all counts.

As he contemplated his error, he heard the sound of shifting changeling flesh below him. Looking away from the nova and down into the empty lands surrounding the former islet, Odo spotted the orange-amber flicker of a Founder changing shape. It approached the islet, rising from below, and then splashed onto the ground beside Odo. It quickly drew up into a humanoid form, and then Laas stood there in his Varalan shape.

Just as Indurane had earlier, Laas began without prefacing his remarks in any way. "What are we going to do?" he asked, a look of astonishment and confusion on his unlined face. Odo imagined the same expression on his own face. But as surprised as he felt at the turn of events, he also recognized the dangers posed by the dissolution of the Great Link. To begin with, and perhaps most importantly, with its ruling force gone, the Dominion could easily descend into anarchy and chaos.

"I don't know what we're going to do," he answered Laas honestly.

"What's going to happen to the Dominion?" Laas persisted.

I don't know, Odo thought again, but then an answer rose in his mind. Attack Vessel 971 currently orbited the planet, and squadrons of similar starships patrolled vast areas of the surrounding space. Vorta and Jem'Hadar forces stretched throughout in impressive numbers, all controlled by the will of the Founders.

"What's going to happen to the Dominion?" Odo repeated. "Laas, from this point on, you and I *are* the Dominion."

A NOTE ON CHRONOLOGY

Readers of this miniseries will no doubt have noticed that the stories in *Worlds of Star Trek: Deep Space Nine* were not presented chronologically. This was intentional. Just as the previously published *Rising Son* and *The Left Hand of Destiny* doubled back to earlier points in the timeline of *Deep Space Nine* fiction set after the TV series, so too does *Worlds of DS9* shift back and forth as the series progresses, telling tales out of sequence in order to reveal events in a desired order. To borrow a phrase from a certain Emissary, the continuing saga of *Deep Space Nine* should not be considered linear.

However, for those interested in the chronological order of events in *Worlds of DS9*, here it is in Gregorian dates, using the final chapters of *Unity* as a benchmark.

September 29, 2376: Bajor joins the Federation.

October 1: Odo departs the Alpha Quadrant.

October 2: Jake Sisko sets out from his father's home in Kendra Valley.

October 4: Fleet Admiral Akaar addresses the Federation Security Council.

October 8: Ezri Dax leads an away team on Minos Korva.

October 11–12: Dax and Julian Bashir on Trill.

October 14: Dax and Bashir return to Deep Space 9. Shortly thereafter, Bashir takes leave time and travels to Earth.

October 24: Sidau village on Bajor is destroyed; Bajoran Militia officer Major Cenn Desca assigned to Deep Space Nine; Commander Elias Vaughn turns 102.

October 25: Jake Sisko returns to Kendra province, married to Azeni Korena.

October 27: Bashir returns to Deep Space 9.

November 1–10: Ensign Thirishar ch'Thane, Ensign Prynn Tenmei and Commander Phillipa Matthias on Andor; Odo returns to the Dominion.

November 17–22: Quark, Lieutenant Nog and Lieutenant Ro Laren on Ferenginar; Bena, daughter of Grand Nagus Rom and Leeta, born on November 21.

December 2: On Cardassia, the True Way attempts to destabilize and discredit Alon Ghemor's government.

December 16–27: *U.S.S. Yolga* travels to Ananke Alpha; Odo leads an investigation of a nova in the Gamma Quadrant.

December 31: Taran'atar attacks Kira; the Great Link dissolves.